"MINTY SHARPE'S THE SAME AS SHE ALLUS WOS"

—*A Phyllis of the Sierras*

"ARGONAUT EDITION" OF
THE WORKS OF BRET HARTE

SALLY DOWS

A PHYLLIS OF THE SIERRAS

BY

BRET HARTE

ILLUSTRATED

VIGILANS ET AUDAX

P. F. COLLIER & SON
NEW YORK

CONTENTS.

SALLY DOWS.

PROLOGUE.

THE LAST GUN AT SNAKE RIVER.

WHAT had been in the cool gray of that summer morning a dewy country lane, marked only by a few wagon tracks that never encroached upon its grassy border, and indented only by the faint footprints of a crossing fox or coon, was now, before high noon, already crushed, beaten down, and trampled out of all semblance of its former graciousness. The heavy springless jolt of gun‑carriage and caisson had cut deeply through the middle track; the hoofs of crowding cavalry had struck down and shredded the wayside vines and bushes to bury them under a cloud of following dust, and the short, plunging double‑quick of infantry had trodden out this hideous ruin into one dusty level chaos. Along that rudely widened highway useless muskets, torn accoutrements, knapsacks, caps, and articles of clothing were scattered, with here and there the larger wrecks of broken-down wagons, roughly thrown aside into the ditch to make way for the living current. For two hours the greater part of an army corps had passed and repassed that way, but, coming or going, always with faces turned eagerly towards an open slope on the right which ran parallel to the lane. And yet nothing was to be seen there. For two hours a gray and bluish cloud, rent and shaken with explosion after explosion, but always closing and thickening after each discharge, was all that had met their eyes. Nevertheless, into this ominous cloud solid moving masses of men in gray or blue had that morning melted away, or emerged from it only as scattered fragments that crept, crawled, ran, or clung together in groups, to be followed, and overtaken in the rolling vapor.

But for the last half hour the desolated track had stretched empty and deserted. While there was no cessation of the rattling, crackling, and detonations on the fateful slope beyond, it had still been silent. Once or twice it had been crossed by timid, hurry-

ing wings, and frightened and hesitating little
feet, or later by skulkers and stragglers from
the main column who were tempted to enter it
from the hedges and bushes where they had
been creeping and hiding. Suddenly a prolonged yell from the hidden slope beyond —
the nearest sound that had yet been heard
from that ominous distance — sent them to
cover again. It was followed by the furious
galloping of horses in the lane, and a handsome, red-capped officer, accompanied by an
orderly, dashed down the track, wheeled,
leaped the hedge, rode out on the slope and
halted. In another instant a cloud of dust
came whirling down the lane after him.
Out of it strained the heavy shoulders and
tightened chain-traces of six frantic horses
dragging the swaying gun that in this tem-
pest of motion alone seemed passive and
helpless with an awful foreknowledge of its
power. As in obedience to a signal from
the officer they crashed through the hedge
after him, a sudden jolt threw an artillery-
man from the limber before the wheel. A
driver glanced back on the tense chain and
hesitated. "Go on!" yelled the prostrate
man, and the wheel went over him. Another and another gun followed out of the

dust cloud, until the whole battery had de-
ployed on the slope.   Before the drifting
dust had fairly settled, the falling back of
the panting horses with their drivers gave a
momentary glimpse of the nearest gun already in position and of the four erect figures
beside it.   The yell that seemed to have
evoked this sudden apparition again sounded
nearer ; a blinding flash broke from the
gun, which was instantly hidden by the closing group around it, and a deafening crash
with the high ringing of metal ran down the
lane.   A column of white, woolly smoke
arose as another flash broke beside it.   This
was quickly followed by another and another, with a response from the gun first
fired, until the whole slope shook and thun-
dered.   And the smoke, no longer white
and woolly, but darkening and thickening
as with unburnt grains of gunpowder, mingled into the one ominous vapor, and driving along the lane hid even the slope from
view.

The yelling had ceased, but the grinding
and rattling heard through the detonation of
cannon came nearer still, and suddenly there
was a shower of leaves and twigs from the
lower branches of a chestnut-tree near the

broken hedge. As the smoke thinned again a rising and falling medley of flapping hats, tossing horses' heads and shining steel appeared for an instant, advancing tumultuously up the slope. But the apparition was as instantly cloven by flame from the two nearest guns, and went down in a gush of smoke and roar of sound. So level was the delivery and so close the impact that a space seemed suddenly cleared between, in which the whirling of the shattered remnants of the charging cavalry was distinctly seen, and the shouts and oaths of the inextricably struggling mass became plain and articulate. Then a gunner serving the nearest piece suddenly dropped his swab and seized a carbine, for out of the whirling confusion before them a single rider was seen galloping furiously towards the gun.

The red-capped young officer rode forward and knocked up the gunner's weapon with his sword. For in that rapid glance he had seen that the rider's reins were hanging loosely on the neck of his horse, who was still dashing forwards with the frantic impetus of the charge, and that the youthful figure of the rider, — wearing the stripes of a lieutenant, — although still erect, exercised

no control over the animal. The face was
boyish, blond, and ghastly; the eyes were
set and glassy. It seemed as if Death itself were charging the gun.

Within a few feet of it the horse swerved
before a brandished rammer, and striking
the cheeks of the gun-carriage pitched his
inanimate rider across the gun. The hot
blood of the dead man smoked on the hotter
brass with the reek of the shambles, and be-
spattered the hand of the gunner who still
mechanically served the vent. As they
lifted the dead body down the order came
to " cease firing." For the yells from below
had ceased too; the rattling and grinding
were receding with the smoke farther to the
left. The ominous central cloud parted for
a brief moment and showed the unexpected
sun glittering down the slope upon a near
and peaceful river.

The young artillery officer had dismounted
and was now gently examining the dead man.
His breast had been crushed by a fragment
of shell; he must have died instantly. The
same missile had cut the chain of a locket
which slipped from his opened coat. The
officer picked it up with a strange feeling —
perhaps because he was conscious himself of

wearing a similar one, perhaps because it might give him some clue to the man's identity. It contained only the photograph of a pretty girl, a tendril of fair hair, and the word "Sally." In the breast-pocket was a sealed letter with the inscription, "For Miss Sally Dows. To be delivered if I fall by the mudsill's hand." A faint smile came over the officer's face; he was about to hand the articles to a sergeant, but changed his mind and put them in his pocket.

Meantime the lane and woods beyond, and even the slope itself, were crowding with supports and waiting troops. His own battery was still unlimbered, waiting orders. There was a slight commotion in the lane.

"Very well done, captain. Smartly taken and gallantly held."

It was the voice of a general officer passing with his staff. There was a note of pleasant relief in its tone, and the middle-aged, care-drawn face of its owner was relaxed in a paternal smile. The young captain flushed with pleasure.

"And you seem to have had close work too," added the general, pointing to the dead man.

The young officer hurriedly explained.

The general nodded, saluted, and passed on.
But a youthful aide airily lingered.

"The old man's feeling good, Courtland,"
he said. "We've rolled 'em up all along
the line. It's all over now. In point of
fact, I reckon you've fired the last round in
this particular fratricidal engagement."

The last round! Courtland remained silent, looking abstractedly at the man it had
crushed and broken at his feet.

"And I should n't wonder if you got your
gold-leaf for to-day's work. But who's your
sunny Southern friend here?" he added,
following his companion's eyes.

Courtland repeated his story a little more
seriously, which, however, failed to subdue
the young aide's levity. "So he concluded
to stop over," he interrupted cheerfully.
"But," looking at the letter and photograph,
"I say — look here! 'Sally Dows?' Why,
there was another man picked up yesterday
with a letter to the same girl! Doc Murphy
has it. And, by Jove! the same picture
too! — eh? I say, Sally must have gathered
in the boys, and raked down the whole pile!
Look here, Courty! you might get Doc
Murphy's letter and hunt her up when this
cruel war is over. Say you're 'fulfilling a

sacred trust!' See? Good idea, old man! Ta-ta!'" and he trotted quickly after his superior.

Courtland remained with the letter and photograph in his hand, gazing abstractedly after him. The smoke had rolled quite away from the fields on the left, but still hung heavily down the south on the heels of the flying cavalry. A long bugle call swelled up musically from below. The freed sun caught the white flags of two field hospitals in the woods and glanced tranquilly on the broad, cypress-fringed, lazy-flowing, and cruel but beautiful Southern river, which had all unseen crept so smilingly that morning through the very heart of the battle.

CHAPTER I.

THE two o'clock express from Redlands to Forestville, Georgia, had been proceeding with the languid placidity of the river whose banks it skirted for more than two hours. But, unlike the river, it had stopped frequently; sometimes at recognized stations and villages, sometimes at the apparition of straw-hatted and linen-coated natives in the solitude of pine woods, where, after a decent interval of cheery conversation with the conductor and engineer, it either took the stranger on board, or relieved him of his parcel, letter, basket, or even the verbal message with which he was charged. Much of the way lay through pine-barren and swampy woods which had never been cleared or cultivated ; much through decayed settlements and ruined villages that had remained unchanged since the War of the Rebellion, now three years past. There were vestiges of the severity of a former military occupation ; the blackened timbers of railway bridges still unrepaired ; and along the line

of a certain memorable march, sections of
iron rails taken from the torn-up track,
roasted in bonfires and bent while red-hot
around the trunks of trees, were still to be
seen. These mementos of defeat seemed
to excite neither revenge nor the energy to
remove them; the dull apathy which had
succeeded the days of hysterical passion
and convulsion still lingered; even the slow
improvement that could be detected was
marked by the languor of convalescence.
The helplessness of a race, hitherto dependent upon certain barbaric conditions or
political place and power, unskilled in invention, and suddenly confronted with the
necessity of personal labor, was visible everywhere. Eyes that but three short years
before had turned vindictively to the North,
now gazed wistfully to that quarter for
help and direction. They scanned eagerly
the faces of their energetic and prosperous
neighbors — and quondam foes — upon the
verandas of Southern hotels and the decks
of Southern steamboats, and were even now
watching from a group in the woods the
windows of the halted train, where the faces
appeared of two men of manifestly different
types, but still alien to the country in dress,
features, and accent.

Two negroes were slowly loading the engine tender from a woodpile. The rich brown smoke of the turpentine knots was filling the train with its stinging fragrance. The elder of the two Northern passengers, with sharp New England angles in his face, impatiently glanced at his watch.

"Of all created shiftlessness, this beats everything! Why could n't we have taken in enough wood to last the ten miles farther to the terminus when we last stopped? And why in thunder, with all this firing up, can't we go faster?"

The younger passenger, whose quiet, well-bred face seemed to indicate more discipline of character, smiled.

"If you really wish to know — and as we 've only ten miles farther to go — I 'll show you *why*. Come with me."

He led the way through the car to the platform and leaped down. Then he pointed significantly to the rails below them. His companion started. The metal was scaling off in thin strips from the rails, and in some places its thickness had been reduced a quarter of an inch, while in others the projecting edges were torn off, or hanging in iron shreds, so that the wheels actually ran on the narrow central strip. It seemed marvelous that the train could keep the track.

"*Now* you know why we don't go more than five miles an hour, and — are thankful that we don't," said the young traveler quietly.

"But this is disgraceful! — criminal!" ejaculated the other nervously.

"Not at their rate of speed," returned the younger man. "The crime would be in going faster. And now you can understand why a good deal of the other progress in this State is obliged to go as slowly over their equally decaying and rotten foundations. You can't rush things here as we do in the North."

The other passenger shrugged his shoulders as they remounted the platform, and the train moved on. It was not the first time that the two fellow-travelers had differed, although their mission was a common one. The elder, Mr. Cyrus Drummond, was the vice-president of a large Northern land and mill company, which had bought extensive tracts of land in Georgia, and the younger, Colonel Courtland, was the consulting surveyor and engineer for the company. Drummond's opinions were a good

deal affected by sectional prejudice, and a
self-satisfied and righteous ignorance of the
actual conditions and limitations of the people with whom he was to deal; while the
younger man, who had served through the
war with distinction, retained a soldier's respect and esteem for his late antagonists,
with a conscientious and thoughtful observation of their character. Although he had
resigned from the army, the fact that he had
previously graduated at West Point with
high honors had given him preferment in this
technical appointment, and his knowledge of
the country and its people made him a valuable counselor. And it was a fact that
the country people had preferred this soldier
with whom they had once personally grap-
pled to the capitalist they had never known
during the struggle.

The train rolled slowly through the woods,
so slowly that the fragrant pine smoke from
the engine still hung round the windows of
the cars. Gradually the " clearings " became
larger; they saw the distant white wooden
colonnades of some planter's house, looking
still opulent and pretentious, although the
fence of its inclosure had broken gaps, and
the gate sagged on its single hinge.

Mr. Drummond sniffed at this damning record of neglect and indifference. "Even if they were ruined, they might still have spent a few cents for nails and slats to enable them to look decent before folks, and not parade their poverty before their neighbors," he said.

"But that's just where you misunderstand them, Drummond," said Courtland, smiling. "They have no reason to keep up an attitude towards their neighbors, who still know them as 'Squire' so-and-so, 'Colonel' this and that, and the 'Judge,' — owners of their vast but crippled estates. They are not ashamed of being poor, which is an accident."

"But they are of working, which is *deliberation*," interrupted Drummond. "They are ashamed to mend their fences themselves, now that they have no slaves to do it for them."

"I doubt very much if some of them know how to drive a nail, for the matter of that," said Courtland, still good-humoredly, "but that's the fault of a system older than themselves, which the founders of the Republic retained. We cannot give them experience in their new condition in one day, and in fact, Drummond, I am very much afraid that for our purposes — and I honnestly believe for *their* good — we must help to keep them for the present as they are."

"Perhaps," said Drummond sarcastically, "you would like to reinstate slavery?"

"No. But I should like to reinstate the *master*. And not for *his* sake alone, but for freedom's sake and *ours*. To be plain: since I have taken up this matter for the company, I have satisfied myself from personal observation that the negro — even more than his master — cannot handle his new condition. He is accustomed to his old traditional task-master, and I doubt if he will work fairly for any other — particularly for those who don't understand him. Don't mistake me: I don't propose to go back to the whip; to that brutal institution, the irresponsible overseer; to the buying and selling, and separation of the family, nor any of the old wrongs; but I propose to make the old master *our overseer*, and responsible to *us*. He is not a fool, and has already learned that it is more profitable to pay wages to his old slaves and have the power of dismissal, like any other employer,

than be obliged, under the old system of enforced labor and life servitude, to undergo
the cost of maintaining incompetence and
idleness. The old sentiment of slave-own-
ing has disappeared before natural common-
sense and selfishness. I am satisfied that
by some such process as this utilizing of the
old master and the new freedom we will be
better able to cultivate our lands than by
buying up their estates, and setting the old
owners adrift, with a little money in their
pockets, as an idle, discontented class to
revive old political dogmas, and foment new
issues, or perhaps set up a dangerous opposition to us."

"You don't mean to say that those infernal niggers would give the preference to
their old oppressors?"

"Dollar for dollar in wages — yes! And
why should n't they? Their old masters
understand them better — and treat them
generally better. They know our interest in
them is only an abstract sentiment, not a
real liking. We show it at every turn. But
we are nearing Redlands, and Major Reed
will, I have no doubt, corroborate my impressions. He insists upon our staying at
his house, although the poor old fellow, I

imagine, can ill afford to entertain company. But he will be offended if we refuse."

"He is a friend of yours, then?" asked Drummond.

"I fought against his division at Stony Creek," said Courtland grimly. "He never tires of talking of it to me — so I suppose I am."

A few moments later the train glided beside the Redlands platform. As the two travelers descended a hand was laid on Courtland's shoulder, and a stout figure in the blackest and shiniest of alpaca jackets, and the whitest and broadest of Panama hats, welcomed him. "Glad to see yo', cun'nel. I reckoned I'd waltz over and bring along the boy," pointing to a grizzled negro servant of sixty who was bowing before them, "to tote yo'r things over instead of using a hack. I have n't run much on horseflesh since the wah — ha! ha! What *I* did n't use up for remounts I reckon yo'r commissary gobbled up with the other live stock, eh?" He laughed heartily, as if the recollections were purely humorous, and again clapped Courtland on the back.

"Let me introduce my friend, Mr. Drummond, Major Reed," said Courtland, smiling.

" Yo' were in the wah, sir ? "

" No — I " — returned Drummond, hesitating, he knew not why, and angry at his own embarrassment.

" Mr. Drummond, the vice-president of the company," interposed Courtland cheerfully, " was engaged in furnishing to us the sinews of war."

Major Reed bowed a little more formally. " Most of us heah, sir, were in the wah some time or other, and if you gentlemen will honah me by joining in a social glass at the hotel across the way, I 'll introduce you to Captain Prendergast, who left a leg at Fair Oaks." Drummond would have declined, but a significant pressure on his arm from Courtland changed his determination. He followed them to the hotel and into the presence of the one-legged warrior (who turned out to be the landlord and barkeeper), to whom Courtland was hilariously introduced by Major Reed as " the man, sir, who had pounded my division for three hours at Stony Creek ! "

Major Reed's house was but a few minutes' walk down the dusty lane, and was presently heralded by the baying of three or four foxhounds and foreshadowed by a

dilapidated condition of picket-fence **and**
stuccoed gate front. Beyond it stretched
the wooden Doric columns of the usual
Southern mansion, dimly seen through the
broad leaves of the horse-chestnut-trees that
shaded it. There were the usual listless
black shadows haunting the veranda and
outer offices — former slaves and still attached house-servants, arrested like lizards
in breathless attitudes at the approach of
strange footsteps, and still holding the brush,
broom, duster, or home implement they had
been lazily using, in their fixed hands. From
the doorway of the detached kitchen, connected by a gallery to the wing of the mansion, " Aunt Martha," the cook, gazed also,
with a saucepan clasped to her bosom, and
her revolving hand with the scrubbing cloth
in it apparently stopped on a dead centre.

Drummond, whose gorge had risen at
these evidences of hopeless incapacity and
utter shiftlessness, was not relieved by the
presence of Mrs. Reed — a soured, disappointed woman of forty, who still carried
in her small dark eyes and thin handsome
lips something of the bitterness and antag-
onism of the typical " Southern rights "
woman ; nor of her two daughters, Octavia

and Augusta, whose languid atrabiliousness seemed a part of the mourning they still wore. The optimistic gallantry and good fellowship of the major appeared the more remarkable by contrast with his cypress-shadowed family and their venomous possibilities. Perhaps there might have been a light vein of Southern insincerity in his good humor. "Paw," said Miss Octavia, with gloomy confidence to Courtland, but with a pretty curl of the hereditary lip, "is about the only 'reconstructed' one of the entire family. We don't make 'em much about yer. But I'd advise yo' friend, Mr. Drummond, if he's coming here carpet-bagging, not to trust too much to paw's 'reconstruction.' It won't wash." But when Courtland hastened to assure her that Drummond was not a "carpet-bagger," was not only free from any of the political intrigue implied under that baleful title, but was a wealthy Northern capitalist simply seeking investment, the young lady was scarcely more hopeful. "I suppose he reckons to pay paw for those niggers yo' stole?" she suggested with gloomy sarcasm.

"No," said Courtland, smiling; "but what if he reckoned to pay those niggers for working for your father and him?"

" If paw is going into trading business with him; if Major Reed — a So'th'n gentleman — is going to keep shop, he ain't such a fool as to believe niggers will work when they ain't obliged to. *That's* been tried over at Mirandy Dows's, not five miles from here, and the niggers are half the time hangin' round here takin' holiday. She put up new quarters for 'em, and tried to make 'em eat together at a long table like those low-down folks up North, and did away with their cabins and their melon patches, and allowed it would get 'em out of lying round too much, and wanted 'em to work over-time and get mo' pay. And the result was that she and her niece, and a lot of poor whites, Irish and Scotch, that she had to pick up ' ' long the river,' do all the work. And her niece Sally was mo' than half Union woman during the wah, and up to all No'th'n tricks and dodges, and swearin' by them; and yet, for all that — the thing won't work."

" But is n't that partly the reason? Is n't her failure a great deal due to this lack of sympathy from her neighbors? Discontent is easily sown, and the negro is still weighted down by superstition; the Fifteenth Amendment did not quite knock off *all* his chains."

"Yes, but that is nothing to *her*. For if there ever was a person in this world who reckoned she was just born to manage everything and everybody, it is Sally Dows!"

"Sally Dows!" repeated Courtland, with a slight start.

"Yes, Sally Dows, of Pineville."

"You say she was half Union, but did she have any relations or — or — friends — in the war — on your side? Any — who — were killed in battle?"

"They were all killed, I reckon," returned Miss Reed darkly. "There was her cousin, Jule Jeffcourt, shot in the cemetery with her beau, who, they say, was Sally's too; there were Chet Brooks and Joyce Masterton, who were both gone on her and both killed too; and there was old Captain Dows himself, who never lifted his head again after Richmond was taken, and drank himself to death. It wasn't considered healthy to be Miss Sally's relations in those times, or to be even wantin' to be one."

Colonel Courtland did not reply. The face of the dead young officer coming towards him out of the blue smoke rose as vividly as on that memorable day. The picture and letter he had taken from the

dead man's breast, which he had retained
ever since; the romantic and fruitless quest
he had made for the fair original in after
days; and the strange and fateful interest
in her which had grown up in his heart
since then, he now knew had only been lulled
to sleep in the busy preoccupation of the
last six months, for it all came back to him
with redoubled force. His present mission
and its practical object, his honest zeal in
its pursuit, and the cautious skill and experience he had brought to it, all seemed to
be suddenly displaced by this romantic and
unreal fantasy. Oddly enough it appeared
now to be the only reality in his life, the
rest was an incoherent, purposeless dream.

"Is — is — Miss Sally married?" he
asked, collecting himself with an effort.

"Married? Yes, to that farm of her
aunt's! I reckon that's the only thing she
cares for."

Courtland looked up, recovering his
usual cheerful calm. "Well, I think that
after luncheon I'll pay my respects to her
family. From what you have just told me
the farm is certainly an experiment worth
seeing. I suppose your father will have no
objection to give me a letter to Miss Dows?"

CHAPTER II.

NEVERTHELESS, as Colonel Courtland rode deliberately towards Dows' Folly, as the new experiment was locally called, although he had not abated his romantic enthusiasm in the least, he was not sorry that he was able to visit it under a practical pretext. It was rather late now to seek out Miss Sally Dows with the avowed intent of bringing her a letter from an admirer who had been dead three years, and whose memory she had probably buried. Neither was it tactful to recall a sentiment which might have been a weakness of which she was ashamed. Yet, clear-headed and logical as Courtland was in his ordinary affairs, he was nevertheless not entirely free from that peculiar superstition which surrounds every man's romance. He believed there was something more than a mere coincidence in his unexpectedly finding himself in such favorable conditions for making her acquaintance. For the rest — if there was any rest — he would simply trust to fate. And so, be-

lieving himself a cool, sagacious **reasoner,**
but being actually, as far as Miss Dows was
concerned, as blind, fatuous, and unreasoning as any of her previous admirers, he rode
complacently forward until he reached the
lane that led to the Dows plantation.

Here a better kept roadway and fence,
whose careful repair would have delighted
Drummond, seemed to augur well for the
new enterprise. Presently, even the old-
fashioned local form of the fence, a slanting zigzag, gave way to the more direct
line of post and rail in the Northern fashion. Beyond it presently appeared a long
low frontage of modern buildings which, to
Courtland's surprise, were entirely new in
structure and design. There was no remi-
niscence of the usual Southern porticoed
gable or columned veranda. Yet it was
not Northern either. The factory-like outline of façade was partly hidden in Cherokee
rose and jessamine.

A long roofed gallery connected the buildings and became a veranda to one. A
broad, well-rolled gravel drive led from the
open gate to the newest building, which
seemed to be the office ; a smaller path di-
verged from it to the corner house, which,

despite its severe simplicity, had a more res-
idential appearance. Unlike Reed's house,
there were no lounging servants or field
hands to be seen; they were evidently attending to their respective duties. Dismount-
ing, Courtland tied his horse to a post at
the office door and took the smaller path to
the corner house.

The door was open to the fragrant afternoon breeze wafted through the rose and
jessamine. So also was a side door opening
from the hall into a long parlor or sitting-
room that ran the whole width of the house.
Courtland entered it. It was prettily furnished, but everything had the air of freshness and of being uncharacteristically new.
It was empty, but a faint hammering was
audible on the rear wall of the house,
through the two open French windows at
the back, curtained with trailing vines,
which gave upon a sunlit courtyard.
Courtland walked to the window. Just
before it, on the ground, stood a small
light ladder, which he gently put aside to
gain a better view of the courtyard as he
put on his hat, and stepped out of the open
window.

In this attitude he suddenly felt his hat

tipped from his head, followed almost instantaneously by a falling slipper, and the distinct impression of a very small foot on the crown of his head. An indescribable sensation passed over him. He hurriedly stepped back into the room, just as a small striped-stockinged foot was as hastily drawn up above the top of the window with the feminine exclamation, " Good gracious me ! "

Lingering for an instant, only to assure himself that the fair speaker had secured her foothold and was in no danger of falling, Courtland snatched up his hat, which had providentially fallen inside the room, and retreated ingloriously to the other end of the parlor. The voice came again from the window, and struck him as being very sweet and clear : —

" Sophy, is that *you ?* "

Courtland discreetly retired to the hall. To his great relief a voice from the outside answered, " Whar, Miss Sally ? "

" What did yo' move the ladder for? Yo' might have killed me."

" Fo' God, Miss Sally, I did n't move no ladder ! "

" Don't tell me, but go down and get my slipper. And bring up some more nails."

Courtland waited silently in the hall. In a few moments he heard a heavy footstep outside the rear window. This was his opportunity. Reëntering the parlor somewhat ostentatiously, he confronted a tall negro girl who was passing through the room carrying a tiny slipper in her hand. " Excuse me," he said politely, " but I could not find any one to announce me. Is Miss Dows at home ? "

The girl instantly whipped the slipper behind her. " Is yo' wanting Miss Mirandy Dows," she asked with great dignity, " oah Miss Sally Dows — her niece ? Miss Mirandy 's bin gone to Atlanta for a week."

" I have a letter for Miss Miranda, but I shall be very glad if Miss Sally Dows will receive me," returned Courtland, handing the letter and his card to the girl.

She received it with a still greater access of dignity and marked deliberation. " It 's clean gone outer my mind, sah, ef Miss Sally is in de resumption of visitahs at dis houah. In fac', sah," she continued, with intensified gravity and an exaggeration of thoughtfulness as the sounds of Miss Sally's hammering came shamelessly from the wall, " I doahn know exac'ly ef she 's engaged playin' de harp, practicin' de languages, or paintin' in oil and watah colors, o' givin' audiences to offishals from de Court House. It might be de houah for de one or de odder. But I 'll communicate wid her, sah, in de budwoh on de uppah flo'." She backed dexterously, so as to keep the slipper behind her, but with no diminution of dignity, out of a side door. In another moment the hammering ceased, followed by the sound of rapid whispering without ; a few tiny twigs and leaves slowly rustled to the ground, and then there was complete silence. He ventured to walk to the fateful window again.

Presently he heard a faint rustle at the other end of the room, and he turned. A sudden tremulousness swept along his pulses, and then they seemed to pause ; he drew a deep breath that was almost a sigh, and remained motionless.

He had no preconceived idea of falling in love with Miss Sally at first sight, nor had he dreamed such a thing possible. Even the girlish face that he had seen in the locket, although it had stirred him with a singular emotion, had not suggested that. And the ideal he had evolved from it was

never a potent presence. But the exqui-
sitely pretty face and figure before him,
although it might have been painted from his
own fancy of her, was still something more
and something unexpected. All that had
gone before had never prepared him for the
beautiful girl who now stood there. It was
a poor explanation to say that Miss Sally was
four or five years older than her picture, and
that later experiences, enlarged capacity, a
different life, and new ambition had impressed her youthful face with a refined mo-
bility; it was a weird fancy to imagine that
the blood of those who had died for her had
in some vague, mysterious way imparted an
actual fascination to her, and he dismissed it.
But even the most familiar spectator, like
Sophy, could see that Miss Sally had the soft-
est pink complexion, the silkiest hair, that
looked as the floss of the Indian corn might
look if curled, or golden spider threads if
materialized, and eyes that were in bright
gray harmony with both; that the frock of
India muslin, albeit home-made, fitted her
figure perfectly, from the azure bows on
her shoulders to the ribbon around her waist;
and that the hem of its billowy skirt
showed a foot which had the reputation of

being the smallest foot south of Mason and Dixon's Line! But it was something more intangible than this which kept Courtland breathless and silent.

"I 'm not Miss Miranda Dows," said the vision with a frankness that was half child-like and half practical, as she extended a lit-tle hand, "but I can talk 'fahm' with yo' about as well as aunty, and I reckon from what Major Reed says heah," holding up the letter between her fingers, "as long as yo' get the persimmons yo' don't mind what kind o' pole yo' knock 'em down with."

The voice that carried this speech was so fresh, clear, and sweet that I am afraid Courtland thought little of its bluntness or its conventional transgressions. But it brought him his own tongue quite unemo-tionally and quietly. "I don't know what was in that note, Miss Dows, but I can hardly believe that Major Reed ever put my present felicity quite in that way."

Miss Sally laughed. Then with a charm-ing exaggeration she waved her little hand towards the sofa.

"There! Yo' naturally wanted a little room for that, co'nnle, but now that yo' 've got it off, — and mighty pooty it was, too,—

yo' can sit down." And with that she sank
down at one end of the sofa, prettily drew
aside a white billow of skirt so as to leave
ample room for Courtland at the other, and
clasping her fingers over her knees, looked
demurely expectant.

"But let me hope that I am not disturbing you unseasonably," said Courtland,
catching sight of the fateful little slipper
beneath her skirt, and remembering the window. "I was so preoccupied in thinking of
your aunt as the business manager of these
estates that I quite forgot that she might
have a lady's hours for receiving."

"We have n't got any company hours,"
said Miss Sally, "and we have n't just now
any servants for company manners, for
we're short-handed in the fields and barns.
When yo' came I was nailing up the laths for
the vines outside, because we could n't spare
carpenters from the factory. But," she added,
with a faint accession of mischief in her
voice, "yo' came to talk about the fahm?"

"Yes," said Courtland, rising but not
to interrupt the work on it. Will you let
me help you nail up the laths on the wall?
I have some experience that way, and we
can talk as we work. Do oblige me!"

The young girl looked at him brightly.

" Well, now, there's nothing mean about *that*. Yo' mean it for sure?"

" Perfectly. I shall feel so much less as if I was enjoying your company under false pretenses."

" Yo' just wait here, then."

She jumped from the sofa, ran out of the room, and returned presently, tying the string of a long striped cotton blouse — evidently an extra one of Sophy's — behind her back as she returned. It was gathered under her oval chin by a tape also tied behind her, while her fair hair was tucked under the usual red bandana handkerchief of the negro housemaid. It is scarcely necessary to add that the effect was bewitching.

" But," said Miss Sally, eying her guest's smartly fitting frock-coat, "yo' 'll spoil yo'r pooty clothes, sure! Take off yo'r coat — don't mind me — and work in yo'r shirt-sleeves."

Courtland obediently flung aside his coat and followed his active hostess through the French window to the platform outside. Above them a wooden ledge or cornice, projecting several inches, ran the whole length

of the building. It was on this that Miss
Sally had evidently found a foothold while
she was nailing up a trellis-work of laths
between it and the windows of the second
floor. Courtland found the ladder, mounted
to the ledge, followed by the young girl, who
smilingly waived his proffered hand to help
her up, and the two gravely set to work.
But in the intervals of hammering and tying up the vines Miss Sally's tongue was not
idle. Her talk was as fresh, as quaint, as
original as herself, and yet so practical and
to the purpose of Courtland's visit as to
excuse his delight in it and her own fascinating propinquity. Whether she stopped
to take a nail from between her pretty lips
when she spoke to him, or whether holding
on perilously with one hand to the trellis
while she gesticulated with the hammer,
pointing out the divisions of the plantation
from her coign of vantage, he thought she
was as clear and convincing to his intellect
as she was distracting to his senses.

She told him how the war had broken
up their old home in Pineville, sending her
father to serve in the Confederate councils
of Richmond, and leaving her aunt and herself to manage the property alone; how the

estate had been devastated, the house destroyed, and how they had barely time to
remove a few valuables; how, although *she*
had always been opposed to secession and
the war, she had not gone North, preferring
to stay with her people, and take with them
the punishment of the folly she had foreseen.
How after the war and her father's death
she and her aunt had determined to "recon-
struct *themselves*" after their own fashion
on this bit of property, which had survived
their fortunes because it had always been
considered valueless and unprofitable for
negro labor.   How at first they had under-
gone serious difficulty, through the incompetence and ignorance of the freed laborer,
and the equal apathy and prejudice of their
neighbors.   How they had gradually succeeded with the adoption of new methods
and ideas that she herself had conceived,
which she now briefly and clearly stated.
Courtland listened with a new, breathless,
and almost superstitious interest: they were
his own theories — perfected and demon-
strated!

   "But you must have had capital for
this?"

   Ah, yes! that was where they were for-

tunate. There were some French cousins
with whom she had once stayed in Paris,
who advanced enough to stock the estate.
There were some English friends of her
father's, old blockade runners, who had
taken shares, provided them with more capital, and imported some skilled laborers and
a kind of steward or agent to represent them.
But they were getting on, and perhaps it was
better for their reputation with their neighbors that they had not been *beholden* to
the "No'th." Seeing a cloud pass over
Courtland's face, the young lady added with
an affected sigh, and the first touch of feminine coquetry which had invaded their wholesome *camaraderie :* —

"Yo' ought to have found us out *before,*
co'nnle."

For an impulsive moment Courtland felt
like telling her then and there the story of
his romantic quest; but the reflection that
they were standing on a narrow ledge with
no room for the emotions, and that Miss
Sally had just put a nail in her mouth and
a start might be dangerous, checked him.
To this may be added a new jealousy of her
previous experiences, which he had not felt
before. Nevertheless, he managed to say
with some effusion : —

"But I hope we are not too late *now*. I think my principals are quite ready and able to buy up any English or French investor now or to come."

"Yo' might try yo' hand on that one," said Miss Sally, pointing to a young fellow who had just emerged from the office and was crossing the courtyard. "He's the English agent."

He was square-shouldered and round-headed, fresh and clean looking in his white flannels, but with an air of being utterly distinct and alien to everything around him, and mentally and morally irreconcilable to it. As he passed the house he glanced shyly at it; his eye brightened and his manner became self-conscious as he caught sight of the young girl, but changed again when he saw her companion. Courtland likewise was conscious of a certain uneasiness; it was one thing to be helping Miss Sally *alone*, but certainly another thing to be doing so under the eye of a stranger; and I am afraid that he met the stony observation of the Englishman with an equally cold stare. Miss Sally alone retained her languid ease and self-possession. She called out, "Wait a moment, Mr. Champney," slipped lightly down the ladder, and leaning against it with one foot on its lowest rung awaited his approach.

" I reckoned yo' might be passing by," she said, as he came forward. " Co'nnle Court-land," with an explanatory wave of the hammer towards her companion, who re-mained erect and slightly stiffened on the cornice, " is no relation to those figures along the frieze of the Redlands Court House, but a No'th'n officer, a friend of Major Reed's, who 's come down here to look after So'th'n property for some No'th'n cap-italists. Mr. Champney," she continued, turning and lifting her eyes to Courtland as she indicated Champney with her hammer, "when he is n't talking English, seeing Eng-lish, thinking English, dressing English, and wondering why God did n't make everything English, is trying to do the same for *his* folks. Mr. Champney, Co'nnle Courtland. Co'nnle Courtland, Mr. Champney ! " The two men bowed formally. " And now, Co'nnle, if yo' ll come down, Mr. Champney will show yo' round the fahm. When yo' 've got through yo' ll find me here at work."

Courtland would have preferred, and half looked for her company and commentary on this round of inspection, but he concealed his disappointment and descended. It did not exactly please him that Champney seemed relieved, and appeared to accept him as a *bona fide* stranger who could not possibly interfere with any confidential relations that he might have with Miss Sally. Nevertheless, he met the Englishman's offer to accompany him with polite gratitude, and they left the house together.

In less than an hour they returned. It had not even taken that time for Courtland to discover that the real improvements and the new methods had originated with Miss Sally; that she was virtually the controlling influence there, and that she was probably retarded rather than assisted by the old-fashioned and traditional conservatism of the company of which Champney was steward. It was equally plain, however, that the young fellow was dimly conscious of this, and was frankly communicative about it.

" You see, over there they work things in a different way, and, by Jove! they can't understand that there is any other, don't you know? They're always wigging me as if I could help it, although I've tried to explain the nigger business, and all that, don't you know? They want Miss Dows to refer her plans to me, and expect me to report on them, and then they'll submit them to the Board and wait for its decision. Fancy Miss Dows doing that! But, by Jove! they can't conceive of her *at all* over there, don't you know?"

"Which Miss Dows do you mean?" asked Courtland dryly.

"Miss Sally, of course," said the young fellow briskly. "*She* manages everything — her aunt included. She can make those niggers work when no one else can, a word or smile from her is enough. She can make terms with dealers and contractors — her own terms, too — when they won't look at *my* figures. By Jove! she even gets points out of those traveling agents and inventors, don't you know, who come along the road with patents and samples. She got one of those lightning-rod and wire-fence men to show her how to put up an arbor for her trailing roses. Why, when I first saw *you* up on the cornice, I thought you were some other chap that she'd asked — don't you know — that is, at first, of course! — you know what I mean — ha, by Jove! — before we were introduced, don't you know."

"I think I *offered* to help Miss Dows,"

said Courtland with a quickness that he at once regretted.

"So did *he*, don't you know? Miss Sally does not *ask* anybody. Don't you see? a fellow don't like to stand by and see a young lady like her doing such work." Vaguely aware of some infelicity in his speech, he awkwardly turned the subject: "I don't think I shall stay here long, myself."

"You expect to return to England?" asked Courtland.

"Oh, no! But I shall go out of the company's service and try my own hand. There's a good bit of land about three miles from here that's in the market, and I think I could make something out of it. A fellow ought to settle down and be his own master," he answered tentatively, "eh?"

"But how will Miss Dows be able to spare you?" asked Courtland, uneasily conscious that he was assuming an indifference.

"Oh, I'm not much use to her, don't you know—at least not *here*. But I might, if I had my own land and if we were neighbors. I told you *she* runs the place, no matter who's here, or whose money is invested."

"I presume you are speaking now of young Miss Dows?" said Courtland dryly.

"Miss Sally — of course — always," said Champney simply. "She runs the shop."

"Were there not some French investors — relations of Miss Dows? Does anybody represent *them?*" asked Courtland pointedly.

Yet he was not quite prepared for the naïve change in his companion's face. "No. There was a sort of French cousin who used to be a good deal to the fore, don't you know? But I rather fancy he did n't come here to look after the *property*," returned Champney with a quick laugh. "I think the aunt must have written to his friends, for they 'called him off,' and I don't think Miss Sally broke her heart about him. She 's not that sort of girl — eh? She could have her pick of the State if she went in for that sort of thing — eh?"

Although this was exactly what Courtland was thinking, it pleased him to answer in a distrait sort of fashion, "Certainly, I should think so," and to relapse into an apparently business abstraction.

"I think I won't go in," continued Champney as they neared the house again. "I suppose you 'll have something more to say to Miss Dows. If there 's anything else

you want of *me*, come to the office. But
she'll know.   And — er — er — if you're
— er — staying long in this part of the
country, ride over and look me up, don't
you know? and have a smoke and a julep;
I have a boy who knows how to mix them,
and I've some old brandy sent me from the
other side.   Good-by."

More awkward in his kindliness than in
his simple business confidences, but apparently equally honest in both, he shook Courtland's hand and walked away.   Courtland
turned towards the house.   He had seen the
farm and its improvements; he had found
some of his own ideas practically discounted;
clearly there was nothing left for him to do
but to thank his hostess and take his leave.
But he felt far more uneasy than when he
had arrived; and there was a singular sense
of incompleteness in his visit that he could
not entirely account for.   His conversation
with Champney had complicated — he knew
not why — his previous theories of Miss
Dows, and although he was half conscious
that this had nothing to do with the business
that brought him there, he tried to think
that it had.   If Miss Sally was really — a —
a — distracting element to contiguous man,

It was certainly something to be considered in a matter of business of which she would take a managerial part. It was true that Champney had said she was "not that sort of girl," but this was the testimony of one who was clearly under her influence. He entered the house through the open French window. The parlor was deserted. He walked through the front hall and porch; no one was there. He lingered a few moments, a slight chagrin beginning to mingle with his uneasiness. She might have been on the lookout for him. She or Sophy must have seen him returning. He would ring for Sophy, and leave his thanks and regrets for her mistress. He looked for a bell, touched it, but on being confronted with Sophy, changed his mind and asked to *see* Miss Dows. In the interval between her departure and the appearance of Miss Sally he resolved to do the very thing which he had dismissed from his thoughts but an hour before as ill-timed and doubtful. He had the photograph and letter in his pocket; he would make them his excuse for personally taking leave of her.

She entered with her fair eyebrows lifted in a pretty surprise.

"I declare to goodness, I thought yo''d ridden over to the red barn and gone home from there. I got through my work on the vines earlier than I thought. One of Judge Garret's nephews dropped in in time to help me with the last row. Yo' need n't have troubled yo'self to send up for me for mere company manners, but Sophy says yo' looked sort of 'anxious and particular' when yo' asked for me — so I suppose yo' want to see me for something."

Mentally objurgating Sophy, and with an unpleasant impression in his mind of the unknown neighbor who had been helping Miss Sally in his place, he nevertheless tried to collect himself gallantly.

"I don't know what my expression conveyed to Sophy," he said with a smile, "but I trust that what I have to tell you may be interesting enough to make you forget my second intrusion." He paused, and still smiling continued: "For more than three years, Miss Dows, you have more or less occupied my thoughts; and although we have actually met to-day only for the first time, I have during that time carried your image with me constantly. Even this meeting, which was only the result of an accident,

I had been seeking for three years. I find you here under your own peaceful vine and fig-tree, and yet three years ago you came to me out of the thunder-cloud of battle."

" My good gracious ! " said Miss Sally.

She had been clasping her knee with her linked fingers, but separated them and leaned backward on the sofa with affected consternation, but an expression of growing amusement in her bright eyes. Courtland saw the mistake of his tone, but it was too late to change it now. He handed her the locket and the letter, and briefly, and perhaps a little more seriously, recounted the incident that had put him in possession of them. But he entirely suppressed the more dramatic and ghastly details, and his own superstition and strange prepossession towards her.

Miss Sally took the articles without a tremor, or the least deepening or paling of the delicate, faint suffusion of her cheek. When she had glanced over the letter, which appeared to be brief, she said, with smiling, half-pitying tranquillity : —

" Yes ! — it *was* that poor Chet Brooks, sure ! I heard that he was killed at Snake River. It was just like him to rush in and get killed the first pop ! And all for nothing, too, — pure foolishness ! "

Shocked, yet relieved, but uneasy under both sensations, Courtland went on blindly:

"But he was not the only one, Miss Dows. There was another man picked up who also had your picture."

"Yes — Joyce Masterton. They sent it to me. But you did n't kill *him*, too?"

"I don't know that I personally killed either," he said a little coldly. He paused, and continued with a gravity which he could not help feeling very inconsistent and even ludicrous: "They were brave men, Miss Dows."

"To have worn my picture?" said Miss Sally brightly.

"To have *thought* they had so much to live for, and yet to have willingly laid down their lives for what they believed was right."

"Yo' did n't go huntin' me for three years to tell *me*, a So'th'n girl, that So'th'n men know how to fight, did yo', co'nnle?" returned the young lady, with the slightest lifting of her head and drooping of her blue-veined lids in a divine hauteur. "They were always ready enough for that, even among themselves. It was much easier for these pooah boys to fight a thing out than think it out, or work it out. Yo' folks in the No'th learned to do all three; that's where you got the grip on us. Yo' look surprised, co'nnle."

"I did n't expect you would look at it — quite in — in — that way," said Courtland awkwardly.

"I am sorry I disappointed yo' after yo' 'd taken such a heap o' trouble," returned the young lady with a puzzling assumption of humility as she rose and smoothed out her skirts, " but I could n't know exactly what yo' might be expecting after three years; if I *had*, I might have put on mo'ning." She stopped and adjusted a straying tendril of her hair with the sharp corner of the dead man's letter. " But I thank yo', all the same, co'nnle. It was real good in yo' to think of toting these things over here." And she held out her hand frankly.

Courtland took it with the sickening consciousness that for the last five minutes he had been an unconscionable ass. He could not prolong the interview after she had so significantly risen. If he had only taken his leave and kept the letter and locket for a later visit, perhaps when they were older friends! It was too late now. He bent over her hand for a moment, again thanked her for her courtesy, and withdrew. A moment later she heard the receding beat of his horse's hoofs on the road.

She opened the drawer of a brass-handled cabinet, and after a moment's critical survey of her picture in the dead man's locket, tossed it and the letter into the recesses of the drawer. Then she stopped, removed her little slipper from her foot, looked at *that*, too, thoughtfully, and called "Sophy!"

" Miss Sally?" said the girl, reappearing at the door.

" Are you sure you did not move that ladder?"

" I 'clare to goodness, Miss Sally, I never teched it!"

Miss Sally directed a critical glance at her handmaiden's red-coifed head. "No," she said to herself softly, " it felt nicer than wool, anyway!"

CHAPTER III.

IN spite of the awkward termination of his visit, — or perhaps *because* of it, — Courtland called again at the plantation within the week. But this time he was accompanied by Drummond, and was received by Miss Miranda Dows, a tall, aquiline-nosed spinster of fifty, whose old-time politeness had become slightly affected, and whose old beliefs had given way to a half-cynical acceptance of new facts. Mr. Drummond, delighted with the farm and its management, was no less fascinated by Miss Sally, while Courtland was now discreet enough to divide his attentions between her and her aunt, with the result that he was far from participating in Champney's conviction of Miss Miranda's unimportance. To the freedmen she still represented the old implacable task-mistress, and it was evident that they superstitiously believed that she still retained a vague power of overriding the Fourteenth Amendment at her pleasure, and was only to be restrained by the media-

tion of the good-humored and sensible Miss
Sally. Courtland was quick to see the value
of this influence in the transition state of
the freedmen, and pointed it out to his principal. Drummond's previous doubts and
skepticism, already weakened by Miss Sally's fascinations, vanished entirely at this
prospect of beneficially utilizing these lingering evils of slavery. He was convinced,
he was even enthusiastic. The foreign investors were men to be bought out; the estate improved and enlarged by the company,
and the fair owners retained in the management and control. Like most prejudiced
men, Drummond's conversion was sudden
and extreme, and, being a practical man,
was at once acted upon. At a second and
third interview the preliminaries were arranged, and in three weeks from Courtland's
first visit, the Dows' plantation and part of
Major Reed's were merged in the "Drummond Syndicate," and placed beyond financial uncertainty. Courtland remained to
represent the company as superintendent at
Redlands, and with the transfer of the English investments Champney retired, as he
had suggested, to a smaller venture of his
own, on a plantation a few miles distant

which the company had been unable to secure.

During this interval Courtland had frequent interviews with Miss Sally, and easy and unrestrained access to her presence. He had never again erred on the side of romance or emotion ; he had never again referred to the infelix letter and photograph ; and, without being obliged to confine himself strictly to business affairs, he had maintained an even, quiet, neighborly intercourse with her. Much of this was the result of his own self-control and soldierly training, and gave little indication of the deeper feeling that he was conscious lay beneath it. At times he caught the young girl's eyes fixed upon him with a mischievous curiosity. A strange thrill went through him ; there are few situations so subtle and dangerous as the accidental confidences and understandings of two young people of opposite sex, even though the question of any sentimental inclination be still in abeyance. Courtland knew that Miss Sally remembered the too serious attitude he had taken towards her past. She might laugh at it, and even resent it, but she *knew* it, remembered it, knew that *he* did, and this precious

knowledge was confined to themselves. It
was in their minds when there was a pause
in their more practical and conventional conversation, and was even revealed in the ex-
cessive care which Miss Sally later took to
avert at the right moment her mischievously smiling eyes. Once she went farther.
Courtland had just finished explaining to
her a plan for substituting small farm buildings for the usual half-cultivated garden-
patches dear to the negro field - hand, and
had laid down the drawings on the table in
the office, when the young lady, leaning
against it with her hands behind her, fixed
her bright gray eyes on his serious face.

"I vow and protest, co'nnle," she said,
dropping into one of the quaint survivals of
an old-time phraseology peculiar to her people, "I never allowed yo' could just give
yo'self up to business, soul and body, as yo'
do, when I first met yo' that day."

"Why, what did you think me?" he
asked quickly.

Miss Sally, who had a Southern aptitude
for gesture, took one little hand from behind her, twirled it above her head with a
pretty air of disposing of some airy nothing
in a presumably masculine fashion, and
said, "Oh, *that.*"

"I am afraid I did not impress you then as a very practical man," he said, with a faint color.

"I thought you roosted rather high, co'nnle, to pick up many worms in the mo'ning. But," she added with a dazzling smile, "I reckon from what yo' said about the photograph, yo' thought *I* was n't exactly what yo' believed I ought to be, either."

He would have liked to tell her then and there that he would have been content if those bright, beautiful eyes had never kindled with anything but love or womanly aspiration; that that soft, lazy, caressing voice had never been lifted beyond the fireside or domestic circle; that the sunny, tendriled hair and pink ears had never inclined to anything but whispered admiration; and that the graceful, lithe, erect figure, so independent and self-contained, had been satisfied to lean only upon his arm for support. He was conscious that this had been in his mind when he first saw her; he was equally conscious that she was more bewilderingly fascinating to him in her present inaccessible intelligence and practicality.

"I confess," he said, looking into her eyes with a vague smile, "I did not expect you

would be so forgetful of some one who had
evidently cared for you."

"Meaning Mr. Chet Brooks, or Mr. Joyce
Masterton, or both. That 's like most yo'
men, co'nnle. Yo' reckon because a girl
pleases yo' she ought to be grateful all her
life — and yo'rs, too! Yo' think different
now! But yo' need n't act up to it quite so
much." She made a little deprecating gesture with her disengaged hand as if to ward
off any retaliating gallantry. "I ain't speaking for myself, co'nnle. Yo' and me are good
enough friends. But the girls round here
think yo' 're a trifle too much taken up with
rice and niggers. And looking at it even
in yo'r light, co'nnle, it ain't *business.* Yo'
want to keep straight with Major Reed, so
it would be just as well to square the major's woman folks. Tavy and Gussie Reed
ain't exactly poisonous, co'nnle, and yo' might
see one or the other home from church next
Sunday. The Sunday after that, just to
show yo' ain't particular, and that yo' go
in for being a regular beau, yo' might walk
home with *me.* Don't be frightened — I 've
got a better gown than this. It 's a new one,
just come home from Louisville, and I 'll wear
it for the occasion."

He did not dare to say that the quaint frock she was then wearing — a plain " checked " household gingham used for children's pinafores, with its ribbons of the same pattern, gathered in bows at the smart apron pockets — had become a part of her beauty, for he was already hopelessly conscious that she was lovely in anything, and he might be impelled to say so. He thanked her gravely and earnestly, but without gallantry or effusion, and had the satisfaction of seeing the mischief in her eyes increase in proportion to his seriousness, and heard her say with affected concern: " Bear up, co'nnle! Don't let it worry yo' till the time comes," and took his leave.

On the following Sunday he was present at the Redlands Episcopal Church, and after the service stood with outward composure but some inward chafing among the gallant youth who, after the local fashion, had ranged themselves outside the doors of the building. He was somewhat surprised to find Mr. Champney, evidently as much out of place as himself, but less self-contained, waiting in the crowd of expectant cavaliers. Although convinced that the young Englishman had come only to see Miss Sally, he was

glad to share his awkward isolation with another stranger, and greeted him pleasantly.
The Dows' pew, being nearer to the entrance
than the Reeds', gave up its occupants first.
Colonel Courtland lifted his hat to Miss
Miranda and her niece at the same moment
that Champney moved forward and ranged
himself beside them. Miss Sally, catching
Courtland's eye, showed the whites of her
own in a backward glance of mischievous
significance to indicate the following Reeds.
When they approached, Courtland joined
them, and finding himself beside Miss Octavia entered into conversation. Apparently
the suppressed passion and sardonic melancholy of that dark-eyed young lady spurred
him to a lighter, gayer humor even in proportion as Miss Sally's good-natured levity
and sunny practicality always made him
serious.   They presently fell to the rear with
other couples, and were soon quite alone.

A little haughty, but tall and erect in her
well-preserved black grenadine dress, which
gave her the appearance of a youthful but
implacable widow, Miss Reed declared she
had not seen the co'nnle for "a coon's age,"
and certainly had not expected to have
the honor of his company as long as there

were niggers to be elevated or painted to
look like white men. She hoped that he and
paw and Sally Dows were happy! They
had n't yet got so far as to put up a nigger
preacher in the place of Mr. Symes, their
rector, but she understood that there was
some talk of running Hannibal Johnson —
Miss Dows' coachman — for county judge
next year! No! she had not heard that the
co'nnle *himself* had thought of running for
the office! He might laugh at her as much
as he liked — he seemed to be in better spirits than when she first saw him — only she
would like to know if it was " No'th'n style "
to laugh coming home from church? Of
course if it *was* she would have to adopt it
with the Fourteenth Amendment. But, just
now, she noticed the folks were staring at
them, and Miss Sally Dows had turned
round to look. Nevertheless, Miss Octavia's
sallow cheek nearest the colonel — the sunny
side — had taken a faint brunette's flush,
and the corners of her proud mouth were
slightly lifted.

" But, candidly, Miss Reed, don't you
think that you would prefer to have old
Hannibal, whom you know, as county judge,
than a stranger and a Northern man like
me?"

Miss Reed's dark eyes glanced sideways at the handsome face and elegant figure beside her. Something like a saucy smile struggled to her thin lips.

" There might n't be much to choose, co 'nnle."

" I admit it. We should both acknowledge our mistress, and be like wax in her hands."

" Yo' ought to make that pooty speech to Sally Dows, she 's generally mistress around here. But,' she added, suddenly fixing her eyes on him, " how does it happen that yo' ain't walking with her instead of that Englishman ? Yo' know that it 's as plain as day that he took that land over there just to be near her, when he was no longer agent."

But Courtland was always master of himself and quite at ease regarding Miss Sally when not in that lady's presence. " You forget," he said smilingly, " that I 'm still a stranger and know little of the local gossip ; and if I did know it, I am afraid we did n't bargain to buy up with the *land* Mr. Champney's personal interest in the *landlady.*"

" Yo' 'd have had your hands full, for I reckon she 's pooty heavily mortgaged in

that fashion, already," returned Miss Reed
with more badinage than spitefulness in the
suggestion. "And Mr. Champney was run
pooty close by a French cousin of hers when
he was here. Yo' have n't got any French
books to lend me, co'nnle — have yo'? Paw
says you read a heap of French, and I find
it mighty hard to keep up *my* practice since
I left the Convent at St. Louis, for paw
don't know what sort of books to order, and
I reckon he makes awful mistakes sometimes."

The conversation here turning upon polite
literature, it appeared that Miss Octavia's
French reading, through a shy, proud innocence and an imperfect knowledge of the
wicked subtleties of the language, was somewhat broad and unconventional for a young
lady. Courtland promised to send her some
books, and even ventured to suggest some
American and English novels not intensely
" No'th'n " nor " metaphysical " — according to the accepted Southern beliefs. A
new respect and pitying interest in this
sullen, solitary girl, cramped by tradition,
and bruised rather than enlightened by sad
experiences, came over him. He found himself talking quite confidentially to the lifted

head, arched eyebrows, and aquiline nose
beside him, and even thinking what a handsome high-bred *brother* she might have been
to some one. When they had reached the
house, in compliance with the familiar custom, he sat down on one of the lower steps
of the veranda, while she, shaking out her
skirt, took a seat a step or two above him.
This enabled him, after the languid local
fashion, to lean on his elbow and gaze up
into the eyes of the young lady, while she
with equal languor looked down upon him.
But in the present instance Miss Reed
leaned forward suddenly, and darting a
sharp quick glance into his very consciousness said : —

"And yo' mean to say, co'nnle, there's
nothing between yo' and Sally Dows ? "

Courtland neither flushed, trembled, grew
confused, nor prevaricated.

"We are good friends, I think," he replied quietly, without evasion or hesitation.

Miss Reed looked at him thoughtfully,
"I reckon that is so — and no more. And
that's why yo' 've been so lucky in everything," she said slowly.

"I don't think I quite understand," returned Courtland, smiling. "Is this a para-
dox — or a consolation ? "

"It's the *truth*," said Miss Reed gravely. "Those who try to be anything more to Sally Dows lose their luck."

"That is — are rejected by her. Is she really so relentless?" continued Courtland gayly.

"I mean that they lose their luck in everything. Something is sure to happen. And *she* can't help it either."

"Is this a Sibylline warning, Miss Reed?'

"No. It's nigger superstition. It came from Mammy Judy, Sally's old nurse. It's part of their regular Hoo-doo. She bewitched Miss Sally when she was a baby, so that everybody is bound to *her* as long as they care for her, and she is n't bound to *them* in any way. All their luck goes to her as soon as the spell is on them," she added darkly.

"I think I know the rest," returned Courtland with still greater solemnity. "You gather the buds of the witch-hazel in April when the moon is full. You then pluck three hairs from the young lady's right eyebrow when she is n't looking"—

"Yo' can laugh, co'nnle, for yo' 're lucky — because yo' 're free."

"I'm not so sure of that," he said gal-

lantly, " for I ought to be riding at this
moment over to the Infirmary to visit my
Sunday sick. If being made to pleasantly
forget one's time and duty is a sign of witch-
craft I am afraid Mammy Judy's enchant-
ments were not confined to only one Southern young lady."

The sound of quick footsteps on the gravel
path caused them both to look up. A surly
looking young fellow, ostentatiously booted
and spurred, and carrying a heavy rawhide
riding-whip in his swinging hand, was approaching them. Deliberately, yet with uneasy self-consciousness, ignoring the presence
of Courtland, he nodded abruptly to Miss
Reed, ascended the steps, brushed past them
both without pausing, and entered the house.

" Is that yo'r manners, Mr. Tom?" called
the young lady after him, a slight flush rising to her sallow cheek. The young man
muttered something from the hall which
Courtland did not catch. "It's Cousin
Tom Higbee," she explained half disdain-
fully. "He's had some ugliness with his
horse, I reckon; but paw ought to teach
him how to behave. And — I don't think
he likes No'th'n men," she added gravely.

Courtland, who had kept his temper with

his full understanding of the intruder's
meaning, smiled as he took Miss Reed's
hand in parting. "That's quite enough
explanation, and I don't know why it
should n't be even an apology."

Yet the incident left little impression on
him as he strolled back to Redlands. It
was not the first time he had tasted the dregs
of former sectional hatred in incivility and
discourtesy, but as it seldom came from his
old personal antagonists — the soldiers —
and was confined to the callow youth, previous non-combatants and politicians, he
could afford to overlook it. He did not see
Miss Sally during the following week.

CHAPTER IV.

On the next Sunday he was early at
church. But he had perhaps accented the
occasion by driving there in a light buggy
behind a fast thoroughbred, possibly selected
more to the taste of a smart cavalry officer
than an agricultural superintendent. He
was already in a side pew, his eyes dreamily
fixed on the prayer-book ledge before him,
when there was a rustle at the church door,
and a thrill of curiosity and admiration
passed over the expectant congregation. It
was the entrance of the Dows party, Miss
Sally well to the fore. She was in her new
clothes, the latest fashion in Louisville, the
latest but two in Paris and New York.

It was over twenty years ago. I shall not
imperil the effect of that lovely vision by
recalling to the eye of to-day a fashion of
yesterday. Enough, that it enabled her to
set her sweet face and vapory golden hair
in a horseshoe frame of delicate flowers, and
to lift her oval chin out of a bewildering
mist of tulle. Nor did a certain light polo-

naise conceal the outlines of her charming
figure. Even those who were constrained to
whisper to each other that "Miss Sally"
must "be now going on twenty-five," did so
because she still carried the slender graces
of seventeen. The organ swelled as if to welcome her; as she took her seat a ray of sunlight, that would have been cruel and searching to any other complexion, drifted across
the faint pink of her cheeks, and nestling in
her nebulous hair became itself transfigured.
A few stained-glass Virtues on the windows
did not come out of this effulgence as triumphantly, and it was small wonder that the
devotional eyes of the worshipers wandered
from them to the face of Sally Dows.

When the service was over, as the congregation filed slowly into the aisle, Courtland slipped mutely behind her. As she
reached the porch he said in an undertone:
"I brought my horse and buggy. I thought
you might possibly allow me to drive" —
But he was stopped by a distressful knitting
of her golden brows. "No," she said quickly,
but firmly, "you must not — it won't do."
As Courtland hesitated in momentary perplexity, she smiled sweetly: "We'll walk
round by the cemetery, if you like; it will

take about as long as a drive." Courtland
vanished, gave hurried instructions and a
dollar to a lounging negro, and rejoined Miss
Sally as the delighted and proud freedman
drove out of the gate. Miss Sally heaved a
slight sigh as the gallant equipage passed.
"It was a mighty pooty turnout, co'nnle,
and I'd have just admired to go, but it
would have been rather hard on the other
folks. There's the Reeds and Maxwells
and Robertsons that are too pooah to keep
blood horses, and too proud to ride behind
anything else. It would n't be the right
thing for us to go whirling by, scattering
our dust over them." There was something
so subtly pleasant in this implied partner-
ship of responsibility, that Courtland forgot
the abrupt refusal and thought only of the
tact that prompted it. Nevertheless, here a
spell seemed to fall upon his usually ready
speech. Now that they were together for
the first time in a distinctly social fashion,
he found himself vacantly, meaninglessly
silent, content to walk beside this charming,
summery presence, brushed by its delicate
draperies, and inhaling its freshness. Presently it spoke.

"It would take more than a thousand feet

of lumber to patch up the cowsheds beyond the Moseley pasture, and an entirely new building with an improved dairy would require only about two thousand more. All the old material would come in good for fencing, and could be used with the new post and rails. Don't yo' think it would be better to have an out-and-out new building?"

"Yes, certainly," returned Courtland a little confusedly. He had not calculated upon this practical conversation, and was the more disconcerted as they were passing some of the other couples, who had purposely lingered to overhear them.

"And," continued the young girl brightly, "the freight question is getting to be a pretty serious one. Aunt Miranda holds some shares in the Briggsville branch line, and thinks something could be done with the directors for a new tariff of charges if she put a pressure on them; Tyler says that there was some talk of their reducing it one sixteenth per cent. before we move this year's crop."

Courtland glanced quickly at his companion's face. It was grave, but there was the faintest wrinkling of the corner of the eye-

lid nearest him. "Had we not better leave
these serious questions until to-morrow?"
he said, smiling.

Miss Sally opened her eyes demurely.
"Why, yo' seemed *so* quiet, I reckoned
yo' must be full of business this morning;
but if yo' prefer company talk, we'll change
the subject. They say that yo' and Miss
Reed did n't have much trouble to find one
last Sunday. She don't usually talk much,
but she keeps up a power of thinking. I
should reckon," she added, suddenly eying
him critically, "that yo' and she might have
a heap o' things to say to each other. She's
a good deal in yo' fashion, co'nnle, she don't
forget, but " — more slowly — " I don't
know that *that's* altogether the best thing
for *yo'!*"

Courtland lifted his eyes with affected
consternation. "If this is in the light of
another mysterious warning, Miss Dows, I
warn you that my intellect is already totter-
ing with them. Last Sunday Miss Reed
thrilled me for an hour with superstition
and Cassandra-like prophecy. Don't things
ever happen accidentally here, and without
warning?"

"I mean," returned the young lady with

her usual practical directness, " that Tave Reed remembers a good many horrid things about the wah that she ought to forget, but don't. But," she continued, looking at him curiously, " she allows she was mighty cut up by her cousin's manner to yo'."

" I am afraid that Miss Reed was more annoyed than I was," said Courtland. " I should be very sorry if she attached any importance to it," he added earnestly.

" And *yo'* don't ? " continued Miss Sally.

" No. Why should I ? " She noticed, however, that he had slightly drawn himself up a little more erect, and she smiled as he continued, " I dare say I should feel as he does if I were in his place."

" But *yo'* wouldn't do anything underhanded," she said quietly. As he glanced at her quickly she added dryly : " Don't trust too much to people always acting in yo' fashion, co'nnle. And don't think too much nor too little of what yo' hear here. Yo' 're just the kind of man to make a good many silly enemies, and as many foolish friends. And I don't know which will give yo' the most trouble. Only don't yo' underrate *either*, or hold yo' head so high, yo' don't see what's crawlin' around yo'. That's why, in a copperhead swamp, a horse is bitten oftener than a hog."

She smiled, yet with knitted brows and such a pretty affectation of concern for her companion that he suddenly took heart.

" I wish I had *one* friend I could call my own," he said boldly, looking straight into her eyes. "I'd care little for other friends, and fear no enemies."

" Yo' 're right, co'nnle," she said, ostentatiously slanting her parasol in a marvelous simulation of hiding a purely imaginative blush on a cheek that was perfectly infantine in its unchanged pink; "company talk is much pootier than what we 've been saying. And — meaning me — for I reckon yo' would n't say that of any other girl but the one yo' 're walking with — what 's the matter with *me?*"

He could not help smiling, though he hesitated. " Nothing! but others have been disappointed."

" And that bothers *yo'?*"

" I mean *I* have as yet had no right to put your feelings to any test, while " —

" Poor Chet had, yo' were going to say ! Well, here we are at the cemetery! I reckoned yo' were bound to get back to the

dead again before we'd gone far, and that's
why I thought we might take the cemetery
on our way. It may put me in a more
proper frame of mind to please yo'."

As he raised his eyes he could not repress
a slight start. He had not noticed before
that they had passed through a small gate-
way on diverging from the road, and was
quite unprepared to find himself on the edge
of a gentle slope leading to a beautiful valley, and before him a long vista of tombs,
white head-stones and low crosses, edged by
drooping cypress and trailing feathery vines.
Some vines had fallen and been caught in
long loops from bough to bough, like fu-
neral garlands, and here and there the tops of
isolated palmettos lifted a cluster of hearse-
like plumes. Yet in spite of this dominance
of sombre but graceful shadow, the drooping
delicacy of dark-tasseled foliage and leafy
fringes, and the waving mourning veils of
gray, translucent moss, a glorious vivifying
Southern sun smiled and glittered everywhere as through tears. The balm of bay,
southernwood, pine, and syringa breathed
through the long alleys; the stimulating
scent of roses moved with every zephyr, and
the closer odors of jessamine, honeysuckle,

and orange flowers hung heavily in the hol-
lows.   It   seemed   to   Courtland   like   the
mourning of beautiful and youthful widow-
hood, seductive even in its dissembling trap-
pings, provocative in the contrast of its own
still strong virility.   Everywhere the grass
grew thick and luxuriant ; the quick earth
was teeming with the germination of the
dead below.

They moved slowly along side by side,
speaking only of the beauty of the spot and
the glory of that summer day, which seemed
to have completed its perfection here.   Perhaps from the heat, the overpowering perfume, or some unsuspected sentiment, the
young lady became presently as silent and
preoccupied as her companion.   She began
to linger and loiter behind, hovering like a
butterfly over some flowering shrub or clus-
tered sheaf of lilies, until, encountered suddenly in her floating draperies, she might
have been taken for a somewhat early and
far too becoming ghost.   It seemed to him,
also, that her bright eyes were slightly
shadowed by a gentle thoughtfulness.   He
moved close to her side with an irresistible
impulse of tenderness, but she turned suddenly, and saying, " Come ! " moved at a

quicker pace down a narrow side path. Courtland followed. He had not gone far before he noticed that the graves seemed to fall into regular lines, the emblems became cheaper and more common; wooden head and foot stones of one monotonous pattern took the place of carved freestone or marble, and he knew that they had reached that part of the cemetery reserved for those who had fallen in the war. The long lines drawn with military precision stretched through the little valley, and again up the opposite hill in an odd semblance of hollow squares, ranks, and columns. A vague recollection of the fateful slope of Snake River came over him. It was intensified as Miss Sally, who was still preceding him, suddenly stopped before an isolated mound bearing a broken marble shaft and a pedestal with the inscription, " Chester Brooks." A few withered garlands and immortelles were lying at its base, but encircling the broken shaft was a perfectly fresh, unfaded wreath.

" You never told me he was buried here! " said Courtland quickly, half shocked at the unexpected revelation. " Was he from this State ? "

" No, but his regiment was," said Miss Sally, eying the wreath critically.

"And this wreath, is it from you?" continued Courtland gently.

"Yes, I thought yo' 'd like to see something fresh and pooty, instead of those stale ones."

"And were they also from you?" he asked even more gently.

"Dear no! They were left over from last anniversary day by some of the veterans. That 's the only one I put there — that is — I got Mr. Champney to leave it here on his way to his house. He lives just yonder, yo' know."

It was impossible to resist this invincible naïveté. Courtland bit his lip as the vision arose before him of this still more naïf English admirer bringing hither, at Miss Sally's bidding, the tribute which she wished to place on the grave of an old lover to please a *third* man. Meantime, she had put her two little hands behind her back in the simulated attitude of "a good girl," and was saying half smilingly, and he even thought half wistfully : —

"Are yo' satisfied?"

"Perfectly."

"Then let 's go away. It 's mighty hot here."

They turned away, and descending the slope again reëntered the thicker shade of the main avenue. Here they seemed to have left the sterner aspect of Death. They walked slowly; the air was heavy with the hot incense of flowers; the road sinking a little left a grassy bank on one side. Here Miss Sally halted and listlessly seated herself, motioning Courtland to do the same. He obeyed eagerly. The incident of the wreath had troubled him, albeit with contending sensations. She had given it to please *him;* why should *he* question the manner, or torment himself with any retrospective thought? He would have given worlds to have been able to accept it lightly or gallantly, — with any other girl he could; but he knew he was trembling on the verge of a passionate declaration; the magnitude of the stake was too great to be imperiled by a levity of which she was more a mistress than himself, and he knew that his sentiment had failed to impress her. His pride kept him from appealing to her strangely practical nature, although he had recognized and accepted it, and had even begun to believe it an essential part of the strong fascination she had over him. But being neither

a coward nor a weak, hesitating idealist,
when he deliberately took his seat beside
her he as deliberately made up his mind to
accept his fate, whatever it might be, then
and there.

Perhaps there was something of this in
his face. " I thought yo' were looking a
little white, co'nnle," she said quietly, "and
I reckoned we might sit down a spell,
and then take it slowly home. Yo' ain't
accustomed to the So'th'n sun, and the air
in the hollow *was* swampy." As he made
a slight gesture of denial, she went on with
a pretty sisterly superiority: " That 's the
way of yo' No'th'n men. Yo' think yo' can
do everything just as if yo' were reared
to it, and yo' never make allowance for different climates, different blood, and different
customs. That 's where yo' slip up."

But he was already leaning towards her
with his dark earnest eyes fixed upon her in
a way she could no longer mistake. " At
the risk of slipping up again, Miss Dows,"
he said gently, dropping into her dialect
with utterly unconscious flattery, " I am
going to ask you to teach me everything *you*
wish, to be all that *you* demand — which
would be far better. You have said we were

good friends; I want you to let me hope to be more. I want you to overlook my deficiencies and the differences of my race and let me meet you on the only level where I can claim to be the equal of your own people — that of loving you. Give me only the same chance you gave the other poor fellow who sleeps yonder — the same chance you gave the luckier man who carried the wreath for you to put upon his grave."

She had listened with delicately knitted brows, the faintest touch of color, and a half-laughing, half-superior disapprobation. When he had finished, she uttered a plaintive little sigh. " Yo' ought n't to have said that, co'nnle, but yo' and me are too good friends to let even *that* stand between us. And to prove it to yo' I 'm going to forget it right away — and so are yo'."

" But I cannot," he said quickly; " if I could I should be unworthy of even your friendship. If you must reject it, do not make me feel the shame of thinking you believe me capable of wanton trifling. I know that this avowal is abrupt to you, but it is not to me. You have known me only for three months, but these three months have been to me the realization of three years' dreaming!'" As she remained looking at him with bright, curious eyes, but still shaking her fair head distressedly, he moved nearer and caught her hand in the little pale lilac thread glove that was, nevertheless, too wide for her small fingers, and said appealingly: "But why should *you* forget it? Why must it be a forbidden topic? What is the barrier? Are you no longer free? Speak, Miss Dows — give me some hope. Miss Dows! — Sally!"

She had drawn herself away, distressed, protesting, her fair head turned aside, until with a slight twist and narrowing of her hand she succeeded in slipping it from the glove which she left a prisoner in his eager clasp. "There! Yo' can keep the glove, co'nnle," she said, breathing quickly. "Sit down! This is not the place nor the weather for husking frolics! Well! — yo' want to know *why* yo' must n't speak to me in that way. Be still, and I 'll tell yo'."

She smoothed down the folds of her frock, sitting sideways on the bank, one little foot touching the road. "Yo' must n't speak that way to me," she went on slowly, "because it 's as much as yo' company 's wo'th, as much as *our* property 's wo'th, as much maybe as yo' life's wo'th! Don't lift yo' comb, co'nnle ; if you don't care for *that*, others may. Sit still, I tell yo'! Well, yo' come here from the No'th to run this property for money — that's square and fair business ; *that* any fool here can understand — it's No'th'n style ; it don't interfere with these fools' family affairs ; it don't bring into their blood any No'th'n taint; it don't divide their clannishness ; it don't separate father and son, sister and brother ; and even if yo' got a foothold here and settled down, they know they can always outvote yo' five to one! But let these same fools know that yo' 're courtin' a So'th'n girl known to be ' Union ' during the wah, that girl who has laughed at their foolishness ; let them even *think* that he wants that girl to mix up the family and the race and the property for him, and there ain't a young or old fool that believes in So'th'n isolation as the price of So'th'n salvation that would n't rise against yo'! There is n't one that would n't make shipwreck of yo'r syndicate and yo'r capital and the prosperity of Redlands for the next four years to come, and think they were doing right! They began to suspect yo' from the first! They suspected yo'

when yo' never went anywhere, but stuck
close to the fahm and me. That's why I
wanted yo' to show yourself among the
girls; they wouldn't have minded yo' flirting with them with the chance of yo' breaking yo' heart over Tave Reed or Lympy
Morris! They're fools enough to believe
that a snub or a jilt from a So'th'n girl would
pay them back for a lost battle or a ruined
plantation!"

For the first time Miss Sally saw Courtland's calm blood fly to his cheek and
kindle in his eye. "You surely do not expect *me* to tolerate this blind and insolent
interference!" he said, rising to his feet.

She lifted her ungloved hand in deprecation. "Sit still, co'nnle. Yo''ve been a
soldier, and yo' know what duty is. Well!
what's yo' duty to yo' company?"

"It neither includes my private affairs
nor regulates the beating of my heart. I
will resign."

"And leave me and Aunt Miranda and
the plantation?"

"No! The company will find another
superintendent to look after your aunt's
affairs and carry out our plans. And you,
Sally — you will let me find you a home

and fortune North? There is work for me there; there is room for you among my people."

She shook her head slowly with a sweet but superior smile. " No, co'nnle! I did n't believe in the wah, but the least I could do was to stand by my folks and share the punishment that I knew was coming from it. I despise this foolishness as much as yo', but I can't run away from it. Come, co'nnle, I won't ask yo' to forget this; mo', I 'll even believe yo' *meant* it, but yo' 'll promise me yo' won't speak of it again as long as yo' are with the company and Aunt Miranda and me! There must n't be more — there must n't even *seem* to be more — between us."

"But then I may hope?" he said, eagerly grasping her hand.

"I promise nothing, for yo' must not even have *that* excuse for speaking of this again, either from anything I do or may seem to do." She stopped, released her hand, as her eyes were suddenly fixed on the distance. Then she said with a slight smile, but without the least embarrassment or impatience: "There 's Mr. Champney coming here now. I reckon he 's looking to see if that wreath is safe."

Courtland looked up quickly. He could see the straw hat of the young Englishman just above the myrtle bushes in a path intersecting the avenue. A faint shadow crossed his face. "Let me know one thing more," he said hurriedly. "I know I have no right to ask the question, but has — has — has Mr. Champney anything to do with your decision?"

She smiled brightly. "Yo' asked just now if yo' could have the same chance he and Chet Brooks had. Well, poor Chet is dead, and Mr. Champney — well! — wait and see." She lifted her voice and called, "Mr. Champney!" The young fellow came briskly towards them; his face betrayed a slight surprise, but no discomfiture, as he recognized her companion.

"Oh, Mr. Champney," said Miss Sally plaintively, "I 've lost my glove somewhere near pooah Brooks's tomb in the hollow. Won't you go and fetch it, and come back here to take me home? The co'nnle has got to go and see his sick niggers in the hospital." Champney lifted his hat, nodded genially to Courtland, and disappeared below the cypresses on the slope. "Yo' must n't be mad," she said, turning in explanation to her companion, " but we have been here too long already, and it 's better that I should be seen coming home with him than yo'."

" Then this sectional interference does not touch him ? " said Courtland bitterly.

" No. He 's an Englishman ; his father was a known friend of the Confederacy, and bought their cotton bonds."

She stopped, gazing into Courtland's face with a pretty vague impatience and a slight pouting of her lip.

" Co'nnle ! "

" Miss Sally."

" Yo' say yo' had known me for three years before yo' saw me. Well, we met once before we ever spoke to each other ! "

Courtland looked in her laughing eyes with admiring wonder. " When ? " he asked.

" The first day yo' came ! Yo' moved the ladder when I was on the cornice, and I walked all over yo' head. And, like a gentleman, yo' never said a word about it. I reckon I stood on yo' head for five minutes."

" Not as long as that," said Courtland laughing, " if I remember rightly."

" Yes," said Miss Sally with dancing eyes. " I, a So'th'n girl, actually set my foot on

the head of a No'th'n scum of a co'nnle!
My!"

"Let that satisfy your friends then."

"No! *I* want to apologize. Sit down,
co'nnle."

"But, Miss Sally" —

"Sit down, quick!"

He did so, seating himself sideways on
the bank. Miss Sally stood beside him.

"Take off yo' hat, sir."

He obeyed smilingly. Miss Sally suddenly slipped behind him. He felt the soft
touch of her small hands on his shoulders;
warm breath stirred the roots of his hair,
and then — the light pressure on his scalp
of what seemed the lips of a child.

He leaped to his feet, yet before he could
turn completely round — a difficulty the
young lady had evidently calculated upon
— he was too late! The floating draperies
of the artful and shameless Miss Sally were
already disappearing among the tombs in
the direction of the hollow.

CHAPTER V.

THE house occupied by the manager of the Drummond Syndicate in Redlands — the former residence of a local lawyer and justice of the peace — was not large, but had an imposing portico of wooden Doric columns, which extended to the roof and fronted the main street. The all-pervading creeper closely covered it ; the sidewalk before it was shaded by a row of broad-leaved ailantus. The front room, with French windows opening on the portico, was used by Colonel Courtland as a general office ; beyond this a sitting-room and din-ing-room overlooked the old-fashioned gar-den with its detached kitchen and inevitable negro cabin. It was a close evening ; there were dark clouds coming up in the direction of the turnpike road, but the leaves of the ailantus hung heavy and motionless in the hush of an impending storm. The sparks of lazily floating fireflies softly expanded and went out in the gloom of the black foliage, or in the dark recesses of the office,

whose windows were widely open, and whose
lights Courtland had extinguished when he
brought his armchair to the portico for
coolness. One of these sparks beyond the
fence, although alternately glowing and
paling, was still so persistent and station-
ary that Courtland leaned forward to watch
it more closely, at which it disappeared, and
a voice from the street said : - –

" Is that you, Courtland ? "

" Yes. Come in, won't you ? "

The voice was Champney's, and the light
was from his cigar. As he opened the gate
and came slowly up the steps of the portico
the usual hesitation of his manner seemed
to have increased. A long sigh trilled the
limp leaves of the ailantus and as quickly
subsided. A few heavy perpendicular rain-
drops crashed and spattered through the
foliage like molten lead.

" You've just escaped the shower," said
Courtland pleasantly. He had not seen
Champney since they parted in the cemetery
six weeks before.

" Yes ! — I — I thought I'd like to have
a little talk with you, Courtland," said
Champney. He hesitated a moment before
the proffered chair, and then added, with a

cautious glance towards the street, " Had n't
we better go inside ? "

" As you like. But you 'll find it wofully
hot. We 're quite alone here ; there 's nobody in the house, and this shower will drive
any loungers from the street." He was quite
frank, although their relations to each other
in regard to Miss Sally were still so unde-
fined as to scarcely invite his confidence.

Howbeit Champney took the proffered
chair and the glass of julep which Courtland
brought him.

" You remember my speaking to you of
Dumont ? " he said hesitatingly, " Miss
Dows' French cousin, you know? Well —
he 's coming here : he 's got property here
— those three houses opposite the Court
House. From what I hear, he 's come over
with a lot of new-fangled French ideas on
the nigger question — rot about equality and
fraternity, don't you know — and the highest
education and highest offices for them. You
know what the feeling is here already ? You
know what happened at the last election at
Coolidgeville — how the whites would n't let
the niggers go to the polls and the jolly row
that was kicked up over it ? Well, it looks
as if that sort of thing might happen *here*,

don't you know, if Miss Dows takes up these ideas."

"But I 've reason to suppose — I mean," said Courtland correcting himself with some deliberation, "that any one who knows Miss Dows' opinions knows that these are not her views. Why should she take them up?"

"Because she takes *him* up," returned Champney hurriedly; "and even if she did n't believe in them herself, she 'd have to share the responsibility with him in the eyes of every unreconstructed rowdy like Tom Higbee and the rest of them. They 'd make short work of her niggers all the same."

"But I don't see why she should be made responsible for the opinions of her cousin, nor do I exactly know what 'taking him up' means," returned Courtland quietly.

Champney moistened his dry lips with the julep and uttered a nervous laugh. "Suppose we say her husband — for that's what his coming back here means. Everybody knows that; you would, too, if you ever talked with her about anything but business."

A bright flash of lightning that lit up the

faces of the two men would have revealed Champney's flushed features and Courtland's lack of color had they been looking at each other. But they were not, and the long reverberating crash of thunder which followed prevented any audible reply from Courtland, and covered his agitation.

For without fully accepting Champney's conclusions he was cruelly shocked at the young man's utterance of them. He had scrupulously respected the wishes of Miss Sally and had faithfully — although never hopelessly — held back any expression of his own love since their conversation in the cemetery. But while his native truthfulness and sense of honor had overlooked the seeming insincerity of her attitude towards Champney, he had never justified his own tacit participation in it, and the concealment of his own pretensions before his possible rival. It was true that she had forbidden him to openly enter the lists with her admirers, but Champney's innocent assumption of his indifference to her and his consequent half confidences added poignancy to his story. There seemed to be only one way to extricate himself, and that was by a quarrel. Whether he did or did not believe Champney's story, whether it was only the jealous exaggeration of a rival, or Miss Sally was actually deceiving them both, his position had become intolerable.

" I must remind you, Champney," he said, with freezing deliberation, "that Miss Miranda Dows and her niece now represent the Drummond Company equally with myself, and that you cannot expect me to listen to any reflections upon the way they choose to administer their part in its affairs, either now, or to come. Still less do I care to discuss the idle gossip which can affect only the *private* interests of these ladies, with which neither you nor I have any right to interfere."

But the naïveté of the young Englishman was as invincible as Miss Sally's own, and as fatal to Courtland's attitude. " Of course I haven't any *right*, you know," he said, calmly ignoring the severe preamble of his companion's speech, " but I say ! hang it all ! even if a fellow has no chance *himself*, he don't like to see a girl throw herself and her property away on a man like that."

" One moment, Champney," said Courtland, under the infection of his guest's simplicity, abandoning his former superior atti-

tude. "You say you have no chance. Do
you want me to understand that you are
regularly a suitor of Miss Dows?"

"Y-e-e-s," said the young fellow, but with
the hesitation of conscientiousness rather
than evasion. "That is — you know I *was*.
But don't you see, it could n't be. It
would n't do, you know. If those clannish
neighbors of hers — that Southern set — suspected that Miss Sally was courted by an
Englishman, don't you know — a poacher on
their preserves — it would be all up with her
position on the property and her influence
over them. I don't mind telling you that's
one reason why I left the company and took
that other plantation. But even that did n't
work; they had their suspicions excited already."

"Did Miss Dows give that as a reason
for declining your suit?" asked Courtland
slowly.

"Yes. You know what a straightforward girl she is. She did n't come no rot
about 'not expecting anything of the kind,'
or about 'being a sister to me,' and all that,
for, by Jove! she's always more like a fellow's sister, don't you know, than his girl.
Of course, it was hard lines for me, but I

suppose she was about right." He stopped, and then added with a kind of gentle persistency : " *You* think she was about right, don't you ? "

With what was passing in Courtland's mind the question seemed so bitterly ironical that at first he leaned half angrily forward, in an unconscious attempt to catch the speaker's expression in the darkness. "I should hardly venture to give an opinion," he said, after a pause. "Miss Dows' relations with her neighbors are so very peculiar. And from what you tell me of her cousin it would seem that her desire to placate them is not always to be depended upon."

"I'm not finding fault with *her*, you know," said Champney hastily. "I'm not such a beastly cad as that ; I would n't have spoken of my affairs at all, but you asked, you know. I only thought, if she was going to get herself into trouble on account of that Frenchman, you might talk to her — she 'd listen to you, because she 'd know you only did it out of business reasons. And they 're really business reasons, you know. I suppose you don't think much of my business capacity, colonel, and you would n't go much on my judgment — especially now ; but I 've

been here longer than you and " — he lowered his voice slightly and dragged his chair
nearer Courtland — " I don't like the looks
of things here. There's some devilment
plotting among those rascals. They 're only
awaiting an opportunity ; a single flash would
be enough to set them in a blaze, even if the
fire was n't lit and smouldering already like
a spark in a bale of cotton. I 'd cut the
whole thing and clear out if I did n't think
it would make it harder for Miss Dows,
who would be left alone."

" You 're a good fellow, Champney," said
Courtland, laying his hand on the young
man's shoulder with a sudden impulse, " and
I forgive you for overlooking any concern
that *I* might have. Indeed," he added, with
an odd seriousness and a half sigh, " it 's
not strange that you should. But I must
remind you that the Dowses are strictly the
agents and tenants of the company I represent, and that their rights and property
under that tenancy shall not be interfered
with by others as long as I am here. I have
no right, however," he added gravely, " to
keep Miss Dows from imperiling them by
her social relations."

Champney rose and shook hands with him

4 Bret Harte

awkwardly. " The shower seems to be holding up," he said, " and I 'll toddle along before it starts afresh. Good-night ! I say —
you did n't mind my coming to you this way,
did you? By Jove! I thought you were
a little stand-offish at first. But you know
what I meant ? "

" Perfectly, and I thank you." They
shook hands again. Champney stepped
from the portico, and, reaching the gate,
seemed to vanish as he had come, out of the
darkness.

The storm was not yet over ; the air had
again become close and suffocating. Courtland remained brooding in his chair.
Whether he could accept Champney's news
as true or not, he felt that he must end this
suspense at once. A half-guilty consciousness that he was thinking more of it in reference to his own passion than his duty to
the company did not render his meditations
less unpleasant. Yet while he could not
reconcile Miss Sally's confidences in the
cemetery concerning the indifference of her
people to Champney's attentions with what
Champney had just told him of the reasons
she had given *him* for declining them, I am
afraid he was not shocked by her peculiar

ethics. A lover seldom finds fault with his mistress for deceiving his rival, and is as little apt to consider the logical deduction that she could deceive him also, as Othello was to accept Brabantio's warning. The masculine sense of honor which might have resented the friendship of a man capable of such treachery did not hesitate to accept the love of a woman under the same conditions. Perhaps there was an implied compliment in thus allowing her to take the sole ethical responsibility, which few women would resist.

In the midst of this gloomy abstraction Courtland suddenly raised his head and listened.

" Cato."

" Yes, sah."

There was a sound of heavy footsteps in the hall coming from the rear of the house, and presently a darker bulk appeared in the shadowed doorway. It was his principal overseer — a strong and superior negro, selected by his fellow-freedmen from among their number in accordance with Courtland's new régime.

" Did you come here from the plantation or the town ? "

" The town, sah."

"I think you had better keep out of the town in the evenings for the present," said Courtland in a tone of quiet but positive authority.

"Are dey goin' to bring back de ole 'patter rollers,'[1] sah?" asked the man with a slight sneer.

"I don't know," returned Courtland calmly, ignoring his overseer's manner. "But if they did you must comply with the local regulations unless they conflict with the Federal laws, when you must appeal to the Federal authorities. I prefer you should avoid any trouble until you are sure."

"I reckon they won't try any games on me," said the negro with a short laugh.

Courtland looked at him intently.

"I thought as much! You're carrying arms, Cato! Hand them over."

The overseer hesitated for a moment, and then unstrapped a revolver from his belt, and handed it to Courtland.

"Now how many of you are in the habit of going round the town armed like this?"

"Only de men who 've been insulted, sah."

[1] The "patrol" or local police who formerly had the surveillance of slaves.

" And how have *you* been insulted ? "

" Marse Tom Higbee down in de market reckoned it was high time fancy niggers was drov into de swamp, and I allowed that loafers and beggars had better roost high when workin' folks was around, and Marse Tom said he 'd cut my haht out."

" And do you think your carrying a revolver will prevent him and his friends performing that operation if you provoked them ? "

"You said we was to pertect ourse'fs, sah," returned the negro gloomily. " What foh den did you drill us to use dem rifles in de armory ? "

" To defend yourselves *together* under orders if attacked, not to singly threaten with them in a street row. Together, you would stand some chance against those men ; separately they could eat you up, Cato."

" I would n't trust too much to some of dem niggers standing together, sah," said Cato darkly. " Dey 'd run before de old masters — if they did n't run to 'em. Shuah ! "

A fear of this kind had crossed Courtland's mind before, but he made no present comment. " I found two of the armory rifles

in the men's cabins yesterday," he resumed
quietly. " See that it does not occur again!
They must not be taken from the armory
except to defend it."

" Yes, sah."

There was a moment of silence. Then it
was broken by a sudden gust that swept
through the columns of the portico, stirring
the vines. The broad leaves of the ailantus
began to rustle; an ominous pattering followed; the rain had recommenced. And as
Courtland rose and walked towards the
open window its blank panes and the interior of the office were suddenly illuminated by a gleam of returning lightning.

He entered the office, bidding Cato follow, and lit the lamp above his desk. The
negro remained standing gloomily but re-
spectfully by the window.

" Cato, do you know anything of Mr.
Dumont — Miss Dows' cousin ? '

The negro's white teeth suddenly flashed
in the lamplight. " Ya! ha! I reckon,
sah."

" Then he's a great friend of your people ? "

" I don't know about dat, sah. But he's
a pow'ful enemy of de Reeds and de Higbees ! "

" On account of his views, of course ? "

" 'Deed no ! " said Cato with an astounded air. "Jess on account of de vendetta ! "

" The vendetta ? "

" Yes, sah. De old blood quo'll of de families. It 's been goin' on over fifty years, sah. De granfader, fader, and brudder of de Higbees was killed by de granfader, fader, and brudder of de Doomonts. De Reeds chipped in when all de Higbees was played out, fo' dey was relations, but dey was chawed up by some of de Dowses, first cousins to de Doomonts."

" What ? Are the Dows in this vendetta ? "

" No, sah. No mo'. Dey 's bin no man in de family since Miss Sally's fader died — dat 's let de Dows out fo' ever. De las' shootin' was done by Marse Jack Doomont, who crippled Marse Tom Higbee's brudder Jo, and den skipped to Europe. Dey say he 's come back, and is lying low over at Atlanty. Dar 'll be lively times ef he comes here to see Miss Sally."

" But he may have changed his ideas while living abroad, where this sort of thing is simple murder."

The negro shook his head grimly. " Den

he wouldn't come, sah. No, sah. He knows
dat Tom Higbee's bound to go fo' him or
leave de place, and Marse Jack would n't
mind settlin' *him* too as well as his brudder,
for de scores is agin' de Doomonts yet. And
Marse Jack ain't no slouch wid a scatter
gun."

At any other time the imminence of this
survival of a lawless barbarism of which he
had heard so much would have impressed
Courtland; now he was only interested in it
on account of the inconceivable position in
which it left Miss Sally. Had she anything to do with this baleful cousin's return, or was she only to be a helpless victim
of it?

A white, dazzling, and bewildering flash
of lightning suddenly lit up the room, the
porch, the dripping ailantus, and the flooded
street beyond. It was followed presently
by a crash of thunder, with what seemed
to be a second fainter flash of lightning,
or rather as if the first flash had suddenly
ignited some inflammable substance. With
the long reverberation of the thunder still
shaking the house, Courtland slipped quickly
out of the window and passed down to the
gate.

"Did it strike anything, sah?" said the startled negro, as Courtland returned.

"Not that I can see," said his employer shortly. "Go inside, and call Zoë and her daughter from the cabin and bring them in the hall. Stay till I come. Go!—I'll shut the windows myself."

"It must have struck somewhere, sah, shuah! Deh's a pow'ful smell of sulphur right here," said the negro as he left the room.

Courtland thought so too, but it was a kind of sulphur that he had smelled before — on the battlefield! For when the door was closed behind his overseer he took the lamp to the opposite wall and examined it carefully. There was the distinct hole made by a bullet which had missed Cato's head at the open window by an inch.

CHAPTER VI.

In an instant Courtland had regained
complete possession of himself. His distracting passion — how distracting he had
never before realized — was gone! His
clear sight — no longer distorted by sentiment — had come back; he saw everything
in its just proportion — his duty, the plantation, the helpless freedman threatened by
lawless fury; the two women — no longer
his one tantalizing vision, but now only a
passing detail of the work before him. He
saw them through no aberrating mist of tenderness or expediency — but with the single
directness of the man of action.

The shot had clearly been intended for
Cato. Even if it were an act of mere personal revenge, it showed a confidence and
security in the would-be assassin that beto-
kened coöperation and an organized plan.
He had availed himself of the thunder-
storm, the flash and long reverberating roll
of sound — an artifice not unknown to border
ambush — to confuse discovery at the in-

stant. Yet the attack might be only an isolated one; or it might be the beginning of
a general raid upon the Syndicate's freedmen. If the former he could protect Cato
from its repetition by guarding him in the
office until he could be conveyed to a place
of safety; if the latter, he must at once collect the negroes at their quarters, and take
Cato with him. He resolved upon the latter course. The quarters were half a mile
from the Dows' dwelling — which was two
miles away.

He sat down and wrote a few lines to Miss
Dows stating that, in view of some threatened disturbances in the town, he thought it
advisable to keep the negroes in their quarters, whither he was himself going. He sent
her his housekeeper and the child, as they
had both better remain in a place of security
until he returned to town. He gave the
note to Zoë, bidding her hasten by the back
garden across the fields. Then he turned to
Cato.

"I am going with you to the quarters to-
night," he said quietly, "and you can carry
your pistol back to the armory yourself."
He handed him the weapon. The negro received it gratefully, but suddenly cast a

searching glance at his employer. Courtland's face, however, betrayed no change.
When Zoë had gone, he continued tranquilly, "We will go by the back way through
the woods." As the negro started slightly,
Courtland continued in the same even tone :
"The sulphur you smelled just now, Cato, was
the smoke of a gun fired at *you* from the
street. I don't propose that the shot shall
be repeated under the same advantages."

The negro became violently agitated. "It
was dat sneakin' hound, Tom Higbee," he
said huskily.

Courtland looked at him sharply. "Then
there was something more than *words* passed
between him and you, Cato. What happened? Come, speak out!"

"He lashed me with his whip, and I gib
him one right under the yeah, and drupped
him," said Cato, recovering his courage with
his anger at the recollection. "I had a right
to defend myse'f, sah."

"Yes, and I hope you'll be able to do it,
now," said Courtland calmly, his face giving no sign of his conviction that Cato's fate
was doomed by that single retaliating blow,
"but you'll be safer at the quarters." He
passed into his bedroom, took a revolver

from his bedhead and a derringer from the drawer, both of which he quickly slipped beneath his buttoned coat, and returned.

" When we are in the fields, clear of the house, keep close by my side, and even try to keep step with me. What you have to say, say *now;* there must be no talking to betray our position — we must go silently, and you'll have enough to do to exercise your eyes and ears. I shall stand between you and any attack, but I expect you to obey orders without hesitation." He opened the back door, motioned to Cato to pass out, followed him, locked the door behind them, and taking the negro's arm walked beside the low palings to the end of the garden, where they climbed the fence and stood upon the open field beyond.

Unfortunately, it had grown lighter with the breaking of the heavy clouds, and gusty gleams of moonlight chased each other over the field, or struck a glitter from standing rain-pools between the little hillocks. To cross the open field and gain the fringe of woods on the other side was the nearest way to the quarters, but for the moment was the most exposed course ; to follow the hedge to the bottom of the field and the boundary

fence and then cross at right angles, in its
shadow, would be safer, but they would lose
valuable time.   Believing that Cato's venge-
ful assailant was still hovering near with his
comrades, Courtland cast a quick glance
down the shadowy line of Osage hedge beside them.   Suddenly Cato grasped his arm
and pointed in the same direction, where the
boundary fence he had noticed — a barrier
of rough palings — crossed the field.   With
the moon low on the other side of it, it was a
mere black silhouette, broken only by bright
silver openings and gaps along its surface
that indicated the moonlit field beyond.   At
first Courtland saw nothing else.   Then he
was struck by the fact that these openings
became successively and regularly eclipsed,
as with the passing of some opaque object
behind them.   It was a file of men on the
other side of the fence, keeping in its shelter
as they crossed the field towards his house.
Roughly calculating from the passing ob-
scurations, there must have been twelve or
fifteen in all.

He could no longer doubt their combined
intentions, nor hesitate how to meet them.
He must at once make for the quarters with
Cato, even if he had to cross that open field

before them. He knew that they would avoid injuring him personally, in the fear of possible Federal and political complications, and he resolved to use that fear to insure Cato's safety. Placing his hands on the negro's shoulders, he shoved him forwards, falling into a " lock step" so close behind him that it became impossible for the most expert marksman to fire at one without imperiling the other's life. When half way across the field he noticed that the shadows seen through the openings of the fence had paused. The ambushed men had evidently seen the double apparition, understood it, and, as he expected, dared not fire. He reached the other side with Cato in safety, but not before he saw the fateful shadows again moving, and this time in their own direction. They were evidently intending to pursue them. But once within the woods Courtland knew that his chances were equal. He breathed more freely. Cato, now less agitated, had even regained something of his former emotional combativeness which Courtland had checked. Although far from confident of his henchman's prowess in an emergency, the prospect of getting him safe into the quarters seemed brighter.

It was necessary, also, to trust to his superior wood-craft and knowledge of the locality, and Courtland still walking between him and his pursuers and covering his retreat allowed him to lead the way. It lay over ground that was beginning to slope gently; the underbrush was presently exchanged for springy moss, the character of the trees changed, the black trunks of cypresses made the gloom thicker. Trailing vines and parasites brushed their faces, a current of damp air seemed to flow just above the soil in which their lower limbs moved sluggishly as through stagnant water. As yet there was no indication of pursuit. But Courtland felt that it was not abandoned. Indeed, he had barely time to check an exclamation from the negro, before the dull gallop of horse-hoofs in the open ahead of them was plain to them both. It was a second party of their pursuers, mounted, who had evidently been sent to prevent their final egress from the woods, while those they had just evaded were no doubt slowly and silently following them on foot. They were to be caught between two fires!

"What is there to the left of us?" whispered Courtland quickly.

" De swamp."

Courtland set his teeth together. His dull-witted companion had evidently walked them both into the trap! Nevertheless, his resolve was quickly made. He could already see through the thinning fringe of timber the figures of the mounted men in the moonlight.

" This should be the boundary line of the plantation? This field beside us is ours? " he said interrogatively.

" Yes," returned the negro, " but de quarters is a mile furder."

"Good! Stay here until I come back or call you; I 'm going to talk to these fellows. But if you value your life, don't *you* speak nor stir."

He strode quickly through the intervening trees and stepped out into the moonlight. A suppressed shout greeted him, and half a dozen mounted men, masked and carrying rifles, rode down towards him, but he remained quietly waiting there, and as the nearest approached him, he made a step forward and cried, " Halt! "

The men pulled up sharply and mechanically at that ring of military imperiousness.

" What are you doing here? " said Courtland.

" We reckon that 's *our* business, co'nnle."

" It 's *mine*, when you 're on property that I control."

The man hesitated and looked interrogatively towards his fellows. " I allow you 've got us there, co'nnle," he said at last with the lazy insolence of conscious power, " but I don't mind telling you we 're wanting a nigger about the size of your Cato. We hain't got anything agin *you*, co'nnle ; we don't want to interfere with *your* property, and *your* ways, but we don't calculate to have strangers interfere with *our* ways and *our* customs. Trot out your nigger — you No'th'n folks don't call *him* ' property,' you know — and we 'll clear off your land."

" And may I ask what you want of Cato ? " said Courtland quietly.

" To show him that all the Federal law in h—ll won't protect him when he strikes a white man ! " burst out one of the masked figures, riding forward.

" Then you compel me to show *you*," said Courtland immovably, " what any Federal citizen may do in the defense of Federal law. For I 'll kill the first man that attempts to lay hands upon him on my property. Some of you, who have already tried to assassinate him in cold blood, I have met before in less dishonorable warfare than this, and *they* know I am able to keep my word."

There was a moment's silence; the barrel of the revolver he was holding at his side glistened for an instant in the moonlight, but he did not move. The two men rode up to the first speaker and exchanged words. A light laugh followed, and the first speaker turned again to Courtland with a mocking politeness.

"Very well, co'nnle, if that's your opinion, and you allow we can't follow our game over your property, why, we reckon we'll have to give way *to those who can.* Sorry to have troubled *you.* Good-night."

He lifted his hat ironically, waved it to his followers, and the next moment the whole party were galloping furiously towards the high road.

For the first time that evening a nervous sense of apprehension passed over Courtland. The impending of some unknown danger is always more terrible to a brave man than the most overwhelming odds that he can see and realize. He felt instinctively that they had uttered no vague bravado to cover up their defeat; there was still some advan-

tage on which they confidently reckoned —
but what? Was it only a reference to the
other party tracking them through the
woods on which their enemies now solely
relied? He regained Cato quickly; the
white teeth of the foolishly confident negro
were already flashing his imagined triumph
to his employer. Courtland's heart grew
sick as he saw it.

"We 're not out of the woods yet, Cato,"
he said dryly; "nor are they. Keep your
eyes and ears open, and attend to me. How
long can we keep in the cover of these
woods, and still push on in the direction of
the quarters?"

"There 's a way roun' de edge o' de
swamp, sah, but we 'd have to go back a
spell to find it."

"Go on!"

"And dar 's moccasins and copperheads
lying round here in de trail! Dey don't go
for *us* ginerally — but," he hesitated, "white
men don't stand much show."

"Good! Then it is as bad for those who
are chasing us as for me. That will do.
Lead on."

They retraced their steps cautiously, until
the negro turned into a lighter by-way. A

strange mephitic odor seemed to come from sodden leaves and mosses that began to ooze under their feet. They had picked their way in silence for some minutes; the stunted willows and cypress standing farther and farther apart, and the openings with clumps of sedge were frequent. Courtland was beginning to fear this exposure of his follower, and had moved up beside him, when suddenly the negro caught his arm, and trembled violently. His lips were parted over his teeth, the whites of his eyes glistened, he seemed gasping and speechless with fear.

"What's the matter, Cato?" said Courtland glancing instinctively at the ground beneath. "Speak, man! — have you been bitten?"

The word seemed to wring an agonized cry from the miserable man.

"Bitten! No; but don't you hear 'em coming, sah! God Almighty! don't you hear dat?"

"What?"

"De dogs! de houns! — *de bloodhouns!* Dey've set 'em loose on me!"

It was true! A faint baying in the distance was now distinctly audible to Courtland. He knew now plainly the full, cruel

purport of the leader's speech, — those who
could go anywhere were tracking their
game!

Every trace of manhood had vanished
from the negro's cowering frame. Courtland laid his hand assuringly, appealingly,
and then savagely on his shoulder.

"Come! Enough of this! I am here,
and will stand by you, whatever comes.
These dogs are no more to be feared than
the others. Rouse yourself, man, and at
least help *me* make a fight of it."

"No! no!" screamed the terrified man.
"Lemme go! Lemme go back to de Mas-
sas! Tell 'em I 'll come! Tell 'em to call
de houns off me, and I 'll go quiet! Lemme
go!" He struggled violently in his companion's grasp.

In all Courtland's self-control, habits of
coolness, and discipline, it is to be feared
there was still something of the old Berser-
ker temper. His face was white, his eyes
blazed in the darkness; only his voice kept
that level distinctness which made it for a
moment more terrible than even the baying
of the tracking hounds to the negro's ear.
"Cato," he said, "attempt to run now, and,
by God! I 'll save the dogs the trouble of

grappling your living carcass! Come here!
Up that tree with you!" pointing to a
swamp magnolia. "Don't move as long as
I can stand here, and when I'm down — but
not till then — save yourself — the best you
can."

He half helped, half dragged, the now
passive African to the solitary tree; as the
bay of a single hound came nearer, the
negro convulsively scrambled from Courtland's knee and shoulder to the fork of
branches a dozen feet from the ground.
Courtland drew his revolver, and, stepping
back a few yards into the open, awaited the
attack.

It came unexpectedly from behind. A
sudden yelp of panting cruelty and frenzied
anticipation at Courtland's back caused
him to change front quickly, and the dripping fangs and snaky boa-like neck of a
gray weird shadow passed him. With an
awful supernaturalness of instinct, it kept
on in an unerring line to the fateful tree.
But that dread directness of scent was
Courtland's opportunity. His revolver
flashed out in an aim as unerring. The
brute, pierced through neck and brain,
dashed on against the tree in his impetus,

and then rolled over against it in a quivering bulk. Again another bay coming from the same direction told Courtland that his pursuers had outflanked him, and the whole pack were crossing the swamp. But he was prepared ; again the same weird shadow, as spectral and monstrous as a dream, dashed out into the brief light of the open, but this time it was stopped, and rolled over convulsively before it had crossed. Flushed, with the fire of fight in his veins, Courtland turned almost furiously from the fallen brutes at his feet to meet the onset of the more cowardly hunters whom he knew were at his heels. At that moment it would have fared ill with the foremost. No longer the calculating steward and diplomatic manager, no longer the cool-headed arbiter of conflicting interests, he was ready to meet them, not only with the intrepid instincts of a soldier, but with an aroused partisan fury equal to their own. To his surprise no one followed; the baying of a third hound seemed to be silenced and checked ; the silence was broken only by the sound of distant disputing voices and the uneasy trampling of hoofs. This was followed by two or three rifle shots in the distance, but

not either in the direction of the quarters
nor the Dows' dwellinghouse. There evidently was some interruption in the pursuit,
— a diversion of some kind had taken place,
— but what he knew not. He could think
of no one who might have interfered on his
behalf, and the shouting and wrangling
seemed to be carried on in the accents of the
one sectional party. He called cautiously
to Cato. The negro did not reply. He
crossed to the tree and shook it impatiently.
Its boughs were empty; Cato was gone!
The miserable negro must have taken advantage of the first diversion in his favor to
escape. But where, and how, there was nothing left to indicate.

As Courtland had taken little note of the
trail, he had no idea of his own whereabouts.
He knew he must return to the fringe of
cypress to be able to cross the open field
and gain the negro quarters, where it was
still possible that Cato had fled. Taking a
general direction from the few stars visible
above the opening, he began to retrace his
steps. But he had no longer the negro's
woodcraft to guide him. At times his feet
were caught in trailing vines which seemed
to coil around his ankles with ominous sug-

gestiveness ; at times the yielding soil beneath his tread showed his perilous proxim-
ity to the swamp, as well as the fact that
he was beginning to incline towards that
dread circle which is the hopeless instinct
of all lost and straying humanity. Luckily
the edge of the swamp was more open, and
he would be enabled to correct his changed
course again by the position of the stars.
But he was becoming chilled and exhausted
by these fruitless efforts, and at length, after
a more devious and prolonged détour, which
brought him back to the swamp again, he
resolved to skirt its edge in search of some
other mode of issuance. Beyond him, the
light seemed stronger, as of a more extended
opening or clearing, and there was even a
superficial gleam from the end of the swamp
itself, as if from some *ignis fatuus* or the
glancing of a pool of unbroken water. A
few rods farther brought him to it and a
full view of the unencumbered expanse.
Beyond him, far across the swamp, he could
see a hillside bathed in the moonlight with
symmetrical lines of small white squares
dotting its slopes and stretching down into
a valley of gleaming shafts, pyramids, and
tombs. It was the cemetery; the white

squares on the hillside were the soldiers' graves. And among them even at that distance, uplifting solemnly, like a reproachful phantom, was the broken shaft above the dust of Chester Brooks.

With the view of that fateful spot, which he had not seen since his last meeting there with Sally Dows, a flood of recollection rushed upon him. In the white mist that hung low along the farther edge of the swamp he fancied he could see again the battery smoke through which the ghostly figure of the dead rider had charged his gun three years before ; in the vapory white plumes of a funereal plant in the long avenue he was reminded of the light figure of Miss Sally as she appeared at their last meeting. In another moment, in his already dazed condition, he might have succumbed to some sensuous memory of her former fascinations, but he threw it off savagely now, with a quick and bitter recalling of her deceit and his own weakness. Turning his back upon the scene with a half-superstitious tremor, he plunged once more into the trackless covert. But he was conscious that his eyesight was gradually growing dim and his strength failing. He was obliged from

time to time to stop and rally his sluggish
senses, that seemed to grow heavier under
some deadly exhalation that flowed around
him. He even seemed to hear familiar
voices, — but that must be delusion. At
last he stumbled. Throwing out an arm to
protect himself, he came heavily down upon
the ooze, striking a dull, half-elastic root
that seemed — it must have been another delusion — to move beneath him, and even —
so confused were his senses now — to strike
back angrily upon his prostrate arm. A
sharp pain ran from his elbow to shoulder
and for a moment stung him to full consciousness again. There were voices surely,
— the voices of their former pursuers ! If
they were seeking to revenge themselves
upon him for Cato's escape, he was ready
for them. He cocked his revolver and stood
erect. A torch flashed through the wood.
But even at that moment a film came over
his eyes; he staggered and fell.

An interval of helpless semi-consciousness
ensued. He felt himself lifted by strong
arms and carried forward, his arm hanging
uselessly at his side. The dank odor of the
wood was presently exchanged for the free
air of the open field ; the flaming pine-knot

torches were extinguished in the bright
moonlight. People pressed around him,
but so indistinctly he could not recognize
them. All his consciousness seemed cen-
tred in the burning, throbbing pain of his
arm. He felt himself laid upon the gravel ;
the sleeve cut from his shoulder, the cool
sensation of the hot and bursting skin bared
to the night air, and then a soft, cool, and
indescribable pressure upon a wound he had
not felt before. A voice followed, — high,
lazily petulant, and familiar to him, and yet
one he strove in vain to recall.

"De Lawdy-Gawd save us, Miss Sally !
Wot yo' doin' dah ? Chile ! Chile ! Yo' 'll
kill yo'se'f, shuah ! "

The pressure continued, strange and potent even through his pain, and was then
withdrawn. And a voice that thrilled him
said : —

"It's the only thing to save him ! Hush,
ye chattering black crow ! Say anything
about this to a living soul, and I 'll have yo'
flogged ! Now trot out the whiskey bottle
and pour it down him."

CHAPTER VII.

WHEN Courtland's eyes opened again, he was in bed in his own room at Redlands, with the vivid morning sun occasionally lighting up the wall whenever the closely drawn curtains were lightly blown aside by the freshening breeze. The whole events of the night might have been a dream but for the insupportable languor which numbed his senses, and the torpor of his arm, that, swollen and discolored, lay outside the coverlet on a pillow before him. Cloths that had been wrung out in iced water were replaced upon it from time to time by Sophy, Miss Dows' housekeeper, who, seated near his bedhead, was lazily fanning him. Their eyes met.

"Broken?" he said interrogatively, with a faint return of his old deliberate manner, glancing at his helpless arm.

"Deedy no, cunnle! Snake bite," responded the negress.

"Snake bite!" repeated Courtland with languid interest, "what snake?"

"Moccasin o' copperhead — if you doun know yo'se'f which," she replied. "But it's all right now, honey! De pizen's draw'd out and clean gone. Wot yer feels now is de whiskey. De whiskey *stays*, sah. It gets into de lubrications of de skin, sah, and has to be abso'bed."

Some faint chord of memory was touched by the girl's peculiar vocabulary.

"Ah," said Courtland quickly, "you 're Miss Dows' Sophy. Then you can tell me "—

"Nuffin, sah! absomlutely nuffin!" interrupted the girl, shaking her head with impressive official dignity. "It's done gone fo'bid by de doctor! Yo' 're to lie dar and shut yo'r eye, honey," she added, for the moment reverting unconsciously to the native maternal tenderness of her race, "and yo' 're not to bodder yo'se'f ef school keeps o' not. De medical man say distinctly, sah," she concluded, sternly recalling her duty again, "no conversation wid de patient."

But Courtland had winning ways with all dependents. "But you will answer me *one* question, Sophy, and I 'll not ask another. Has "— he hesitated in his still uncertainty as to the actuality of his experience and its probable extent — " has — Cato — escaped ? "

" If yo' mean dat sassy, bull-nigger oberseer of yo'se, cunnle, *he's* safe, yo' bet ! " returned Sophy sharply. " Safe in his own quo'tahs night afo' las', after braggin' about the bloodhaowns he killed ; and safe ober the county line yes'day moan'in, after kicking up all dis rumpus. If dar is a sassy, highfalutin' nigger I jiss 'spises — its dat black nigger Cato o' yo'se ! Now," — relenting — " yo' jiss wink yo' eye, honey, and don't excite yo'se'f about sach black trash ; drap off to sleep comfor'ble. Fo' you do'an get annuder word out o' Sophy, shuah ! "

As if in obedience, Courtland closed his eyes. But even in his weak state he was conscious of the blood coming into his cheek at Sophy's relentless criticism of the man for whom he had just periled his life and position. Much of it he felt was true ; but how far had he been a dupe in his quixotic defense of a quarrelsome blusterer and cowardly bully ? Yet there was the unmistakable shot and cold-blooded attempt at Cato's assassination ! And there were the bloodhounds sent to track the unfortunate man ! That was no dream — but a brutal inexcusable fact !

The medical practitioner of Redlands he remembered was conservative, old-fashioned, and diplomatic. But his sympathies had been broadened by some army experiences, and Courtland trusted to some soldierly and frank exposition of the matter from him. Nevertheless, Dr. Maynard was first healer, and, like Sophy, professionally cautious. The colonel had better not talk about it now. It was already two days old; the colonel had been nearly forty-eight hours in bed. It was a regrettable affair, but the natural climax of long-continued political and racial irritation — and not without *great* provocation! Assassination was a strong word; could Colonel Courtland swear that Cato was actually *aimed at*, or was it not merely a demonstration to frighten a bullying negro? It might have been necessary to teach him a lesson — which the colonel by this time ought to know could only be taught to these inferior races by *fear*. The bloodhounds! Ah, yes! — well, the bloodhounds were, in fact, only a part of that wholesome discipline. Surely Colonel Courtland was not so foolish as to believe that, even in the old slave-holding days, planters sent dogs after runaways to mangle and destroy *their own property?* They might as well, at once, let them escape! No, sir! They were used only to frighten and drive the niggers out of swamps, brakes, and hiding-places — as no nigger had ever dared to face 'em. Cato might lie as much as he liked, but everybody knew *who* it was that killed Major Reed's hounds. Nobody blamed the colonel for it, — not even Major Reed, — but if the colonel had lived a little longer in the South, he'd have known it was n't necessary to do that in self-preservation, as the hounds would never have gone for a white man. But that was not a matter for the colonel to bother about *now*. He was doing well; he had slept nearly thirty hours; there was no fever, he must continue to doze off the exhaustion of his powerful stimulant, and he, the doctor, would return later in the afternoon.

Perhaps it was his very inability to grasp in that exhausted state the full comprehension of the doctor's meaning, perhaps because the physical benumbing of his brain was stronger than any mental excitement, but he slept again until the doctor reappeared. " You 're doing well enough now, colonel," said the physician, after a brief examination of his patient, " and I think we can afford to wake you up a bit, and even let you move your arm. You're luckier than poor Tom Higbee, who won't be able to set his leg to the floor for three weeks to come. I have n't got all the buckshot out of it yet that Jack Dumont put there the other night."

Courtland started slightly. Jack Dumont! That was the name of Sally Dows' cousin of whom Champney had spoken! He had resolutely put aside from his returning memory the hazy recollection of the young girl's voice — the last thing he had heard that night — and the mystery that seemed to surround it. But there was no delusion in this cousin — his rival, and that of the equally deceived Champney. He controlled himself and repeated coldly: —

" Jack Dumont ! "

" Yes. But of course you knew nothing of all that, while you were off in the swamp there. Yet, by Jingo ! it was Dumont's shooting Higbee that helped *you* to get off your nigger a darned sight more than *your* killing the dogs."

" I don't understand," returned Courtland coldly.

"Well, you see, Dumont, who had taken up No'th'n principles, I reckon, more to goad the Higbees and please Sally Dows than from any conviction, came over here that night. Whether he suspected anything was up, or wanted to dare Higbee for bedevilment, or was only dancing attendance on Miss Sally, no one knows. But he rode slap into Higbee's party, called out, 'If you 're out hunting, Tom, here 's a chance for your score!' meaning their old vendetta feud, and brings his shot-gun up to his shoulder. Higbee was n't quick enough, Dumont lets fly, drops Higbee, and then gallops off chased by the Reeds to avenge Higbee, and followed by the whole crowd to see the fun, which was a little better than nigger-driving. And that let you and Cato out, colonel."

"And Dumont?"

"Got clean away to Foxboro' Station, leaving another score on his side for the Reeds and Higbees to wipe out as best they can. You No'th'n men don't believe in these sort of things, colonel, but taken as a straight dash and bit o' raiding, that stroke of Sally Dows' cousin was mighty fine!"

Courtland controlled himself with difficulty. The doctor had spoken truly. The hero of this miserable affair was *her* cousin — *his rival!* And to him — perhaps influenced by some pitying appeal of Miss Sally for the man she had deceived — Courtland owed his life! He instinctively drew a quick, sharp breath.

" Are you in pain? "

" Not at all. When can I get up? "

" Perhaps to-morrow."

" And this arm? "

" Better not use it for a week or two." He stopped, and, glancing paternally at the younger man, added gravely but kindly : " If you 'll take my unprofessional advice, Colonel Courtland, you 'll let this matter simmer down. It won't hurt you and your affairs here that folks have had a taste of your quality, and the nigger a lesson that his fellows won't forget."

" I thank you," returned Courtland coldly ; " but I think I already understand my duty to the company I represent and the Government I have served."

" Possibly, colonel," said the doctor quietly ; " but you 'll let an older man remind you and the Government that you can't change the habits or relations of two

distinct races in a few years. Your friend,
Miss Sally Dows — although not quite in my
way of thinking — has never attempted *that*."

"I am fully aware that Miss Dows pos-
sesses diplomatic accomplishments and
graces that I cannot lay claim to," returned
Courtland bitterly.

The doctor lifted his eyebrows slightly and
changed the subject.

When he had gone, Courtland called for
writing materials. He had already made
up his mind, and one course alone seemed
proper to him. He wrote to the president
of the company, detailing the circumstances
that had just occurred, admitting the alleged
provocation given by his overseer, but pointing out the terrorism of a mob-law which
rendered his own discipline impossible. He
asked that the matter be reported to Washington, and some measures taken for the
protection of the freedmen. In the mean
time he begged to tender his own resignation,
but he would stay until his successor was
appointed, or the safety of his employees
secured. Until then, he should act upon his
own responsibility and according to his
judgment. He made no personal charges,
mentioned no names, asked for no exem-

plary prosecution or trial of the offenders, but only demanded a safeguard against a repetition of the offense. His next letter, although less formal and official, was more difficult. It was addressed to the commandant of the nearest Federal barracks, who was an old friend and former companion-in-arms. He alluded to some conversation they had previously exchanged in regard to the presence of a small detachment of troops at Redlands during the elections, which Courtland at the time, however, had diplomatically opposed. He suggested it now as a matter of public expediency and prevention. When he had sealed the letters, not caring to expose them to the espionage of the local postmaster or his ordinary servants, he intrusted them to one of Miss Sally's own henchmen, to be posted at the next office, at Bitter Creek Station, ten miles distant.

Unfortunately, this duty accomplished, the reaction consequent on his still weak physical condition threw him back upon himself and his memory. He had resolutely refused to think of Miss Sally; he had been able to withstand the suggestions of her in the presence of her handmaid — supposed to be

potent in nursing and herb-lore — whom she
had detached to wait upon him, and he had
returned politely formal acknowledgments
to her inquiries. He had determined to continue this personal avoidance as far as possible until he was relieved, on the ground of
that *business* expediency which these events
had made necessary. She would see that
he was only accepting the arguments with
which she had met his previous advances.
Briefly, he had recourse to that hopeless
logic by which a man proves to himself that
he has no reason for loving a certain woman,
and is as incontestably convinced by the
same process that he has. And in the midst
of it he weakly fell asleep, and dreamed
that he and Miss Sally were walking in the
cemetery ; that a hideous snake concealed
among some lilies, over which the young
girl was bending, had uplifted its triangular
head to strike. That he seized it by the
neck, struggled with it until he was nearly
exhausted, when it suddenly collapsed and
shrunk, leaving in his palm the limp, crushed,
and delicately perfumed little thread glove
which he remembered to have once slipped
from her hand.

When he awoke, that perfume seemed to

be still in the air, distinct from the fresh
but homelier scents of the garden which
stole through the window. A sense of delicious coolness came with the afternoon
breeze, that faintly trilled the slanting slats
of the blind with a slumberous humming as
of bees. The golden glory of a sinking
southern sun was penciling the cheap paper
on the wall with leafy tracery and glowing
arabesques. But more than that, the calm
of some potent influence — or some unseen
presence — was upon him, which he feared
a movement might dispel. The chair at the
foot of his bed was empty. Sophy had gone
out. He did not turn his head to look
further; his languid eyes falling aimlessly
upon the carpet at his bedside suddenly di-
lated. For they fell also on the " smallest
foot in the State."

He started to his elbow, but a soft hand
was laid gently yet firmly upon his shoulder,
and with a faint rustle of muslin skirts Miss
Sally rose from an unseen chair at the head
of his bed, and stood beside him.

" Don't stir, co'nnle, I did n't sit where
I could look in yo'r face for fear of waking
yo'. But I 'll change seats now." She
moved to the chair which Sophy had va-

cated, drew it slightly nearer the bed, and sat down.

"It was very kind of you — to come," said Courtland hesitatingly, as with a strong effort he drew his eyes away from the fascinating vision, and regained a certain cold composure, "but I am afraid my illness has been greatly magnified. I really am quite well enough to be up and about my business, if the doctor would permit it. But I shall certainly manage to attend to my duty to-morrow, and I hope to be at your service."

"Meaning that yo' don't care to see me *now*, co'nnle," she said lightly, with a faint twinkle in her wise, sweet eyes. "I thought of that, but as my business would n't wait, I brought it to yo'." She took from the folds of her gown a letter. To his utter amazement it was the one he had given his overseer to post to the commandant that morning. To his greater indignation the seal was broken.

"Who has dared?" he demanded, half rising.

Her little hand was thrust out half deprecatingly. "No one yo' can fight, co'nnle; only *me*. I don't generally open other folks' letters, and I would n't have done it for *my-self;* I did for yo'."

" For me?"

" For yo'. I reckoned what yo' *might* do, and I told Sam to bring *me* the letters first. I did n't mind what yo' wrote to the com-pany — for they 'll take care of yo', and their own eggs are all in the same basket. I did n't open *that* one, but I did *this* when I saw the address. It was as I expected, and yo' 'd given yo'self away! For if yo' had those soldiers down here, yo' 'd have a row, sure! Don't move, co'nnle, *yo'* may not care for that, it 's in *yo'r* line. But folks will say that the soldiers were n't sent to pre-vent *rioting*, but that Co'nnle Courtland was using his old comrades to keep order on his property at Gov'ment expense. Hol' on! Hol' on! co'nnle," said the little figure, ris-ing and waving its pretty arms with a mis-chievous simulation of terrified deprecation. " Don't shoot! Of course yo' did n't mean *that*, but that 's about the way that So'th'n men will put it to yo'r Gov'ment. For," she continued, more gently, yet with the shrewd-est twinkle in her gray eyes, " if yo' really thought the niggers might need Federal pro-tection, yo' 'd have let *me* write to the com-

mandant to send an escort — not to *yo* , but
to *Cato* — that *he* might be able to come
back in safety. Yo' 'd have had yo'r soldiers ; I 'd have had back my nigger, which "
— demurely — " yo' don't seem to worry yo'-
self much about, co'nnle ; and there is n't a
So'th'n man would have objected. But,"
still more demurely, and affectedly smooth-
ing out her crisp skirt with her little hands,
" yo' have n't been troubling me much with
yo'r counsel lately."

A swift and utterly new comprehension
swept over Courtland. For the first time in
his knowledge of her he suddenly grasped
what was, perhaps, the true conception of
her character. Looking at her clearly now,
he understood the meaning of those pliant
graces, so unaffected and yet always controlled by the reasoning of an unbiased
intellect ; her frank speech and plausible
intonations ! Before him stood the true-born
daughter of a long race of politicians ! All
that he had heard of their dexterity, tact,
and expediency rose here incarnate, with the
added grace of womanhood. A strange
sense of relief — perhaps a dawning of hope
— stole over him.

" But how will this insure Cato's safety

hereafter, or give protection to the others?" he said, fixing his eyes upon her.

"The future won't concern *yo'* much, co'nnle, if as yo' say here yo'r resignation is sent in, and yo'r successor appointed," she replied, with more gravity than she had previously shown.

"But you do not think I will leave *you* in this uncertainty," he said passionately. He stopped suddenly, his brow darkened. "I forgot," he added coldly, "you will be well protected. Your — *cousin* — will give you the counsel of race — and — closer ties."

To his infinite astonishment, Miss Sally leaned forward in her chair and buried her laughing face in both of her hands. When her dimples had become again visible, she said with an effort, "Don't yo' think, co'nnle, that as a peacemaker my cousin was even a bigger failure than yo'self?"

"I don't understand," stammered Courtland.

"Don't yo' think," she continued, wiping her eyes demurely, "that if a young woman about my size, who had got perfectly tired and sick of all this fuss made about *yo'*, because yo' were a No'th'n man, managing niggers — if that young woman wanted to show her people what sort of a radical and abolitionist a *So'th'n* man of their own sort might become, she 'd have sent for Jack Dumont as a sample? Eh? Only, I declare to goodness, *I* never reckoned that he and Higbee would revive the tomfooling of the vendetta, and take to shootin' each other at once."

"And your sending for your cousin was only a feint to protect me?" said Courtland faintly.

"Perhaps he did n't have to be *sent for*, co'nnle," she said, with a slight touch of coquetry. "Suppose we say, I *let him come*. He 'd be hanging round, for he has property here, and wanted to get me to take it up with mine in the company. I knew what his new views and ideas were, and I thought I 'd better consult Champney — who, being a foreigner, and an older resident than yo', was quite neutral. He did n't happen to tell *yo'* anything about it — did he, co'nnle?" she added with a grave mouth, but an indescribable twinkle in her eyes.

Courtland's face darkened. "He did — and he further told me, Miss Dows, that he himself was your suitor, and that you had refused him because of the objections of your people."

She raised her eyes to his swiftly and dropped them.

" And yo' think I ought to have accepted him ? " she said slowly.

" No ! but — you know — you told me " — he began hurriedly. But she had already risen, and was shaking out the folds of her dress.

" We 're not talking *business* co'nnle — and business was my only excuse for coming here, and taking Sophy's place. I 'll send her in to yo', now."

" But, Miss Dows ! — Miss Sally ! "

She stopped — hesitated — a singular weakness for so self-contained a nature — and then slowly produced from her pocket a second letter — the one that Courtland had directed to the company. "I did n't read *this* letter, as I just told yo' co'nnle, for I reckon I know what 's in it, but I thought I 'd bring it with me too, in case *yo' changed yo'r mind*."

He raised himself on his pillow as she turned quickly away ; but in that single vanishing glimpse of her bright face he saw what neither he nor any one else had ever seen upon the face of Sally Dows — a burning blush !

"Miss Sally!" He almost leaped from the bed, but she was gone. There was another rustle at the door — the entrance of Sophy.

"Call her back, Sophy, quick!" he said.

The negress shook her turbaned head. "Not much, honey! When Miss Sally say she goes — she done gone, shuah!"

"But, Sophy!" Perhaps something in the significant face of the girl tempted him; perhaps it was only an impulse of his forgotten youth. "Sophy!" appealingly — "tell me! — is Miss Sally engaged to her cousin?"

"Wat dat?" said Sophy in indignant scorn. "Miss Sally engaged to dat Dumont! What fo'? Yo' 're crazy! No!"

"Nor Champney? Tell me, Sophy, has she a *lover?*"

For a moment the whites of Sophy's eyes were uplifted in speechless scorn. "Yo' ask dat! Yo' lyin' dar wid dat snake-bit arm! Yo' lyin' dar, and Miss Sally — who has only to whistle to call de fust quality in de State raoun her — coming and going here wid you, and trotting on yo'r arrants — and yo' ask dat! Yes! she has a lover, and what's mo', she *can't help it;* and yo' 're her lover; and what's mo', *yo'* can't help it either! And yo' can't back out of it now — bo'fe of yo' — nebber! Fo' yo' 're hers, and she's yo'rs — fo' ebber. For she sucked yo' blood."

"What!" gasped Courtland, aghast at what he believed to be the sudden insanity of the negress.

"Yes! Whar's yo'r eyes? whar's yo'r years? who's yo' dat yo' did n't see nor heah nuffin? When dey dragged yo' outer de swamp dat night — wid de snake-bite fresh on yo'r arm — did n't *she*, dat poh chile! — dat same Miss Sally — frow herself down on yo', and put dat baby mouf of hers to de wound and suck out de pizen and sabe de life ob yo' at de risk ob her own? Say? And if dey's any troof in Hoodoo, don't dat make yo' one blood and one soul! Go way, white man! I'm sick of yo'. Stop dar! Lie down dar! Hol' on, co'nnle, for massy's sake. Well, dar — I 'll call her back!"

And she did!

"Look here — don't you know — it rather took me by surprise," said Champney, a few days later, with a hearty grip of the colonel's uninjured hand; "but I don't bear

malice, old fellow, and, by Jove! it was
such a sensible, all-round, business-like
choice for the girl to make that no wonder
we never thought of it before. Hang it
all, you see a fellow was always so certain
it would be something out of the way and
detrimental, don't you know, that would
take the fancy of a girl like that — somebody like that cousin of hers or Higbee, or
even *me*, by Jove that we never thought of
looking beyond our noses — never thought
of the *business!* And *you* all the time so
cold and silent and matter-of-fact about it!
But I congratulate you! You've got the
business down on a safe basis now, and
what's more, you've got the one woman
who can run it."

They say he was a true prophet. At least
the Syndicate affairs prospered, and in
course of time even the Reeds and the Higbees participated in the benefits. There
were no more racial disturbances; only the
districts polled a peaceful and *smaller* Democratic majority at the next election. There
were not wanting those who alleged that
Colonel Courtland had simply become *Mrs.
Courtland's superintendent;* that she had
absorbed him as she had every one who had

come under her influence, and that she would not rest until she had made him a Senator (to represent Mrs. Courtland) in the councils of the nation. But when I last dined with them in Washington, ten years ago, I found them both very happy and comfortable, and I remember that Mrs. Courtland's remarks upon Federal and State interests, the proper education of young girls, and the management of the family, were eminently wise and practical.

THE CONSPIRACY OF MRS. BUNKER.

PART I.

On the northerly shore of San Francisco Bay a line of bluffs terminates in a promontory, at whose base, formed by the crumbling débris of the cliff above, there is a narrow stretch of beach, salt meadow, and scrub oak. The abrupt wall of rock behind it seems to isolate it as completely from the mainland as the sea before it separates it from the opposite shore. In spite of its contiguity to San Francisco, — opposite also, but hidden by the sharp reëntering curve of coast, — the locality was wild, uncultivated, and unfrequented. A solitary fisherman's cabin half hidden in the rocks was the only trace of habitation. White drifts of sea-gulls and pelican across the face of the cliff, gray clouds of sandpipers rising from the beach, the dripping flight of ducks

over the salt meadows, and the occasional
splash of a seal from the rocks, were the
only signs of life that could be seen from
the decks of passing ships. And yet the
fisherman's cabin was occupied by Zephas
Bunker and his young wife, and he had
succeeded in wresting from the hard soil
pasturage for a cow and goats, while his
lateen-sailed fishing-boat occasionally rode
quietly in the sheltered cove below.

Three years ago Zephas Bunker, an ex-
whaler, had found himself stranded on a
San Francisco wharf and had "hired out"
to a small Petaluma farmer. At the end of
a year he had acquired little taste for the
farmer's business, but considerable for the
farmer's youthful daughter, who, equally
weary of small agriculture, had consented
to elope with him in order to escape it.
They were married at Oakland; he put his
scant earnings into a fishing-boat, discovered
the site for his cabin, and brought his bride
thither. The novelty of the change pleased
her, although perhaps it was but little advance on her previous humble position. Yet
she preferred her present freedom to the
bare restricted home life of her past; the
perpetual presence of the restless sea was a

relief to the old monotony of the wheat
field and its isolated drudgery. For Mary's
youthful fancy, thinly sustained in childhood by the lightest literary food, had neither been stimulated nor disillusioned by
her marriage. That practical experience
which is usually the end of girlish romance
had left her still a child in sentiment. The
long absences of her husband in his fishing-
boat kept her from wearying of or even
knowing his older and unequal companionship; it gave her a freedom her girlhood
had never known, yet added a protection
that suited her still childish dependency,
while it tickled her pride with its equality.
When not engaged in her easy household
duties in her three-roomed cottage, or the
care of her rocky garden patch, she found
time enough to indulge her fancy over the
mysterious haze that wrapped the invisible
city so near and yet unknown to her; in the
sails that slipped in and out of the Golden
Gate, but of whose destination she knew
nothing; and in the long smoke trail of the
mail steamer which had yet brought her no
message. Like all dwellers by the sea, her
face and her thoughts were more frequently
turned towards it; and as with them, it also

seemed to her that whatever change was coming into her life would come across that vast unknown expanse. But it was here that Mrs. Bunker was mistaken.

It had been a sparkling summer morning. The waves were running before the dry northwest trade winds with crystalline but colorless brilliancy. Sheltered by the high, northerly bluff, the house and its garden were exposed to the untempered heat of the cloudless sun refracted from the rocky wall behind it. Some tarpaulin and ropes lying among the rocks were sticky and odorous; the scrub oaks and manzañita bushes gave out the aroma of baking wood; occasionally a faint pot-pourri fragrance from the hot wild roses and beach grass was blown along the shore; even the lingering odors of Bunker's vocation, and of Mrs. Bunker's cooking, were idealized and refined by the saline breath of the sea at the doors and windows. Mrs. Bunker, in the dazzling sun, bending over her peas and lettuces with a small hoe, felt the comfort of her brown holland sun-bonnet. Secure in her isolation, she unbuttoned the neck of her gown for air, and did not put up the strand of black hair that had escaped over her shoulder. It was very hot in the lee of the bluff, and very quiet in that still air. So quiet that she heard two distinct reports, following each other quickly, but very faint and far. She glanced mechanically towards the sea. Two merchantmen in midstream were shaking out their wings for a long flight, a pilot boat and coasting schooner were rounding the point, but there was no smoke from their decks. She bent over her work again, and in another moment had forgotten it. But the heat, with the dazzling reflection from the cliff, forced her to suspend her gardening, and stroll along the beach to the extreme limit of her domain. Here she looked after the cow that had also strayed away through the tangled bush for coolness. The goats, impervious to temperature, were basking in inaccessible fastnesses on the cliff itself that made her eyes ache to climb. Over an hour passed, she was returning, and had neared her house, when she was suddenly startled to see the figure of a man between her and the cliff. He was engaged in brushing his dusty clothes with a handkerchief, and although he saw her coming, and even moved slowly towards her, continued his occupation with a half-impatient, half-abstracted air.

Her feminine perception was struck with the circumstance that he was in deep black, with scarcely a gleam of white showing even at his throat, and that he wore a tall black hat. Without knowing anything of social customs, it seemed to her that his dress was inconsistent with his appearance there.

" Good-morning," he said, lifting his hat with a preoccupied air. " Do you live here ? "

" Yes," she said wonderingly.

" Anybody else ? "

" My husband."

" I mean any other people ? Are there any other houses ? " he said with a slight impatience.

" No."

He looked at her and then towards the sea. " I expect some friends who are coming for me in a boat. I suppose they can land easily here ? "

" Did n't you yourself land here just now ? " she said quickly.

He half hesitated, and then, as if scorning an equivocation, made a hasty gesture over her shoulder and said bluntly, " No, I came over the cliff."

" Down the cliff ? " she repeated incredulously.

"Yes," he said, glancing at his clothes; "it was a rough scramble, but the goats showed me the way."

"And you were up on the bluff all the time?" she went on curiously.

"Yes. You see — I "— he stopped suddenly at what seemed to be the beginning of a prearranged and plausible explanation, as if impatient of its weakness or hypocrisy, and said briefly, "Yes, I was there."

Like most women, more observant of his face and figure, she did not miss this lack of explanation. He was a very good-looking man of middle age, with a thin, proud, high-bred face, which in a country of bearded men had the further distinction of being smoothly shaven. She had never seen any one like him before. She thought he looked like an illustration of some novel she had read, but also somewhat melancholy, worn, and tired.

"Won't you come in and rest yourself?" she said, motioning to the cabin.

"Thank you," he said, still half absently. "Perhaps I'd better. It may be some time yet before they come."

She led the way to the cabin, entered the living room — a plainly furnished little **apartment** between the bedroom and the

kitchen — pointed to a large bamboo arm-
chair, and placed a bottle of whiskey and
some water on the table before him. He
thanked her again very gently, poured out
some spirits in his glass, and mixed it with
water. But when she glanced towards him
again he had apparently risen without tast-
ing it, and going to the door was standing
there with his hand in the breast of his buttoned frock coat, gazing silently towards the
sea. There was something vaguely historical
in his attitude — or what she thought might
be historical — as of somebody of great importance who had halted on the eve of some
great event at the door of her humble cabin.

His apparent unconsciousness of her and
of his surroundings, his preoccupation with
something far beyond her ken, far from
piquing her, only excited her interest the
more. And then there was such an odd sadness in his eyes.

" Are you anxious for your folks' coming ? " she said at last, following his out-
look.

" I — oh no ! " he returned, quickly recalling himself, " they 'll be sure to come —
sooner or later. No fear of that," he added,
half smilingly, half wearily.

Mrs. Bunker passed into the kitchen, where, while apparently attending to her household duties, she could still observe her singular guest. Left alone, he seated himself mechanically in the chair, and gazed fixedly at the fireplace. He remained a long time so quiet and unmoved, in spite of the marked ostentatious clatter Mrs. Bunker found it necessary to make with her dishes, that an odd fancy that he was scarcely a human visitant began to take possession of her. Yet she was not frightened. She remembered distinctly afterwards that, far from having any concern for herself, she was only moved by a strange and vague admiration of him.

But her prolonged scrutiny was not without effect. Suddenly he raised his dark eyes, and she felt them pierce the obscurity of her kitchen with a quick, suspicious, impatient penetration, which as they met hers gave way, however, to a look that she thought was gently reproachful. Then he rose, stretched himself to his full height, and approaching the kitchen door leaned listlessly against the door-post.

"I don't suppose you are ever lonely here?"

" No, sir."

" Of course not. You have yourself and husband. Nobody interferes with you. You are contented and happy together."

Mrs. Bunker did not say, what was the fact, that she had never before connected the sole companionship of her husband with her happiness. Perhaps it had never occurred to her until that moment how little it had to do with it. She only smiled gratefully at the change in her guest's abstraction.

" Do you often go to San Francisco? " he continued.

" I have never been there at all. Some day I expect we will go there to live."

" I would n't advise you to," he said, looking at her gravely. " I don't think it will pay you. You 'll never be happy there as here. You 'll never have the independence and freedom you have here. You 'll never be your own mistress again. But how does it happen you never were in San Francisco? " he said suddenly.

If he would not talk of himself, here at least was a chance for Mrs. Bunker to say something. She related how her family had emigrated from Kansas across the plains and had taken up a "location" at Contra Costa. How she didn't care for it, and how she came to marry the seafaring man who brought her here — all with great simplicity and frankness and as unreservedly as to a superior being — albeit his attention wandered at times, and a rare but melancholy smile that he had apparently evoked to meet her conversational advances became fixed occasionally. Even his dark eyes, which had obliged Mrs. Bunker to put up her hair and button her collar, rested upon her without seeing her.

"Then your husband's name is Bunker?" he said when she paused at last. "That's one of those Nantucket Quaker names — sailors and whalers for generations — and yours, you say, was MacEwan. Well, Mrs. Bunker, *your* family came from Kentucky to Kansas only lately, though I suppose your father calls himself a Free-States man. You ought to know something of farming and cattle, for your ancestors were old Scotch Covenanters who emigrated a hundred years ago, and were great stock raisers."

All this seemed only the natural omniscience of a superior being. And Mrs.

Bunker perhaps was not pained to learn that her husband's family was of a lower degree than her own. But the stranger's knowledge did not end there. He talked of her husband's business — he explained the vast fishing resources of the bay and coast. He showed her how the large colony of Italian fishermen were inimical to the interests of California and to her husband — particularly as a native American trader. He told her of the volcanic changes of the bay and coast line, of the formation of the rocky ledge on which she lived. He pointed out to her its value to the Government for defensive purposes, and how it naturally commanded the entrance of the Golden Gate far better than Fort Point, and that it ought to be in its hands. If the Federal Government did not buy it of her husband, certainly the State of California should. And here he fell into an abstraction as deep and as gloomy as before. He walked to the window, paced the floor with his hand in his breast, went to the door, and finally stepped out of the cabin, moving along the ledge of rocks to the shore, where he stood motionless.

Mrs. Bunker had listened to him with parted lips and eyes of eloquent admiration.

She had never before heard any one talk like *that*—she had not believed it possible that any one could have such knowledge. Perhaps she could not understand all he said, but she would try to remember it after he had gone. She could only think now how kind it was of him that in all this mystery of his coming, and in the singular sadness that was oppressing him, he should try to interest her. And thus looking at him, and wondering, an idea came to her.

She went into her bedroom and took down her husband's heavy pilot overcoat and sou'wester, and handed them to her guest.

"You'd better put them on if you're going to stand there," she said.

"But I am not cold," he said wonderingly.

"But you might be *seen*," she said simply.

It was the first suggestion that had passed between them that his presence there was a secret. He looked at her intently, then he smiled and said, "I think you're right, for many reasons," put the pilot coat over his frock coat, removed his hat with the gesture of a bow, handed it to her, and placed the sou'wester in its stead. Then for an instant he hesitated as if about to speak, but Mrs.

Bunker, with a delicacy that she could not herself comprehend at the moment, hurried back to the cabin without giving him an opportunity.

Nor did she again intrude upon his meditations. Hidden in his disguise, which to her eyes did not, however, seem to conceal his characteristic figure, he wandered for nearly an hour under the bluff and along the shore, returning at last almost mechanically to the cabin, where, oblivious of his surroundings, he reseated himself in silence by the table with his cheek resting on his hand. Presently, her quick, experienced ear detected the sound of oars in their rowlocks; she could plainly see from her kitchen window a small boat with two strangers seated at the stern being pulled to the shore. With the same strange instinct of delicacy, she determined not to go out lest her presence might embarrass her guest's reception of his friends. But as she turned towards the living room she found he had already risen and was removing his hat and pilot coat. She was struck, however, by the circumstance that not only did he exhibit no feeling of relief at his deliverance, but that a half-cynical, half-savage expression had

taken the place of his former melancholy.
As he went to the door, the two gentlemen
hastily clambered up the rocks to greet him.

" Jim reckoned it was you hangin' round
the rocks, but I could n't tell at that distance. Seemed you borrowed a hat and
coat. Well — it 's all fixed, and we 've no
time to lose. There 's a coasting steamer
just dropping down below the Heads, and it
will take you aboard. But I can tell you
you 've kicked up a h—ll of a row over
there." He stopped, evidently at some
sign from her guest. The rest of the man's
speech followed in a hurried whisper, which
was stopped again by the voice she knew.
" No. Certainly not." The next moment
his tall figure was darkening the door of
the kitchen ; his hand was outstretched.
" Good-by, Mrs. Bunker, and many thanks
for your hospitality. My friends here," he
turned grimly to the men behind him,
" think I ought to ask you to keep this a
secret even from your husband. *I don't !*
They also think that I ought to offer you
money for your kindness. *I don't !* But
if you will honor me by keeping this ring in
remembrance of it " — he took a heavy seal
ring from his finger — " it 's the only bit of

jewelry I have about me — I'll be very glad. Good-by!" She felt for a moment the firm, soft pressure of his long, thin fingers around her own, and then — he was gone. The sound of retreating oars grew fainter and fainter and was lost. The same reserve of delicacy which now appeared to her as a duty kept her from going to the window to watch the destination of the boat. No, he should go as he came, without her supervision or knowledge.

Nor did she feel lonely afterwards. On the contrary, the silence and solitude of the isolated domain had a new charm. They kept the memory of her experience intact, and enabled her to refill it with his presence. She could see his tall figure again pausing before her cabin, without the incongruous association of another personality; she could hear his voice again, unmingled with one more familiar. For the first time, the regular absence of her husband seemed an essential good fortune instead of an accident of their life. For the experience belonged to *her*, and not to him and her together. He could not understand it; he would have acted differently and spoiled it. She should not tell him anything of it, in spite of the stranger's suggestion, which, of course, he had only made because he did n't know Zephas as well as she did. For Mrs. Bunker was getting on rapidly; it was her first admission of the conjugal knowledge that one's husband is inferior to the outside estimate of him. The next step — the belief that he was deceiving *her* as he was *them* — would be comparatively easy.

Nor should she show him the ring. The stranger had certainly never said anything about that! It was a heavy ring, with a helmeted head carved on its red carnelian stone, and what looked like strange letters around it. It fitted her third finger perfectly; but *his* fingers were small, and he had taken it from his little finger. She should keep it herself. Of course, if it had been money, she would have given it to Zephas; but the stranger knew that she would n't take money. How firmly he had said that " I don't! " She felt the warm blood fly to her fresh young face at the thought of it. He had understood her. She might be living in a poor cabin, doing all the housework herself, and her husband only a fisherman, but he had treated her like a lady.

And so the afternoon passed. The outlying fog began to roll in at the Golden
Gate, obliterating the headland and stretching a fleecy bar across the channel as if
shutting out from vulgar eyes the way that
he had gone. Night fell, but Zephas had
not yet come. This was unusual, for he
was generally as regular as the afternoon
"trades" which blew him there. There
was nothing to detain him in this weather
and at this season. She began to be vaguely
uneasy; then a little angry at this new
development of his incompatibility. Then
it occurred to her, for the first time in her
wifehood, to think what she would do if he
were lost. Yet, in spite of some pain, terror,
and perplexity at the possibility, her dominant thought was that she would be a free
woman to order her life as she liked.

It was after ten before his lateen sail
flapped in the little cove. She was waiting
to receive him on the shore. His good-humored hirsute face was slightly apologetic
in expression, but flushed and disturbed
with some new excitement to which an extra
glass or two of spirits had apparently added
intensity. The contrast between his evident
indulgence and the previous abstemiousness

of her late guest struck her unpleasantly. " Well — I declare," she said indignantly, " so *that's* what kept you ! "

" No," he said quickly ; " there 's been awful times over in 'Frisco ! Everybody just wild, and the Vigilance Committee in session. Jo Henderson 's killed ! Shot by Wynyard Marion in a duel ! He 'll be lynched, sure as a gun, if they ketch him."

" But I thought men who fought duels always went free."

" Yes, but this ain't no common duel ; they say the whole thing was planned beforehand by them Southern fire-eaters to get rid o' Henderson because he 's a Northern man and anti-slavery, and that they picked out Colonel Marion to do it because he was a dead shot. They got him to insult Henderson, so he was bound to challenge Marion, and that giv' Marion the chyce of weppings. It was a reg'lar put up job to kill him."

" And what 's all this to lo with you ? " she asked, with irritation.

" Hold on, won't you ! and I 'll tell you. I was pickin' up nets off Saucelito about noon, when I was hailed by one of them Vigilance tugs, and they set me to stand off and on the shore and watch that Marion

did n't get away, while they were scoutin'
inland. Ye see *the duel took place just
over the bluff there — behind ye —* and they
allowed that Marion had struck away north
for Mendocino to take ship there. For after
overhaulin' his second's boat, they found
out that they had come away from Saucelito
alone. But they sent a tug around by sea
to Mendocino to head him off there, while
they 're closin' in around him inland.
They 're bound to catch him sooner or later.
But you ain't listenin', Mollie ? "

She was — in every fibre — but with her
head turned towards the window, and the
invisible Golden Gate through which the
fugitive had escaped. For she saw it all
now — that glorious vision — her high-bred,
handsome guest and Wynyard Marion were
one and the same person. And this rough,
commonplace man before her — her own
husband — had been basely set to capture
him !

PART II.

During that evening and the next Mrs.
Bunker, without betraying her secret, or exciting the least suspicion on the part of her
husband, managed to extract from him not

only a rough description of Marion which tallied with her own impressions, but a short history of his career. He was a famous politician who had held high office in the South; he was an accomplished lawyer; he had served in the army; he was a fiery speaker; he had a singular command of men. He was unmarried, but there were queer stories of his relations with some of the wives of prominent officials, and there was no doubt that he used them in some of his political intrigues. He, Zephas, would bet something that it was a woman who had helped him off! Did she speak?

Yes, she had spoken. It made her sick to sit there and hear such stories! Because a man did not agree with some people in politics it was perfectly awful to think how they would abuse him and take away his character! Men were so awfully jealous, too; if another man happened to be superior and fine-looking there was n't anything bad enough for them to say about him! No! she was n't a slavery sympathizer either, and had n't anything to do with man politics, although she was a Southern woman, and the MacEwans had come from Kentucky and owned slaves. Of course, he, Zephas, whose ancestors were Cape Cod Quakers and had always been sailors, could n't understand. She did not know what he meant by saying "what a long tail our cat's got," but if he meant to call her a cat, and was going to use such language to her, he had better have stayed in San Francisco with his Vigilance friends. And perhaps it would have been better if he had stayed there before he took her away from her parents at Martinez. Then she would n't have been left on a desert rock without any chance of seeing the world, or ever making any friends or acquaintances!

It was their first quarrel. Discreetly made up by Mrs. Bunker in some alarm at betraying herself; honestly forgiven by Zephas in a rude, remorseful consciousness of her limited life. One or two nights later, when he returned, it was with a mingled air of mystery and satisfaction. "Well, Mollie," he said cheerfully, "it looks as if your pets were not as bad as I thought them."

"My pets!" repeated Mrs. Bunker, with a faint rising of color.

"Well, I call these Southern Chivs your pets, Mollie, because you stuck up for them so the other night. But never mind that now. What do you suppose has happened? Jim Rider, you know, the Southern banker and speculator, who's a regular big Injin among the ' Chivs,' he sent Cap Simmons down to the wharf while I was unloadin' to come up and see him. Well, I went, and what do y'u think? He told me he was gettin' up an American Fishin' Company, and wanted me to take charge of a first-class schooner on shares. Said he heard of me afore, and knew I was an American and a white man, and just the chap ez could knock them Eytalians outer the market."

"Yes," interrupted Mrs. Bunker quickly, but emphatically, " the fishing interest ought to be American and protected by the State, with regular charters and treaties."

"I say, Mollie," said her astonished but admiring husband, "you've been readin' the papers or listenin' to stump speakin' sure."

"Go on," returned Mrs. Bunker impatiently, " and say what happened next."

" Well," returned Zephas, " I first thought, you see, that it had suthin' to do with that Marion business, particklerly ez folks allowed he was hidin' somewhere yet, and they wanted me to run him off. So I thought

Rider might as well know that I was n't to
be bribed, so I ups and tells him how I 'd
been lyin' off Saucelito the other day workin'
for the other side agin him. With that he
laughs, says he did n't want any better friends
than me, but that I must be livin' in the
backwoods not to know that Wynyard Marion had escaped, and was then at sea on his
way to Mexico or Central America. Then
we agreed to terms, and the long and short
of it is, Mollie, that I 'm to have the schooner
with a hundred and fifty dollars a month,
and ten per cent. shares after a year! Looks
like biz, eh, Mollie, old girl? but you don't
seem pleased."

She had put aside the arm with which he
was drawing her to him, and had turned her
white face away to the window. So *he* had
gone — this stranger — this one friend of
her life — she would never see him again,
and all that would ever come of it was this
pecuniary benefit to her husband, who had
done nothing. He would not even offer her
money, but he had managed to pay his debt
to her in this way that their vulgar poverty
would appreciate. And this was the end of
her dream!

"You don't seem to take it in, Mollie,"

continued the surprised Zephas. " It means a house in 'Frisco and a little cabin for you on the schooner when you like."

" I don't want it ! I won't have it ! I shall stay here," she burst out with a half-passionate, half-childish cry, and ran into her bedroom, leaving the astonished Zephas helpless in his awkward consternation.

" By Gum ! I must take her to 'Frisco right off, or she 'll be havin' the high strikes here alone. I oughter knowed it would come to this ! " But although he consulted " Cap " Simmons the next day, who informed him it was all woman's ways when " struck," and advised him to pay out all the line he could at such delicate moments, she had no recurrence of the outbreak. On the contrary, for days and weeks following she seemed calmer, older, and more " growed up ; " although she resisted changing her seashore dwelling for San Francisco, she accompanied him on one or two of his " deep sea " trips down the coast, and seemed happier on their southern limits. She had taken to reading the political papers and speeches, and some cheap American histories. Captain Bunker's crew, profoundly convinced that their skipper's wife was a " woman's

rights " fanatic, with the baleful qualities of
" sea lawyer " superadded, marveled at his
bringing her.

It was on returning home from one of
these trips that they touched briefly at San
Francisco, where the Secretary of the Fishing Company came on board. Mrs. Bunker
was startled to recognize in him one of the
two gentlemen who had taken Mr. Marion
off in the boat, but as he did not appear to
recognize her even after an awkward introduction by her husband, she would have recovered her equanimity but for a singular
incident. As her husband turned momentarily away, the Secretary, with a significant
gesture, slipped a letter into her hand. She
felt the blood rush to her face as, with a
smile, he moved away to follow her husband.
She came down to the little cabin and impatiently tore open the envelope, which bore
no address. A small folded note contained
the following lines : —

" I never intended to burden you with my
confidence, but the discretion, tact, and courage you displayed on our first meeting, and
what I know of your loyalty since, have
prompted me to trust myself again to your

kindness, even though you are now aware whom you have helped, and the risks you ran. My friends wish to communicate with me and to forward to me, from time to time, certain papers of importance, which, owing to the tyrannical espionage of the Government, would be discovered and stopped in passing through the express or post-office. These papers will be left at your house, but here I must trust entirely to your wit and judgment as to the way in which they should be delivered to my agent at the nearest Mexican port. To facilitate your action, your husband will receive directions to pursue his course as far south as Todos Santos, where a boat will be ready to take charge of them when he is sighted. I know I am asking a great favor, but I have such confidence in you that I do not even ask you to commit yourself to a reply to this. If it can be done I know that you will do it; if it cannot, I will understand and appreciate the reason why. I will only ask you that when you are ready to receive the papers you will fly a small red pennant from the little flagstaff among the rocks. Believe me, your friend and grateful debtor,

" W. M."

Mrs. Bunker cast a hasty glance around her, and pressed the letter to her lips. It was a sudden consummation of her vaguest, half-formed wishes, the realization of her wildest dreams! To be the confidante of the gallant but melancholy hero in his lonely exile and persecution was to satisfy all the unformulated romantic fancies of her girlish reading; to be later, perhaps, the Flora Macdonald of a middle-aged Prince Charlie did not, however, evoke any ludicrous associations in her mind. Her feminine fancy exalted the escaped duelist and alleged assassin into a social martyr. His actual small political intrigues and ignoble aims of office seemed to her little different from those aspirations of royalty which she had read about — as perhaps they were. Indeed, it is to be feared that in foolish little Mrs. Bunker, Wynyard Marion had found the old feminine adoration of pretension and privilege which every rascal has taken advantage of since the flood.

Howbeit, the next morning after she had returned and Zephas had sailed away, she flew a red bandana handkerchief on the little flagstaff before the house. A few hours later, a boat appeared mysteriously

from around the Point. Its only occupant
— a common sailor — asked her name, and
handed her a sealed package. Mrs. Bunker's invention had already been at work.
She had created an aunt in Mexico, for
whom she had, with some ostentation, made
some small purchases while in San Francisco. When her husband spoke of going
as far south as Todos Santos, she begged
him to deliver the parcel to her aunt's messenger, and even addressed it boldly to her.
Inside the outer wrapper she wrote a note
to Marion, which, with a new and amazing
diffidence, she composed and altered a dozen
times, at last addressing the following in a
large, school-girl hand : " Sir, I obey your
commands to the last. Whatever your oppressors or enemies may do, you can always
rely and trust upon She who in deepest
sympathy signs herself ever, Mollie Rosalie
MacEwan." The substitution of her maiden
name in full seemed in her simplicity to be
a delicate exclusion of her husband from the
affair, and a certain disguise of herself to
alien eyes. The superscription, " To Mrs.
Marion MacEwan from Mollie Bunker, to
be called for by hand at Todos Santos," also
struck her as a marvel of ingenuity. The

package was safely and punctually delivered by Zephas, who brought back a small packet directed to her, which on private examination proved to contain a letter addressed to " J. E. Kirby, to be called for," with the hurried line : " A thousand thanks, W. M." Mrs. Bunker drew a long, quick breath. He might have written more ; he might have — but the wish remained still unformulated. The next day she ran up a signal ; the same boat and solitary rower appeared around the Point, and took the package. A week later, when her husband was ready for sea, she again hoisted her signal. It brought a return package for Mexico, which she inclosed and readdressed, and gave to her husband. The recurrence of this incident apparently struck a bright idea from the simple Zephas.

" Look here, Mollie, why don't you come *yourself* and see your aunt. I can't go into port without a license, and them port charges cost a heap o' red tape, for they 've got a Filibuster scare on down there just now, but you can go ashore in the boat and I 'll get permission from the Secretary to stand off and wait for you there for twenty-four hours." Mrs. Bunker flushed and paled at the thought. She could see him ! The letter would be sufficient excuse, the distrust suggested by her husband would give color to her delivering it in person. There was perhaps a brief twinge of conscience in taking this advantage of Zephas' kindness, but the next moment, with that peculiar logic known only to the sex, she made the unfortunate man's suggestion a condonation of her deceit. *She* had n't asked to go ; *he* had offered to take her. He had only himself to thank.

Meantime the political excitement in which she had become a partisan without understanding or even conviction, presently culminated with the Presidential campaign and the election of Abraham Lincoln. The intrigues of Southern statesmen were revealed in open expression, and echoed in California by those citizens of Southern birth and extraction who had long held place, power, and opinion there. There were rumors of secession, of California joining the South, or of her founding an independent Pacific Empire. A note from " J. E. Kirby " informed Mrs. Bunker that she was to carefully retain any correspondence that might be in her hands until further orders, almost at the same time that

Zephas as regretfully told her that his projected Southern trip had been suspended.
Mrs. Bunker was disappointed, and yet, in
some singular conditions of her feelings, felt
relieved that her meeting with Marion was
postponed. It is to be feared that some dim
conviction, unworthy a partisan, that in the
magnitude of political events her own petty
personality might be overlooked by her hero
tended somewhat to her resignation.

Meanwhile the seasons had changed.
The winter rains had set in ; the trade
winds had shifted to the southeast, and the
cottage, although strengthened, enlarged,
and made more comfortable through the
good fortunes of the Bunkers, was no longer
sheltered by the cliff, but was exposed to
the full strength of the Pacific gales. There
were long nights when she could hear the
rain fall monotonously on the shingles, or
startle her with a short, sharp reveille on
the windows ; there were brief days of flying clouds and drifting sunshine, and intervals of dull gray shadow, when the heaving
white breakers beyond the Gate slowly lifted
themselves and sank before her like wraiths
of warning. At such times, in her accepted
solitude, Mrs. Bunker gave herself up to

strange moods and singular visions ; the
more audacious and more striking it seemed
to her from their very remoteness, and the
difficulty she was beginning to have in ma-
terializing them. The actual personality of
Wynyard Marion, as she knew it in her one
interview, had become very shadowy and
faint in the months that passed, yet when
the days were heavy she sometimes saw
herself standing by his side in some vague
tropical surroundings, and hailed by the multitude as the faithful wife and consort of the
great Leader, President, Emperor — she
knew not what! Exactly how this was to
be managed, and the manner of Zephas'
effacement from the scene, never troubled
her childish fancy, and, it is but fair to say,
her woman's conscience. In the logic before
alluded to, it seemed to her that all ethical
responsibility for her actions rested with the
husband who had unduly married her. Nor
were those visions always roseate. In the
wild declamation of that exciting epoch
which filled the newspapers there was talk
of short shrift with traitors. So there were
days when the sudden onset of a squall of
hail against her window caused her to start
as if she had heard the sharp fusillade of

that file of muskets of which she had sometimes read in history.

One day she had a singular fright. She
had heard the sound of oars falling with a
precision and regularity unknown to her.
She was startled to see the approach of a
large eight-oared barge rowed by men in uniform, with two officers wrapped in cloaks in
the stern sheets, and before them the glitter
of musket barrels. The two officers appeared to be conversing earnestly, and occasionally pointing to the shore and the bluff
above. For an instant she trembled, and
then an instinct of revolt and resistance followed. She hurriedly removed the ring,
which she usually wore when alone, from her
finger, slipped it with the packet under the
mattress of her bed, and prepared with blazing eyes to face the intruders. But when
the boat was beached, the two officers, with
scarcely a glance towards the cottage, proceeded leisurely along the shore. Relieved,
yet it must be confessed a little piqued at
their indifference, she snatched up her hat
and sallied forth to confront them.

" I suppose you don't know that this is
private property ? " she said sharply.

The group halted and turned towards her.

The orderly, who was following, turned his face aside and smiled. The younger officer demurely lifted his cap. The elder, gray, handsome, in a general's uniform, after a moment's half-astounded, half-amused scrutiny of the little figure, gravely raised his gauntleted fingers in a military salute.

"I beg your pardon, madam, but I am afraid we never even thought of that. We are making a preliminary survey for the Government with a possible view of fortifying the bluff. It is very doubtful if you will be disturbed in any rights you may have, but if you are, the Government will not fail to make it good to you." He turned carelessly to the aide beside him. "I suppose the bluff is quite inaccessible from here?"

"I don't know about that, general. They say that Marion, after he killed Henderson, escaped down this way," said the young man.

"Indeed, what good was that? How did he get away from here?"

"They say that Mrs. Fairfax was hanging round in a boat, waiting for him. The story of the escape is all out now."

They moved away with a slight perfunctory bow to Mrs. Bunker, only the younger officer noting that the pert, pretty little Western woman was n't as sharp and snappy to his superior as she had at first promised to be.

She turned back to the cottage astounded, angry, and vaguely alarmed. Who was this Mrs. Fairfax who had usurped her fame and solitary devotion? There was no woman in the boat that took him off; it was equally well known that he went in the ship alone. If they had heard that some woman was with him here — why should they have supposed it was Mrs. Fairfax? Zephas might know something — but he was away. The thought haunted her that day and the next. On the third came a more startling incident.

She had been wandering along the edge of her domain in a state of restlessness which had driven her from the monotony of the house when she heard the barking of the big Newfoundland dog which Zephas had lately bought for protection and company. She looked up and saw the boat and its solitary rower at the landing. She ran quickly to the house to bring the packet. As she entered she started back in amazement. For the sitting-room was already in possession

of a woman who was seated calmly by the
table.

The stranger turned on Mrs. Bunker that
frankly insolent glance and deliberate examination which only one woman can give
another. In that glance Mrs. Bunker felt
herself in the presence of a superior, even
if her own eyes had not told her that in
beauty, attire, and bearing the intruder was
of a type and condition far beyond her own,
or even that of any she had known. It was
the more crushing that there also seemed to
be in this haughty woman the same incon-
gruousness and sharp contrast to the plain
and homely surroundings of the cottage that
she remembered in *him*.

" Yo' aw Mrs. Bunker, I believe," she
said in languid Southern accents. " How
de doh ? "

" I am Mrs. Bunker," said Mrs. Bunker
shortly.

" And so this is where Cunnle Marion
stopped when he waited fo' the boat to take
him off," said the stranger, glancing lazily
around, and delaying with smiling insolence
the explanation she knew Mrs. Bunker was
expecting. " The cunnle said it was a pooh
enough place, but I don't see it. I reckon,

however, he was too worried to judge and glad enough to get off. Yo' ought to have made him talk — he generally don't want much prompting to talk to women, if they 're pooty."

" He did n't seem in a hurry to go," said Mrs. Bunker indignantly. The next moment she saw her error, even before the cruel, handsome smile of her unbidden guest revealed it.

" I thought so," she said lazily; "this *is* the place and here 's where the cunnle stayed. Only yo' ought n't have given him and yo'self away to the first stranger quite so easy. The cunnle might have taught yo' *that* the two or three hours he was with yo'."

" What do you want with me ? " demanded Mrs. Bunker angrily.

" I want a letter yo' have for me from Cunnle Marion."

" I have nothing for you," said Mrs. Bunker. " I don't know who you are."

" You ought to, considering you 've been acting as messenger between the cunnle and me," said the lady coolly.

" That 's not true," said Mrs. Bunker hotly, to combat an inward sinking.

The lady rose with a lazy, languid grace,

walked to the door and called still lazily, "O Pedro!"

The solitary rower clambered up the rocks and appeared on the cottage threshold.

"Is this the lady who gave you the letters for me and to whom you took mine?"

"Si, señora."

"They were addressed to a Mr. Kirby," said Mrs. Bunker sullenly. "How was I to know they were for Mrs. Kirby?"

"Mr. Kirby, Mrs. Kirby, and myself are all the same. You don't suppose the cunnle would give my real name and address? Did you address yo'r packet to *his* real name or to some one else. Did you let your husband know who they were for?"

Oddly, a sickening sense of the meanness of all these deceits and subterfuges suddenly came over Mrs. Bunker. Without replying she went to her bedroom and returned with Colonel Marion's last letter, which she tossed into her visitor's lap.

"Thank yo', Mrs. Bunker. I'll be sure to tell the cunnle how careful yo' were not to give up his correspondence to everybody. It'll please him mo' than to hear yo' are wearing his ring — which everybody knows — before people."

"He gave it to me — he — he knew I would n't take money," said Mrs. Bunker indignantly.

"He did n't have any to give," said the lady slowly, as she removed the envelope from her letter and looked up with a dazzling but cruel smile. "A So'th'n gentleman don't fill up his pockets when he goes out to fight. He don't tuck his maw's Bible in his breast-pocket, clap his dear auntie's locket big as a cheese plate over his heart, nor let his sole leather cigyar case that his gyrl gave him lie round him in spots when he goes out to take another gentleman's fire. He leaves that to Yanks!"

"Did you come here to insult my husband?" said Mrs. Bunker in the rage of desperation.

"To insult yo' husband! Well — I came here to get a letter that his wife received from his political and natural enemy and — perhaps *I did!*" With a side glance at Mrs. Bunker's crimson cheek she added carelessly, "I have nothing against Captain Bunker; he 's a straightforward man and must go with his kind. He helped those hounds of Vigilantes because he believes in them. We could n't bribe him if we wanted to. And we don't."

If she only knew something of this woman's relations to Marion — which she only instinctively suspected — and could retaliate upon her, Mrs. Bunker felt she would have given up her life at that moment.

"Colonel Marion seems to find plenty that he can bribe," she said roughly, "and I've yet to know who *you* are to sit in judgment on them. You've got your letter, take it and go! When he wants to send you another through me, somebody else must come for it, not you. That's all!"

She drew back as if to let the intruder pass, but the lady, without moving a muscle, finished the reading of her letter, then stood up quietly and began carefully to draw her handsome cloak over her shoulders. "Yo' want to know who I am, Mrs. Bunker," she said, arranging the velvet collar under her white oval chin. "Well, I'm a So'th'n woman from Figinya, and I'm Figinyan first, last, and all the time." She shook out her sleeves and the folds of her cloak. "I believe in State rights and slavery — if you know what that means. I hate the North, I hate the East, I hate the West. I hate this nigger Government, I'd kill that man Lincoln quicker than lightning!" She began

to draw down the fingers of her gloves, holding her shapely hands upright before her.
" I 'm hard and fast to the Cause. I gave up
house and niggers for it." She began to
button her gloves at the wrist with some
difficulty, tightly setting together her beautiful lips as she did so.   " I gave up my husband for it, and I went to the man who loved
it better and had risked more for it than
ever he had. Cunnle Marion 's my friend.
I 'm Mrs. Fairfax, Josephine Hardee that
was ; *his* disciple and follower.   Well, may·
be those puritanical No'th'n folks might give
it another name ! "

She moved slowly towards the door, but
on the threshold paused, as Colonel Marion
had, and came back to Mrs. Bunker with an
outstretched hand.   " I don't see that yo'
and me need quo'll.   I didn't come here
for that.   I came here to see yo'r husband,
and seeing *yo'* I thought it was only right
to talk squarely to yo', as yo' understand I
would n't talk to yo'r husband.   Mrs. Bunker, I want yo'r husband to take me away
— I want him to take me to the cunnle. If
I tried to go in any other way I 'd be
watched, spied upon and followed, and only
lead those hounds on his track. I don't

expect yo' to *ask* yo' husband for me, but only not to interfere when I do."

There was a touch of unexpected weakness in her voice and a look of pain in her eyes which was not unlike what Mrs. Bunker had seen and pitied in Marion. But they were the eyes of a woman who had humbled her, and Mrs. Bunker would have been unworthy her sex if she had not felt a cruel enjoyment in it. Yet the dominance of the stranger was still so strong that she did not dare to refuse the proffered hand. She, however, slipped the ring from her finger and laid it in Mrs. Fairfax's palm.

"You can take that with you," she said, with a desperate attempt to imitate the other's previous indifference. "I should n't like to deprive you and *your friend* of the opportunity of making use of it again. As for *my* husband, I shall say nothing of you to him as long as you say nothing to him of me — which I suppose is what you mean."

The insolent look came back to Mrs. Fairfax's face. "I reckon yo' 're right," she said quietly, putting the ring in her pocket as she fixed her dark eyes on Mrs. Bunker, "and the ring may be of use again. Good-by, Mrs. Bunker."

She waved her hand carelessly, and turning away passed out of the house. A moment later the boat and its two occupants pushed from the shore, and disappeared round the Point.

Then Mrs. Bunker looked round the room, and down upon her empty finger, and knew that it was the end of her dream. It was all over now — indeed, with the picture of that proud, insolent woman before her she wondered if it had ever begun. This was the woman she had allowed herself to think *she* might be. This was the woman *he* was thinking of when he sat there; this was the Mrs. Fairfax the officers had spoken of, and who had made her — Mrs. Bunker —the go-between for their love-making! All the work that she had done for him, the deceit she had practiced on her husband, was to bring him and this woman together! And they both knew it, and had no doubt laughed at her and her pretensions!

It was with a burning cheek that she thought how she had intended to go to Marion, and imagined herself arriving perhaps to find that shameless woman already there. In her vague unformulated longings she had never before realized the degradation into which her foolish romance might lead her. She saw it now ; that humiliating moral lesson we are all apt to experience in the accidental display of our own particular vices in the person we hate, she had just felt in Mrs. Fairfax's presence. With it came the paralyzing fear of her husband's discovery of her secret. Secure as she had been in her dull belief that he had in some way wronged her by marrying her, she for the first time began to doubt if this con- doned the deceit she had practiced on him. The tribute Mrs. Fairfax had paid him — this appreciation of his integrity and honesty by an enemy and a woman like herself — troubled her, frightened her, and filled her with her first jealousy ! What if this wo- man should tell him all ; what if she should make use of him as Marion had of her ! Zephas was a strong Northern partisan, but was he proof against the guileful charms of such a devil ? She had never thought before of questioning his fidelity to her ; she suddenly remembered now some rough pleas- antries of Captain Simmons in regard to the inconstancy of his calling. No ! there was but one thing for her to do : she would make a clean breast to him ; she would tell

him everything she had done except the fatal
fancy that compelled her to it! She began
to look for his coming now with alternate
hope and fear — with unabated impatience!
The night that he should have arrived passed
slowly; morning came, but not Zephas.
When the mist had lifted she ran impatiently to the rocks and gazed anxiously
towards the lower bay. There were a few
gray sails scarce distinguishable above the
grayer water — but they were not his. She
glanced half mechanically seaward, and her
eyes became suddenly fixed. There was no
mistake! She knew the rig! — she could
see the familiar white lap-streak as the vessel careened on the starboard tack — it was
her husband's schooner slowly creeping out
of the Golden Gate!

PART III.

Her first wild impulse was to run to the
cove, for the little dingey always moored
there, and to desperately attempt to over-
take him. But the swift consciousness of
its impossibility was followed by a dull, bewildering torpor, that kept her motionless,
helplessly following the vessel with straining

7 Bret Harte

eyes, as if they could evoke some response
from its decks. She was so lost in this occupation that she did not see that a pilot-
boat nearly abreast of the cove had put out
a two-oared gig, which was pulling quickly
for the rocks. When she saw it, she trembled with the instinct that it brought her
intelligence. She was right; it was a brief
note from her husband, informing her that
he had been hurriedly dispatched on a short
sea cruise; that in order to catch the tide he
had not time to go ashore at the bluff, but
he would explain everything on his return.
Her relief was only partial; she was already
experienced enough in his vocation to know
that the excuse was a feeble one. He could
easily have "fetched" the bluff in tacking
out of the Gate and have signaled to her to
board him in her own boat. The next day
she locked up her house, rowed round the
Point to the Embarcadero, where the Bay
steamboats occasionally touched and took up
passengers to San Francisco. Captain Simmons had not seen her husband this last
trip; indeed, did not know that he had gone
out of the Bay. Mrs. Bunker was seized
with a desperate idea. She called upon the
Secretary of the Fishing Trust. That gentle-

man was business-like, but neither expansive
nor communicative. Her husband had *not*
been ordered out to sea by them; she ought
to know that Captain Bunker was now
his own master, choosing his own fishing
grounds, and his own times and seasons.
He was not aware of any secret service for
the Company in which Captain Bunker was
engaged. He hoped Mrs. Bunker would
distinctly remember that the little matter of
the duel to which she referred was an old
bygone affair, and never anything but a personal matter, in which the Fishery had no
concern whatever, and in which *he* certainly
should not again engage. He would advise
Mrs. Bunker, if she valued her own good,
and especially her husband's, to speedily
forget all about it. These were ugly times,
as it was. If Mrs. Bunker's services had
not been properly rewarded or considered it
was certainly a great shame, but really *he*
could not be expected to make it good. Certain parties had cost him trouble enough
already. Besides, really, she must see that
his position between her husband, whom he
respected, and a certain other party was a
delicate one. But Mrs. Bunker heard no
more. She turned and ran down the stair-

case, carrying with her a burning cheek and blazing eye that somewhat startled the complacent official.

She did not remember how she got home again. She had a vague recollection of passing through the crowded streets, wondering if the people knew that she was an outcast, deserted by her husband, deceived by her ideal hero, repudiated by her friends! Men had gathered in knots before the newspaper offices, excited and gesticulating over the bulletin boards that had such strange legends as " The Crisis," "Details of an Alleged Conspiracy to Overthrow the Government," "The Assassin of Henderson to the Fore Again," " Rumored Arrests on the Mexican Frontier." Sometimes she thought she understood the drift of them; even fancied they were the outcome of her visit — as if her very presence carried treachery and suspicion with it — but generally they only struck her benumbed sense as a dull, meaningless echo of something that had happened long ago. When she reached her house, late that night, the familiar solitude of shore and sea gave her a momentary relief, but with it came the terrible conviction that she had forfeited her right to it, that when her husband came back it would be hers no longer, and that with their meeting she would know it no more. For through all her childish vacillation and imaginings she managed to cling to one steadfast resolution. She would tell him *everything*, and know the worst. Perhaps he would never come; perhaps she should not be alive to meet him.

And so the days and nights slowly passed. The solitude which her previous empty deceit had enabled her to fill with such charming visions now in her awakened remorse seemed only to protract her misery. Had she been a more experienced, though even a more guilty, woman she would have suffered less. Without sympathy or counsel, without even the faintest knowledge of the world or its standards of morality to guide her, she accepted her isolation and friendlessness as a necessary part of her wrongdoing. Her only criterion was her enemy — Mrs. Fairfax — and *she* could seek her relief by joining her lover; but Mrs. Bunker knew now that she herself had never had one — and was alone! Mrs. Fairfax had broken openly with her husband; but *she* had *deceived* hers, and the experience and reckoning were still to come. In her miserable confession it was not strange that this half child, half woman, sometimes looked towards that gray sea, eternally waiting for her, — that sea which had taken everything from her and given her nothing in return, — for an obliterating and perhaps exonerating death !

The third day of her waiting isolation was broken upon by another intrusion. The morning had been threatening, with an opaque, motionless, livid arch above, which had taken the place of the usual flying scud and shaded cloud masses of the rainy season. The whole outlying ocean, too, beyond the bar, appeared nearer, and even seemed to be lifted higher than the Bay itself, and was lit every now and then with wonderful clearness by long flashes of breaking foam like summer lightning. She knew that this meant a southwester, and began, with a certain mechanical deliberation, to set her little domain in order against the coming gale. She drove the cows to the rude shed among the scrub oaks, she collected the goats and young kids in the corral, and replenished the stock of fuel from the woodpile. She was quite hidden in the shrubbery when she saw a boat making slow headway against the wind towards the little cove where but a moment before she had drawn up the dingey beyond the reach of breaking seas. It was a whaleboat from Saucelito containing a few men. As they neared the landing she recognized in the man who seemed to be directing the boat the second friend of Colonel Marion — the man who had come with the Secretary to take him off, but whom she had never seen again. In her present horror of that memory she remained hidden, determined at all hazards to avoid a meeting. When they had landed, one of the men halted accidentally before the shrubbery where she was concealed as he caught his first view of the cottage, which had been invisible from the point they had rounded.

" Look here, Bragg," he said, turning to Marion's friend, in a voice which was distinctly audible to Mrs. Bunker. " What are we to say to these people ? "

" There 's only one," returned the other. " The man 's at sea. His wife 's here. She 's all right."

" You said she was one of us ? "

" After a fashion. She 's the woman who helped Marion when he was here. I reckon he made it square with her from the begin-

ning, for she forwarded letters from him
since. But you can tell her as much or as
little as you find necessary when you see
her."

"Yes, but we must settle that *now*," said
Bragg sharply, "and I propose to tell her
nothing. I 'm against having any more pet-
ticoats mixed up with our affairs. I propose
to make an examination of the place without
bothering our heads about her."

"But we must give some reason for coming here, and we must ask her to keep dark,
or we 'll have her blabbing to the first person she meets," urged the other.

"She 's not likely to see anybody before
night, when the brig will be in and the men
and guns landed. Move on, and let Jim
take soundings off the cove, while I look
along the shore. It 's just as well that
there 's a house here, and a little cover like
this " — pointing to the shrubbery — "to
keep the men from making too much of
a show until after the earthworks are up.
There are sharp eyes over at the Fort."

"There don't seem to be any one in the
house now," returned the other after a moment's scrutiny of the cottage, "or the
woman would surely come out at the bark-

ing of the dog, even if she had n't seen us. Likely she 's gone to Saucelito."

"So much the better. Just as well that she should know nothing until it happens. Afterwards we 'll settle with the husband for the price of possession ; he has only a squatter's rights. Come along ; we 'll have bad weather before we get back round the Point again, but so much the better, for it will keep off any inquisitive longshore cruisers."

They moved away. But Mrs. Bunker, stung through her benumbed and brooding consciousness, and made desperate by this repeated revelation of her former weakness, had heard enough to make her feverish to hear more. She knew the intricacies of the shrubbery thoroughly. She knew every foot of shade and cover of the clearing, and creeping like a cat from bush to bush she managed, without being discovered, to keep the party in sight and hearing all the time. It required no great discernment, even for an inexperienced woman like herself, at the end of an hour, to gather their real purpose. It was to prepare for the secret landing of an armed force, disguised as laborers, who, under the outward show of quarrying in the bluff, were to throw up breastworks, and fortify the craggy shelf. The landing was fixed for that night, and was to be effected by a vessel now cruising outside the Heads.

She understood it all now. She remembered Marion's speech about the importance of the bluff for military purposes; she remembered the visit of the officers from the Fort opposite. The strangers were stealing a march upon the Government, and by night would be in possession. It was perhaps an evidence of her newly awakened and larger comprehension that she took no thought of her loss of home and property, — perhaps there was little to draw her to it now, — but was conscious only of a more terrible catastrophe — a catastrophe to which she was partly accessory, of which any other woman would have warned her husband — or at least those officers of the Fort whose business it was to — Ah, yes! the officers of the Fort — only just opposite to her! She trembled, and yet flushed with an inspiration. It was not too late yet — why not warn them *now?*

But how? A message sent by Saucelito and the steamboat to San Francisco — the usual way — would not reach them to-night. To go herself, rowing directly across in the

dingey, would be the only security of success. If she could do it? It was a long
pull — the sea was getting up — but she
would try.

She waited until the last man had stepped
into the boat, in nervous dread of some one
remaining. Then, when the boat had vanished round the Point again, she ran back
to the cottage, arrayed herself in her husband's pilot coat, hat, and boots, and launched
the dingey. It was a heavy, slow, but luckily a stanch and seaworthy boat. It was not
until she was well off shore that she began
to feel the full fury of the wind and waves,
and knew the difficulty and danger of her
undertaking. She had decided that her
shortest and most direct course was within a
few points of the wind, but the quartering
of the waves on the broad bluff bows of the
boat tended to throw it to leeward, a movement that, while it retarded her forward progress, no doubt saved the little craft from
swamping. Again, the feebleness and short-
ness of her stroke, which never impelled her
through a rising wave, but rather lifted her
half way up its face, prevented the boat from
taking much water, while her steadfast gaze,
fixed only on the slowly retreating shore,

kept her steering free from any fatal nervous vacillation, which the sight of the
threatening seas on her bow might have produced. Preserved through her very weakness, ignorance, and simplicity of purpose,
the dingey had all the security of a drifting
boat, yet retained a certain gentle but persistent guidance. In this feminine fashion
she made enough headway to carry her
abreast of the Point, where she met the re-
flux current sweeping round it that carried
her well along into the channel, now sluggish
with the turn of the tide. After half an
hour's pulling, she was delighted to find herself again in a reverse current, abreast of her
cottage, but steadily increasing her distance
from it. She was, in fact, on the extreme
outer edge of a vast whirlpool formed by the
force of the gale on a curving lee shore, and
was being carried to her destination in a
semicircle around that bay which she never
could have crossed. She was moving now
in a line with the shore and the Fort, whose
flagstaff, above its green, square, and white
quarters, she could see distinctly, and whose
lower water battery and landing seemed to
stretch out from the rocks scarcely a mile
ahead. Protected by the shore from the

fury of the wind, and even of the sea, her
progress was also steadily accelerated by the
velocity of the current, mingling with the
ebbing tide. A sudden fear seized her.
She turned the boat's head towards the
shore, but it was swept quickly round again;
she redoubled her exertions, tugging frantically at her helpless oars. She only succeeded in getting the boat into the trough of
the sea, where, after a lurch that threatened
to capsize it, it providentially swung around
on its short keel and began to drift stern on.
She was almost abreast of the battery now;
she could hear the fitful notes of a bugle
that seemed blown and scattered above her
head; she even thought she could see some
men in blue uniforms moving along the little
pier. She was passing it; another fruitless
effort to regain her ground, but she was
swept along steadily towards the Gate, the
whitening bar, and the open sea.

She knew now what it all meant. This
was what she had come for; this was the
end! Beyond, only a little beyond, just a
few moments longer to wait, and then, out
there among the breakers was the rest that
she had longed for but had not dared to
seek. It was not her fault; they could not

blame *her*. He would come back and never
know what had happened — nor even know
how she had tried to atone for her deceit.
And he would find his house in possession
of — of — those devils ! No ! No ! she
must not die yet, at least not until she had
warned the Fort. She seized the oars again
with frenzied strength ; the boat had stopped
under the unwonted strain, staggered, tried
to rise in an uplifted sea, took part of it
over her bow, struck down Mrs. Bunker
under half a ton of blue water that wrested
the oars from her paralyzed hands like play-
things, swept them over the gunwale, and
left her lying senseless in the bottom of the
boat.

.   .   .   .

"Hold har-rd — or you 'll run her
down."

"Now then, Riley, — look alive, — is it
slapin' ye are ! "

"Hold yer jaw, Flanigan, and stand
ready with the boat-hook. Now then, hold
har-rd ! "

The sudden jarring and tilting of the
water-logged boat, a sound of rasping timbers, the swarming of men in shirtsleeves
and blue trousers around her, seemed to

rouse her momentarily, but she again fainted away.

When she struggled back to consciousness once more she was wrapped in a soldier's jacket, her head pillowed on the shirtsleeve of an artillery corporal in the stern sheets of that eight-oared government barge she had remembered. But the only officer was a bareheaded, boyish lieutenant, and the rowers were an athletic but unseamanlike crew of mingled artillerymen and infantry.

"And where did ye drift from, darlint?"

Mrs. Bunker bridled feebly at the epithet.

"I didn't drift. I was going to the Fort."

"The Fort, is it?"

"Yes. I want to see the general."

"Wad n't the liftenant do ye? Or shure there's the adjutant; he's a foine man."

"Silence, Flanigan," said the young officer sharply. Then turning to Mrs. Bunker he said, "Don't mind *him*, but let his wife take you to the canteen, when we get in, and get you some dry clothes."

But Mrs. Bunker, spurred to convalescence at the indignity, protested stiffly, and demanded on her arrival to be led at once to the general's quarters. A few officers, who had been attracted to the pier by the rescue, acceded to her demand.

She recognized the gray-haired, handsome man who had come ashore at her house. With a touch of indignation at her treatment, she briefly told her story. But the general listened coldly and gravely with his eyes fixed upon her face.

" You say you recognized in the leader of the party a man you had seen before. Under what circumstances ? "

Mrs. Bunker hesitated with burning cheeks. " He came to take Colonel Marion from our place."

" When you were hiding him, — yes, we 've heard the story. Now, Mrs. Bunker, may I ask you what you, as a Southern sympathizer, expect to gain by telling me this story ? "

But here Mrs. Bunker burst out. " I am not a Southern sympathizer! Never! Never! Never! I 'm a Union woman, — wife of a Northern man. I helped that man before I knew who he was. Any Christian, Northerner or Southerner, would have done the same ! "

Her sincerity and passion were equally unmistakable. The general rose, opened the door of the adjoining room, said a few words to an orderly on duty, and returned. " What you are asking of me, Mrs. Bunker, is almost as extravagant and unprecedented as your story. You must understand, as well as your husband, that if I land a force on your property it will be to *take possession* of it in the name of the Government, for Government purposes."

" Yes, yes," said Mrs. Bunker eagerly; " I know that. I am willing; Zephas will be willing."

" And," continued the general, fixing his eyes on her face, " you will also understand that I may be compelled to detain you here as a hostage for the safety of my men."

" Oh no! no! please!" said Mrs. Bunker, springing up with an imploring feminine gesture; " I am expecting my husband. He may be coming back at any moment; I must be there to see him *first!* Please let me go back, sir, with your men; put me anywhere ashore between them and those men that are coming. Lock me up; keep me a prisoner in my own home; do anything else if you think I am deceiving you; but don't keep me here to miss him when he comes!"

"But you can see him later," said the general.

"But I must see him *first*," said Mrs. Bunker desperately. "I must see him first, for — for — *he knows nothing of this*. He knows nothing of my helping Colonel Marion; he knows nothing of — how foolish I have been, and — he must not know it from others! There!" It was out at last. She was sobbing now, but her pride was gone. She felt relieved, and did not even notice the presence of two or three other officers, who had entered the room, exchanged a few hurried words with their superior, and were gazing at her in astonishment.

The general's brow relaxed, and he smiled. "Very well, Mrs. Bunker; it shall be as you like, then. You shall go and meet your husband with Captain Jennings here," — indicating one of the officers, — "who will take charge of you and the party."

"And," said Mrs. Bunker, looking imploringly through her wet but pretty lashes at the officer, "he won't say anything to Zephas, either?"

"Not a syllable," said Captain Jennings

gravely. " But while the tug is getting ready, general, had n't Mrs. Bunker better go to Mrs. Flanigan ? "

" I think not," said the general, with a significant look at the officer as he gallantly offered his arm to the astonished Mrs. Bunker, " if she will allow me the pleasure of taking her to my wife."

There was an equally marked respect in the manner of the men and officers as Mrs. Bunker finally stepped on board the steam tug that was to convey the party across the turbulent bay. But she heeded it not, neither did she take any concern of the still furious gale, the difficult landing, the preternatural activity of the band of sappers, who seemed to work magic with their picks and shovels, the shelter tents that arose swiftly around her, the sheds and bush inclosures that were evoked from the very ground beneath her feet ; the wonderful skill, order, and discipline that in a few hours converted her straggling dominion into a formal camp, even to the sentinel, who was already calmly pacing the rocks by the landing as if he had being doing it for years ! Only one thing thrilled her — the sudden outburst, fluttering and snapping of the national flag from

her little flagstaff. He would see it — and
perhaps be pleased!

And indeed it seemed as if the men had
caught the infection of her anxiety, for when
her strained eyes could no longer pierce the
murky twilight settling over the Gate, one
came running to her to say that the lookout
had just discovered through his glass a close-
reefed schooner running in before the wind.
It was her husband, and scarcely an hour
after night had shut in the schooner had
rounded to off the Point, dropped her boat,
and sped away to anchorage. And then
Mrs. Bunker, running bareheaded down the
rocks, breaking in upon the hurried explanation of the officer of the guard, threw herself
upon her husband's breast, and sobbed and
laughed as if her heart would break!

Nor did she scarcely hear his hurried comment to the officer and unconscious corroboration of her story : how a brig had raced
them from the Gate, was heading for the
bar, but suddenly sheered off and put away
to sea again, as if from some signal from the
headland. " Yes — the bluff," interrupted
Captain Jennings bitterly, "I thought of
that, but the old man said it was more diplomatic just now to *prevent* an attempt than
even to successfully resist it."

But when they were alone again in their little cottage, and Zephas' honest eyes — with no trace of evil knowledge or suspicion in their homely, neutral lightness — were looking into hers with his usual simple trustfulness, Mrs. Bunker trembled, whimpered, and — I grieve to say — basely funked her boasted confession. But here the Deity which protects feminine weakness intervened with the usual miracle. As he gazed at his wife's troubled face, an apologetic cloud came over his rugged but open brow, and a smile of awkward deprecating embarrassment suffused his eyes. " I declare to goodness, Mollie, but I must tell you suthin, although I guess I did n't kalkilate to say a word about it. But, darn it all, I can't keep it in. No! Lookin' inter that innercent face o' yourn " — pressing her flushing cheeks between his cool brown hands — " and gazing inter them two truthful eyes " — they blinked at this moment with a divine modesty — " and thinkin' of what you 've just did for your kentry — like them revolutionary women o' '76 — I feel like a darned swab of a traitor myself. Well! what I want ter tell you is this : Ye know, or ye 've heard me tell o' that Mrs. Fairfax, as left her hus-

band for that fire-eatin' Marion, and stuck
to him through thick and thin, and stood
watch and watch with him in this howlin'
Southern rumpus they're kickin' up all
along the coast, as if she was a man herself.
Well, jes as I hauled up at the wharf at
'Frisco, she comes aboard.

"'You're Cap Bunker?' she says.

"'That's me, ma'am,' I says.

"'You're a Northern man and you go
with your kind,' sez she; 'but you're a
white man, and thar's no cur blood in you.'
But you ain't listenin', Mollie; you're
dead tired, lass," — with a commiserating
look at her now whitening face, — "and I'll
haul in line and wait. Well, to cut it short,
she wanted me to take her down the coast
a bit to where she could join Marion. She
said she'd been shook by his friends, followed by spies — and, blame my skin, Mollie, ef that proud woman didn't break down
and *cry* like a baby. Now, Mollie, what got
me in all this, was that them Chivalry folks
— ez was always jawin' about their 'Southern dames' and their 'Ladye fairs,' and
always runnin' that kind of bilge water
outer their scuppers whenever they careened
over on a fair wind — was jes the kind to

throw off on a woman when they did n't
want her, and I kinder thought I 'd like *her*
to see the difference betwixt the latitude o'
Charleston and Cape Cod. So I told her I
did n't want the jewelry and dimons she
offered me, but if she would come down to
the wharf, after dark, I 'd smuggle her
aboard, and I 'd allow to the men that she
was *your auntie* ez I was givin' a free passage to! Lord! dear! think o' me takin'
the name o' Mollie Bunker's aunt in vain
for that sort o' woman! Think o' me," continued Captain Bunker with a tentative
chuckle, " sort o' pretendin' to hand yo'r
auntie to Kernel Marion for — for his lady
love! I don't wonder ye 's half frighted and
half laffin'," he added, as his wife uttered
a hysterical cry; " it *was* awful! But it
worked, and I got her off, and wot 's more I
got her shipped to Mazatlan, where she 'll
join Marion, and the two are goin' back to
Virginy, where I guess they won't trouble
Californy again. Ye know now, deary," he
went on, speaking with difficulty through
Mrs. Bunker's clinging arms and fast dripping tears, " why I did n't heave to to say
' good-by.' But it 's all over now — I 've
made a clean breast of it, Mollie — and
don't you cry! "

But it was *not* all over. For a moment later Captain Bunker began to fumble in his waistcoat pocket with the one hand that was not clasping his wife's waist. "One thing more, Mollie; when I left her and refused to take any of her dimons, she put a queer sort o' ring into my hand, and told me with a kind o' mischievious, bedevilin' smile, that I must keep it to remember her by. Here it is — why, Mollie lass! are you crazy?"

She had snatched it from his fingers and was running swiftly from the cottage out into the tempestuous night. He followed closely, until she reached the edge of the rocks. And only then, in the struggling, fast-flying moonlight, she raised a passionate hand, and threw it far into the sea!

As he led her back to the cottage she said she was jealous, and honest Captain Bunker, with his arm around her, felt himself the happiest man in the world!

.   .   .   .

From that day the flag flew regularly over the rocky shelf, and, in time, bugles and morning drumbeats were wafted from it to the decks of passing ships. For the Federal Government had adjudged the land for its own use, paid Captain Bunker a handsome sum for its possession, and had discreetly hidden the little cottage of Mrs. Bunker and its history forever behind bastion and casemate.

THE TRANSFORMATION OF BUCKEYE CAMP.

PART I.

THE tiny lights that had been far scattered and intermittent as fireflies all along the dark stream at last dropped out one by one, leaving only the three windows of "Parks' Emporium" to pierce the profoundly wooded banks of the South Fork. So all-pervading was the darkness that the mere opening of the "Emporium" front door shot out an illuminating shaft which revealed the whole length of the little main street of "Buckeye," while the simple passing of a single figure before one of the windows momentarily eclipsed a third of the settlement. This undue preëminence given to the only three citizens of Buckeye who were still up at ten o'clock seemed to be hardly justified by their outward appearance, which was that of ordinary long-bearded and long-booted river bar miners. Two sat upon the counter with their hands upon their knees, the third leaned beside the open window.

It was very quiet. The faint, far barking of a dog, or an occasional subdued murmur from the river shallows, audible only when the wind rose slightly, helped to intensify their solitude. So supreme had it become that when the man at the window at last continued his conversation meditatively, with his face towards it, he seemed to be taking all Nature into his confidence.

" The worst thing about it is, that the only way we can keep her out of the settlement is by the same illegal methods which we deplore in other camps. We have always boasted that Buckeye could get along without Vigilance Committees or Regulators."

"Yes, and that was because we started it on the principle of original selection, which we are only proposing to continue," replied one of the men on the counter. " So there 's nothing wrong about our sending a deputation to wait upon her, to protest against her settling here, and give her our reasons."

"Yes, only it has all the impudence with-

out the pluck of the Regulators. You demand what you are afraid to enforce. Come,
Parks, you know she has all the rights on
her side. Look at it squarely. She pro-
poses to open a store and sell liquor and
cigars, which she serves herself, in the
broken-down *tienda* which was regularly
given to her people by the Spanish grantee
of the land we're squatting on. It's not
her fault but ours if we've adopted a line
of rules, which don't agree with hers, to
govern the settlers on *her* land, nor should
she be compelled to follow them. Nor because we justify *our* squatting here, on the
ground that the Spanish grant is n't con-
firmed yet, can we forbid her squatting
under the same right."

"But look at the moral question, Brace.
Consider the example; the influence of such
a shop, kept by such a woman, on the community! We have the right to protect
ourselves — the majority."

"That's the way the lynchers talk," returned Brace. "And I'm not so sure
about there being any moral question yet.
You are assuming too much. There is no
reason why she should n't run the *tienda* as
decently — barring the liquor sale, which,

however, is legal, and for which she can get
a license — as a man could, and without interfering with our morals."

"Then what is the use of our rules?"

"They were made for those who consented
to adopt them, as we all did. They still
bind *us*, and if we don't choose to buy her
liquor or cigars that will dispose of her and
her *tienda* much more effectually than your
protest. It's a pity she's a lone unprotected
woman. Now if she only had a husband" —

"She carries a dagger in her garter."

This apparently irrelevant remark came
from the man who had not yet spoken, but
who had been listening with the languid unconcern of one who, relinquishing the labor
of argument to others, had consented to
abide by their decision. It was met with a
scornful smile from each of the disputants,
perhaps even by an added shrug of the
shoulders from the woman's previous de-
fender! *He* was evidently not to be taken
in by extraneous sentiment. Nevertheless,
both listened as the speaker, slowly feeling
his knees as if they were his way to a difficult subject, continued with the same suggestion of stating general fact, but waiving
any argument himself. "Clarkson of An-

gels allows she's got a free, gaudy, picter-
covered style with the boys, but that she can
be gilt-edged when she wants to. Rowley
Meade — him ez hed his skelp pulled over
his eyes at one stroke, foolin' with a she
bear over on Black Mountain — allows it
would be rather monotonous in him at-
temptin' any familiarities with her. Bul-
strode's brother, ez was in Marysville, said
there was a woman — like to her, but not
her — ez made it lively for the boys with a
game called 'Little Monte,' and he dropped
a hundred dollars there afore he came away.
They do say that about seven men got shot
in Marysville on account o' this one, or from
some oneasiness that happened at her shop.
But then," he went on slowly and deferen-
tially as the faces of the two others were
lowered and became fixed, " *she* says she
tired o' drunken rowdies, — there's a same-
ness about 'em, and it don't sell her pipes
and cigars, and that's *why* she's coming
here. Thompson over at Dry Creek sez that
that's where our reputation is playin' us!
'We've got her as a reward o' virtoo, and
be d—d to us.' But," cautiously, "Thompson ain't drawed a sober breath since Christmas."

The three men looked in each other's faces in silence. The same thought occurred to each; the profane Thompson was right, and the woman's advent was the logical sequence of their own ethics. Two years previously, the Buckeye Company had found gold on the South Fork, and had taken up claims. Composed mainly of careful, provident, and thoughtful men, — some of cultivation and refinement, — they had adopted a certain orderly discipline for their own guidance solely, which, however, commended itself to later settlers, already weary of the lawlessness and reckless freedom which usually attended the inception of mining settlements. Consequently the birth of Buckeye was accompanied with no dangerous travail; its infancy was free from the diseases of adolescent communities. The settlers, without any express prohibition, had tacitly dispensed with gambling and drinking saloons; following the unwritten law of example, had laid aside their revolvers, and mingled together peacefully when their labors were ended, without a single peremptory regulation against drinking and playing, or carrying lethal weapons. Nor had there been any test of fitness or

qualification for citizenship through previous virtue. There were one or two gamblers, a skillful duelist, and men who still
drank whiskey who had voluntarily sought
the camp. Of some such antecedents was
the last speaker. Probably with two wives
elsewhere, and a possible homicidal record,
he had modestly held aloof from obtrusive
argument.

" Well, we must have a meeting and put
the question squarely to the boys to-morrow," said Parks, gazing thoughtfully from
the window. The remark was followed by
another long silence. Beyond, in the darkness, Buckeye, unconscious of the momentous
question awaiting its decision, slept on
peacefully.

" I brought the keg of whiskey and
brandy from Red Gulch to-day that Doctor
Duchesne spoke of," he resumed presently.
" You know he said we ought to have some
in common stock that he could always rely
upon in emergencies, and for use after the
tule fever. I did n't agree with him, and
told him how I had brought Sam Denver
through an attack with quinine and arrow-
root, but he laughed and wanted to know
if we 'd ' resolved ' that everybody should

hereafter have the Denver constitution. That's the trouble with those old army surgeons, — they never can get over the 'heroics' of their past. Why he told Parson Jennings that he'd rather treat a man for jim-jams than one that was dying for want of stimulants. However, the liquor is here, and one of the things we must settle tomorrow is the question if it ought not to be issued only on Duchesne's prescription. When I made that point to him squarely, he grinned again, and wanted to know if I calculated to put the same restriction on the sale of patent medicines and drugs generally."

" 'N powder 'n shot," contributed the indifferent man.

" Perhaps you'd better take a look at the liquor, Saunders," said Parks, dismissing the ethical question. "*You* know more about it than we do. It ought to be the best."

Saunders went behind the counter, drew out two demijohns, and, possibly from the force of habit, selected *three* mugs from the crockery and poured some whiskey into each, before he could check himself.

" Perhaps we had better compare tastes," said Brace blandly. They all sipped their liquor slowly and in silence. The decision was favorable. "Better try some with water to see how it mixes," said Saunders, lazily filling the glasses with a practiced hand. This required more deliberation, and they drew their chairs to the table and sat down. A slight relaxation stole over the thoughtful faces of Brace and Parks, a gentle perspiration came over the latter's brow, but the features and expression of Saunders never changed. The conversation took a broader range; politics and philosophy entered into it; literature and poetry were discussed by Parks and Brace, Saunders still retaining the air of a dispassionate observer, ready to be convinced, but abstaining from argument — and occasionally replenishing the glasses. There was felt to be no inconsistency between their present attitude and their previous conversation; rather it proved to them that gentlemen could occasionally indulge in a social glass together without frequenting a liquor saloon. This was stated with some degree of effusion by Parks and assented to with singular enthusiasm by Brace; Saunders nodding. It was also observed with great penetration by Brace that in having really *good*, specially selected liquor like that, the great danger of the intoshikat'n 'fx

— he corrected himself with great deliberation, "the intoxicating effects" — of adulter-
ated liquors sold in drinking saloons was
obviated. Mr. Brace thought also that the
vitiated quality of the close air of a crowded
saloon had a great deal to do with it —
the excess of carbon — hic — he begged
their pardon — carbonic acid gas undoubtedly rendered people "slupid and steepy."
"But here, from the open window," he
walked dreamily to it and leaned out admir-
ingly towards the dark landscape that softly
slumbered without, "one could drink in only
health and poetry."

"Wot's that?" said Saunders, looking up.

"I said health and poetry," returned
Brace with some dignity. "I repeat" —

"No. I mean wot's that noise? Listen."

They listened so breathlessly that the soft
murmur of the river seemed to flow in upon
them. But above it quite distinctly came
the regular muffled beat of horse-hoofs in
the thick dust and the occasional rattle of
wheels over rocky irregularities. But still
very far and faint, and fading like the noises
in a dream. Brace drew a long breath;
Parks smiled and softly closed his eyes.
But Saunders remained listening.

"That was over *our* road, near the turn-pike !" he said musingly. "That's queer; thar ain't any of the boys away to-night, and that's a wagon. It's some one comin' here. Hark to that! There it is again."

It was the same sound but more distinct and nearer, and then was lost again.

"They're dragging through the river sand that's just abreast o' Mallory's. Stopped there, I reckon. No! pushin' on again. Hear 'em grinding along the gravel over Hamilton's trailin's? Stopped agin — that's before Somerville's shanty. What's gone o' them now? Maybe they've lost the trail and got onto Gray's slide through the woods. It's no use lookin'; ye could n't see anything in this nigger dark. Hol' on! If they 're comin' through the woods, ye 'll hear 'em again jest off here. Yes! by thunder! here they are."

This time the clatter and horse-hoofs were before them, at the very door. A man's voice cried, "Whoa!" and there was a sudden bound on the veranda. The door opened; for an instant the entrance appeared to be filled with a mass of dazzling white flounces, and a figure which from waist to crown was impenetrably wrapped and swathed in black lace. Somewhere beneath its folds a soft Spanish, yet somewhat childish voice cried, "Tente. Hol' on," turned and vanished. This was succeeded by the apparition of a silent, swarthy Mexican, who dropped a small trunk at their feet and vanished also. Then the white-flounced and black-laced figure reappeared as the departing wagon rattled away, glided to the centre of the room, placed on the trunk a small foot, whose low-quartered black satin slipper seemed to be held only by the toe, threw back with both hands the black lace mantilla, which was pinned by a red rose over her little right ear, and with her hands slightly extended and waving softly said, "Mira caballeros! 'Ere we are again, boys! Viva! Aow ees your mother? Aow ees that for high? Behold me! just from Pike!"

Parks and Brace, who had partly risen, fell back hopelessly in their chairs again and gazed at the figure with a feeble smile of vacuous pain and politeness. At which it advanced, lowered its black eyes mischievously over the table and the men who sat there, poured out a glass of the liquor, and said: "I look towards you, boys! Don't

errise. You are just a leetle weary, eh?
A leetle. Oh yes! a leetle tired of crookin'
your elbow — eh? Don't care if the school
keep! — eh? Don't want any pie! Want
to go 'ome, eh?"

But here Mr. Parks rose with slight difficulty, but unflinching dignity, and leaned
impressively over the table, "May I ashk —
may I be permitted to arsk, madam, to what
we may owe the pleasure of thish — of this
— visit?"

Her face and attitude instantly changed.
Her arms dropped and caught up the mantilla with a quick but not ungraceful sweep,
and in apparently a single movement she was
draped, wrapped, and muffled from waist to
crown as before. With a slight inclination
of her head, she said in quite another voice:
"Si, señor. I have arrive here because in
your whole great town of Booki there is not
so much as one" — she held up a small
brown finger — " as much as *one* leetle light
or fire like thees; be-cause in this grand
pueblo there is not one peoples who have
not already sleep in his bed but thees!
Bueno! I have arrive all the same like a
leetle bird, like the small fly arrive to the
light! not to *you* — only to *the light!* I

go not to my casa for she is dark, and to-
night she have nothing to make the fire or
bed. I go not to the 'otel — there is not
one" — the brown finger again uplifted —
— "'otel in Booki! I make the 'otel — the
Fonda — in my hoose mañana — to - mor-
row! To-night I and Sanchicha make the
bed for us 'ere. Sanchicha, she stands herself now over in the street. We have mooch
sorrow we have to make the caballeros mooch
tr-rouble to make disposition of his house.
But what will you?"

There was another awkward silence, and
then Saunders, who had been examining the
intruder with languid criticism, removed his
pipe from his mouth and said quietly: —

"That's the woman you're looking for —
Jovita Mendez!"

PART II.

The rest of that interview has not been
recorded. Suffice it that a few minutes later
Parks, Brace, and Saunders left the Emporium, and passed the night in the latter's
cabin, leaving the Emporium in possession
of Miss Mendez and her peon servant; that
at the earliest dawn the two women and

their baggage were transferred to the old adobe house, where, however, a Mexican workman had already arrived, and with a basketful of red tiles was making it habitable. Buckeye, which was popularly supposed to sleep with one eye on the river, and always first repaired there in the morning to wash and work, was only awake to the knowledge of the invasion at noon. The meeting so confidently spoken of the night before had *not* been called. Messrs. Parks and Brace were suffering from headaches — undoubtedly a touch of tule chill. Saunders, at work with his partner in Eagle Bar, was as usual generous with apparently irrelevant facts on all subjects — but that of the strangers. It would seem as if the self-constituted Committee of Safety had done nothing.

And nothing whatever seemed to happen! Thompson of Angels, smoking a meditative pipe at noon on the trail noticed the repairing of the old adobe house, casually spoke of it on his return to his work, without apparent concern or exciting any comment. The two Billinger brothers saw Jovita Mendez at the door of her house an hour later, were themselves seen conversing with her

by Jim Barker, but on returning to their
claim, neither they nor Barker exhibited
any insurrectionary excitement. Later on,
Shuttleworth was found in possession of two
bundles of freshly rolled corn-husk cigar-
ettes, and promised to get his partner some
the next day, but that gentleman anticipated
him. By nightfall nearly all Buckeye had
passed in procession before the little house
without exhibiting any indignation or protest. That night, however, it seemed as if
the events for which the Committee was
waiting were really impending. The adult
female population of Buckeye consisted of
seven women — wives of miners. That they
would submit tamely to the introduction of
a young, pretty, and presumably dangerous
member of their own sex was not to be supposed. But whatever protest they made did
not pass beyond their conjugal seclusion,
and was apparently not supported by their
husbands. Two or three of them, under the
pretext of sympathy of sex, secured interviews with the fair intruder, the result of
which was not, however, generally known.
But a few days later Mrs. " Bob " Carpenter — a somewhat brick-dusty blonde — was
observed wearing some black netting and a

heavily flounced skirt, and Mrs. Shuttleworth in her next visit to Fiddletown wore
her Paisley shawl affixed to her chestnut
hair by a bunch of dog - roses, and wrapped
like a plaid around her waist. The seven
ladies of Buckeye, who had never before
met, except on domestic errands to each
other's houses or on Sunday attendance at
the " First Methodist Church " at Fiddletown, now took to walking together, or in
their husbands' company, along the upper
bank of the river — the one boulevard of
Buckeye. The third day after Miss Mendez' arrival they felt the necessity of immediate shopping expeditions to Fiddletown.
This operation had hitherto been confined
to certain periods, and restricted to the laying in of stores of rough household stuffs;
but it now apparently included a wider
range and more ostentatious quality. Parks'
Emporium no longer satisfied them, and this
unexpected phase of the situation was practically brought home to the proprietor in
the necessity of extending the more inoffen-
sive and peaceful part of his stock. And
when, towards the end of the week, a cart-
load of pretty fixtures, mirrors, and furniture arrived at the *tienda*, there was a

renewed demand at the Emporium for articles not in stock, and the consequent diverting of custom to Fiddletown. Buckeye found itself face to face with a hitherto undreamt of and preposterous proposition. It seemed that the advent of the strange woman, without having yet produced any appreciable effect upon the men, had already insidiously inveigled the adult female population into ostentatious extravagance.

At the end of a week the little adobe house was not only rendered habitable, but was even made picturesque by clean white curtains at its barred windows, and some bright, half-Moorish coloring of beams and rafters. Nearly the whole ground floor was given up to the saloon of the *tienda*, which consisted of a small counter at one side, containing bottles and glasses, and another, flanking it, with glass cases, containing cigars, pipes, and tobacco, while the centre of the room was given up to four or five small restaurant tables. The staff of Jovita was no longer limited to Sanchicha, but had been augmented by a little old man of indefinite antiquity who resembled an Aztec idol, and an equally old Mexican, who looked not unlike a brown-tinted and veined to-

bacco leaf himself, and might have stood
for a sign. But the genius of the place, its
omnipresent and all-pervading goddess, was
Jovita! Smiling, joyous, indefatigable in
suavity and attention ; all-embracing in her
courtesies ; frank of speech and eye ; quick
at repartee and deftly handling the slang
of the day and the locality with a childlike
appreciation and an infantine accent that
seemed to redeem it from vulgarity or un-
feminine boldness ! Few could resist the
volatile infection of her presence. A smile
was the only tribute she exacted, and good-
humor the rule laid down for her guests.
If it occasionally required some mental agil-
ity to respond to her banter, a Californian
gathering was, however, seldom lacking in
humor. Yet she was always the principal
performer to an admiring audience. Perhaps there was security in this multitude of
admirers ; perhaps there was a saving grace
in this humorous trifling. The passions are
apt to be serious and solitary, and Jovita
evaded them with a jest, — which, if not always delicate or witty, was effective in securing the laughter of the majority and the
jealousy of none.

At the end of the week another peculiarity was noticed. There was a perceptible increase of the Mexican population, who had always hitherto avoided Buckeye. On Sunday an Irish priest from El Pásto said mass in a patched-up corner of the old Mission ruin opposite Rollinson's Ford. A few lounging " Excelsior " boys were equally astonished to see Jovita's red rose crest and black mantilla glide by, and followed her unvarying smile and jesting salutation up to the shadow of the crumbling portal. At vespers nearly all Buckeye, hitherto virtuously skeptical and good-humoredly secure in Works without Faith, made a point of attending ; it was alleged by some to see if Jovita's glossy Indian-inky eyes would suffer aberration in her devotions. But the rose-crested head was never lifted from the well-worn prayer-book or the brown hands which held a certain poor little cheap rosary like a child's string of battered copper coins. Buckeye lounged by the wall through the service with respectful tolerance and uneasy shifting legs, and came away. But the apparently simple event did not end there. It was unconsciously charged with a tremendous import to the settlement. For it was discovered the next day by Mrs. " Bob " Carpenter

and Nan Shuttleworth that the Methodist
Church at Fiddletown was too far away,
and Buckeye ought to have a preacher of its
own. Seats were fitted up in the loft of
Carpenter's store-house, where the Reverend Henry McCorkle held divine service,
and instituted a Bible class. At the end of
two weeks it appeared that Jovita's invasion
— which was to bring dissipation and ruin
to Buckeye — had indirectly brought two
churches! A chilling doubt like a cold mist
settled along the river. As the two rival
processions passed on the third Sunday, Jo
Bateman, who had been in the habit of re-
clining on that day in his shirt-sleeves under
a tree, with a novel in his hand, looked
gloomily after them. Then knocking the
ashes from his pipe, he rose, shook hands
with his partners, said apologetically that he
had lately got into the habit of *respecting
the Sabbath*, and was too old to change
again, and so shook the red dust of Buckeye from his feet and departed.

As yet there had not been the slightest
evidence of disorderly conduct on the part
of the fair proprietress of the *tienda*, nor
her customers, nor any drunkenness or riot-
ous disturbance that could be at all attrib-

uted to her presence. There was, it is true, considerable hilarity, smoking, and some gambling there until a late hour, but this could not be said to interfere with the rest and comfort of other people. A clue to the mystery of so extraordinary a propriety was given by Jovita herself. One day she walked into Parks' Emporium and demanded an interview with the proprietor.

"You have made the rules for thees Booki?"

"Yes—that is—I and my friends have."

"And when one shall not have mind the rule—when one have say, 'No! damn the rule,' what shall you make to him? Shall you aprison him?"

Mr. Parks hastened to say with a superior, yet engaging smile that it never had been necessary, as the rules were obligatory upon the honor and consent of all—and were never broken. "Except," he added, still more engagingly, "she would remember, in her case—with their consent."

"And your caballeros break not the rules?"

"No."

"Then they shall not break the rules of me—at *my tienda !* Look! I have made the rule that I shall not have a caballero drunk at my house; I have made the rule that I shall not sell him the aguardiente when he have too mooch. I have made the rule that when he gamble too mooch, when he put up too mooch money, I say 'No!' I will not that he shall! I make one more rule: that he shall not quarrel nor fight in my house. When he quarrel and fight, I say 'Go! Vamos! Get out!'"

"And very good rules they are too, Miss Mendez."

Jovita fixed her shining black eyes on the smiling Parks. "And when he say, 'No, nevarre, damn the rules!' When he come drunk, remain drunk, play high and fight, *you* will not poonish him? *you* will not take him out?"

"Well, you see, the fact is, I have not the power."

"Are you not the Alcalde?"

"No. There is a Justice of the Peace at Fiddletown, but even he could do nothing to enforce your rules. But if anything should happen, you can make a complaint to him."

"Bueno. You have not the power; *I* have. I make not the complaint to Fiddletown. I make the complaint to José Perez,

to Manuel, to Antonio, to Sanchicha — she
is a strong one! I say 'Chook him out.'
They chook him out! they remove him! He
does not r-r-remain. Enough. Bueno. Gra-
cias, señor, good-a-by!'"

She was gone. For the next four days
Parks was in a state of some anxiety — but
it appeared unnecessarily so. Whether the
interview had become known along the river
did not transpire, but there seemed to be no
reason for Miss Mendez to enforce her rules.
It was said that once, when Thompson of
Angels was a little too noisy, he had been
quietly conducted by his friends from the
tienda without the intervention of José.
The frequenters of the saloon became its
police.

Yet the event — long protracted — came
at last! It was a dry, feverish, breezeless
afternoon, when the short, echoless explosion
of a revolver puffed out on the river, followed by another, delivered so rapidly that
they seemed rolled into one. There was no
mistaking that significant repetition. *One*
shot might have been an accident; *two*
meant intention. The men dropped their
picks and shovels and ran — ran as they
never before ran in Buckeye — ran mechan-

ically, blindly groping at their belts and
pockets for the weapons that hung there no
longer; ran aimlessly, as to purpose, but following instinctively with hurried breath and
quivering nostrils the cruel scent of powder
and blood. Ran until, reaching the *tienda*,
the foremost stumbled over the body of
Shuttleworth; came upon the half-sitting,
half-leaning figure of Saunders against its
adobe wall! The doors were barred and
closed, and even as the crowd charged furiously forward, a window was sharply shut
above, in their very face.

"Stand back, gentlemen! Lift him up.
What's the row? What is it, Saunders?
Who did it? Speak, man!"

But Saunders, who was still supporting
himself against the wall, only looked at
them with a singular and half-apologetic
smile, and then leaned forward as if to catch
the eye of Shuttleworth, who was recovering consciousness in the uplifted arms of his
companions. But neither spoke.

"It's some d—d Greaser inside!" said
Thompson, with sudden ferocity. "Some
of her cursed crew! Break down the doors,
boys!"

"Stop!"

It was the voice of Shuttleworth, speaking with an effort. He was hard hit, somewhere in the groin; pain and blood were coming with consciousness and movement, and his face was ghastly. Yet there was the same singular smile of embarrassment which Saunders had worn, and a touch of invincible disgust in his voice as he stammered quickly, " Don't be d—d fools ! It 's no one in *there*. It 's only me and *him !* He 'll tell you that. Won't you, Saunders ? "

" Yes," said Saunders, leaning anxiously forward, with a brightening face. " D—n it all — can't you see ? It 's only — only us."

" You and me, that 's all," repeated Shuttleworth, with a feverish laugh. " Only our d—d foolishness ! Think of it, boys ! He gave me the lie, and I drew ! "

" Both of us full, you know — reg'lar beasts," said Saunders, sinking back against the wall. " Kick me, somebody, and finish me off."

" I don't see any weapons here," said Brace gravely, examining the ground.

" They 're inside," said Shuttleworth with tremulous haste. " We began it in there — just like hogs, you know ! Did n't we, Saunders ? " bitterly.

" You bet," said Saunders faintly. " Reg-'lar swine."

Parks looked graver still, and as he passed a handkerchief around the wounded man's thigh, said : " But I don't see where you got your pistols, and how you got out here."

" Clinched, you know; sorter rolled over out here — and — and — oh, d—n it — don't talk ! "

" He means," said Shuttleworth still feebly, " that we — we — grabbed *another man's* six-shooter and — and — he that is — and they — he —he and me grabbed each other, and — don't you see — ? " but here, becoming more involved and much weaker, he discreetly fainted away.

And that was all Buckeye ever knew of the affair ! For they refused to speak of it again, and Dr. Duchesne gravely forbade any further interrogation. Both men's re-volvers were found undischarged in their holsters, hanging in their respective cabins. The balls which were afterwards extracted from the two men singularly disappeared ; Dr. Duchesne asserting with a grim smile that they had swallowed them.[1]

[1] It was a frontier superstition that the ball extracted from a gunshot wound, if swallowed by the wounded

Nothing could be ascertained of the facts at the *tienda*, which at that hour of the day appeared to have been empty of customers, and was occupied only by Miss Mendez and her retainers. All surmises as to the real cause of the quarrel and the reason for the reticence of the two belligerents were suddenly and unexpectedly stopped by their departure from Buckeye as soon as their condition permitted, on the alleged opinion of Dr. Duchesne that the air of the river was dangerous to their convalescence. The momentary indignation against the *tienda* which the two combatants had checked, eventually subsided altogether. After all, the fight had taken place *outside ;* it was not even proven that the provocation had been given *at* the *tienda !* Its popularity was undiminished.

PART III.

It was the end of the rainy season, and a wet night. Brace and Parks were looking from the window over the swollen river, with faces quite as troubled as the stream below. Nor was the prospect any longer the same.

man, prevented inflammation or any supervening complications.

In the past two years Buckeye had grown
into a city. They could now count a half
dozen church spires from the window of the
three-storied brick building which had taken
the place of the old wooden Emporium, but
they could also count the brilliantly lit windows of an equal number of saloons and
gambling-houses which glittered through the
rain, or, to use the words of a local critic,
"Shone seven nights in the week to the
Gospel shops' *one!*" A difficulty had arisen
which the two men had never dreamed of,
and a struggle had taken place between the
two rival powers, which was developing a
degree of virulence and intolerance on both
sides that boded no good to Buckeye. The
disease which its infancy had escaped had
attacked its adult growth with greater vio-
lence. The new American saloons which
competed with Jovita Mendez' Spanish
venture had substituted a brutal masculine
sincerity for her veiled feminine methods.
There was higher play, deeper drinking,
darker passion. Yet the opposition, after
the fashion of most reformers, were casting
back to the origin of the trouble in Jovita,
and were confounding principles and growth.
"If it had not been for her the rule would

never have been broken." "If there was to be a cleaning out of the gambling houses, she must go first!"

The sounds of a harp and a violin played in the nearest saloon struggled up to them with the opening and shutting of its swinging baize inner doors. There was boisterous chanting from certain belated revelers in the next street which had no such remission. The brawling of the stream below seemed to be echoed in the uneasy streets; the quiet of the old days had departed with the sedate, encompassing woods that no longer fringed the river bank; the restful calm of Nature had receded before the dusty outskirts of the town.

"It's mighty unfortunate, too," said Brace moodily, "that Shuttleworth and Saunders, who have n't been in the place since their row, have come over from Fiddle-town to-day, and are hanging around town. They have n't said anything that I know of, but their *presence* is quite enough to revive the old feeling against her shop. The Committee," he added bitterly, "will be sure to say that not only the first gambling, but the first shooting in Buckeye took place there. If they get up that story again — no matter how quiet *she* has become since — no matter what *you* may say as mayor — it will go hard with her. What's that now?"

They listened breathlessly. Above the brawling of the river, the twanging of the harp-player, and the receding shouts of the revelers, they could hear the hollow wooden sidewalks resounding with the dull, monotonous trampling of closely following feet. Parks rose with a white face.

" Brace ! "

" Yes ! "

" Will you stand by me — and *her ?* "

" Stand by *you and her ?* Eh? What? Good God! Parks! — you don't mean to say you — it's gone as far as *that ?* "

" Will you or won't you? "

The sound of the trampling had changed to a shuffling on the pavement below, and then footsteps began to ascend the stairs.

Brace held out his hand quickly and grasped that of Parks as the door opened to half a dozen men. They were evidently the ringleaders of the crowd below. There was no hesitation or doubt in their manner ; the unswerving directness which always characterized those illegal demonstrations lent it something of dignity. Nevertheless, Car-

penter, the spokesman, flushed slightly before Parks' white, determined face.

"Come, Parks, you know what we're
after," he said bluntly. "We did n't come
here to parley. We knew *your* sentiments
and what *you* think is your duty. We know
what we consider *ours* — and so do you.
But we're here to give you a chance, either
as mayor, or, if you prefer it, as the oldest
citizen here, to take a hand in our business
to-night. We're not ashamed of what we're
going to do, and we're willing to abide by
it ; so there's no reason why we should n't
speak aboveboard of it to you. We even
invite you to take part in our last ' call ' to-
night at the Hall."

"Go!" whispered Brace quickly, "*you'll
gain time !*"

Parks' face changed, and he turned to
Carpenter. "Enough," he said gravely.
"I reserve what I have to say of these pro-
ceedings till I join you there." He stopped,
whispered a few words to Brace, and then
disappeared as the men descended the stairs,
and, joining the crowd on the pavement,
proceeded silently towards the Town Hall.
There was nothing in the appearance of that
decorous procession to indicate its unlawful

character or the recklessness with which it was charged.

There were thirty or forty men already seated in the Hall. The meeting was brief and to the point. The gambling saloons were to be "cleaned out" that night, the tables and appliances thrown into the street and burnt, the doors closed, and the gamblers were to be conducted to the outskirts of the town and forbidden to enter it again on pain of death.

"Does this yer refer to Jovita Mendez' saloon?" asked a voice.

To their surprise the voice was not Parks' but Shuttleworth's. It was also a matter to be noted that he stood a little forward of the crowd, and that there was a corresponding movement of a dozen or more men from Fiddletown who apparently were part of the meeting.

The chairman (No. 10) said there was to be no exception, and certainly not for the originator of disorder in Buckeye! He was surprised that the question should be asked by No. 72, who was an old resident of Buckeye, and who, with No. 73, had suffered from the character of that woman's saloon.

"That's jest it," said Shuttleworth, "and

ez I reckon that *Saunders and me* did all the
disorder there was, and had to turn ourselves
out o' town on account of it, I don't see jest
where *she* could come into this affair. Only,"
he turned and looked around him, "in one
way! And that way, gentlemen, would be
for her to come here and boot one half o'
this kempany out o' town, and shoot the
other half! You hear me!—that's so!"
He stopped, tugged a moment at his cravat
and loosened his shirt-collar as if it impeded
his utterance, and went on. "I've got to
say suthin' to you gentlemen about me and
Saunders and this woman; I've got to say
suthin' that's hard for a white man to say,
and him a married man, too—I've got to
say that me and Saunders never had no
qu'oll, never had *no fight* at her shop: I've
got to say that me and Saunders got shot by
Jovita Mendez for *insultin' her*—for tryin'
to treat her as if she was the common dirt of
the turnpike—and served us right! I've
got to say that Saunders and me made a bet
that for all her airs she was n't no better
than she might be, and we went there drunk
to try her—and that we got left, with two
shots into us like hounds as we were! That's
so!—was n't it, Saunders?"

" With two shots inter us like hounds ez we were," repeated Saunders with deliberate precision.

" And I 've got to say suthin' more, gen'le-men," continued Shuttleworth, now entirely removing his coat and vest, and apparently shaking himself free from any extraneous trammels. " I 've got to say this — I 've got to say that thar ain't a man in Buckeye, from Dirty Dick over yon to the mayor of this town, ez has n't tried the same thing on and got left — got left, without shootin' maybe, more 's the pity, but got left all the same! And I 've got to say," lifting his voice, " *that ef that 's what you call disor-derliness in her* — if that 's what yo'r turn-in' this woman out o' town for — why " —

He stopped, absolutely breathless and gasping. For there was a momentary shock of surprise and shame, and then he was overborne by peal after peal of inextin-guishable laughter. But it was the laughter that precipitated doubt, enlightened justice, cleared confusion, and — saved them !

In vain a few struggled to remind them that the question of the *other* saloons was still unaffected. It was lost in the motion enthusiastically put and carried that the

Committee should instantly accompany Saunders and Shuttleworth to Jovita's saloon to make an apology in their presence. Five minutes later they halted hilariously before its door. But it was closed, dark, and silent!

Their sudden onset and alarm brought Sanchicha to the half-opened door. " Ah, yes! the Señorita? Bueno! She had just left for Fiddletown with the Señor Parks, the honorable mayor. They had been married only a few moments before by the Reverend Mr. McCorkle!"

THEIR UNCLE FROM CALI-FORNIA.

PART I.

It was bitterly cold. When night fell over Lakeville, Wisconsin, the sunset, which had flickered rather than glowed in the western sky, took upon itself a still more boreal tremulousness, until at last it seemed to fade away in cold blue shivers to the zenith. Nothing else stirred; in the crisp still air the evening smoke of chimneys rose threadlike and vanished. The stars were early, pale, and pitiless; when the later moonlight fell, it appeared only to whiten the stiffened earth like snow, except where it made a dull, pewter-like film over the three frozen lakes which encompassed the town.

The site of the town itself was rarely beautiful, and its pioneers and founders had carried out the suggestions they had found there with loving taste and intelligence.

Themselves old *voyageurs*, trappers, and traders, they still loved Nature too well to exclude her from the restful homes they had achieved after years of toiling face to face with her. So a strip of primeval forest on the one side, and rolling level prairie on the other, still came up to the base of the hill, whereon they had built certain solid houses, which a second generation had beautified and improved with modern taste, but which still retained their old honesty of foundation and wholesome rustic space. These yet stood among the old trees, military squares, and broad sloping avenues of the town. Seen from the railway by day, the regularity of streets and blocks was hidden by environing trees; there remained only a picturesque lifting of rustic gardens, brown roofs, gables, spires, and cupolas above the mirroring lake : seen from the railway this bitter night, the invisible terraces and streets were now pricked out by symmetrical lines and curves of sparkling lights, which glittered through the leafless boughs and seemed to encircle the hill like a diadem.

Central in the chiefest square, and yet preserving its old lordly isolation in a wooded garden, the homestead of Enoch

Lane stood with all its modern additions and improvements. Already these included not only the latest phases of decoration, but various treasures brought by the second generation from Europe, which they were wont to visit, but from which they always contentedly returned to their little provincial town. Whether there was some instinctive yearning, like the stirred sap of great forests, in their wholesome pioneer blood, or whether there was some occult fascination in the pretty town-crested hill itself, it was still certain that the richest inhabitants always preferred to live in Lakeville. Even the young, who left it to seek their fortune elsewhere, came back to enjoy their success under the sylvan vaults of this vast ancestral roof. And that was why, this 22d of December, 1870, the whole household of Gabriel Lane was awaiting the arrival from California of his brother, Sylvester Lane, at the old homestead which he had left twenty years ago.

"And you don't know how he looks?" said Kitty Lane to her father.

"I do, perfectly; rather chubby, with blue eyes, curly hair, fair skin, and blushes when you speak to him."

" Papa ! "

" Eh ? — Oh, well, he *used* to. You see
that was twenty-five years ago, when he left
here for boarding-school. He ran away from
there, as I told you; went to sea, and finally
brought up at San Francisco."

" And you have n't had any picture, or
photograph of him, since ? "

" No — that is — I say ! — you have n't,
any of you, got a picture of Sylvester, have
you ? " he turned in a vague parentheti-
cal appeal to the company of relatives and
friends collected in the drawing-room after
dinner.

" Cousin Jane has ; she knows all about
him ! "

But it appeared that Cousin Jane had
only heard Susan Marckland say that Ed-
ward Bingham had told her that he was in
California when " Uncle Sylvester " had
been nearly hanged by a Vigilance Committee for protecting a horse thief or a gambler,
or some such person. This was felt to be
ineffective as a personal description.

" He 's sure to wear a big beard ; they all
do when they first come back," said Amos
Gunn, with metropolitan oraculousness.

" He has a big curling mustache, long

silken hair, and broad shoulders," said Marie du Page.

There was such piquant conviction in the manner of the speaker, who was also a very pretty girl, that they all turned towards her, and Kitty quickly said, —

"But *you 've* never seen him?"

"No — but — " She stopped, and, lifting one shoulder, threw her spirited head sideways, in a pretty deprecatory way, with elevated eyebrows and an expression intended to show the otherwise untranslatable character of her impression. But it showed quite as pleasantly the other fact, that she was the daughter of a foreigner, an old French military explorer, and that she had retained even in Anglo-Saxon Lakeville some of the Gallic animation.

"Well, how many of you girls are going with me to meet him at the station?" said Gabriel, dismissing with masculine promptness the lesser question. "It 's time to be off."

"I 'd like to go," said Kitty, "and so would Cousin Jane; but really, papa, you see if *you* don't know him, and *we* don't either, and you 've got to satisfy yourself that it 's the right man, and then introduce *yourself* and then us — and all this on the platform before everybody — it makes it rather embarrassing for us. And then, as he's your younger brother and we're supposed to be his affectionate nieces, you know, it would make *him* feel *so* ridiculous ! "

" And if he were to *kiss* you," said Marie tragically, " and then turn out not to be him ! "

" So," continued Kitty, " you'd better take Cousin John, who was more in Uncle Sylvester's time, to represent the Past of the family, and perhaps Mr. Gunn " —

" To represent the future, I suppose ? " interrupted Gabriel in a wicked whisper.

" To represent a name that most men of the world in New York and San Francisco know," went on Kitty, without a blush. " It would make recognition and introduction easier. And take an extra fur with you, dear — not for *him* but for yourself. I suppose he's lived so much in the open air as to laugh at our coddling."

" I don't know about that," said her father thoughtfully ; " the last telegram I have from him, *en route*, says he's half frozen, and wants a close carriage sent to the station."

" Of course," said Marie impatiently, " you forget the poor creature comes from burning cañons and hot golden sands and perpetual sunshine."

" Very well ; but come along, Marie, and see how I 've prepared his room," and as her father left the drawing-room Kitty carried off her old schoolfellow upstairs.

The room selected for the coming Sylvester had been one of the elaborate guest-chambers, but was now stripped of its more luxurious furniture and arranged with picturesque yet rural extravagance. A few rare buffalo, bear, and panther skins were disposed over the bare floor, and even displayed gracefully over some elaborately rustic chairs. The handsome French bedstead had been displaced for a small wrought-iron ascetic-looking couch covered with a gorgeously striped Mexican blanket. The fireplace had been dismantled of its steel grate, and the hearth extended so as to allow a pile of symmetrically heaped moss-covered hickory logs to take its place. The walls were covered with trophies of the chase, buck-horns and deer-heads, and a number of Indian arrows stood in a sheaf in the corners beside a few modern guns and rifles.

"Perfectly lovely," said Marie, "but" — with a slight shiver of her expressive shoulders — "a little cold and outdoorish, eh?"

"Nonsense," returned Kitty dictatorially, "and if he *is* cold, he can easily light those logs. They always build their open fires under a tree. Why, even Mr. Gunn used to do that when he was camping out in the Adirondacks last summer. I call it perfectly comfortable and *so* natural." Nevertheless, they had both tucked their chilly hands under the fleecy shawls they had snatched from the hall for this hyperborean expedition.

"You have taken much pains for him, Kaitee," said Marie, with her faintest foreign intonation. "You will like this strange uncle — you?"

"He is a wonderful man, Marie; he's been everywhere, seen everything, and done everything out there. He's fought duels, been captured by Indians and tied to a stake to be tortured. He's been leader of a Vigilance Committee, and they say that he has often shot and killed men himself. I'm afraid he's been rather wicked, you know. He's lived alone in the woods like a hermit without seeing a soul, and then, again, he's been a chief among the Indians, with Heaven knows how many Indian wives! They called him 'The Pale-faced Thunder-bolt,' my dear, and 'The Young Man who Swallows the Lightning,' or something like that."

"And what can he want here?" asked Marie.

"To see us, my dear," said Kitty loftily; "and then, too, he has to settle something about *his* share of the property; for you know grandpa left a share of it to him. Not that he's ever bothered himself about it, for he's rich, — a kind of Monte Cristo, you know, — with a gold mine and an island off the coast, to say nothing of a whole county that he owns, that is called after him, and millions of wild cattle that he rides among and lassos! It's dreadfully hard to do. You know you take a long rope with a slip-knot, and you throw it around your head so, and " —

"Hark!" said Marie, with a dramatic start, and her finger on her small mouth, "he comes!"

There was the clear roll of wheels along the smooth, frozen carriage sweep towards

the house, the sharp crisp click of hoofs on
stone, the opening of heavy doors, the sudden sparkling invasion of frigid air, the uplifting of voices in greeting, — but all familiar ! There were Gabriel Lane's cheery,
hopeful tones, the soprano of Cousin Jane
and Cousin Emma, the baritone of Mr.
Gunn, and the grave measured oratorical
utterance of Parson Dexter, who had joined
the party at the station; but certainly the
accents of no *stranger*. Had he come ?
Yes, for his name was just then called, and
the quick ear of Marie had detected a light,
lounging, alien footstep cross the cold strip
of marble vestibule. The two girls exchanged a rapid glance ; each looked into
the mirror, and then interrogatively at the
other, nodded their heads affirmatively, and
descended to the drawing-room. A group
had already drawn round the fire, and a
small central figure, who, with its back
turned towards them, was still enwrapped in
an enormous overcoat of rich fur, was engaged in presenting an alternate small var-
nished leather boot to the warmth of the
grate. As they entered the room the heavy
fur was yielded up with apparent reluctance,
and revealed to the astonished girls a man

of ordinary stature with a slight and elegant figure set off by a traveling suit of irreproachable cut. His light reddish-yellow hair, mustache, and sunburned cheek, which seemed all of one color and outline, made it impossible to detect the gray of the one or the hollowness of the other, and gave no indication of his age. Yet there was clearly no mistake. Here was Gabriel Lane seizing their nervously cold fingers and presenting them to their "Uncle Sylvester."

Far from attempting to kiss Kitty, the stranger for an instant seemed oblivious of the little hand she offered him in the half-preoccupied bow he gave her. But Marie was not so easily passed over, and, with her audacious face challenging his, he abstractedly imparted to the shake of her hand something of the fervor that he should have shown his relative. And, then, still warming his feet on the fender, he seemed to have forgotten them both.

"Accustomed as you have been, sir," said the Reverend Mr. Dexter, seizing upon an awkward silence, and accenting it laboriously, "perhaps I should say *inured* as you have been to the exciting and stirring incidents of a lawless and adventurous community, you doubtless find in a pastoral, yet cultivated and refined, seclusion like Lakeville a degree of " —

" Oh, several degrees," said Uncle Sylvester, blandly flicking bits of buffalo hair from his well-fitting trousers; " it 's colder, you know — much colder."

" I was referring to a less material contrast," continued Mr. Dexter, with a resigned smile; " yet, as to the mere question of cold, I am told, sir, that in California there are certain severe regions of altitude — although the mean temperature " —

" I suppose out in California you fellows would say our temperature was a darned sight *meaner*, eh ? " broke in Amos Gunn, with a confidential glance at the others, as if offering a humorous diversion suited to the Californian taste. Uncle Sylvester did not, however, smile. Gazing critically at Gunn, he said thoughtfully : " I think not ; I 've even known men killed for saying less than that," and turned to the clergyman. " You are quite right ; some of the higher passes are very cold. I was lost in one of them in '56 with a small party. We were seventy miles from any settlement, we had had nothing to eat for thirty-six hours ; our campfire, melting the snow, sank twelve feet below the surface." The circle closed eagerly around him, Marie, Kitty, and Cousin Jane pressing forward with excited faces; even the clergyman assumed an expression of profound interest. "A man by the name of Thompson, I think," continued Uncle Sylvester, thoughtfully gazing at the fire, "was frozen a few yards away. Towards morning, having been fifty-eight hours without food, our last drop of whiskey exhausted, and the fire extinguished, we found " —

"Yes, yes!" said half a dozen voices.

"We found," continued Uncle Sylvester, rubbing his hands cheerfully, "we found it — exceedingly cold. Yes — *exceedingly* cold!"

There was a dead silence.

"But you escaped!" said Kitty breathlessly.

"I think so. I think we all escaped — that is, except Thompson, if his name *was* Thompson; it might have been Parker," continued Uncle Sylvester, gazing with a certain languid astonishment on the eager faces around him.

"But *how* did you escape?"

"Oh, somehow! I don't remember exactly. I don't think," he went on reflectively, " that we had to eat Thompson — if it was *him* — at least not then. No " — with a faint effort of recollection — " that would have been another affair. Yes," assuringly to the eager, frightened eyes of Cousin Jane, " you are quite right, that was something altogether different. Dear me ; one quite mixes up these things. Eh ? "

A servant had entered, and after a hurried colloquy with Gabriel, the latter turned to Uncle Sylvester —

" Excuse me, but I think there must be some mistake ! We brought up your luggage with you — two trunks — in the station wagon. A man has just arrived with three more, which he says are yours."

" There should be five in all, I think," said Uncle Sylvester thoughtfully.

" Maybe there are, sir, I did n't count exactly," said the servant.

" All right," said Uncle Sylvester cheerfully, turning to his brother. "You can put them in my room or on the landing, except two marked ' L ' in a triangle. They contain some things I picked up for you and the girls. We 'll look them over in the morning. And, if you don't mind, I 'll excuse myself now and go to bed."

"But it's only half past ten," said Gabriel remonstratingly. "You don't, surely, go to bed at half past ten?"

"I do when I travel. Travel is *so* exhausting. Good-night! Don't let anybody disturb themselves to come with me."

He bowed languidly to the company, and disappeared with a yawn gracefully disguised into a parting smile.

"Well!" said Cousin Jane, drawing a long breath.

"I don't believe it's your Uncle Sylvester at all!" said Marie vivaciously. "It's some trick that Gabriel is playing upon us. And he's not even a good actor — he forgets his part."

"And, then, five trunks for one single man! Heavens! what can he have in them?" said Cousin Emma.

"Perhaps his confederates, to spring out upon us at night, after everybody's asleep."

"Are you sure you remembered him, papa?" said Kitty *sotto voce.*

"Certainly. And, my dear child, he knows all the family history as well as you do; and" — continued her father with a slight laugh that did not, however, conceal a certain seriousness that was new to him — "I only wish I understood as much about the property as he does. By the way, Amos," he broke off suddenly, turning to the young man, "he seemed to know your people."

"Most men in the financial world do," said Gunn a little superciliously.

"Yes; but he asked me if you had n't a relative of some kind in Southern California or Mexico."

A slight flush — so slight that only the keen, vivaciously observant eyes of Marie noticed it — passed over the young man's face.

"I believe it is a known fact that our branch of the family never emigrated from their native town," he said emphatically. "The Gunns were rather peculiar and particular in that respect."

"Then there were no offshoots from the old *stock*," said Gabriel.

Nevertheless, this pet joke of Gabriel's did not dissipate the constraint and disappointment left upon the company by Uncle Sylvester's unsatisfying performance and early withdrawal, and they separated soon after, Kitty and Marie being glad to escape upstairs together. On the landing they met two of the Irish housemaids in a state of agitated exhaustion. It appeared that the

" sthrange gintleman " had requested that his bed be remade from bedclothes and bedding *always carried with him in his trunks!* From their apologetic tone it was evident that he had liberally rewarded them. " Shure, Miss," protested Norah, in deprecation of Kitty's flashing eye, " there 's thim that 's lived among shnakes and poysin riptiles and faverous disayses that 's particklar av the beds and sheets they lie on. Hisht! Howly Mother! it 's something else he 's wanting now ! "

The door of Uncle Sylvester's room had slowly opened, and a blue pyjama'd sleeve appeared, carefully depositing the sheaf of bows and arrows outside the door. " I say, Norah, or Bridget there, some of you take those infernal things away. And look out, will you, for the arrowheads are deadly poison. The fool who got 'em did n't know they were African, and not Indian at all! And hold on ! " The hand vanished, and presently reappeared holding two rifles. " And take these away, too ! They 're loaded, capped, and *not* on the half-cock! A jar, a fall, the slightest shock is enough to send them off ! "

" I 'm dreadfully sorry that you should

find it so uncomfortable in our house, Uncle Sylvester," said Kitty, with a flushed cheek and vibrating voice.

"Oh, it's you — is it?" said Uncle Sylvester's voice cheerfully. "I thought it was Bridget out there. No, I don't intend to find it uncomfortable. That's why I'm putting these things outside. But, for Heaven's sake, don't *you* touch them. Leave that to the ineffable ass who put them there. Good-night!"

The door closed; the whispering voices of the girls faded from the corridor; the lights were lowered in the central hall, only the red Cyclopean eye of an enormous columnar stove, like a lighthouse, gleamed through the darkness. Outside, the silent night sparkled, glistened, and finally paled. Towards morning, having invested the sturdy wooden outer walls of the house and filmed with delicate tracery every available inch of window pane, it seemed stealthily to invade the house itself, stilling and chilling it as it drew closer around its central heart of warmth and life. Only once the frigid stillness was broken by the opening of a door and steps along the corridor. This was preceded by an acrid smell of burning bark.

It was subtle enough to permeate the upper floor and the bedroom of Marie du Page, who was that night a light and nervous sleeper. Peering from her door, she could see, on the lower corridor, the extraordinary spectacle of Uncle Sylvester, robed in a gorgeous Japanese dressing-gown of quilted satin trimmed with the fur of the blue fox, candle in hand, leisurely examining the wall of the passage. Presently, drawing out a foot-rule from his pocket, he actually began to measure it! Miss Du Page saw no more. Hurriedly closing her door, she locked and bolted it, firmly convinced that Gabriel Lane was harboring in the guise of Uncle Sylvester a somnambulist, a maniac, or an impostor.

PART II.

" It does n't seem as if Uncle Sylvester was any the more comfortable for having his own private bedding with him," said Kitty Lane, entering Marie's room early the next morning. " Bridget found him curled up in his furs like a cat asleep on the drawing-room sofa this morning."

Marie started; she remembered her last

night's vision. But some instinct — she knew not what — kept her from revealing it at this moment. She only said a little ironically : —

"Perhaps he missed the wild freedom of his barbaric life in a small bedroom."

"No. Bridget says he said something about being smoked out of his room by a ridiculous wood fire. The idea! As if a man brought up in the woods could n't stand a little smoke. No — that 's his excuse! Marie! — do you know what I firmly believe ? "

"No," said Marie quickly.

"I firmly believe that poor man is ashamed of his past rough life, and does everything he can to forget it. That 's why he affects those ultra-civilized and effeminate ways, and goes to the other extreme, as people always do."

"Then you think he 's really reformed, and is n't likely to take an impulse to rob and murder anybody again ? "

"Why, Marie, what nonsense ! "

Nevertheless, Uncle Sylvester appeared quite fresh and cheerful at breakfast. It seemed that he had lit the fire before undressing, but the green logs were piled so far into the room that the smoke nearly suffocated him. Fearful of alarming the house by letting the smoke escape through the door, he opened the window, and when it had partly dispersed, sought refuge himself from the arctic air of his bedroom in the drawing-room. So far the act did not seem inconsistent with his sanity, or even intelligence and consideration for others. But Marie fixed upon him a pair of black, audacious eyes.

" Did you ever walk in your sleep, Mr. Lane ? "

" No ; but " — thoughtfully breaking an egg — " I have ridden, I think."

" In your sleep ? Oh, do tell us all about it ! " said Cousins Jane and Emma in chorus.

Uncle Sylvester cast a resigned glance out of the window. " Oh, yes — certainly ; it is n't much. You see at one time I was in the habit of making long monotonous journeys, and they were often exhausting, and," he added, becoming wearied as if at the recollection, " always dreadfully tiresome. As the trail was sometimes very uncertain and dangerous, I rode a very surefooted mule that could go anywhere where there was space big enough to set her small hoofs upon. One night I was coming down the slope of a mountain towards a narrow valley and river that were crossed by an old, abandoned flume, of which nothing was now left but the upright trestle-work and long horizontal string-piece. As the trail was very difficult and the mule's pace was slow, I found myself dozing at times, and at last I must have fallen asleep. I think I must have been awakened by a singular regularity in the movement of the mule — or else it was the monotony of step that had put me to sleep and the cessation of it awakened me. You see, at first I was not certain that I was n't really dreaming. For the trail seemed to have disappeared; the wall of rock on one side had vanished also, and there appeared to be nothing ahead of me but the opposite hillside."

Uncle Sylvester stopped to look out of the window at a passing carriage. Then he went on. "The moon came out, and I saw what had happened. The mule, either of her own free will, or obeying some movement I had given the reins in my sleep, had swerved from the trail, got on top of the flume, and was actually walking across the valley on the narrow string-piece, a foot wide, half a mile long, and sixty feet from the ground.

I knew," he continued, examining his napkin thoughtfully, "that she was perfectly sure-footed, and that if I kept quiet she could make the passage, but I suddenly remembered that midway there was a break and gap of twenty feet in the continuous line, and that the string-piece was too narrow to allow her to turn round and retrace her steps."

"Good heavens!" said Cousin Jane.

"I beg your pardon?" said Uncle Sylvester politely.

"I only said, 'Good heavens!' Well?" she added impatiently.

"Well?" repeated Uncle Sylvester vaguely. "Oh, that's all. I only wanted to explain what I meant by saying I had ridden in my sleep."

"But," said Cousin Jane, leaning across the table with grim deliberation and emphasizing each word with the handle of her knife, "how — did — you — and — that — mule get down?"

"Oh, with slings and ropes, you know — so," demonstrating by placing his napkin-ring in a sling made of his napkin.

"And I suppose you carried the slings and ropes with you in your five trunks!" gasped Cousin Jane.

"No. Fellows on the river brought 'em in the morning. Mighty spry chaps, those river miners."

"Very!" said Cousin Jane.

Breakfast over, they were not surprised that their sybaritic guest excused himself from an inspection of the town in the frigid morning air, and declined joining a skating party to the lake on the ground that he could keep warmer indoors with half the exertion. An hour later found him standing before the fire in Gabriel Lane's study, looking languidly down on his elder brother.

"Then, as far as I can see," he said quietly, "you have made ducks and drakes of your share of the property, and that virtually you are in the hands of this man Gunn and his father."

"You're putting it too strongly," said Gabriel deprecatingly. "In the first place, my investments with Gunn's firm are by no means failures, and they only hold as security a mortgage on the forest land below the hill. It's scarcely worth the money. I would have sold it long ago, but it had been a fancy of father's to keep it wild land for the sake of old times and the healthiness of the town."

"There used to be a log cabin there, where the old man had a habit of camping out whenever he felt cramped by civilization up here, was n't there?" said Uncle Sylvester meditatively.

"Yes," said Gabriel impatiently; "it 's still there — but to return to Mr. Gunn. He has taken a fancy to Kitty, and even if *I* could not lift the mortgage, there 's some possibility that the land would still remain in the family."

"I think I 'll drive over this afternoon and take a look at the old shanty if this infernal weather lets up."

"Yes; but just now, my dear Sylvester, let us attend to business. I want to show you those investments."

"Oh, certainly; trot 'em out," said his brother, plucking up a simulation of interest as he took a seat at the table.

From a drawer of his desk Gabriel brought out a bundle of prospectuses and laid them before Uncle Sylvester.

A languid smile of recognition lit up the latter's face. "Ah! yes," he said, glancing at them. "The old lot: 'Carmelita,' 'Santa Maria,' and 'Preciosa!' Just as I imagined — and yet who 'd have thought of seeing

them *here !* A good deal rouged and pow-
dered, Miss Carmelita, since I first knew
you! Considerably bolstered up by miraculous testimony to your powers, my dear
Santa Maria, since the day I found you out,
to my cost! And you too, Preciosa! — a
precious lot of money I dropped on you in
the old days ! "

"You are joking," said Gabriel, with an
uneasy smile. " You don't mean to imply
that this stock is old and worthless ? "

" There is n't a capital in America or
Europe where for the last five years it
has n't been floated with a new character
each time. My dear Gabriel, that stock
is n't worth the paper it is printed on."

" But it is impossible that an experienced
financier like Gunn could be deceived ! "

" I 'm sorry to hear *that.*"

"Come, Sylvester ! confess you 've taken
a prejudice against Gunn from your sudden
dislike of his son ! And what have you
against him ? "

" I could n't say exactly," said Uncle
Sylvester reflectively. " It may be his eyes,
or only his cravat ! But," rising cheerfully
and placing his hand lightly on his brother's
shoulder, "don't *you* worry yourself about

that stock, old man; *I'll* see that somebody else has the worry and you the cash. And as to the land and — Kitty — well, you hold on to them both until you find out which the young man is really after."

"And then?" said Gabriel, with a smile.

"Don't give him either! But, I say, haven't we had enough business this morning? Let's talk of something else. Who's the French girl?"

"Marie? She's the daughter of Jules du Page — don't you remember? — father's friend. When Jules died, it was always thought that father, who had half adopted her as a child, would leave her some legacy. But you know that father died without making a will, and that — rich as he was — his actual assets were far less than we had reason to expect. Kitty, who felt the disappointment as keenly as her friend, I believe would have divided her own share with her. It's odd, by the way, that father could have been so deceived in the amount of his capital, or how he got rid of his money in a way that we knew nothing of. Do you know, Sylvester, I've sometimes suspected" —

"What?" said Uncle Sylvester suddenly. The bored languor of his face had abruptly vanished. Every muscle was alert; his gray eyes glittered.

"That he advanced money to Du Page, who lost it, or that they speculated together," returned Gabriel, who, following Uncle Sylvester's voice only, had not noticed the change of expression.

"That would seem to be a weakness of the Lane family," said Uncle Sylvester grimly, with a return of his former carelessness. "But that is not *your* own opinion — that's a suggestion of some one else?"

"Well," said Gabriel, with a laugh and a slight addition of color, "it *was* Gunn's theory. As a man of the world and a practical financier, you know."

"And you've talked with *him* about it?"

"Yes. It was a matter of general wonder years ago."

"Very likely — but, just now, don't you think we've had enough financial talk?" said Uncle Sylvester, with a bored contraction of his eyebrows. "Come," looking around the room, "you've changed the interior of the old house."

"Yes. Unfortunately, just after father's death it was put in the hands of a local architect or builder, one of father's old friends, but not a very skillful workman, who made changes while the family were away. That's why your present bedroom, which was father's old study, had a slice taken off it to make the corridor larger, and why the big chimney and hearthstone are still there, although the fireplace is modernized. That was Flint's stupidity."

" Whose stupidity?" asked Uncle Sylvester, trimming his nails.

" Flint's — the old architect."

" Why didn't you make him change it back again?"

" He left Lakeville shortly after, and I brought an architect from St. Louis after I returned from Europe. But nothing could be done to your room without taking down the chimney, so it remained as Flint left it."

" That reminds me, Gabriel, I'm afraid I spoke rather cavalierly to Kitty, last night, about the arrangements of the room. The fact is, I've taken a fancy to it, and should like to fit it up myself. Have I your permission?"

" Certainly, my dear Sylvester."

" I've some knickknacks in my trunks, and I'll do it at once."

" As you like."

" And you'll see that I am not disturbed; and you 'll explain it to Kitty, with my apologies ? "

" Yes."

" Then I'm off."

Gabriel glanced at his brother with a perplexed smile. Here was the bored traveler, explorer, gold - seeker, soldier of fortune, actually as pleased as a girl over the prospect of arranging his room ! He called after him, " Sylvester ! "

" Yes."

" I say, if you could, you know, just try to interest these people to-night with some of your adventures — something told *seriously*, you know, as if you really were in earnest — I 'd be awfully obliged to you. The fact is, — you 'll excuse me, — but they think you don't come up to your reputation."

" They want a story ? "

" Yes, — one of your experiences."

" I 'll give them one. Ta-ta ! "

For the rest of the day Uncle Sylvester was invisible, although his active presence in his room was betrayed by the sound of hammering and moving of furniture. As the remainder of the party were skating on

the lake, this eccentricity was not remarked
except by one, — Marie du Page, — who
on pretense of a slight cold had stayed at
home. But with her suspicions of the former
night, she had determined to watch the singular relative of her friend. Added to a
natural loyalty to the Lanes, she was moved
by a certain curiosity and fascination towards this incomprehensible man.

The house was very quiet when she stole
out of her room and passed softly along the
corridor; she examined the wall carefully
to discover anything that might have excited
the visitor's attention. There were a few
large engravings hanging there; could he
have designed to replace them by some
others? Suddenly she was struck with the
distinct conviction that the wall of the corridor did not coincide with the wall of his
room as represented by the line of the door.
There was certainly a space between the two
walls unaccounted for. This was undoubtedly what had attracted *his* attention; but
what *business* was it of his?

She reflected that she had seen in the
wall of the conservatory an old closed staircase, now used as shelves for dried herbs
and seeds, which she had been told was the

old-time communication between the garden and Grandfather Lane's study, — the room now occupied by the stranger. Perhaps it led still farther, and thus accounted for the space. Determined to satisfy herself, she noiselessly descended to the conservatory. There, surely, was the staircase, — a narrow flight of wooden steps encumbered with packages of herbs, — losing itself in upper darkness. By the aid of a candle she managed to grope and pick her way up step by step. Then she paused. The staircase had abruptly ended on the level of the study, now cut off from it by the new partition. She was in a stifling inclosure, formed by the walls, scarcely eighteen inches wide. It was made narrower by a singular excrescence on the old wall, which seemed to have been a bricked closet, now half destroyed and in ruins. She turned to descend, when a strange sound from Uncle Sylvester's room struck her ear. It was the sound of tapping on the floor close to the partition, within a foot of where she was standing. At the same moment there was a decided movement of the plank of the flooring beneath the partition : it began to slide slowly, and then was gradually withdrawn into the room. With prompt presence of mind, she instantly extinguished her candle and drew herself breathlessly against the partition.

When the plank was entirely withdrawn, a ray of light slipped through the opening, revealing the bare rafters of the floor, and a hand and arm inserted under the partition, groping as if towards the bricked closet. As the fingers of the exploring hand were widely extended, Marie had no difficulty in recognizing on one of them a peculiar signet ring which Uncle Sylvester wore. A swift impulse seized her. To the audacious Marie impulse and action were the same thing. Bending stealthily over the aperture, she suddenly snatched the ring from the extended finger. The hand was quickly withdrawn with a start and uncontrolled exclamation, and she availed herself of that instant to glide rapidly down the stairs.

She regained her room stealthily, having the satisfaction a moment later of hearing Uncle Sylvester's door open and the sound of his footsteps in the corridor. But he was evidently unable to discover any outer ingress to the inclosure, or believed the loss of his ring an accident, for he presently returned. Meantime, what was she to do?

Tell Kitty of her discovery, and show the ring? No — not yet! Oddly enough, now that she had the ring, taken from his wicked finger in the very act, she found it as difficult as ever to believe in his burglarious design. She must wait. The mischief — if there had been mischief — was done ; the breaking in of the bricked closet was, from the appearance of the ruins, a bygone act. Could it have been some youthful escapade of Uncle Sylvester's, the scene of which he was revisiting as criminals are compelled to do? And had there been anything taken from the closet — or was its destruction a part of the changes in the old house? How could she find out without asking Kitty? There was one way. She remembered that Mr. Gunn had once shown a great deal of interest to Kitty about the old homestead, and even of old Mr. Lane's woodland cabin. She would ask *him.* It was a friendly act, for Kitty had not of late been very kind to him.

The opportunity presented itself at dusk, as Mr. Gunn, somewhat abstracted, stood apart at the drawing-room window. Marie hoped he had enjoyed himself while skating ; her stupid cold had kept her indoors. She

had amused herself rambling about the old
homestead ; it was such a queer place, so
full of old nooks and corners and unaccount-
able spaces. Just the place, she would
think, where old treasures might have been
stored. Eh ?

Mr. Gunn had not spoken — he had only
coughed. But in the darkness his eyes were
fixed angrily on her face. Without observing it, she went on. She knew he was interested in the old house ; she had heard him
talk to Kitty about it : had Kitty ever said
anything about some old secret hoarding
place ?

No, certainly not ! And she was mistaken,
he never was interested in the house ! He
could not understand what had put that idea
in her head ! Unless it was this ridiculous,
shady stranger in the guise of an uncle
whom they had got there. It was like his
affectation !

" Oh, dear, no," said Marie, with unmistakable truthfulness, " *he* did not say anything. But," with sudden inconsistent ag-
gression, " is *that* the way you speak to
Kitty of her uncle ? "

Really he did n't know — he was joking
only, and he was afraid he must just now

ask her to excuse him. He had received letters that made it possible that he might be called suddenly to New York at any moment. Marie stared. It was evident that he had proposed to Kitty and been rejected! But she was no nearer her discovery.

Nor was there the least revelation in the calm, half-bored, yet good-humored presence of the wicked uncle at dinner. So indifferent did he seem, not only to his own villainy but even to the loss it had entailed, that she had a wild impulse to take the ring from her pocket and display it on her own finger before him then and there. But the conviction that he would in some way be equal to the occasion prevented her. The dinner passed off with some constraint, no doubt emanating from the conscious Kitty and Gunn. Nevertheless, when they had returned to the drawing-room, Gabriel rubbed his hands expectantly.

"I prevailed on Sylvester this morning to promise to tell us some of his experiences — something *complete* and satisfactory this time. Eh?"

Uncle Sylvester, warming his cold blood before the fire, looked momentarily forgetful and — disappointing. Cousins Jane and Emma shrugged their shoulders.

"Eh," said Uncle Sylvester absently, "er — er — oh yes! Well" (more cheerfully), "about what, eh?"

"Let it be," said Marie pointedly, fixing her black magnetic eyes on the wicked stranger, "let it be something about the *discovery* of gold, or a buried *treasure hoard*, or a robbery."

To her intense disgust Uncle Sylvester, far from being discomfited or confused, actually looked pleased, and his gray eyes thawed slightly.

"Certainly," he said. "Well, then! Down on the San Joaquin River there was an old chap — one of the earliest settlers — in fact, he'd come on from Oregon before the gold discovery. His name, dear me!" — continued Uncle Sylvester, with an effort of memory and apparently beginning already to lose his interest in the story — "was — er — Flint."

As Uncle Sylvester paused here, Cousin Jane broke in impatiently. "Well, that's not an uncommon name. There was an old carpenter here in your father's time who was called Flint."

"Yes," said Uncle Sylvester languidly. "But there is, or was, something uncommon about it — and that's the point of the story, for in the old time Flint and Gunn were of the same stock."

"Is this a Californian joke?" said Gunn, with a forced smile on his flushed face. "If so, spare me, for it's an old one."

"It's much older *history*, Mr. Gunn," said Uncle Sylvester blandly, "which I remember from a boy. When the first Flint traded near Sault Sainte Marie, the Canadian *voyageurs* literally translated his name into Pierre à Fusil, and he went by that name always. But when the English superseded the French in numbers and language the name was literally translated back again into 'Peter Gunn,' which his descendants bear."

"A labored form of the old joke," said Gunn, turning contemptuously away.

"But the story," said Cousins Jane and Emma. "The story of the gold discovery — never mind the names."

"Excuse me," said Uncle Sylvester, placing his hand in the breast of his coat with a delightful exaggeration of offended dignity. "But, doubts having been cast upon my preliminary statement, I fear I must decline proceeding further." Nevertheless, he smiled unblushingly at Miss Du Page as he followed Gunn from the room.

The next morning those who had noticed the strained relations of Miss Kitty and Mr. Gunn were not surprised that the latter was recalled on pressing business to New York by the first train; but it was a matter of some astonishment to Gabriel Lane and Marie du Page that Uncle Sylvester should have been up early, and actually accompanied that gentleman as far as the station! Indeed, the languid explorer and gold-seeker exhibited remarkable activity, and, clad in a rough tourist suit, announced, over the breakfast-table, his intention of taking a long tramp through the woods, which he had not revisited since a boy. To this end he had even provided himself with a small knapsack, and for once realized Kitty's ideal of his character.

"Don't go too far," said Gabriel, "for, although the cold has moderated, the barometer is falling fast, and there is every appearance of snow. Take care you are not caught in one of our blizzards."

"But *you* are all going on the lake to skate!" protested Uncle Sylvester.

"Yes; for the very reason that it may be

our last chance ; but should it snow we shall be nearer home than you may be."

Nevertheless, when it came on to snow, as Gabriel had predicted, the skating party was by no means so near home as he had imagined. A shrewd keenness and some stimulating electric condition of the atmosphere had tempted the young people far out on the lake, and they had ignored the first fall of fine grayish granulations that swept along the icy surface like little puffs of dust or smoke. Then the fall grew thicker, the gray sky contracted, the hurrying flakes, dashed against them by a fierce northwester, were larger, heavier, and seemed an almost palpable force that held them back. Their skates, already clogged with drift, were beginning to be useless. The bare wind-swept spaces were becoming rarer ; they could only stumble on blindly towards the nearest shore. Nor when they reached it were they yet safe ; they could scarcely stand against the still increasing storm that was fast obliterating the banks and stretch of meadow beyond. Their only hope of shelter was the range of woods that joined the hill. Holding hands in single file, the little party, consisting of Kitty, Marie, and Cousins Jane and Emma — stout-hearted Gabriel leading and Cousin John bringing up the rear — at last succeeded in reaching it, and were rejoiced to find themselves near old Lane's half-ruined cabin. To their added joy and astonishment, whiffs of whirling smoke were issuing from the crumbling chimney. They ran to the crazy door, pushed aside its weak fastening, and found — Uncle Sylvester calmly enjoying a pipe before a blazing fire. A small pickaxe and crowbar were lying upon a mound of freshly turned earth beside the chimney, where the rotten flooring had been torn up.

The tumultuous entrance of the skating party required no explanation; but when congratulations had been exchanged, the wet snow shaken off, and they had drawn round the fire, curious eyes were cast upon the solitary occupant and the pile of earth and débris before him.

"I believe," said Gabriel laughingly, "that you have been so bored here that you have actually played at gold-hunting for amusement."

Uncle Sylvester took the pipe from his mouth and nodded.

"It's a common diversion of yours," said Marie audaciously.

Uncle Sylvester smiled sweetly.

"And have you been successful *this time?*" asked Marie.

"I got the color."

"Eh?"

Uncle Sylvester rose and placed himself with his back to the fire, gently surveying the assembled group.

"I was interrupted in a story of gold-digging last evening," he said blandly. "How far had I got?"

"You were down on the San Joaquin River in the spring of '50, with a chap named Flint," chorused Cousins Jane and Emma promptly.

"Ah! yes," said Uncle Sylvester. "Well, in those days there was a scarcity of money in the diggings. Gold dust there was in plenty, but no *coin*. You can fancy it was a bother to weigh out a pinch of dust every time you wanted a drink of whiskey or a pound of flour; but there was no other legal tender. Pretty soon, however, a lot of gold and silver pieces found their way into circulation in our camp and the camps around us. They were foreign — old French and English coins. Here's one of them that I kept." He took from his pocket a gold coin and handed it to Gabriel.

Lane rose to his feet with an exclamation : " Why, this is like the louis-d'or that grandfather saved through the war and gave to father."

Uncle Sylvester took the coin back, placed it in his left eye, like a monocle, and winked gravely at the company.

"It is the *same!*" he went on quietly. " I was interested, for I had a good memory, and I remembered that, as a boy, grandfather had shown me one of those coins and told me he was keeping them for old Jules du Page, who did n't believe in banks and bank-notes. Well, I traced them to a trader called Flint, who was shipping gold dust from Stockton to Peter Gunn & Sons, in New York."

" To whom ? " asked Gabriel quickly.

" Old Gunn — the father of your friend ! " said Uncle Sylvester blandly. " We talked the matter over on our way to the station this morning. Well, to return. Flint only said that he had got them from a man called Thompson, who had got them from somebody else in exchange for goods. A year or two afterwards this same Thompson happened to be frozen up with me in Star vation Camp. When he thought he was dying he confessed that he had been bribed by Flint to say what he had said, but that he believed the coins were stolen. Meantime, Flint had disappeared. Other things claimed my attention. I had quite forgotten him, until one night, five years afterwards, I blundered into a deserted mining-camp, by falling asleep on my mule, who carried me across a broken flume, but — I think I told you that story already."

"You never finished it," said Cousin Jane sharply.

"Let me do so now, then. I was really saved by some Indians, who took me for a spirit up aloft there in the moonlight and spread the alarm. The first white man they brought me was a wretched drunkard known to the boys as ' Old Fusil,' or ' Fusel Oil,' who went into delirium tremens at the sight of me. Well, who do you suppose he turned out to be ? Flint ! Flint played out and ruined ! Cast off and discarded by his relations in New York — the foundation of whose fortunes he had laid by the villainy they had accepted and condoned. For Flint, as the carpenter of the old homestead, had discovered the existence of a bricked closet in the wall of father's study, partitioned it off so that he could break into it without detection and rifle it at his leisure, and who had thus carried off that part of grandfather's hoard which father had concealed there. He knew it could never be missed by the descendants. But, through haste or ignorance, he *did not touch the papers* and documents also hidden there. And *they* told of the existence of grandfather's second *cache*, or hiding-place, beneath this hearth, and were left for me to discover."

He coolly relit his pipe, fixed his eyes on Marie without apparently paying attention to the breathless scrutiny of the others, and went on : " Flint, *alias* Pierre à Fusil, *alias* Gunn, died a maniac. I resolved to test the truth of his story. I came here. I knew the old homestead, as a boy who had wandered over every part of it, far better than you, Gabriel, or any one. The elder Gunn had only heard of it through the criminal disclosure of his relative, and only wished to absorb it through his son in time, and thus obliterate all trace of Flint's outrage. I recognized the room perfectly — thanks to our dear Kitty, who had taken up the carpet, which thus disclosed the loose plank before the closet that was hidden by the partition. Under pretext of rearranging the room—for which Kitty will forgive me—I spent the day behind a locked door, making my way through the partition. There I found the rifled closet, but the papers intact. They contained a full description of the sum taken by Flint, and also of a larger sum buried in a cask beside this chimney. I had just finished unearthing it a few moments before you came. I had at first hoped to offer it to the family as a Christmas gift to-morrow, but"— He stopped and sucked slowly at his pipe.

"We anticipated you," said Gabriel laughing.

"No," said Uncle Sylvester coolly. "But because it don't happen to belong to *you* at all! According to the paper I have in my pocket, which is about as legal a document as I ever saw, it is father's free gift to Miss Marie du Page."

Kitty threw her arms around her white and breathless friend with a joyful cry, and honest Gabriel's face shone with unselfish gratification.

"For yourself, my dear Gabriel, you must be satisfied with the fact that Messrs. Peter Gunn & Sons will take back your wildcat stock at the price you paid for it. It is the price they pay for their share in this little transaction, as I had the honor of pointing out to Mr. Gunn on our way to the station this morning."

"Then you think that young Mr. Gunn knew that Flint was his relation, and that he had stolen father's money," said Kitty, "and that Mr. Gunn only wanted to " — She stopped, with flashing eyes.

"I think he would have liked to have made an arrangement, my dear, that would keep the secret and the property in the family," said Uncle Sylvester. "But I don't think he suspected the existence of the second treasure here."

"And then, sir," said Cousin Jane, "it appears that all these wretched, unsatisfactory scraps of stories you were telling us were nothing after all but " —

"My way of telling *this* one," said Uncle Sylvester.

As the others were eagerly gathering around the unearthed treasure, Marie approached him timidly, all her audacity gone, tears in her eyes, and his ring held hesitatingly between her fingers. "How can I thank you — and how *can* you ever forgive me ? "

" Well," said Uncle Sylvester, gazing at her critically, " you might keep the ring to think over it."

A PHYLLIS OF THE SIERRAS.

CONTENTS.

A PHYLLIS OF THE SIERRAS.

CHAPTER I.

WHERE the great highway of the Sierras nears the summit, and the pines begin to show sterile reaches of rock and waste in their drawn-up files, there are signs of occasional departures from the main road, as if the weary traveller had at times succumbed to the long ascent, and turned aside for rest and breath again. The tired eyes of many a dusty passenger on the old overland coach have gazed wistfully on those sylvan openings, and imagined recesses of primeval shade and virgin wilderness in their dim perspectives. Had he descended, however, and followed one of these diverging paths, he would have come upon some rude wagon track, or "log-slide," leading from a clearing on the slope, or the ominous saw-mill, half hidden in the forest it was slowly decimating. The woodland hush might have been broken by the sound of water passing over some unseen dam in the hollow, or the hiss of escaping steam and throb of an invisible engine in the covert.

Such, at least, was the experience of a young fellow of five-and-twenty, who, knapsack on back and stick in hand, had turned aside from the highway and entered the woods one pleasant afternoon in July. But he was evidently a deliberate pedestrian, and not a recent deposit of the proceeding stage-coach; and although his stout walking-shoes were covered with dust, he had neither the habitual slouch and slovenliness of the tramp, nor the hurried fatigue and growing negligence of and involuntary wayfarer. His clothes, which were strong and serviceable, were better fitted for their present usage than the ordinary garments of the Californian travellers, which were too apt to be either above or below their requirements. But perhaps the stranger's greatest claim to originality was the absence of any weapon in his equipment. He carried neither rifle nor gun in his hand, and his narrow leathern belt was empty of either knife or revolver.

A half-mile from the main road, which seemed to him to have dropped out of sight the moment he had left it, he came upon a half-cleared area, where the hastily-cut stumps of pines, of irregular height, bore an odd resemblance to the broken columns of some vast and ruined temple. A few fallen shafts, denuded of their bark and tessellated branches, sawn into symmetrical cylinders, lay beside the stumps, and lent themselves to the illusion. But the freshly-cut chips, so damp that they still clung in layers to each other as they had fallen from the axe, and the stumps themselves, still wet and viscous from their drained life-blood, were redolent of an odor of youth and freshness.

The young man seated himself on one of the logs and deeply inhaled the sharp balsamic fragrance—albeit with a slight cough and a later hurried respiration. This, and a certain drawn look about his upper lip, seemed to indicate, in spite of his strength and color, some pulmonary weakness. He, however, rose after a moment's rest with undiminished energy and cheerfulness, readjusted his knapsack, and began to lightly pick his way across the fallen timber. A few paces on, the muffled whir of machinery became more audible, with the lazy, monotonous command of "Gee thar," from some unseen ox-driver. Presently, the slow, deliberately-swaying heads of a team of oxen emerged from the bushes, followed by the clanking chain of the "skids" of sawn planks, which they were ponderously dragging with that ostentatious submissiveness peculiar to their species. They had nearly passed him when there was a sudden hitch in the procession. From where he stood he could see that a projecting plank had struck a pile of chips and become partly imbedded in it. To run to the obstruction and, with a few dexterous strokes and the leverage of his stout stick, dislodge the plank was the work not only of the moment but of an evidently energetic hand. The teamster looked back and merely nodded his appreciation, and with a "Gee up! Out of that, now!" the skids moved on.

"Much obliged, there!" said a hearty voice, as if supplementing the teamster's imperfect acknowledgment.

The stranger looked up. The voice came from the open, sashless, shutterless window of a rude building—a mere shell of boards and beams half hidden in the still leafy covert before him. He had completely overlooked it in his approach, even as he had ignored the nearer throbbing of the machinery, which was so violent as to impart a decided tremor to the slight edifice, and to shake the speaker so strongly that he was obliged while speaking to steady himself by the sashless frame of the window at which he stood. He had a face of good-natured and alert intelligence, a master's independence and authority of manner, in spite of his blue jean overalls and flannel shirt.

"Don't mention it," said the stranger, smiling with equal but more deliberate good-humor. Then, seeing that his interlocutor still lingered a hospitable moment in spite of his quick eyes and the jarring impatience of the machinery, he added hesitatingly, "I fancy I've wandered off the track a bit. Do you know a Mr. Bradley—somewhere here?"

The stranger's hesitation seemed to be more from some habitual conscientiousness of statement than awkwardness. The man in the window replied, "I'm Bradley."

"Ah! Thank you: I've a letter for you —somewhere. Here it is." He produced a note from his breast-pocket. Bradley stooped to a sitting posture in the window. "Pitch it up." It was thrown and caught cleverly. Bradley opened it, read it hastily, smiled and nodded, glanced behind him as if to implore further delay from the impatient machinery, leaned perilously from the window, and said,—

"Look here! Do you see that silver-fir straight ahead?"

"Yes."

"A little to the left there's a trail. Follow it and skirt along the edge of the canyon until you see my house. Ask for my wife—that's Mrs. Bradley—and give her your letter. Stop!" He drew a carpenter's pencil from his pocket, scrawled two or three words across the open sheet and tossed it back to the stranger. "See you at tea! Excuse me—Mr. Mainwaring— we're short-handed—and—the engine—" But here he disappeared suddenly.

Without glancing at the note again, the stranger quietly replaced it in his pocket, and struck out across the fallen trunks towards the silver-fir. He quickly found the trail indicated by Bradley, although it was faint and apparently worn by a single pair of feet as a shorter and private cut from some more travelled path. It was well for the stranger that he had a keen eye or he would have lost it; it was equally fortunate that he had a mountaineering instinct, for a sudden profound deepening of the blue mist seen dimly through the leaves before him caused him to slacken his steps. The trail bent abruptly to the right; a gulf fully two thousand feet deep was at his feet! It was the Great Canyon.

At the first glance it seemed so narrow that a rifle-shot could have crossed its tranquil depths; but a second look at the comparative size of the trees on the opposite mountain convinced him of his error. A nearer survey of the abyss also showed him that instead of its walls being perpendicular they were made of successive ledges or terraces to the valley below. Yet the air was so still, and the outlines so clearly cut, that they might have been only the reflections of the mountains around him cast upon the placid mirror of a lake. The spectacle arrested him, as it arrested all men, by some occult power beyond the mere attraction of beauty or magnitude; even the teamster never passed it without the tribute of a stone or broken twig tossed into its immeasurable profundity.

Reluctantly leaving the spot, the stranger turned with the trail that now began to skirt its edge. This was no easy matter, as the undergrowth was very thick, and the foliage dense to the perilous brink of the precipice. He walked on, however, wondering why Bradley had chosen so circuitous and dangerous a route to his house, which naturally would be some distance back from the canyon. At the end of ten minutes' struggling through the "brush," the trail became vague, and, to all appearances, ended. Had he arrived? The thicket was as dense as before; through the interstices of leaf and spray he could see the blue void of the canyon at his side, and he even fancied that the foliage ahead of him was more symmetrical and less irregular, and was touched here and there with faint bits of color. To complete his utter mystification, a woman's voice, very fresh, very youthful, and by no means un-

musical, rose apparently from the circum-
ambient air. He looked hurriedly to the
right and left, and even hopelessly into the
trees above him.

"Yes," said the voice, as if renewing a
suspended conversation, "it was too funny
for anything. There were the two Missouri
girls from Skinner's, with their auburn
hair ringleted, my dear, like the old
'Books of Beauty'—in white frocks and
sashes of an unripe greenish yellow, that
puckered up your mouth like persimmons.
One of them was speechless from good be-
havior, and the other—well! the other was
so energetic she called out the figures before the fiddler did, and shrieked to my
vis-à-vis to dance up to the entire stranger
—meaning *me,* if you please."

The voice appeared to come from the
foliage that overhung the canyon, and the
stranger even fancied he could detect
through the shimmering leafy veil something that moved monotonously to and fro.
Mystified and impatient, he made a hurried stride forward, his foot struck a
wooden step, and the next moment the
mystery was made clear. He had almost
stumbled upon the end of a long veranda

that projected over the abyss before a low, modern dwelling, till then invisible, nestling on its very brink. The symmetrically-trimmed foliage he had noticed were the luxuriant Madeira vines that hid the rude pillars of the veranda; the moving object was a rocking-chair, with its back towards the intruder, that disclosed only the brown hair above, and the white skirts and small slippered feet below, of a seated female figure. In the mean time, a second voice from the interior of the house had replied to the figure in the chair, who was evidently the first speaker:—

"It must have been very funny; but as long as Jim is always bringing somebody over from the mill, I don't see how *I* can go to those places. You were lucky, my dear, to escape from the new Division Superintendent last night; he was insufferable to Jim with his talk of his friend the San Francisco millionaire, and to me with his cheap society airs. I do hate a provincial fine gentleman."

The situation was becoming embarrassing to the intruder. At the apparition of the woman, the unaffected and simple directness he had previously shown in his equally abrupt contact with Bradley had fled utterly; confused by the awkwardness of his arrival, and shocked at the idea of overhearing a private conversation, he stepped hurriedly on the veranda.

"Well? go on!" said the second voice impatiently. "Well, who else was there? *What* did you say? I don't hear you. What's the matter?"

The seated figure had risen from her chair, and turned a young and pretty face somewhat superciliously towards the stranger, as she said in a low tone to her unseen auditor, "Hush! there is somebody here."

The young man came forward with an awkwardness that was more boyish than rustic. His embarrassment was not lessened by the simultaneous entrance from the open door of a second woman, apparently as young as and prettier than the first.

"I trust you'll excuse me for—for—being so wretchedly stupid," he stammered, "but I really thought, you know, that—that—I was following the trail to—to—the front of the house, when I stumbled in—in here."

Long before he had finished, both women, by some simple feminine intuition, were relieved and even prepossessed by his voice and manner. They smiled graciously. The later-comer pointed to the empty chair. But with his habit of pertinacious conscientiousness the stranger continued, "It was regularly stupid, wasn't it?—and I ought to have known better. I should have turned back and gone away when I found out what an ass I was likely to be, but I was—afraid—you know, of alarming you by the noise."

"Won't you sit down?" said the second lady, pleasantly.

"Oh, thanks! I've a letter here—I"—he transferred his stick and hat to his left hand as he felt in his breast-pocket with his right. But the action was so awkward that the stick dropped on the veranda. Both women made a movement to restore it to its embarrassed owner, who, however, quickly anticipated them. "Pray don't mind it," he continued, with accelerated breath and heightened color. "Ah, here's the letter!" He produced the note Bradley had returned to him. "It's mine, in fact —that is, I brought it to Mr. Bradley. He said I was to give it to—to—to—Mrs. Bradley." He paused, glancing embarrassedly from the one to the other.

"I'm Mrs. Bradley," said the prettiest one, with a laugh. He handed her the letter. It ran as follows:—

"DEAR BRADLEY—Put Mr. Mainwaring through as far as he wants to go, or hang him up at The Lookout, just as he likes. The Bank's behind him, and his hat's chalked all over the Road; but he don't care much about being on velvet. That ain't his style—and you'll like him. He's somebody's son in England. B."

Mrs. Bradley glanced simply at the first sentence. "Pray sit down, Mr. Mainwaring," she said gently; "or, rather, let me first introduce my cousin—Miss Macy."

"Thanks," said Mainwaring, with a bow to Miss Macy, "but I—I—I—think," he added conscientiously, "you did not notice that your husband had written something across the paper."

Mrs. Bradley smiled, and glanced at her husband's indorsement—"All right. Wade in." "It's nothing but Jim's slang," she said, with a laugh and a slightly heightened color. "He ought not to have sent you by that short cut; it's a bother, and even dangerous for a stranger. If you had come directly to *us* by the road, without making your first call at the mill," she added, with a touch of coquetry, "you would have had a pleasanter walk, and seen *us* sooner. I suppose, however, you got off the stage at the mill?"

"I was not on the coach," said Mainwaring, unfastening the strap of his knapsack. "I walked over from Lone Pine Flat."

"Walked!" echoed both women in simultaneous astonishment.

"Yes," returned Mainwaring simply, laying aside his burden and taking the proffered seat. "It's a very fine bit of country."

"Why, it's fifteen miles," said Mrs. Bradley, glancing horror-stricken at her cousin. "How dreadful! And to think Jim could have sent you a horse to Lone Pine. Why, you must be dead!"

"Thanks, I'm all right! I rather enjoyed it, you know."

"But," said Miss Macy, glancing wonderingly at his knapsack, "you must want something, a change—or some refreshment —after fifteen miles."

"Pray don't disturb yourself," said Mainwaring, rising hastily, but not quickly enough to prevent the young girl from slipping past him into the house, whence she rapidly returned with a decanter and glasses.

"Perhaps Mr. Mainwaring would prefer to go into Jim's room and wash his hands and put on a pair of slippers?" said Mrs. Bradley, with gentle concern.

"Thanks, no. I really am not tired. I sent some luggage yesterday by the coach to the Summit Hotel," he said, observing the women's eyes still fixed upon his knapsack. "I dare say I can get them if I want them. I've got a change here," he continued, lifting the knapsack as if with a sudden sense of its incongruity with its surroundings, and depositing it on the end of the veranda.

"Do let it remain where it is," said Mrs. Bradley, greatly amused, "and pray sit still and take some refreshment. You'll make yourself ill after your exertions," she added, with a charming assumption of matronly solicitude.

"But I'm not at all deserving of your sympathy," said Mainwaring, with a laugh. "I'm awfully fond of walking, and my usual constitutional isn't much under this."

"Perhaps you were stronger than you are now," said Mrs. Bradley, gazing at him with a frank curiosity that, however, brought a faint deepening of color to his cheek.

"I dare say you're right," he said suddenly, with an apologetic smile. "I quite forgot that I'm a sort of an invalid, you know, travelling for my health. I'm not very strong here," he added, lightly tapping his chest, that now, relieved of the bands of his knapsack, appeared somewhat thin and hollow in spite of his broad shoulders. His voice, too, had become less clear and distinct.

Mrs. Bradley, who was still watching him, here rose potentially. "You ought to take more care of yourself," she said. "You should begin by eating this biscuit, drinking that glass of whiskey, and making yourself more comfortable in Jim's room until we can get the spare room fixed a little."

"But I am not to be sent to bed—am I?" asked Mainwaring, in half-real, half-amused consternation.

"I'm not so sure of that," said Mrs. Bradley, with playful precision. "But for the present we'll let you off with a good wash and a nap afterwards in that rocking-chair, while my cousin and I make some little domestic preparations. You see," she added with a certain proud humility, "we've got only one servant—a Chinaman, and there are many things we can't leave to him."

The color again rose in Mainwaring's cheek, but he had tact enough to reflect that any protest or hesitation on his part at that moment would only increase the difficulties of his gentle entertainers. He allowed himself to be ushered into the house by Mrs. Bradley, and shown to her husband's room, without perceiving that Miss Macy had availed herself of his absence to run to the end of the veranda, mischievously try to lift the discarded knapsack to her own pretty shoulder, but, failing, heroically stagger with it into the passage and softly deposit it at his door. This done, she pantingly rejoined her cousin in the kitchen.

"Well," said Mrs. Bradley, emphatically. *"Did* you ever? Walking fifteen miles for pleasure — and with such lungs!"

"And that knapsack!" added Louise Macy, pointing to the mark in her little palm where the strap had imbedded itself in the soft flesh.

"He's nice, though; isn't he?" said Mrs. Bradley, tentatively.

"Yes," said Miss Macy, "he isn't, certainly, one of those provincial fine gentlemen you object to. But *did* you see his shoes? I suppose they make the miles go quickly, or seem to measure less by comparison."

"They're probably more serviceable than those high-heeled things that Captain Greyson hops about in."

"But the Captain always rides—and rides very well—you know," said Louise, reflectively. There was a moment's pause.

"I suppose Jim will tell us all about him," said Mrs. Bradley, dismissing the subject, as she turned her sleeves back over her white arms, preparatory to grappling certain culinary difficulties.

"Jim," observed Miss Macy, shortly, "in my opinion, knows nothing more than his note says. That's like Jim."

"There's nothing more to know, really," said Mrs. Bradley, with a superior air. "He's undoubtedly the son of some Englishman of fortune, sent out here for his health."

"Hush!"

Miss Macy had heard a step in the passage. It halted at last, half irresolutely, before the open door of the kitchen, and the stranger appeared with an embarrassed air.

But in his brief absence he seemed to have completely groomed himself, and stood there, the impersonation of close-cropped, clean, and wholesome English young manhood. The two women appreciated it with cat-like fastidiousness.

"I beg your pardon; but really you're going to let a fellow do something for you," he said, "just to keep him from looking like a fool. I really can do no end of things, you know, if you'll try me. I've done some camping-out, and can cook as well as the next man."

The two women made a movement of smiling remonstrance, half coquettish, and half superior, until Mrs. Bradley, becoming conscious of her bare arms and the stranger's wandering eyes, colored faintly, and said with more decision:—

"Certainly not. You'd only be in the way. Besides, you need rest more than we do. Put yourself in the rocking-chair in the veranda, and go to sleep until Mr. Bradley comes."

Mainwaring saw that she was serious, and withdrew, a little ashamed at his familiarity into which his boyishness had betrayed him. But he had scarcely seated himself in the rocking-chair before Miss Macy appeared, carrying with both hands a large tin basin of unshelled peas.

"There," she said pantingly, placing her burden in his lap, "if you really want to help, there's something to do that isn't very fatiguing. You may shell these peas."

"*Shell* them—I beg pardon, but how?" he asked, with smiling earnestness.

"How? Why, I'll show you—look."

She frankly stepped beside him, so close that her full-skirted dress half encompassed him and the basin in a delicious confusion, and, leaning over his lap, with her left hand picked up a pea-cod, which, with a single movement of her charming little right thumb, she broke at the end, and stripped the green shallow of its tiny treasures.

He watched her with smiling eyes; her own, looking down on him, were very bright and luminous. "There; that's easy enough," she said, and turned away.

"But—one moment, Miss—Miss—?"

"Macy," said Louise.

"Where am I to put the shells?"

"Oh! throw them down there—there's room enough."

She was pointing to the canyon below. The veranda actually projected over its brink, and seemed to hang in mid air above it. Mainwaring almost mechanically threw his arm out to catch the incautious girl, who had stepped heedlessly to its extreme edge.

"How odd! Don't you find it rather dangerous here?" he could not help saying. "I mean—you might have had a railing that wouldn't intercept the view and yet be safe?"

"It's a fancy of Mr. Bradley's," returned the young girl carelessly. "It's all like this. The house was built on a ledge against the side of the precipice, and the road suddenly drops down to it."

"It's tremendously pretty, all the same, you know," said the young man thoughtfully, gazing, however, at the girl's rounded chin above him.

"Yes," she replied curtly. "But this isn't working. I must go back to Jenny. You can shell the peas until Mr. Bradley comes home. He won't be long."

She turned away, and reëntered the house. Without knowing why, he thought her withdrawal abrupt, and he was again feeling his ready color rise with the suspicion of either having been betrayed by the young girl's innocent fearlessness into some unpardonable familiarity, which she had quietly resented, or of feeling an ease and freedom in the company of these two women that were inconsistent with respect, and should be restrained.

He, however, began to apply himself to the task given to him with his usual conscientiousness of duty, and presently acquired a certain manual dexterity in the operation. It was "good fun" to throw the cast-off husks into the mighty unfathomable void before him, and watch them linger with suspended gravity in mid air for a moment—apparently motionless—

until they either lost themselves, a mere vanishing black spot in the thin ether, or slid suddenly at a sharp angle into unknown shadow. How deuced odd for him to be sitting here in this fashion! It would be something to talk of hereafter, and yet,—he stopped—it was not at all in the line of that characteristic adventure, uncivilized novelty, and barbarous freedom which for the last month he had sought and experienced. It was not at all like his meeting with the grizzly last week while wandering in a lonely canyon; not a bit in the line of his chance acquaintance with that notorious ruffian, Spanish Jack, or his witnessing with his own eyes that actual lynching affair at Angels. No! Nor was it at all characteristic, according to his previous ideas of frontier rural seclusion—as for instance the Pike County cabin of the family where he stayed one night, and where the handsome daughter asked him what his Christian name was. No! These two young women were very unlike her; they seemed really quite the equals of his family and friends in England,—perhaps more attractive,—and yet, yes, it was this very attractiveness that

alarmed his inbred social conservatism regarding women. With a man it was very
different; that alert, active, intelligent husband, instinct with the throbbing life of
his saw-mill, creator and worker in one,
challenged his unqualified trust and admiration.

He had become conscious for the last
minute or two of thinking rapidly and becoming feverishly excited; of breathing
with greater difficulty, and a renewed tendency to cough. The tendency increased
until he instinctively put aside the pan
from his lap and half rose. But even that
slight exertion brought on an accession of
coughing. He put his handkerchief to his
lips, partly to keep the sound from disturbing the women in the kitchen, partly
because of a certain significant taste in
his mouth which he unpleasantly remembered. When he removed the handkerchief
it was, as he expected, spotted with blood.
He turned quickly and reëntered the house
softly, regaining the bedroom without at-
tracting attention. An increasing faint-
ness here obliged him to lie down on the
bed until it should pass.

Everything was quiet. He hoped they

would not discover his absence from the
veranda until he was better; it was
deucedly awkward that he should have had
this attack just now—and after he had
made so light of his previous exertions.
They would think him an effeminate fraud,
these two bright, active women and that
alert, energetic man. A faint color came
into his cheek at the idea, and an uneasy
sense that he had been in some way foolishly imprudent about his health. Again,
they might be alarmed at missing him
from the veranda; perhaps he had better
have remained there; perhaps he ought to
tell them that he had concluded to take
their advice and lie down. He tried to
rise, but the deep blue chasm before the
window seemed to be swelling up to meet
him, the bed slowly sinking into its oblivious profundity. He knew no more.

He came to with the smell and taste of
some powerful volatile spirit, and the
vague vision of Mr. Bradley still standing
at the window of the mill and vibrating
with the machinery; this changed presently to a pleasant lassitude and lazy
curiosity as he perceived Mr. Bradley
smile and apparently slip from the window

of the mill to his bedside. "You're all right now," said Bradley, cheerfully.

He was feeling Mainwaring's pulse. Had he really been ill and was Bradley a doctor?

Bradley evidently saw what was passing in his mind. "Don't be alarmed," he said gayly. "I'm not a doctor, but I practise a little medicine and surgery on account of the men at the mill, and accidents, you know. You're all right now; you've lost a little blood: but in a couple of weeks in this air we'll have that tubercle healed, and you'll be as right as a trivet."

"In a couple of weeks!" echoed Mainwaring, in faint astonishment. "Why, I leave here to-morrow."

"You'll do nothing of the kind," said Mrs. Bradley, with smiling peremptoriness, suddenly slipping out from behind her husband. "Everything is all perfectly arranged. Jim has sent off messengers to your friends, so that if you can't come to them, they can come to you. You see you can't help yourself! If you *will* walk fifteen miles with such lungs, and then frighten people to death, you must abide by the consequences."

"You see the old lady has fixed you," said Bradley, smiling; "and she's the master here. Come, Mainwaring, you can send any other message you like, and have who and what you want here; but *here* you must stop for a while."

"But did I frighten you really?" stammered Mainwaring, faintly, to Mrs. Bradley.

"Frighten us!" said Mrs. Bradley. "Well, look there!"

She pointed to the window, which commanded a view of the veranda. Miss Macy had dropped into the vacant chair, with her little feet stretched out before her, her cheeks burning with heat and fire, her eyes partly closed, her straw hat hanging by a ribbon round her neck, her brown hair clinging to her ears and forehead in damp tendrils, and an enormous palm-leaf fan in each hand violently playing upon this charming picture of exhaustion and abandonment.

"She came tearing down to the mill, bare-backed on our half-broken mustang, about half an hour ago, to call me 'to help you,'" explained Bradley. "Heaven knows how she managed to do it!"

CHAPTER II.

The medication of the woods was not overestimated by Bradley. There was surely some occult healing property in that vast reservoir of balmy and resinous odors over which The Lookout beetled and clung, and from which at times the pure exhalations of the terraced valley seemed to rise. Under its remedial influence and a conscientious adherence to the rules of absolute rest and repose laid down for him, Mainwaring had no return of the hemorrhage. The nearest professional medical authority, hastily summoned, saw no reason for changing or for supplementing Bradley's intelligent and simple treatment, although astounded that the patient had been under no more radical or systematic cure than travel and exercise. The women especially were amazed that Mainwaring had taken "nothing for it," in their habitual experience of an unfettered pill-and-elixir-consuming democracy. In their knowledge of the thousand "panaceas" that filled the shelves of the general store, this singular abstention of their guest seemed to indicate a national peculiarity.

His bed was moved beside the low window, from which he could not only view the veranda but converse at times with its occupants, and even listen to the book which Miss Macy, seated without, read aloud to him. In the evening Bradley would linger by his couch until late, beguiling the tedium of his convalescence with characteristic stories and information which he thought might please the invalid. For Mainwaring, who had been early struck with Bradley's ready and cultivated intelligence, ended by shyly avoiding the discussion of more serious topics, partly because Bradley impressed him with a suspicion of his own inferiority, and partly because Mainwaring questioned the taste of Bradley's apparent exhibition of his manifest superiority. He learned accidentally that this mill-owner and backwoodsman was a college-bred man; but the practical application of that education to the ordinary affairs of life was new to the young Englishman's traditions, and

grated a little harshly on his feelings. He
would have been quite content if Bradley
had, like himself and fellows he knew,
undervalued his training, and kept his
gifts conservatively impractical. The
knowledge also that his host's education
naturally came from some provincial institution unlike Oxford and Cambridge may
have unconsciously affected his general
estimate. I say unconsciously, for his
strict conscientiousness would have rejected any such formal proposition.

Another trifle annoyed him. He could
not help noticing also that although Bradley's manner and sympathy were confidential and almost brotherly, he never made
any allusion to Mainwaring's own family
or connections, and, in fact, gave no indication of what he believed was the national curiosity in regard to strangers.
Somewhat embarrassed by this indifference, Mainwaring made the occasion of
writing some letters home an opportunity
for laughingly alluding to the fact that he
had made his mother and his sisters fully
aware of the great debt they owed the
household of The Lookout.

"They'll probably all send you a round

robin of thanks, except, perhaps, my next brother, Bob."

Bradley contented himself with a gesture of general deprecation, and did not ask *why* Mainwaring's young brother should contemplate his death with satisfaction. Nevertheless, some time afterwards Miss Macy remarked that it seemed hard that the happiness of one member of a family should depend upon a calamity to another. "As for instance ?" asked Mainwaring, who had already forgotten the circumstance. "Why, if you had died and your younger brother succeeded to the baronetcy, and become Sir Robert Mainwaring," responded Miss Macy, with precision. This was the first and only allusion to his family and prospective rank. On the other hand, he had —through naive and boyish inquiries, which seemed to amuse his entertainers— acquired, as he believed, a full knowledge of the history and antecedents of the Bradley household. He knew how Bradley had brought his young wife and her cousin to California and abandoned a lucrative law practice in San Francisco to take possession of this mountain mill and woodland,

which he had acquired through some professional service.

"Then you are a barrister really?" said
Mainwaring, gravely.

Bradley laughed. "I'm afraid I've had
more practice—though not as lucrative a
one—as surgeon or doctor."

"But you're regularly on the rolls, you
know; you're entered as Counsel, and all
that sort of thing?" continued Mainwaring, with great seriousness.

"Well, yes," replied Bradley, much
amused. "I'm afraid I must plead guilty
to that."

"It's not a bad sort of thing," said Mainwaring, naively, ignoring Bradley's amusement. "I've got a cousin who's gone in
for the law. Got out of the army to do it
—too. He's a sharp fellow."

"Then you *do* allow a man to try many
trades—over there," said Miss Macy, demurely.

"Yes, sometimes," said Mainwaring,
graciously, but by no means certain that
the case was at all analogous.

Nevertheless, as if relieved of certain
doubts of the conventional quality of his
host's attainments, he now gave himself up

to a very hearty and honest admiration of Bradley. "You know it's awfully kind of him to talk to a fellow like me who just pulled through, and never got any prizes at Oxford, and don't understand the half of these things," he remarked confidentially to Mrs. Bradley. "He knows more about the things we used to go in for at Oxford than lots of our men, and he's never been there. He's uncommonly clever."

"Jim was always very brilliant," returned Mrs. Bradley, indifferently, and with more than even conventionally polite wifely deprecation; "I wish he were more practical."

"Practical! Oh, I say, Mrs. Bradley! Why, a fellow that can go in among a lot of workmen and tell them just what to do —an all-round chap that can be independent of his valet, his doctor, and his—banker! By Jove—*that's* practical!"

"I mean," said Mrs. Bradley, coldly, "that there are some things that a gentleman ought not to be practical about nor independent of. Mr. Bradley would have done better to have used his talents in some more legitimate and established way."

Mainwaring looked at her in genuine

surprise. To his inexperienced observation Bradley's intelligent energy and, above all, his originality, ought to have been priceless in the eyes of his wife—the American female of his species. He felt that slight shock which most loyal or logical men feel when first brought face to face with the easy disloyalty and incomprehensible logic of the feminine affections. Here was a fellow, by Jove, that any woman ought to be proud of, and—and—he stopped blankly. He wondered if Miss Macy sympathized with her cousin.

Howbeit, this did not affect the charm of their idyllic life at The Lookout. The precipice over which they hung was as charming as ever in its poetic illusions of space and depth and color; the isolation of their comfortable existence in the tasteful yet audacious habitation, the pleasant routine of daily tasks and amusements, all tended to make the enforced quiet and inaction of his convalescence a lazy recreation. He was really improving; more than that, he was conscious of a certain satisfaction in this passive observation of novelty that was healthier and perhaps *truer* than his previous passion for adventure and that febrile

desire for change and excitement which he
now felt was a part of his disease. Nor
were incident and variety entirely absent
from this tranquil experience. He was one
day astonished at being presented by Bradley with copies of the latest English newspapers, procured from Sacramento, and he
equally astonished his host, after profusely
thanking him, by only listlessly glancing
at their columns. He estopped a proposed
visit from one of his influential countrymen ; in the absence of his fair entertainers at their domestic duties, he extracted
infinite satisfaction from Foo-Yup, the
Chinese servant, who was particularly detached for his service. From his invalid
coign of vantage at the window he was observant of all that passed upon the veranda, that al-fresco audience-room of The
Lookout, and he was good-humoredly conscious that a great many eccentric and
peculiar visitors were invariably dragged
thither by Miss Macy, and goaded into
characteristic exhibition within sight and
hearing of her guest, with a too evident
view, under the ostentatious excuse of extending his knowledge of national character or mischievously shocking him.

"When you are strong enough to stand Captain Gashweiler's opinions of the Established Church and Chinamen," said Miss Macy, after one of these revelations, "I'll get Jim to bring him here, for really he swears so outrageously that even in the broadest interests of international understanding and good-will neither Mrs. Bradley nor myself could be present."

On another occasion she provokingly lingered before his window for a moment with a rifle slung jauntily over her shoulder. "If you hear a shot or two don't excite yourself, and believe we're having a lynching case in the woods. It will be only me. There's some creature—confess, you expected me to say 'critter'—hanging round the barn. It may be a bear. Good-by." She missed the creature,— which happened to be really a bear,—much to Mainwaring's illogical satisfaction. "I wonder why," he reflected, with vague uneasiness, "she doesn't leave all that sort of thing to girls like that tow-headed girl at the blacksmith's."

It chanced, however, that this blacksmith's tow-headed daughter, who, it may be incidentally remarked, had the additional eccentricities of large black eyes and large white teeth, came to the fore in quite another fashion. Shortly after this, Mainwaring being able to leave his room and join the family board, Mrs. Bradley found it necessary to enlarge her domestic service, and arranged with her nearest neighbor, the blacksmith, to allow his daughter to come to The Lookout for a few days to "do the chores" and assist in the housekeeping, as she had on previous occasions. The day of her advent Bradley entered Mainwaring's room, and, closing the door mysteriously, fixed his blue eyes, kindling with mischief, on the young Englishman.

"You are aware, my dear boy," he began with affected gravity, "that you are now living in a land of liberty, where mere artificial distinctions are not known, and where Freedom from her mountain heights generally levels all social positions. I think you have graciously admitted that fact."

"I know I've been taking a tremendous lot of freedom with you and yours, old man, and it's a deuced shame," interrupted Mainwaring, with a faint smile.

"And that nowhere," continued Bradley, with immovable features, "does equality exist as perfectly as above yonder unfathomable abyss, where you have also, doubtless, observed the American eagle proudly soars and screams defiance."

"Then that was the fellow that kept me awake this morning, and made me wonder if I was strong enough to hold a gun again."

"That wouldn't have settled the matter," continued Bradley, imperturbably. "The case is simply this: Miss Minty Sharpe, that blacksmith's daughter, has once or twice consented, for a slight emolument, to assist in our domestic service for a day or two, and she comes back again to-day. Now, under the ægis of that noble bird whom your national instincts tempt you to destroy, she has on all previous occasions taken her meals with us, at the same table, on terms of perfect equality. She will naturally expect to do the same now. Mrs. Bradley thought it proper, therefore, to warn you, that, in case your health was not quite equal to this democratic simplicity, you could still dine in your room."

"It would be great fun—if Miss Sharpe won't object to my presence."

"But it must not be 'great fun,'" returned Bradley, more seriously; "for Miss Minty's perception of humor is probably as keen as yours, and she would be quick to notice it. And, so far from having any objection to you, I am inclined to think that we owe her consent to come to her desire of making your acquaintance."

"She will find my conduct most exemplary," said Mainwaring, earnestly.

"Let us hope so," concluded Bradley, with unabated gravity. "And, now that you have consented, let me add from my own experience that Miss Minty's lemonpies alone are worthy of any concession."

The dinner-hour came. Mainwaring, a little pale and interesting, leaning on the arm of Bradley, crossed the hall, and for the first time entered the dining-room of the house where he had lodged for three weeks. It was a bright, cheerful apartment, giving upon the laurels of the rocky hillside, and permeated, like the rest of the house, with the wholesome spice of the valley—an odor that, in its pure desiccating property, seemed to obliterate all flavor of alien human habitation, and even to dominate and etherealize the appetizing smell of the viands before them. The bare,

shining, planed, boarded walls appeared
to resent any decoration that might have
savored of dust, decay, or moisture. The
four large windows and long, open door,
set in scanty strips of the plainest spotless
muslin, framed in themselves pictures of
woods and rock and sky of limitless depth,
color, and distance, that made all other
adornment impertinent. Nature, invading
the room at every opening, had banished
Art from those neutral walls.

"It's like a picnic, with comfort," said
Mainwaring, glancing round him with boyish appreciation. Miss Minty was not yet
there; the Chinaman was alone in attendance. Mainwaring could not help whispering, half mischievously, to Louise,
"You draw the line at Chinamen, I suppose ?"

"*We* don't, but *he* does," answered the
young girl. "He considers us his social inferiors. But—hush!"

Minty Sharpe had just entered the room,
and was advancing with smiling confidence
towards the table. Mainwaring was a little
startled; he had seen Minty in a holland
sun-bonnet and turned up skirt crossing
the veranda, only a moment before; in the

brief instant between the dishing-up of
dinner and its actual announcement she
had managed to change her dress, put on
a clean collar, cuffs, and a large jet brooch,
and apply some odorous unguent to her
rebellious hair. Her face, guiltless of
powder or cold cream, was still shining
with the healthy perspiration of her last
labors as she promptly took the vacant
chair beside Mainwaring.

"Don't mind me, folks," she said cheerfully, resting her plump elbow on the table,
and addressing the company generally, but
gazing with frank curiosity into the face
of the young man at her side. "It was a
keen jump, I tell yer, to get out of my old
duds inter these, and look decent inside o'
five minutes. But I reckon I ain't kept
yer waitin' long—least of all this yer sick
stranger. But you're looking pearter than
you did. You're wonderin' like ez not
where I ever saw ye before?" she continued, laughing. "Well, I'll tell you. Last
week! I'd kem over yer on a chance of
seein' Jenny Bradley, and while I was
meanderin' down the veranda I saw you
lyin' back in your chair by the window
drowned in sleep, like a baby. Lordy! I

mout hev won a pair o' gloves, but I reckoned you were Loo's game, and not mine."

The slightly constrained laugh which
went round the table after Miss Minty's
speech was due quite as much to the faint
flush that had accented Mainwaring's own
smile as to the embarrassing remark itself.
Mrs. Bradley and Miss Macy exchanged
rapid glances.   Bradley, who alone retained his composure, with a slight flicker
of amusement in the corner of his eye and
nostril, said quickly: "You see, Mainwaring, how nature stands ready to help your
convalescence at every turn.   If Miss
Minty had only followed up her healing
opportunity, your cure would have been
complete."

"Ye mout hev left some o' that pretty
talk for *him* to say," said Minty, taking
up her knife and fork with a slight shrug,
"and you needn't call me *Miss* Minty
either, jest because there's kempeny present."

"I hope you won't look upon me as company, Minty, or I shall be obliged to call
you 'Miss' too," said Mainwaring, unexpectedly regaining his usual frankness.

Bradley's face brightened; Miss Minty

raised her black eyes from her plate with still broader appreciation.

"There's nothin' mean about that," she said, showing her white teeth. "Well, what's *your* first name?"

"Not as pretty as yours, I'm afraid. It's Frank."

"No it ain't, it's Francis! You reckon to be Sir Francis some day," she said gravely. "You can't play any Frank off on me. You wouldn't do it on *her*," she added, indicating Louise with her elbow.

A momentous silence followed. The particular form that Minty's vulgarity had taken had not been anticipated by the two other women. They had, not unreasonably, expected some original audacity or *gaucherie* from the blacksmith's daughter, which might astonish yet amuse their guest, and condone for the situation forced upon them. But they were not prepared for a playfulness that involved themselves in a ridiculous indiscretion. Mrs. Bradley's eyes sought her husband's meaningly; Louise's pretty mouth hardened. Luckily the cheerful cause of it suddenly jumped up from the table, and saying that the stranger was starving, insisted upon

bringing a dish from the other side and
helping him herself plentifully. Mainwaring rose gallantly to take the dish from
her hand, a slight scuffle ensued which
ended in the young man being forced down
in his chair by the pressure of Minty's
strong plump hand on his shoulder.
"There," she said, "ye kin mind your
dinner now, and I reckon we'll give the
others a chance to chip into the conversation," and at once applied herself to the
plate before her.

The conversation presently became general, with the exception that Minty, more
or less engrossed by professional anxiety
in the quality of the dinner and occasional
hurried visits to the kitchen, briefly answered the few polite remarks which
Mainwaring felt called upon to address to
her. Nevertheless, he was conscious,
malgré her rallying allusions to Miss
Macy, that he felt none of the vague yet
half pleasant anxiety with which Louise
was beginning to inspire him. He felt at
ease in Minty's presence, and believed,
rightly or wrongly, that she understood
him as well as he understood her. And
there were certainly points in common be-

tween his two hostesses and their humbler
though proud dependent. The social evo-
lution of Mrs. Bradley and Louise Macy
from some previous Minty was neither remote nor complete; the self-sufficient independence, ease, and quiet self-assertion
were alike in each. The superior position
was still too recent and accidental for
either to resent or criticise qualities that
were common to both. At least, this was
what he thought when not abandoning
himself to the gratification of a conva-
lescent appetite; to the presence of two
pretty women, the sympathy of a genial
friend, the healthy intoxication of the white
sunlight that glanced upon the pine walls,
the views that mirrored themselves in the
open windows, and the pure atmosphere in
which The Lookout seemed to swim.
Wandering breezes of balm and spice
lightly stirred the flowers on the table, and
seemed to fan his hair and forehead with
softly healing breath. Looking up in an
interval of silence, he caught Bradley's
gray eyes fixed upon him with a subdued
light of amusement and affection, as of an
elder brother regarding a schoolboy's
boisterous appetite at some feast. Main-

waring laid down his knife and fork with
a laughing color, touched equally by Bradley's fraternal kindliness and the consciousness of his gastronomical powers.

"Hang it, Bradley; look here! I know
my appetite's disgraceful, but what can a
fellow do? In such air, with such viands
and such company! It's like the bees getting drunk on Hybla and Hymettus, you
know. I'm not responsible!"

"It's the first square meal I believe
you've really eaten in six months," said
Bradley, gravely. "I can't understand
why your doctor allowed you to run down
so dreadfully."

"I reckon you ain't as keerful of yourself, you Britishers, ez us," said Minty.
"Lordy! Why there's Pop invests in more
patent medicines in one day than you have
in two weeks, and he'd make two of you.
Mebbe your folks don't look after you
enough."

"I'm a splendid advertisement of what
your care and your medicines have done,"
said Mainwaring, gratefully, to Mrs. Bradley; "and if you ever want to set up a
'Cure' here, I'm ready with a ten-page testimonial."

"Have a care, Mainwaring," said Bradley, laughing, "that the ladies don't take you at your word. Louise and Jenny have been doing their best for the last year to get me to accept a flattering offer from a Sacramento firm to put up a hotel for tourists on the site of The Lookout. Why, I believe that they have already secretly in their hearts concocted a flaming prospectus of 'Unrivalled Scenery' and 'Health-giving Air,' and are looking forward to Saturday night hops on the piazza."

"Have you really, though?" said Mainwaring, gazing from the one to the other.

"We should certainly see more company than we do now, and feel a little less out of the world," said Louise, candidly. "There are no neighbors here—I mean the people at the Summit are not," she added, with a slight glance towards Minty.

"And Mr. Bradley would find it more profitable—not to say more suitable to a man of his position—than this wretched saw-mill and timber business," said Mrs. Bradley, decidedly.

Mainwaring was astounded; was it possible they considered it more dignified for a lawyer to keep a hotel than a saw-mill?

12 Bret Harte

Bradley, as if answering what was passing in his mind, said mischievously, "I'm not sure, exactly, what my position is, my dear, and I'm afraid I've declined the hotel on business principles. But, by the way, Mainwaring, I found a letter at the mill this morning from Mr. Richardson. He is about to pay us the distinguished honor of visiting The Lookout, solely on your account, my dear fellow."

"But I wrote him that I was much better, and it wasn't necessary for him to come," said Mainwaring.

"He makes an excuse of some law business with me. I suppose he considers the mere fact of his taking the trouble to come here, all the way from San Francisco, a sufficient honor to justify any absence of formal invitation," said Bradley, smiling.

"But he's only—I mean he's my father's banker," said Mainwaring, correcting himself, "and—you don't keep a hotel."

"Not yet," returned Bradley, with a mischievous glance at the two women, "but The Lookout is elastic, and I dare say we can manage to put him up."

A silence ensued. It seemed as if some shadow, or momentary darkening of the brilliant atmosphere; some film across the mirror-like expanse of the open windows, or misty dimming of their wholesome light, had arisen to their elevation. Mainwaring felt that he was looking forward with unreasoning indignation and uneasiness to this impending interruption of their idyllic life; Mrs. Bradley and Louise, who had become a little more constrained and formal under Minty's freedom, were less sympathetic; even the irrepressible Minty appeared absorbed in the responsibilities of the dinner.

Bradley alone preserved his usual patient good-humor. "We'll take our coffee on the veranda, and the ladies will join us by and by, Mainwaring; besides, I don't know that I can allow you, as an invalid, to go entirely through Minty's bountiful *menu* at present. You shall have the sweets another time."

When they were alone on the veranda, he said, between the puffs of his black brier-wood pipe,—a pet aversion of Mrs. Bradley,—"I wonder how Richardson will accept Minty!"

"If *I* can, I think he *must*," returned Mainwaring, dryly. "By Jove, it will be

great fun to see him; but"——he stopped
and hesitated——"I don't know about the
ladies. I don't think, you know, that
they'll stand Minty again before another
stranger."

Bradley glanced quickly at the young
man; their eyes met, and they both joined
in a superior and, I fear, disloyal smile.
After a pause Bradley, as if in a spirit of
further confidence, took his pipe from his
mouth and pointed to the blue abyss before
them.

"Look at that profundity, Mainwaring,
and think of it ever being bullied and over-
awed by a long veranda-load of gaping,
patronizing tourists, and the idiotic flirting
females of their species. Think of a lot of
over-dressed creatures flouting those severe
outlines and deep-toned distances with
frippery and garishness. You know how
you have been lulled to sleep by that delicious, indefinite, far-off murmur of the
canyon at night—think of it being broken
by a crazy waltz or a monotonous german
—by the clatter of waiters and the pop of
champagne corks. And yet, by thunder,
those women are capable of liking both and
finding no discord in them!"

"Dancing ain't half bad, you know," said Mainwaring, conscientiously, "if a chap's got the wind to do it; and all Americans, especially the women, dance better than we do. But I say, Bradley, to hear you talk, a fellow wouldn't suspect you were as big a Vandal as anybody, with a beastly, howling saw-mill in the heart of the primeval forest. By Jove, you quite bowled me over that first day we met, when you popped your head out of that delirium tremens shaking mill, like the very genius of destructive improvement."

"But that was *fighting* Nature, not patronizing her; and it's a business that pays. That reminds me that I must go back to it," said Bradley, rising and knocking the ashes from his pipe.

"Not *after* dinner, surely!" said Mainwaring, in surprise. "Come now, that's too much like the bolting Yankee of the travellers' books."

"There's a heavy run to get through tonight. We're working against time," returned Bradley. Even while speaking he had vanished within the house, returned quickly—having replaced his dark suit by jean trousers tucked in heavy boots, and a red flannel shirt over his starched white one—and, nodding gayly to Mainwaring, stepped from the lower end of the veranda. "The beggar actually looks pleased to go," said Mainwaring to himself in wonderment.

"Oh! Jim," said Mrs. Bradley, appearing at the door.

"Yes," said Bradley, faintly, from the bushes.

"Minty's ready. You might take her home."

"All right. I'll wait."

"I hope I haven't frightened Miss Sharpe away," said Mainwaring. "She isn't going, surely?"

"Only to get some better clothes, on account of company. I'm afraid you are giving her a good deal of trouble, Mr. Mainwaring," said Mrs. Bradley, laughing.

"She wished me to say good-by to you for her, as she couldn't come on the veranda in her old shawl and sun-bonnet," added Louise, who had joined them. "What do you really think of her, Mr. Mainwaring? I call her quite pretty, at times. Don't you?"

Mainwaring knew not what to say. He could not understand why they could have any special interest in the girl, or care to know what he, a perfect stranger, thought of her. He avoided a direct reply, however, by playfully wondering how Mrs. Bradley could subject her husband to Miss Minty's undivided fascinations.

"Oh, Jim always takes her home—if it's in the evening. He gets along with these people better than we do," returned Mrs. Bradley, dryly. "But," she added, with a return of her piquant Quaker-like co-quettishness, "Jim says we are to devote ourselves to you to-night—in retaliation, I suppose. We are to amuse you, and not let you get excited; and you are to be sent to bed early."

It is to be feared that these latter wise precautions—invaluable for all defenceless and enfeebled humanity—were not carried out: and it was late when Mainwaring eventually retired, with brightened eyes and a somewhat accelerated pulse. For the ladies, who had quite regained that kindly equanimity which Minty had rudely inter-rupted, had also added a delicate and confi-dential sympathy in their relations with

Mainwaring,—as of people who had suffered in common,—and he experienced
these tender attentions at their hands
which any two women are emboldened by
each other's saving presence to show any
single member of our sex. Indeed, he
hardly knew if his satisfaction was the
more complete when Mrs. Bradley, with-
drawing for a few moments, left him alone
on the veranda with Louise and the vast,
omnipotent night.

For a while they sat silent, in the midst
of the profound and measureless calm.
Looking down upon the dim moonlit abyss
at their feet, they themselves seemed a part
of this night that arched above it; the half-
risen moon appeared to linger long enough
at their side to enwrap and suffuse them
with its glory; a few bright stars quietly
ringed themselves around them, and looked
wonderingly into the level of their own
shining eyes. For some vague yearning to
humanity seemed to draw this dark and
passionless void towards them. The vast
protecting maternity of Nature leant
hushed and breathless over the solitude.
Warm currents of air rose occasionally
from the valley, which one might have be-

lieved were sighs from its full and over-
flowing breast, or a grateful coolness swept
their cheeks and hair when the tranquil
heights around them were moved to
slowly respond. Odors from invisible bay
and laurel sometimes filled the air; the
incense of some rare and remoter cultivated meadow beyond their ken, or the
strong germinating breath of leagues of
wild oats, that had yellowed the upland
by day. In the silence and shadow, their
voices took upon themselves, almost without their volition, a far-off confidential
murmur, with intervals of meaning silence
—rather as if their thoughts had spoken
for themselves, and they had stopped wonderingly to listen. They talked at first
vaguely to this discreet audience of space
and darkness, and then, growing bolder,
spoke to each other and of themselves. Invested by the infinite gravity of nature,
they had no fear of human ridicule to
restrain their youthful conceit or the extravagance of their unimportant confes-
sions. They talked of their tastes, of
their habits, of their friends and acquaintances. They settled some points of doc-
trine, duty, and etiquette, with the sweet

seriousness of youth and its all-powerful
convictions. The listening vines would
have recognized no flirtation or love-making in their animated but important
confidences; yet when Mrs. Bradley reappeared to warn the invalid that it was
time to seek his couch, they both coughed
slightly in the nervous consciousness of
some unaccustomed quality in their voices,
and a sense of interruption far beyond
their own or the innocent intruder's ken.

"Well?" said Mrs. Bradley, in the sitting-room as Mainwaring's steps retreated
down the passage to his room.

"Well," said Louise with a slight yawn,
leaning her pretty shoulders languidly
against the door-post, as she shaded her
moonlight-accustomed eyes from the vulgar
brilliancy of Mrs. Bradley's bedroom candle. "Well—oh, he talked a great deal
about 'his people' as he called them, and I
talked about us. He's very nice. You
know in some things he's really like a
boy."

"He looks much better."

"Yes; but he is far from strong yet."

Meantime, Mainwaring had no other
confidant of his impressions than his own

thoughts. Mingled with his exaltation, which was the more seductive that it had no well-defined foundation for existing, and implied no future responsibility, was a recurrence of his uneasiness at the impending visit of Richardson the next day. Strangely enough, it had increased under the stimulus of the evening. Just as he was really getting on with the family, he felt sure that this visitor would import some foreign element into their familiarity, as Minty had done. It was possible they would not like him: now he remembered there was really something ostentatiously British and insular about this Richardson—something they would likely resent. Why couldn't this fellow have come later — or even before? Before what? But here he fell asleep, and almost instantly slipped from this veranda in the Sierras, six thousand miles away, to an ancient terrace, overgrown with moss and tradition, that overlooked the sedate glory of an English park. Here he found himself, restricted painfully by his inconsistent night-clothes, endeavoring to impress his mother and sisters with the singular virtues and excellences of his

American host and hostesses—virtues and excellences that he himself was beginning to feel conscious had become more or less apocryphal in that atmosphere. He heard his mother's voice saying severely, "When you learn, Francis, to respect the opinions and prejudices of your family enough to prevent your appearing before them in this uncivilized aboriginal costume, we will listen to what you have to say of the friends whose habits you seem to have adopted;" and he was frantically indignant that his efforts to convince them that his negligence was a personal oversight, and not a Californian custom, were utterly futile. But even then this vision was brushed away by the bewildering sweep of Louise's pretty skirt across the dreamy picture, and her delicate features and softly-fringed eyes remained the last to slip from his fading consciousness.

The moon rose higher and higher above the sleeping house and softly breathing canyon. There was nothing to mar the idyllic repose of the landscape; only the growing light of the last two hours had brought out in the far eastern horizon a dim white peak, that gleamed faintly among the stars, like a bridal couch spread between the hills fringed with fading nuptial torches. No one would have believed that behind that impenetrable shadow to the west, in the heart of the forest, the throbbing saw-mill of James Bradley was even at that moment eating its destructive way through the conserved growth of Nature and centuries, and that the refined proprietor of house and greenwood, with the glow of his furnace fires on his red shirt, and his alert, intelligent eyes, was the genie of that devastation, and the toiling leader of the shadowy, toiling figures around him.

CHAPTER III.

AMID the beauty of the most uncultivated and untrodden wilderness there are
certain localities where the meaner and
more common processes of Nature take
upon themselves a degrading likeness to
the slovenly, wasteful, and improvident
processes of man. The unrecorded land-
slip disintegrating a whole hillside will
not only lay bare the delicate framework
of strata and deposit to the vulgar eye, but
hurl into the valley a débris so monstrous
and unlovely as to shame even the hideous
ruins left by dynamite, hydraulic, or pick
and shovel; an overflown and forgotten
woodland torrent will leave in some remote hollow a disturbed and ungraceful
chaos of inextricable logs, branches, rock,
and soil that will rival the unsavory details of some wrecked or abandoned settlement. Of lesser magnitude and importance, there are certain natural dust-heaps,

sinks, and cesspools, where the elements have collected the cast-off, broken, and frayed disjecta of wood and field—the sweepings of the sylvan household. It was remarkable that Nature, so kindly considerate of mere human ruins, made no attempt to cover up or disguise these monuments of her own mortality: no grass grew over the unsightly landslides, no moss or ivy clothed the stripped and bleached skeletons of overthrown branch and tree; the dead leaves and withered husks rotted in their open grave uncrossed by vine and creeper. Even the animals, except the lower organizations, shunned those haunts of decay and ruin.

It was scarcely a hundred yards from one of those dreary receptacles that Mr. Bradley had taken leave of Miss Minty Sharpe. The cabin occupied by her father, herself, and a younger brother stood, in fact, on the very edge of the little hollow, which was partly filled with decayed wood, leaves, and displacements of the crumbling bank, with the coal dust and ashes which Mr. Sharpe had added from his forge, that stood a few paces distant at the corner of a cross-road. The

occupants of the cabin had also contributed to the hollow the refuse of their
household in broken boxes, earthenware,
tin cans, and cast-off clothing; and it is
not improbable that the site of the cabin
was chosen with reference to this conve-
nient disposal of useless and encumbering
impedimenta. It was true that the locality offered little choice in the way of
beauty. An outcrop of brown granite—
a portent of higher altitudes—extended a
quarter of a mile from the nearest fringe
of dwarf laurel and "brush" in one direction; in the other an advanced file of
Bradley's woods had suffered from some
long-forgotten fire, and still raised its
blackened masts and broken stumps over
the scorched and arid soil, swept of older
underbrush and verdure. On the other
side of the road a dark ravine, tangled
with briers and haunted at night by owls
and wild cats, struggled wearily on, until
blundering at last upon the edge of the
Great Canyon, it slipped and lost itself
forever in a single furrow of those mighty
flanks. When Bradley had once asked
Sharpe why he had not built his house
in the ravine, the blacksmith had replied:

"That until the Lord had appointed his time, he reckoned to keep his head above ground and the foundations thereof." Howbeit, the ravine, or the "run," as it was locally known, was Minty's only Saturday afternoon resort for recreation or berries. "It was," she had explained, "pow'ful soothin', and solitary."

She entered the house—a rude, square building of unpainted boards—containing a sitting-room, a kitchen, and two bed-rooms. A glance at these rooms, which were plainly furnished, and whose canvas-colored walls were adorned with gorgeous agricultural implement circulars, patent medicine calendars, with polytinted chromos and cheaply-illuminated Scriptural texts, showed her that a certain neatness and order had been preserved during her absence; and, finding the house empty, she crossed the barren and blackened inter-vening space between the back door and her father's forge, and entered the open shed. The light was fading from the sky; but the glow of the forge lit up the dusty road before it, and accented the blackness of the rocky ledge beyond. A small curly-headed boy, bearing a singular likeness to a smudged and blackened crayon drawing of Minty, was mechanically blowing the bellows and obviously intent upon something else; while her father—a powerfully built man, with a quaintly dissatisfied expression of countenance—was with equal want of interest mechanically hammering at a horseshoe. Without noticing Minty's advent, he lazily broke into a querulous drawling chant of some vague religious character:

> "O tur-ren, sinner; tur-ren.
> For the Lord bids you turn—ah!
> O tur-ren, sinner; tur-ren.
> Why will you die?"

The musical accent adapted itself to the monotonous fall of the sledge-hammer; and at every repetition of the word "turn" he suited the action to the word by turning the horseshoe with the iron in his left hand. A slight grunt at the end of every stroke, and the simultaneous repetition of "turn" seemed to offer him amusement and relief. Minty, without speaking, crossed the shop, and administered a sound box on her brother's ear. "Take that, and let me ketch you agen layin' low when my back's turned, to put on your store pants."

"The others had fetched away in the laig," said the boy, opposing a knee and elbow at acute angle to further attack.

"You jest get and change 'em," said Minty.

The sudden collapse of the bellows broke in upon the soothing refrain of Mr. Sharpe, and caused him to turn also.

"It's Minty," he said, replacing the horseshoe on the coals, and setting his powerful arms and the sledge on the anvil with an exaggerated expression of weariness.

"Yes; it's me," said Minty, "and Creation knows it's time I *did* come, to keep that boy from ruinin' us with his airs and conceits."

"Did ye bring over any o' that fever mixter?"

"No. Bradley sez you're loading yerself up with so much o' that bitter bark—kuinine they call it over there—that you'll lift the ruff off your head next. He allows ye ain't got no ague; it's jest wind and dyspepsy. He sez yer's strong ez a hoss."

"Bradley," said Sharpe, laying aside

his sledge with an aggrieved manner which was, however, as complacent as his fatigue and discontent, "ez one of them nat'ral born finikin skunks ez I despise. I reckon he began to give p'ints to his parents when he was about knee-high to Richelieu there. He's on them confidential terms with hisself and the Almighty that he reckons he ken run a saw-mill and a man's insides at the same time with one hand tied behind him. And this finikin is up to his conceit: he wanted to tell me that that yer handy brush dump outside our shanty was unhealthy. Give a man with frills like that his own way and he'd be a sprinkling odor cologne and peppermint all over the country."

"He set your shoulder as well as any doctor," said Minty.

"That's bone-settin', and a nat'ral gift," returned Sharpe, as triumphantly as his habitual depression would admit; "it ain't conceit and finikin got out o' books! Well," he added, after a pause, "wot's happened ?"

Minty's face slightly changed. "Nothin'; I kem back to get some things," she said shortly, moving away.

"And ye saw *him?*"

"Ye-e-s," drawled Minty, carelessly, still retreating.

"Bixby was along here about noon. He says the stranger was suthin' high and mighty in his own country, and them 'Frisco millionaires are quite sweet on him. Where are ye goin' ?"

"In the house."

"Well, look yer, Minty. Now that you're here, ye might get up a batch o' hot biscuit for supper. Dinner was that promiscous and experimental to-day, along o' Richelieu's nat'ral foolin', that I think I could git outside of a little suthin' now, if only to prop up a kind of innard sinkin' that takes me. Ye ken tell me the news at supper."

Later, however, when Mr. Sharpe had quitted his forge for the night and, seated at his domestic board, was, with a dismal presentiment of future indigestion, voraciously absorbing his favorite meal of hot saleratus biscuits swimming in butter, he had apparently forgotten his curiosity concerning Mainwaring and settled himself to a complaining chronicle of the day's mishaps. "Nat'rally, havin' an extra lot o' work on hand and no time for foolin', what does that ornery Richelieu get up and do this mornin'? Ye know them ridiklus specimens that he's been chippin' outer that ledge that the yearth slipped from down the run, and litterin' up the whole shanty with 'em. Well, darn my skin! if he didn't run a heap of 'em, mixed up with coal, unbeknowned to me, in the forge, to make what he called a 'fire essay' of 'em. Nat'rally, I couldn't get a blessed iron hot, and didn't know what had gone of the fire, or the coal either, for two hours, till I stopped work and raked out the coal. That comes from his hangin' round that saw-mill in the woods, and listenin' to Bradley's high-falutin' talk about rocks and strata and sich."

"But Bradley don't go a cent on minin', Pop," said Minty. "He sez the woods is good enough for him; and there's millions to be made when the railroad comes along, and timber's wanted."

"But until then he's got to keep hisself, to pay wages, and keep the mill runnin'. Onless it's, ez Bixby says, that he hopes to get that Englishman to rope in some o' them 'Frisco friends of his to take a hand. Ye didn't have any o' that kind o' talk, did ye?"

"No; not *that* kind o' talk," said Minty.

"Not *that* kind o' talk!" repeated her father with aggrieved curiosity. "Wot kind, then?"

"Well," said Minty, lifting her black eyes to her father's; "I ain't no account, and you ain't no account either. You ain't got no college education, ain't got no friends in 'Frisco, and ain't got no high-toned style; I can't play the pianner, jabber French, nor get French dresses. We ain't got no fancy 'Shallet,' as they call it, with a first-class view of nothing; but only a shanty on dry rock. But, afore *I'd* take advantage of a lazy, gawky boy— for it ain't anything else, though he's good meanin' enough—that happened to fall sick in *my* house, and coax and cosset him, and wrap him in white cotton, and mother him, and sister him, and Aunt Sukey him, and almost dry-nuss him gin'rally, jist to get him sweet on me and on mine, and take the inside track of others—*I'd* be an Injin! And if you'd allow it, Pop, you'd be wuss nor a nigger!"

"Sho!" said her father, kindling with

that intense gratification with which the male receives any intimation of alien feminine weakness. "It ain't that, Minty, I wanter know!"

"It's jist that, Pop; and I ez good ez let 'em know I seed it. I ain't a fool, if some folks do drop their eyes and pertend to wipe the laugh out of their noses with a handkerchief when I let out to speak. I mayn't be good enough kempany—"

"Look yer, Minty," interrupted the blacksmith, sternly, half rising from his seat with every trace of his former weakness vanished from his hardset face; "do you mean to say that they put on airs to ye—to *my* darter?"

"No," said Minty quickly; "the men didn't; and don't you, a man, mix yourself up with women's meannesses. I ken manage 'em, Pop, with one hand."

Mr. Sharpe looked at his daughter's flashing black eyes. Perhaps an uneasy recollection of the late Mrs. Sharpe's remarkable capacity in that respect checked his further rage.

"No. Wot I was sayin'," resumed Minty, "ez that I mayn't be thought by others good enough to keep kempany with baronetts ez is to be—though baronetts mightn't object—but I ain't mean enough to try to steal away some ole woman's darling boy in England, or snatch some likely young English girl's big brother outer the family without sayin' by your leave. How'd you like it if Richelieu was growed up, and went to sea,—and it would be like his peartness,—and he fell sick in some foreign land, and some princess or other skyulged *him* underhand away from us?"

Probably owing to the affair of the specimens, the elder Sharpe did not seem to regard the possible mésalliance of Richelieu with extraordinary disfavor. "That boy is conceited enough with hair ile and fine clothes for anything," he said plaintively. "But didn't that Louise Macy hev a feller already—that Captain Greyson? Wot's gone o' him?"

"That's it," said Minty: "he kin go out in the woods and whistle now. But all the same, she could hitch him in again at any time if the other stranger kicked over the traces. That's the style over there at The Lookout. There ain't ez much heart in them two women put together ez would make a green gal flush up playin' forfeits. It's all in their breed, Pop. Love ain't going to spile their appetites and complexions, give 'em nose-bleed, nor put a drop o' water into their eyes in all their natural born days. That's wot makes me mad. Ef I thought that Loo cared a bit for that child I wouldn't mind; I'd just advise her to make him get up and get—pack his duds out o' camp, and go home and not come back until he had a written permit from his mother, or the other baronet in office."

"Looks sorter ef some one orter interfere," said the blacksmith, reflectively. "'Tain't exackly a case for a vigilance committee, tho' it's agin public morals, this sorter kidnappin' o' strangers. Looks ez if it might bring the country into discredit in England."

"Well, don't *you* go and interfere and havin' folks say ez my nose was put out o' jint over there," said Minty, curtly. "There's another Englishman comin' up from 'Frisco to see him to-morrow. Ef he ain't scooped up by Jenny Bradley he'll guess there's a nigger in the fence somewhere. But there, Pop, let it drop. It's a bad aig, anyway," she concluded, rising from the table, and passing her hands down her frock and her shapely hips, as if to wipe off further contamination of the subject. "Where's Richelieu agin?"

"Said he didn't want supper, and like ez not he's gone over to see that fammerly at the Summit. There's a little girl thar he's sparkin', about his own age."

"His own age!" said Minty, indignantly. "Why, she's double that, if she's a day. Well—if he ain't the triflinest, conceitednest little limb that ever grew! I'd like to know where he got it from—it wasn't mar's style."

Mr. Sharpe smiled darkly. Richelieu's precocious gallantry evidently was not considered as gratuitous as his experimental metallurgy. But as his eyes followed his daughter's wholesome, Phyllis-like figure, a new idea took possession of him: needless to say, however, it was in the line of another personal aggrievement, albeit it took the form of religious reflection.

"It's curous, Minty, wot's foreordained, and wot ain't. Now, yer's one of them high and mighty fellows, after the Lord, ez comes meanderin' around here, and drops off—ez fur ez I kin hear—in a kind o' faint at the first house he kems to, and is taken in and lodged and sumptuously fed; and, nat'rally, they gets their reward for it. Now wot's to hev kept that young feller from coming *here* and droppin' down in my forge, or in this very room, and *you* a tendin' him, and jist layin' over them folks at The Lookout?"

"Wot's got hold o' ye, Pop? Don't I tell ye he had a letter to Jim Bradley?" said Minty, quickly, with an angry flash of color in her cheek.

"That ain't it," said Sharpe confidently; "it's cos he *walked*. Nat'rally, you'd think he'd *ride*, being high and mighty, and that's where, ez the parson will tell ye, wot's merely fi-nite and human wisdom errs! Ef that feller had ridden, he'd have had to come by this yer road, and by this yer forge, and stop a spell like any other. But it was foreordained that he should walk, jest cos it wasn't generally kalkilated and reckoned on. So, *you* had no show."

For a moment, Minty seemed struck

with her father's original theory. But with a vigorous shake of her shoulders she threw it off. Her eyes darkened.

"I reckon you ain't thinking, Pop—" she began.

"I was only sayin' it was curous," he rejoined quietly. Nevertheless, after a pause, he rose, coughed, and going up to the young girl, as she leaned over the dresser, bent his powerful arm around her, and, drawing her and the plate she was holding against his breast, laid his bearded cheek for an instant softly upon her rebellious head. "It's all right, Minty," he said; "ain't it, pet?" Minty's eyelids closed gently under the familiar pressure. "Wot's that in your hair, Minty?" he said tactfully, breaking an embarrassing pause.

"Bar's grease, father," murmured Minty, in a child's voice—the grown-up woman, under that magic touch, having lapsed again into her father's motherless charge of ten years before.

"It's pow'ful soothin', and pretty," said her father.

"I made it myself — do you want some?" asked Minty.

"Not now, girl!" For a moment they slightly rocked each other in that attitude —the man dexterously, the woman with infinite tenderness—and then they separated.

Late that night, after Richelieu had returned, and her father wrestled in his fitful sleep with the remorse of his guilty indulgence at supper, Minty remained alone in her room, hard at work, surrounded by the contents of one of her mother's trunks and the fragments of certain ripped-up and newly-turned dresses. For Minty had conceived the bold idea of altering one of her mother's gowns to the fashion of a certain fascinating frock worn by Louise Macy. It was late when her self-imposed task was completed. With a nervous trepidation that was novel to her, Minty began to disrobe herself preparatory to trying on her new creation. The light of a tallow candle and a large swinging lantern, borrowed from her father's forge, fell shyly on her milky neck and shoulders, and shone in her sparkling eyes, as she stood before her largest mirror—the long glazed door of a kitchen clock which she had placed upon her chest of drawers. Had poor Minty been content with the full, free, and goddess-like outlines that it reflected, she would have been spared her impending disappointment. For, alas! the dress of her model had been framed upon a symmetrically attenuated French corset, and the unfortunate Minty's fuller and ampler curves had under her simple country stays known no more restraining cincture than knew the Venus of Milo. The alteration was a hideous failure, it was neither Minty's statuesque outline nor Louise Macy's graceful contour. Minty was no fool, and the revelation of this slow education of the figure and training of outline—whether fair or false in art—struck her quick intelligence with all its full and hopeless significance. A bitter light sprang to her eyes; she tore the wretched sham from her shoulders, and then wrapping a shawl around her, threw herself heavily and sullenly on the bed. But inaction was not a characteristic of Minty's emotion; she presently rose again, and, taking an old work-box from her trunk, began to rummage in its recesses. It was an old shell-incrusted affair, and the apparent receptacle of such cheap odds and ends of jewelry as she possessed; a hideous cameo ring, the property of the late Mrs. Sharpe, was missing. She again rapidly explored the contents of the box, and then an inspiration seized her, and she darted into her brother's bedroom.

That precocious and gallant Lovelace of ten, despite all sentiment, had basely succumbed to the gross materialism of youthful slumber. On a cot in the corner, half hidden under the wreck of his own careless and hurried disrobing, with one arm hanging out of the coverlid, Richelieu lay supremely unconscious. On the forefinger of his small but dirty hand the missing cameo was still glittering guiltily. With a swift movement of indignation Minty rushed with uplifted palm towards the tempting expanse of youthful cheek that lay invitingly exposed upon the pillow. Then she stopped suddenly.

She had seen him lying thus a hundred times before. On the pillow near him an indistinguishable mass of golden fur—the helpless bulk of a squirrel chained to the leg of his cot; at his feet a wall-eyed cat, who had followed his tyrannous caprices

with the long-suffering devotion of her
sex; on the shelf above him a loathsome
collection of flies and tarantulas in dull
green bottles: a slab of ginger-bread for
light nocturnal refection, and her own pot
of bear's grease. Perhaps it was the
piteous defencelessness of youthful sleep,
perhaps it was some lingering memory of
her father's caress; but as she gazed at
him with troubled eyes, the juvenile repro-
bate slipped back into the baby-boy that
she had carried in her own childish arms
such a short time ago, when the maternal
responsibility had descended with the dead
mother's ill-fitting dresses upon her lank
girlish figure and scant virgin breast—and
her hand fell listlessly at her side.

The sleeper stirred slightly and awoke.
At the same moment, by some mysterious
sympathy, a pair of beady bright eyes appeared in the bulk of fur near his curls,
the cat stretched herself, and even a vague
agitation was heard in the bottles on the
shelf. Richelieu's blinking eyes wandered
from the candle to his sister, and then
the guilty hand was suddenly withdrawn
under the bedclothes.

"No matter, dear," said Minty; "it's

mar's, and you kin wear it when you like, if you'll only ask for it."

Richelieu wondered if he was dreaming! This unexpected mildness—this inexplicable tremor in his sister's voice: it must be some occult influence of the night season on the sisterly mind, possibly akin to a fear of ghosts! He made a mental note of it in view of future favors, yet for the moment he felt embarrassedly gratified. "Ye ain't wantin' anything, Minty," he said affectionately; "a pail o' cold water from the far spring—no nothin'?" He made an ostentatious movement as if to rise, yet sufficiently protracted to prevent any hasty acceptance of his prodigal offer.

"No, dear," she said, still gazing at him with an absorbed look in her dark eyes.

Richelieu felt a slight creepy sensation under that lonely far-off gaze. "Your eyes look awful big at night, Minty," he said. He would have added "and pretty," but she was his sister, and he had the lofty fraternal conviction of his duty in repressing the inordinate vanity of the sex. "Ye're sure ye ain't wantin' nothin'?"

"Not now, dear." She paused a moment, and then said deliberately: "But you

wouldn't mind turnin' out after sun-up
and runnin' an errand for me over to The
Lookout ?"

Richelieu's eyes sparkled so suddenly
that even in her absorption Minty noticed
the change. "But ye're not goin' to tarry
over there, ner gossip—you hear ? Yer to
take this yer message. Yer to say 'that it
will be onpossible for me to come back
there, on account—on account of—' "

"Important business," suggested Richelieu; "that's the perlite style."

"Ef you like." She leaned over the bed
and put her lips to his forehead, still
damp with the dews of sleep, and then to
his long-lashed lids. "Mind Nip!"—the
squirrel—he practically suggested. For
an instant their blond curls mingled on
the pillow. "Now go to sleep," she said
curtly.

But Richelieu had taken her white neck
in the short strangulatory hug of the small
boy, and held her fast. "Ye'll let me put
on my best pants ?"

"Yes."

"And wear that ring ?"

"Yes"—a little sadly.

"Then yer kin count me in, Minty; and

see here"—his voice sank to a confidential whisper—"mebbee some day ye'll be beholden to *me* for a lot o' real jewelry."

She returned slowly to her room, and, opening the window, looked out upon the night. The same moon that had lent such supererogatory grace to the natural beauty of The Lookout, here seemed to have failed, as Minty had, in disguising the relentless limitations of Nature or the cruel bonds of custom. The black plain of granite, under its rays, appeared only to extend its poverty to some remoter barrier; the blackened stumps of the burnt forest stood bleaker against the sky, like broken and twisted pillars of iron. The cavity of the broken ledge where Richelieu had prospected was a hideous chasm of bluish blackness, over which a purple vapor seemed to hover; the "brush dump" beside the house showed a cavern of writhing and distorted objects stiffened into dark rigidity. She had often looked upon the prospect: it had never seemed so hard and changeless; yet she accepted it, as she had accepted it before.

She turned away, undressed herself mechanically, and went to bed. She had an idea that she had been very foolish; that her escape from being still more foolish was something miraculous, and in some measure connected with Providence, her father, her little brother, and her dead mother, whose dress she had recklessly spoiled. But that she had even so slightly touched the bitterness and glory of re-nunciation—as written of heroines and fine ladies by novelists and poets—never entered the foolish head of Minty Sharpe, the blacksmith's daughter.

CHAPTER IV.

IT was a little after daybreak next morning that Mainwaring awoke from the first
unrefreshing night he had passed at The
Lookout. He was so feverish and restless
that he dressed himself at sunrise, and
cautiously stepped out upon the still silent
veranda. The chairs which he and Louise
Macy had occupied were still, it seemed to
him, conspicuously confidential with each
other, and he separated them, but as he
looked down into the Great Canyon at his
feet he was conscious of some undefinable
change in the prospect. A slight mist was
rising from the valley, as if it were the
last of last night's illusions; the first level
sunbeams were obtrusively searching, and
the keen morning air had a dryly practical
insistence which irritated him, until a
light footstep on the farther end of the
veranda caused him to turn sharply.

It was the singular apparition of a small

boy, bearing a surprising resemblance to
Minty Sharpe, and dressed in an unique
fashion. On a tumbled sea of blond curls
a "chip" sailor hat, with a broad red ribbon, rode jauntily. But here the nautical
suggestion changed, as had the desire of
becoming a pirate which induced it. A red
shirt, with a white collar, and a yellow
plaid ribbon tie, that also recalled Minty
Sharpe, lightly turned the suggestion of
his costume to mining. Short black velvet
trousers, coming to his knee, and ostentatiously new short-legged boots, with visible
straps like curling ears, completed the entirely original character of his lower limbs.

Mainwaring, always easily gentle and
familiar with children and his inferiors,
looked at him with an encouraging smile.
Richelieu—for it was he—advanced
gravely and held out his hand, with the
cameo ring apparent. Mainwaring, with
equal gravity, shook it warmly, and removed his hat. Richelieu, keenly observant, did the same.

"Is Jim Bradley out yet?" asked Richelieu, carelessly.

"No; I think not. But I'm Frank
Mainwaring. Will I do?"

Richelieu smiled. The dimples, the white teeth, the dark, laughing eyes, were surely Minty's?

"I'm Richelieu," he rejoined with equal candor.

"Richelieu?"

"Yes. That Frenchman — the Lord Cardinal—you know. Mar saw Forrest do him out in St. Louis."

"Do him?"

"Yes, in the theayter."

With a confused misconception of his meaning, Mainwaring tried to recall the historical dress of the great Cardinal and fit it to the masquerader—if such he were —before him. But Richelieu relieved him by adding,—

"Richelieu Sharpe."

"Oh, that's your *name!*" said Mainwaring, cheerfully. "Then you're Miss Minty's brother. I know her. How jolly lucky!"

They both shook hands again. Richelieu, eager to get rid of the burden of his sister's message, which he felt was in the way of free-and-easy intercourse with this charming stranger, looked uneasily towards the house.

"I say," said Mainwaring, "if you're in a hurry, you'd better go in there and knock. I hear some one stirring in the kitchen."

Richelieu nodded, but first went back to the steps of the veranda, picked up a small blue knotted handkerchief, apparently containing some heavy objects, and repassed Mainwaring.

"What! have you cut it, Richelieu, with your valuables? What have you got there?"

"Specimins, said Richelieu, shortly, and vanished.

He returned presently. "Well, Cardinal, did you see anybody?" asked Mainwaring.

"Mrs. Bradley; but Jim's over to the mill. I'm goin' there."

"Did you see Miss Macy?" continued Mainwaring, carelessly.

"Loo?"

"Loo!—well; yes."

"No. She's philanderin' with Captain Greyson."

"Philandering with Greyson?" echoed Mainwaring, in wonder.

"Yes; on horseback on the ridge."

"You mean she's riding out with Mr. —with Captain Greyson?"

"Yes; ridin' *and* philanderin'," persisted Richelieu.

"And what do you call philandering?"

"Well; I reckon you and she oughter know," returned Richelieu, with a precocious air.

"Certainly," said Mainwaring, with a faint smile. Richelieu really was like Minty.

There was a long silence. This young Englishman was becoming exceedingly uninteresting. Richelieu felt that he was gaining neither profit nor amusement, and losing time. "I'm going," he said.

"Good morning," said Mainwaring, without looking up.

Richelieu picked up his specimens, thoroughly convinced of the stranger's glittering deceitfulness, and vanished.

It was nearly eight o'clock when Mrs. Bradley came from the house. She apologized, with a slightly distrait smile, for the tardiness of the household. "Mr. Bradley stayed at the mill all night, and will not be here until breakfast, when he brings your friend Mr. Richardson with him"—Mainwaring scarcely repressed a movement of impatience—"who arrives early. It's unfortunate that Miss Sharpe can't come to-day."

In his abstraction Mainwaring did not notice that Mrs. Bradley slightly accented Minty's formal appellation, and said carelessly,—

"Oh, that's why her brother came over here so early!"

"Did *you* see him?" asked Mrs. Bradley, almost abruptly.

"Yes. He is an amusing little beggar; but I think he shares his sister's preference for Mr. Bradley. He deserted me here in the veranda for him at the mill."

"Louise will keep you company as soon as she has changed her dress," continued Mrs. Bradley. "She was out riding early this morning with a friend. She's very fond of early morning rides."

"*And* philandering," repeated Mainwaring to himself. It was quite natural for Miss Macy to ride out in the morning, after the fashion of the country, with an escort; but why had the cub insisted on the "philandering"? He had said, *"and* philandering," distinctly. It was a nasty thing for him to say. Any other fellow but he, Mainwaring, might misunderstand the whole thing. Perhaps he ought to warn her—but no! he could not repeat the gossip of a child, and that child the brother of one of her inferiors. But was Minty an inferior? Did she and Minty talk together about this fellow Greyson? At all events, it would only revive the awkwardness of the preceding day, and he resolved to say nothing.

He was rewarded by a half-inquiring, half-confiding look in Louise's bright eyes, when she presently greeted him on the veranda. "She had quite forgotten," she said, "to tell him last night of her morning's engagement; indeed, she had half forgotten *it*. It used to be a favorite practice of hers, with Captain Greyson; but she had lately given it up. She believed she had not ridden since—since—"

"Since when?" asked Mainwaring.

"Well, since you were ill," she said frankly.

A quick pleasure shone in Mainwaring's cheek and eye; but Louise's pretty lids did not drop, nor her faint, quiet bloom deepen. Breakfast was already waiting when Mr. Richardson arrived alone.

He explained that Mr. Bradley had some important and unexpected business which had delayed him, but which, he added, "Mr. Bradley says may prove interesting enough to you to excuse his absence this morning." Mainwaring was not displeased that his critical and observant host was not present at their meeting. Louise Macy was, however, as demurely conscious of the different bearing of the two compatriots. Richardson's somewhat self-important patronage of the two ladies, and that Californian familiarity he had acquired, changed to a certain uneasy deference towards Mainwaring; while the younger Englishman's slightly stiff and deliberate cordiality was, nevertheless, mingled with a mysterious understanding that appeared innate and unconscious. Louise was quick to see that these two men, more widely divergent in quality than any two of her own countrymen, were yet more subtly connected by some unknown sympathy than the most equal of Americans. Minty's prophetic belief of the effect of the two women upon Richardson was certainly true as regarded Mrs. Bradley. The banker—a large material nature—was quickly fascinated by the demure, puritanic graces of that lady, and was inclined to exhibit a somewhat broad and ostentatious gallantry that annoyed Mainwaring. When they were seated alone on the veranda, which the ladies had discreetly left to them, Richardson said,—

"Odd I didn't hear of Bradley's wife before. She seems a spicy, pretty, comfortable creature. Regularly thrown away with him up here."

Mainwaring replied coldly that she was "an admirable helpmeet of a very admirable man," not, however, without an uneasy recollection of her previous confidences respecting her husband. "They have been most thoroughly good and kind to me; my own brother and sister could not have done more. And certainly not with better taste or delicacy," he added, markedly.

"Certainly, certainly," said Richardson, hurriedly. "I wrote to Lady Mainwaring that you were taken capital

care of by some very honest people; and
that—"

"Lady Mainwaring already knows what
I think of them, and what she owes to their
kindness," said Mainwaring, dryly.

"True, true," said Richardson, apologetically. "Of course you must have seen a
good deal of them. I only know Bradley
in a business way. He's been trying to get
the Bank to help him to put up some new
mills here; but we didn't see it. I dare
say he is good company—rather amusing,
eh?"

Mainwaring had the gift of his class of
snubbing by the polite and forgiving oblivion of silence. Richardson shifted uneasily
in his chair, but continued with assumed
carelessness:—

"No; I only knew of this cousin, Miss
Macy. I heard of her when she was visiting some friends in Menlo Park last year.
Rather an attractive girl. They say Colonel Johnson, of Sacramento, took quite a
fancy to her—it would have been a good
match, I dare say, for he is very rich—but
the thing fell through in some way. Then,
they say, *she* wanted to marry that Spaniard, young Pico, of the Amador Ranche;

but his family wouldn't hear of it. Somehow, she's deuced unlucky. I suppose she'll make a mess of it with Captain Greyson she was out riding with this morning."

"Didn't the Bank think Bradley's mills a good investment?" asked Mainwaring quietly, when Richardson paused.

"Not with him in it; he is not a business man, you know."

"I thought he was. He seems to me an energetic man, who knows his work, and is not afraid to look after it himself."

"That's just it. He has got absurd ideas of coöperating with his workmen, you know, and doing everything slowly and on a limited scale. The only thing to be done is to buy up all the land on this ridge, run off the settlers, freeze out all the other mills, and put it into a big San Francisco company on shares. That's the only way we would look at it."

"But you don't consider the investment bad, even from *his* point of view?"

"Perhaps not."

"And you only decline it because it isn't big enough for the Bank?"

"Exactly."

"Richardson," said Mainwaring, slowly rising, putting his hands in his trousers pockets, and suddenly looking down upon the banker from the easy level of habitual superiority, "I wish you'd attend to this thing for me. I desire to make some return to Mr. Bradley for his kindness. I wish to give him what help he wants—in his own way—you understand. I wish it, and I believe my father wishes it, too. If you'd like him to write to you to that effect—"

"By no means, it's not at all necessary," said Richardson, dropping with equal suddenness into his old-world obsequiousness. "I shall certainly do as you wish. It is not a bad investment, Mr. Mainwaring, and as you suggest, a very proper return for their kindness. And, being here, it will come quite naturally for me to take up the affair again."

"And—I say, Richardson."

"Yes, sir?"

"As these ladies are rather short-handed in their domestic service, you know, perhaps you'd better not stay to luncheon or dinner, but go on to the Summit House— it's only a mile or two farther—and

come back here this evening. I shan't
want you until then."

"Certainly!" stammered Richardson.
"I'll just take leave of the ladies!"

"It's not at all necessary," said Mainwaring, quietly; "you would only disturb
them in their household duties. I'll tell
them what I've done with you, if they ask.
You'll find your stick and hat in the passage, and you can leave the veranda by
these steps. By the way, you had better
manage at the Summit to get some one to
bring my traps from here to be forwarded
to Sacramento to-morrow. I'll want a
conveyance, or a horse of some kind, myself, for I've given up walking for a
while; but we can settle about that to-
night. Come early. Good morning!"

He accompanied his thoroughly subjugated countryman—who, however, far from
attempting to reassert himself, actually
seemed easier and more cheerful in his
submission—to the end of the veranda,
and watched him depart. As he turned
back, he saw the pretty figure of Louise
Macy leaning against the doorway. How
graceful and refined she looked in that
simple morning dress! What wonder that

she was admired by Greyson, by Johnson, and by that Spaniard!—no, by Jove, it was *she* that wanted to marry him!

"What have you sent away Mr. Richardson for?" asked the young girl, with a half-reproachful, half-mischievous look in her bright eyes.

"I packed him off because I thought it was a little too hard on you and Mrs. Bradley to entertain him without help."

"But as he was *our* guest, you might have left that to us," said Miss Macy.

"By Jove! I never thought of that," said Mainwaring, coloring in consternation. "Pray forgive me, Miss Macy—but you see I knew the man, and could say it, and you couldn't."

"Well, I forgive you, for you look really so cut up," said Louise, laughing. "But I don't know what Jenny will say of your disposing of her conquest so summarily." She stopped and regarded him more attentively. "Has he brought you any bad news? if so, it's a pity you didn't send him away before. He's quite spoiling our cure."

Mainwaring thought bitterly that he had. "But it's a cure for all that, Miss

Macy," he said, with an attempt at cheerfulness, "and being a cure, you see, there's no longer an excuse for my staying here. I have been making arrangements for leaving here to-morrow."

"So soon?"

"Do you think it soon, Miss Macy?" asked Mainwaring, turning pale in spite of himself.

"I quite forgot—that you were here as an invalid only, and that we owe our pleasure to the accident of your pain."

She spoke a little artificially, he thought, yet her cheeks had not lost their pink bloom, nor her eyes their tranquillity. Had he heard Minty's criticism he might have believed that the organic omission noticed by her was a fact.

"And now that your good work as Sister of Charity is completed, you'll be able to enter the world of gayety again with a clear conscience," said Mainwaring, with a smile that he inwardly felt was a miserable failure. "You'll be able to resume your morning rides, you know, which the wretched invalid interrupted."

Louise raised her clear eyes to his, without reproach, indignation, or even wonder.

He felt as if he had attempted an insult and failed.

"Does my cousin know you are going so soon?" she asked finally.

"No, I did not know myself until to-day. You see," he added hastily, while his honest blood blazoned the lie in his cheek, "I've heard of some miserable business affairs that will bring me back to England sooner that I expected."

"I think you should consider your health more important than any mere business," said Louise. "I don't mean that you should remain *here*," she added with a hasty laugh, "but it would be a pity, now that you have reaped the benefit of rest and taking care of yourself, that you should not make it your only business to seek it elsewhere."

Mainwaring longed to say that within the last half hour, living or dying had become of little moment to him; but he doubted the truth or efficacy of this time-worn heroic of passion. He felt, too, that anything he said was a mere subterfuge for the real reason of his sudden departure. And how was he to question her as to that reason? In escaping from these subterfuges — he was compelled to lie again. With an assumption of changing the subject, he said calmly, "Richardson thought he had met you before—in Menlo Park, I think."

Amazed at the evident irrelevance of the remark, Louise said coldly, that she did not remember having seen him before.

"I think it was at a Mr. Johnson's—or *with* a Mr. Johnson—or perhaps at one of those Spanish ranches—I think he mentioned some name like Pico!"

Louise looked at him wonderingly for an instant, and then gave way to a frank, irrepressible laugh, which lent her delicate but rather set little face all the color he had missed. Partially relieved by her unconcern, and yet mortified that he had only provoked her sense of the ludicrous, he tried to laugh also.

"Then, to be quite plain," said Louise, wiping her now humid eyes, "you want me to understand that you really didn't pay sufficient attention to hear correctly! Thank you; that's a pretty English compliment, I suppose."

"I dare say you wouldn't call it 'philandering'?"

"I certainly shouldn't, for I don't know what 'philandering' means."

Mainwaring could not reply, with Richelieu, "You ought to know"; nor did he dare explain what he thought it meant, and how he knew it. Louise, however, innocently solved the difficulty.

"There's a country song I've heard Minty sing," she said. "It runs—

> Come, Philander, let us be a-marchin',
> Every one for his true love a-sarchin'
> Choose your true love now or never. . . .

Have you been listening to her also?"

"No," said Mainwaring, with a sudden incomprehensible, but utterly irrepressible, resolution; "but *I'm* 'a-marchin',' you know, and perhaps I must 'choose my true love now or never.' Will you help me, Miss Macy?"

He drew gently near her. He had become quite white, but also very manly, and it struck her, more deeply, thoroughly, and conscientiously sincere than any man who had before addressed her. She moved slightly away, as if to rest herself by laying both hands upon the back of the chair.

"Where do you expect to begin your 'sarchin' '?" she said, leaning on the chair and tilting it before her; "or are you as vague as usual as to locality? Is it at some 'Mr. Johnson' or 'Mr. Pico,' or—"

"Here," he interrupted boldly.

"I really think you ought to first tell my cousin that you are going away to-morrow," she said, with a faint smile. "It's such short notice. She's just in there." She nodded her pretty head, without raising her eyes, towards the hall.

"But it may not be so soon," said Mainwaring.

"Oh, then the 'sarchin'' is not so important?" said Louise, raising her head, and looking towards the hall with some uneasy but indefinable feminine instinct.

She was right; the sitting-room door opened, and Mrs. Bradley made her smiling appearance.

"Mr. Mainwaring was just looking for you," said Louise, for the first time raising her eyes to him. "He's not only sent off Mr. Richardson, but he's going away himself to-morrow."

Mrs. Bradley looked from the one to the other in mute wonder. Mainwaring cast an imploring glance at Louise, which had the desired effect. Much more seriously, and in a quaint, business-like way, the young girl took it upon herself to explain to Mrs. Bradley that Richardson had brought the invalid some important news that would, unfortunately, not only shorten his stay in America, but even compel him to leave The Lookout sooner than he expected, perhaps to-morrow. Mainwaring thanked her with his eyes, and then turned to Mrs. Bradley.

"Whether I go to-morrow or next day," he said with simple and earnest directness, "I intend, you know, to see you soon again, either here or in my own home in England. I do not know," he added with marked gravity, "that I have succeeded in convincing you that I have made your family already well known to my people, and that"—he fixed his eyes with a meaning look on Louise—"no matter when, or in what way, you come to them, your place is made ready for you. You may not like them, you know: the governor is getting to be an old man—perhaps too old for young Americans—but *they* will like *you,* and you must put up with that. My mother and sisters know Miss Macy as well as I do, and will make her one of the family."

The conscientious earnestness with which these apparent conventionalities were uttered, and some occult quality of quiet conviction in the young man's manner, brought a pleasant sparkle to the eyes of Mrs. Bradley and Louise.

"But," said Mrs. Bradley, gayly, "our going to England is quite beyond our present wildest dreams; nothing but a windfall, an unexpected rise in timber, or even the tabooed hotel speculation, could make it possible."

"But I shall take the liberty of trying to present it to Mr. Bradley tonight in some practical way that may convince even his critical judgment," said Mainwaring, still seriously. "It will be," he added more lightly, "the famous testimonial of my cure which I promised you."

"And you will find Mr. Bradley so sceptical that you will be obliged to defer your going," said Mrs. Bradley, triumphantly. "Come, Louise, we must not forget that we have still Mr. Mainwaring's present comfort to look after; that Minty has basely deserted us, and that we ourselves must see that the last days of our guest beneath our

roof are not remembered for their priva-
tion."

She led Louise away with a half-mischievous suggestion of maternal propriety,
and left Mainwaring once more alone on
the veranda.

He had done it! Certainly she must
have understood his meaning, and there
was nothing left for him to do but to
acquaint Bradley with his intentions to-
night, and press her for a final answer in
the morning. There would be no in-
delicacy then in asking her for an interview more free from interruption than this
public veranda. Without conceit, he did
not doubt what the answer would be. His
indecision, his sudden resolution to leave
her, had been all based upon the uncertainty of *his* own feelings, the propriety
of *his* declaration, the possibility of some
previous experience of hers that might
compromise *him*. Convinced by her un-
embarrassed manner of her innocence, or
rather satisfied of her indifference to
Richardson's gossip, he had been hurried
by his feelings into an unexpected avowal.
Brought up in the perfect security of his
own social position, and familiarly con-

scious—without vanity—of its importance and power in such a situation, he believed, without undervaluing Louise's charms or independence, that he had no one else than himself to consult. Even the slight uneasiness that still pursued him was more due to his habitual conscientiousness of his own intention than to any fear that she would not fully respond to it. Indeed, with his conservative ideas of proper feminine self-restraint, Louise's calm passivity and undemonstrative attitude were a proof of her superiority; had she blushed overmuch, cried, or thrown herself into his arms, he would have doubted the wisdom of so easy a selection. It was true he had known her scarcely three weeks; if he chose to be content with that, his own accessible record of three centuries should be sufficient for her, and condone any irregularity.

Nevertheless, as an hour slipped away and Louise did not make her appearance, either on the veranda or in the little sitting-room off the hall, Mainwaring became more uneasy as to the incompleteness of their interview. Perhaps a faint suspicion of the inadequacy of her response began to trouble him; but he still fatuously regarded it rather as owing to his own hurried and unfinished declaration. It was true that he hadn't said half what he intended to say; it was true that she might have misunderstood it as the conventional gallantry of the situation, as—terrible thought!—the light banter of the habitual love-making American, to which she had been accustomed; perhaps even now she relegated him to the level of Greyson, and this accounted for her singular impassiveness—an impassiveness that certainly was singular now he reflected upon it—that might have been even contempt. The last thought pricked his deep conscientiousness; he walked hurriedly up and down the veranda, and then, suddenly reëntering his room, took up a sheet of note-paper, and began to write to her:—

"Can you grant me a few moments' interview alone? I cannot bear you should think that what I was trying to tell you when we were interrupted was prompted by anything but the deepest sincerity and conviction, or that I am willing it should be passed over lightly by you or be forgotten. Pray give me a chance of proving it, by saying you will see me.   F. M."

But how should he convey this to her? His delicacy revolted against handing it to her behind Mrs. Bradley's back, or the prestidigitation of slipping it into her lap or under her plate before them at luncheon; he thought for an instant of the Chinaman, but gentlemen—except in that "mirror of nature" the stage—usually hesitate to suborn other people's servants, or entrust a woman's secret to her inferiors. He remembered that Louise's room was at the farther end of the house, and its low window gave upon the veranda, and was guarded at night by a film of white and blue curtains that were parted during the day, to allow a triangular revelation of a pale blue and white draped interior. Mainwaring reflected that the low inside window ledge was easily accessible from the veranda, would afford a capital lodgment for the note, and be quickly seen by the fair occupant of the room on entering. He sauntered slowly past the window; the room was empty, the moment propitious. A slight breeze was stirring the blue ribbons of the curtain; it would be necessary to secure the note with something; he returned along the veranda to the steps, where he had noticed a small irregular stone lying, which had evidently

escaped from Richelieu's bag of treasure
specimens, and had been overlooked by
that ingenuous child. It was of a pretty
peacock-blue color, and, besides securing
a paper, would be sure to attract her attention. He placed his note on the inside
ledge, and the blue stone atop, and went
away with a sense of relief.

Another half hour passed without incident. He could hear the voices of the two
women in the kitchen and dining-room.
After a while they appeared to cease, and
he heard the sound of an opening door. It
then occurred to him that the veranda was
still too exposed for a confidential interview, and he resolved to descend the steps,
pass before the windows of the kitchen
where Louise might see him, and penetrate
the shrubbery, where she might be induced
to follow him. They would not be interrupted nor overheard there.

But he had barely left the veranda before the figure of Richelieu, who had been
patiently waiting for Mainwaring's disappearance, emerged stealthily from the
shrubbery. He had discovered his loss on
handing his "fire assays" to the good-
humored Bradley for later examination,

and he had retraced his way, step by step, looking everywhere for his missing stone with the unbounded hopefulness, lazy persistency, and lofty disregard for time and occupation known only to the genuine boy. He remembered to have placed his knotted bag upon the veranda, and, slipping off his stiff boots slowly and softly, slid along against the wall of the house, looking carefully on the floor, and yet preserving a studied negligence of demeanor, with one hand in his pocket, and his small mouth contracted into a singularly soothing and almost voiceless whistle—Richelieu's own peculiar accomplishment. But no stone appeared. Like most of his genus he was superstitious, and repeated to himself the cabalistic formula: "Losin's seekin's, findin's keepin's"—presumed to be of great efficacy in such cases—with religious fervor. He had laboriously reached the end of the veranda when he noticed the open window of Louise's room, and stopped as a perfunctory duty to look in. And then Richelieu Sharpe stood for an instant utterly confounded and aghast at this crowning proof of the absolute infamy and sickening enormity of Man.

There was *his* stone—*his, Richelieu's, own specimen,* carefully gathered by himself and none other—and now stolen, abstracted, "skyugled," "smouged," "hooked" by this "rotten, skunkified, long-legged, splay-footed, hoss-laughin', nigger-toothed, or'nary despot!" And, worse than all, actually made to do infamous duty as a love token!—a "candy-gift!"—a "philanderin' box!" to *his,* Richelieu's, girl—for Louise belonged to that innocent and vague outside seraglio of Richelieu's boyish dreams —and put atop of a letter to her! and Providence permitted such an outrage! "Wot was he, Richelieu, sent to school for, and organized wickedness in the shape of gorilla Injins like this allowed to ride high horses rampant over Californey!" He looked at the heavens in mute appeal. And then—Providence not immediately interfering—he thrust his own small arm into the window, regained his priceless treasure, and fled swiftly.

A fateful silence ensued. The wind slightly moved the curtain outward, as if in a playful attempt to follow him, and then subsided. A moment later, apparently reenforced by other winds, or sym-

pathizing with Richelieu, it lightly lifted
the unlucky missive and cast it softly from
the window. But here another wind,
lying in wait, caught it cleverly, and tossed
it, in a long curve, into the abyss. For an
instant it seemed to float lazily, as on the
mirrored surface of a lake, until, turning
upon its side, it suddenly darted into utter
oblivion.

When Mainwaring returned from the
shrubbery, he went softly to the window.
The disappearance of the letter and stone
satisfied him of the success of his stratagem, and for the space of three hours relieved his anxiety. But at the end of that
time, finding no response from Louise,
his former uneasiness returned. Was
she offended, or — the first doubt of
her acceptance of him crossed his
mind !

A sudden and inexplicable sense of
shame came upon him. At the same moment, he heard his name called from the
steps, turned—and beheld Minty.

Her dark eyes were shining with a pleasant light, and her lips parted on her white
teeth with a frank, happy smile. She advanced and held out her hand. He took it

with a mingling of disappointment and embarrassment.

"You're wondering why I kem on here, arter I sent word this morning that I kelkilated not to come. Well, 'twixt then and now suthin' 's happened. We've had fine doin's over at our house, you bet! Pop don't know which end he's standin' on; and I reckon that for about ten minutes I didn't know my own name. But ez soon ez I got fairly hold o' the hull thing, and had it put straight in my mind, I sez to myself, Minty Sharpe, sez I, the first thing for you to do now, is to put on yer bonnet and shawl, and trapse over to Jim Bradley's and help them two womenfolks get dinner for themselves and that sick stranger. And," continued Minty, throwing herself into a chair and fanning her glowing face with her apron, "yer I am!"

"But you have not told me *what* has happened," said Mainwaring, with a constrained smile, and an uneasy glance towards the house.

"That's so," said Minty, with a brilliant laugh. "I clean forgot the hull gist of the thing. Well, we're rich folks now—over thar' on Barren Ledge! That onery

brother of mine, Richelieu, hez taken some
of his specimens over to Jim Bradley to
be tested. And Bradley, just to please that
child, takes 'em; and not an hour ago
Bradley comes running, likety switch, over
to Pop to tell him to put up his notices,
for the hull of that ledge where the forge
stands is a mine o' silver and copper.
Afore ye knew it, Lordy! half the folks
outer the Summit and the mill was scattered down thar all over it. Richardson—
that stranger ez knows you—kem thar too
with Jim, and he allows, ef Bradley's essay
is right, it's worth more than a hundred
thousand dollars ez it stands!"

"I suppose I must congratulate you, Miss
Sharpe," said Mainwaring with an attempt
at interest, but his attention still preoccupied with the open doorway.

"Oh, *they* know all about it!" said
Minty, following the direction of his abstracted eyes with a slight darkening of
her own, "I jest kem out o' the kitchen the
other way, and Jim sent 'em a note; but
I allowed I'd tell *you* myself. Specially
ez you are going away to-morrow."

"Who said I was going away to-morrow?" asked Mainwaring, uneasily.

"Loo Macy!"

"Ah—she did? But I may change my mind, you know!" he continued, with a faint smile.

Minty shook her curls decisively. "I reckon *she* knows," she said dryly, "she's got law and gospel for wot she says. But yer she comes. Ask her! Look yer, Loo," she added, as the two women appeared at the doorway, with a certain exaggeration of congratulatory manner that struck Mainwaring as being as artificial aṇd disturbed as his own, "didn't Sir Francis yer say he was going to-morrow?"

"That's what I understood!" returned Louise, with cold astonishment, letting her clear indifferent eyes fall upon Mainwaring. "I do not know that he has changed his mind."

"Unless, as Miss Sharpe is a great capitalist now, she is willing to use her powers of persuasion," added Mrs. Bradley, with a slight acidulous pointing of her usual prim playfulness.

"I reckon Minty Sharpe's the same ez she allus wos, unless more so," returned Minty, with an honest egotism that carried so much conviction to the hearer as to con-

done its vanity. "But I kem yer to do a
day's work, gals, and I allow to pitch in
and do it, and not sit yer swoppin' compli-
ments and keeping *him* from packin' his
duds. Onless," she stopped, and looked
around at the uneasy, unsympathetic circle
with a faint tremulousness of lip that be-
lied the brave black eyes above it, "onless
I'm in yer way."

The two women sprang forward with a
feminine bewildering excess of protesta-
tion; and Mainwaring, suddenly pierced
through his outer selfish embarrassment
to his more honest depths, stammered
quickly—

"Look here, Miss Sharpe, if you think
of running away again, after having come
all the way here to make us share the
knowledge of your good fortune and your
better heart, by Jove! I'll go back with
you."

But here the two women effusively hurried her away from the dangerous prox-
imity of such sympathetic honesty, and a
moment later Mainwaring heard her laughing voice, as of old, ringing in the kitchen.
And then, as if unconsciously responding
to the significant common sense that lay in

her last allusion to him, he went to his
room and grimly began his packing.

He did not again see Louise alone. At
their informal luncheon the conversation
turned upon the more absorbing topic of
the Sharpes' discovery, its extent, and its
probable effect upon the fortunes of the locality. He noticed, abstractedly, that both
Mrs. Bradley and her cousin showed a real
or assumed scepticism of its value. This
did not disturb him greatly, except for its
intended check upon Minty's enthusiasm.
He was more conscious, perhaps,—with a
faint touch of mortified vanity,—that his
own contemplated departure was of lesser
importance than this local excitement.
Yet in his growing conviction that all was
over—if, indeed, it had ever begun—between himself and Louise, he was grateful
to this natural diversion of incident which
spared them both an interval of embarrassing commonplaces. And, with the suspicion of some indefinable insincerity—
either of his own or Louise's—haunting
him, Minty's frank heartiness and out-
spoken loyalty gave him a strange relief.
It seemed to him as if the clear cool breath
of the forest had entered with her homely

garments, and the steadfast truth of Nature were incarnate in her shining eyes. How far this poetic fancy would have been consistent or even coexistent with any gleam of tenderness or self-forgetfulness in Louise's equally pretty orbs, I leave the satirical feminine reader to determine.

It was late when Bradley at last returned, bringing further and more complete corroboration of the truth of Sharpe's good fortune. Two experts had arrived, one from Pine Flat and another from the Summit, and upon this statement Richardson had offered to purchase an interest in the discovery that would at once enable the blacksmith to develop his mine. "I shouldn't wonder, Mainwaring," he added cheerfully, "if he'd put you into it, too, and make your eternal fortune."

"With larks falling from the skies all round you, it's a pity *you* couldn't get put into something," said Mrs. Bradley, straightening her pretty brows.

"I'm not a gold-miner, my dear," said Bradley, pleasantly.

"Nor a gold-finder," returned his wife, with a cruel little depression of her pink nostrils, "but you can work all night in

that stupid mill and then," she added in a
low voice, to escape Minty's attention,
"spend the whole of the next day examining and following up a boy's discovery
that his own relations had been too lazy
and too ignorant to understand and profit
by. I suppose that next you will be hunting up a site on the *other side* of the Canyon, where somebody else can put up a
hotel and ruin your own prospects."

A sensitive shadow of pain quickly
dimmed Bradley's glance—not the first or
last time evidently, for it was gradually
bringing out a background of sadness in
his intelligent eyes. But the next moment
he turned kindly to Mainwaring, and
began to deplore the necessity of his early
departure, which Richardson had already
made known to him with practical and
satisfying reasons.

"I hope you won't forget, my dear fellow, that your most really urgent business
is to look after your health; and if, hereafter, you'll only remember the old Lookout enough to impress that fact upon you,
I shall feel that any poor service I have
rendered you has been amply repaid."

Mainwaring, notwithstanding that he

winced slightly at this fateful echo of Louise's advice, returned the grasp of his friend's hand with an honest pressure equal to his own. He longed now only for the coming of Richardson, to complete his scheme of grateful benefaction to his host.

The banker came fortunately as the conversation began to flag; and Mrs. Bradley's half-coquettish ill-humor of a pretty woman, and Louise's abstracted indifference, were becoming so noticeable as to even impress Minty into a thoughtful taciturnity. The graciousness of his reception by Mrs. Bradley somewhat restored his former ostentatious gallantry, and his self-satisfied, domineering manner had enough masculine power in it to favorably affect the three women, who, it must be confessed, were a little bored by the finer abstractions of Bradley and Mainwaring. After a few moments, Mainwaring rose and, with a significant glance at Richardson to remind him of his proposed conference with Bradley, turned to leave the room. He was obliged to pass Louise, who was sitting by the table. His attention was suddenly arrested by something in her hand with which she was listlessly playing.

It was the stone which he had put on his letter to her.

As he had not been present when Bradley arrived, he did not know that this fateful object had been brought home by his host, who, after receiving it from Richelieu, had put it in his pocket to illustrate his story of the discovery. On the contrary, it seemed that Louise's careless exposure of his foolish stratagem was gratuitously and purposely cruel. Nevertheless, he stopped and looked at her.

"That's a queer stone you have there," he said, in a tone which she recognized as coldly and ostentatiously civil.

"Yes," she replied, without looking up; "it's the outcrop of that mine." She handed it to him as if to obviate any further remark. "I thought you had seen it before."

"The outcrop," he repeated dryly. "That is—it—it—it is the indication or sign of something important that's below it—isn't it?"

Louise shrugged her shoulders sceptically. "It don't follow. It's just as likely to cover rubbish, after you've taken the trouble to look."

"Thanks," he said, with measured gentleness, and passed quietly out of the room.

The moon had already risen when Bradley, with his brierwood pipe, preceded Richardson upon the veranda. The latter threw his large frame into Louise's rocking-chair near the edge of the abyss; Bradley, with his own chair tilted against the side of the house after the national fashion, waited for him to speak. The absence of Mainwaring and the stimulus of Mrs. Bradley's graciousness had given the banker a certain condescending familiarity, which Bradley received with amused and ironical tolerance that his twinkling eyes made partly visible in the darkness.

"One of the things I wanted to talk to you about, Bradley, was that old affair of the advance you asked for from the Bank. We did not quite see our way to it then, and, speaking as a business man, it isn't really a matter of business now; but it has lately been put to me in a light that would make the doing of it possible—you understand? The fact of the matter is this: Sir Robert Mainwaring, the father of the young fellow you've got in your house, is one of our directors and largest shareholders, and I can tell you—if you don't suspect it already—you've been lucky, Bradley—deucedly lucky—to have had him in your house and to have rendered him a service. He's the heir to one of the largest landed estates in his country, one of the oldest county families, and will step into the title some day. But, ahem!" he coughed patronizingly, "you knew all that! No? Well, that charming wife of yours, at least, does; for she's been talking about it. Gad, Bradley, it takes those women to find out anything of that kind, eh?"

The light in Bradley's eyes and his pipe went slowly out together.

"Then we'll say that affair of the advance is as good as settled. It's Sir Robert's wish, you understand,—and this young fellow's wish,—and if you'll come down to the Bank next week we'll arrange it for you; I think you'll admit they're doing the handsome to you and yours. And therefore," he lowered his voice confidentially, "you'll see, Bradley, that it will only be the honorable thing in you, you know, to look upon the affair as finished, and, in fact, to do all you can"—

he drew his chair closer—"to—to—to drop this other foolishness."

"I don't think I quite understand you!" said Bradley, slowly.

"But your wife does, if you don't," returned Richardson, bluntly; "I mean this foolish flirtation between Louise Macy and Mainwaring, which is utterly preposterous. Why, man, it can't possibly come to anything, and it couldn't be allowed for a moment. Look at his position and hers. I should think, as a practical man, it would strike you—"

"Only one thing strikes me, Richardson," interrupted Bradley, in a singularly distinct whisper, rising, and moving nearer the speaker; "it is that you're sitting perilously near the edge of this veranda. For, by the living God, if you don't take yourself out of that chair and out of this house, I won't be answerable for the consequences!"

"Hold on there a minute, will you?" said Mainwaring's voice from the window.

Both men turned towards it. A long leg was protruding from Mainwaring's window; it was quickly followed by the other leg and body of the occupant, and the next moment Mainwaring come towards the two men, with his hands in his pockets.

"Not so loud," he said, looking towards the house.

"Let that man go," said Bradley, in a repressed voice. "You and I, Mainwaring, can speak together afterwards."

"That man must stay until he hears what I have got to say," said Mainwaring, stepping between them. He was very white and grave in the moonlight, but very quiet; and he did not take his hands from his pockets. "I've listened to what he said because he came here on *my* business, which was simply to offer to do you a service. That was all, Bradley, that *I* told him to do. This rot about what he expects of you in return is his own impertinence. If you'd punched his head when he began it, it would have been all right. But since he has begun it, before he goes I think he ought to hear me tell you that I have already *offered* myself to Miss Macy, and she has *refused* me! If she had given me the least encouragement, I should have told you before. Further, I want to say that, in spite of that man's insinuations, I firmly believe that no one is aware of the circumstance except Miss Macy and my-self."

"I had no idea of intimating that any-thing had happened that was not highly honorable and creditable to you and the young lady," began Richardson, hurriedly.

"I don't know that it was necessary for you to have any ideas on the subject at all," said Mainwaring, sternly; "nor that, having been shown how you have insulted this gentleman and myself, you need trouble us an instant longer with your company. You need not come back. I will manage my other affairs myself."

"Very well, Mr. Mainwaring—but— you may be sure that I shall certainly take the first opportunity to explain myself to Sir Robert," returned Richardson as, with an attempt at dignity, he strode away.

There was an interval of silence.

"Don't be too hard upon a fellow, Brad-ley," said Mainwaring, as Bradley re-mained dark and motionless in the shadow. "It is a poor return I'm making you for your kindness, but I swear I never thought of anything like—like—this."

"Nor did I," said Bradley, bitterly.

"I know it, and that's what makes it so

infernally bad for me. Forgive me, won't
you? Think of me, old fellow, as the
wretchedest ass you ever met, but not such
a cad as this would make me!" As Mainwaring stepped out from the moonlight
towards him with extended hand, Bradley
grasped it warmly.

"Thanks—there—thanks, old fellow!
And, Bradley—I say—don't say anything
to your wife, for I don't think she knows
it. And, Bradley—look here—I didn't
like to be anything but plain before that
fellow; but I don't mind telling *you,* now
that it's all over, that I really think Louise
—Miss Macy—didn't altogether understand me either."

With another shake of the hand they
separated for the night. For a long time
after Mainwaring had gone, Bradley remained gazing thoughtfully into the Great
Canyon. He thought of the time when he
had first come there, full of life and enthusiasm, making an ideal world of his
pure and wholesome eyrie on the ledge.
What else he thought will, probably, never
be known until the misunderstanding
of honorable and chivalrous men by a
charming and illogical sex shall incite

the audacious pen of some more daring romancer.

When he returned to the house, he said kindly to his wife, "I have been thinking to-day about your hotel scheme, and I shall write to Sacramento to-night to accept that capitalist's offer."

CHAPTER V.

The sun was just rising. In two years
of mutation and change it had seen the
little cottage clinging like a swallow's nest
to the rocky caves of a great Sierran can-
you give way to a straggling, many-
galleried hotel, and a dozen blackened
chimneys rise above the barren tableland
where once had stood the lonely forge. To
that conservative orb of light and heat
there must have been a peculiar satisfaction in looking down a few hours earlier
upon the battlements and gables of Oldenhurst, whose base was deeply embedded in
the matured foundations and settled traditions of an English county. For the rising
sun had for ten centuries found Oldenhurst in its place, from the heavy stone
terrace that covered the dead-and-forgotten
wall, where a Roman sentinel had once
paced, to the little grating in the cloistered
quadrangle, where it had seen a Cister-

cian brother place the morning dole. It
had daily welcomed the growth of this vast
and picturesque excrescence of the times;
it had smiled every morning upon this
formidable yet quaint incrustation of
power and custom, ignoring, as Oldenhurst itself had ignored, the generations
who possessed it, the men who built it, the
men who carried it with fire and sword,
the men who had lied and cringed for it,
the King who had given it to a favorite, the few brave hearts who had died for
it in exile, and the one or two who had
bought and paid for it. For Oldenhurst
had absorbed all these and more until it
had become a story of the past, incarnate
in stone, greenwood, and flower; it had
even drained the life-blood from adjacent
hamlets, repaying them with tumuli
growths like its own, in the shape of purposeless lodges, quaintly incompetent hospitals and schools, and churches where the
inestimable blessing and knowledge of its
gospel were taught and fostered. Nor had
it dealt more kindly with the gentry within
its walls, sending some to the scaffold, pil-
lorying others in infamous office, reducing a few to poverty, and halting its later

guests with gout and paralysis. It had given them in exchange the dubious immortality of a portrait gallery, from which they stared with stony and equal resignation; it had preserved their useless armor and accoutrements; it had set up their marble effigies in churches or laid them in cross-legged attitudes to trip up the unwary, until in death, as in life, they got between the congregation and the Truth that was taught there. It had allowed an Oldenhurst crusader, with a broken nose like a pugilist, on the strength of his having been twice to the Holy Land, to hide the beautifully illuminated Word from the lowlier worshipper on the humbler benches; it had sent an iconoclastic Bishop of the Reformation to a nearer minster to ostentatiously occupy the place of the consecrated image he had overthrown. Small wonder that crowding the Oldenhurst retainers gradually into smaller space, with occasional Sabbath glimpses of the living rulers of Oldenhurst already in railed-off exaltation, it had forced them to accept Oldenhurst as a synonym of eternity, and left the knowledge of a higher Power to what time they should be turned

out to their longer sleep under the tender
grass of the beautiful outer churchyard.

And even so, while every stone of the
pile of Oldenhurst and every tree in its
leafy park might have been eloquent with
the story of vanity, selfishness, and unequal justice, it had been left to the infinite
mercy of Nature to seal their lips with a
spell of beauty that left mankind equally
dumb; earth, air, and moisture had entered into a gentle conspiracy to soften,
mellow, and clothe its external blemishes
of breach and accident, its irregular design,
its additions, accretions, ruins, and lapses
with a harmonious charm of outline and
color; poets, romancers, and historians had
equally conspired to illuminate the dark
passages and uglier inconsistencies of its
interior life with the glamour of their own
fancy. The fragment of menacing keep,
with its choked oubliettes, became a bower
of tender ivy; the grim story of its crimes,
properly edited by a contemporary bard of
the family, passed into a charming ballad.
Even the superstitious darkness of its religious house had escaped through fallen
roof and shattered wall, leaving only the
foliated and sun-pierced screen of front,

with its rose-window and pinnacle of cross
behind. Pilgrims from all lands had come
to see it; fierce Republicans had crossed
the seas to gaze at its mediæval outlines,
and copy them in wood and stucco on their
younger soil. Politicians had equally
pointed to it as a convincing evidence of
their own principles and in refutation of
each other; and it had survived both. For
it was this belief in its own perpetuity that
was its strength and weakness. And that
belief was never stronger than on this
bright August morning, when it was on the
verge of dissolution. A telegram brought
to Sir Robert Mainwaring had even then
as completely shattered and disintegrated
Oldenhurst, in all it was and all it meant,
as if the brown-paper envelope had been
itself charged with the electric fluid.

Sir Robert Mainwaring, whose family
had for three centuries possessed Oldenhurst, had received the news of his financial ruin; and the vast pile which had
survived the repeated invasion of superstition, force, intrigue, and even progress,
had succumbed to a foe its founders and
proprietors had loftily ignored and left to
Jews and traders. The acquisition of

money, except by despoilment, gift, royal
favor, or inheritance, had been unknown at
Oldenhurst. The present degenerate cus-
todian of its fortunes, staggering under
the weight of its sentimental mortmain
already alluded to, had speculated in order
to keep up its material strength, that was
gradually shrinking through impoverished
land and the ruined trade it had despised.
He had invested largely in California
mines, and was the chief shareholder in a
San Francisco Bank. But the mines had
proved worthless, the Bank had that morning suspended payment, owing to the
failure of a large land and timber company
on the Sierras which it had imprudently
"carried." The spark which had demol-
ished Oldenhurst had been fired from the
new telegraph-station in the hotel above
the great Sierran canyon.

There was a large house-party at Oldenhurst that morning. But it had been a
part of the history of the Mainwarings to
accept defeat gallantly and as became
their blood. Sir Percival,—the second
gentleman on the left as you entered the
library,—unhorsed, dying on a distant
moor, with a handful of followers, aban-

doned by a charming Prince and a miserable cause, was scarcely a greater hero
than this ruined but undaunted gentleman
of eighty, entering the breakfast-room a
few hours later as jauntily as his gout
would permit, and conscientiously dispens-
ing the hospitalities of his crumbling
house. When he had arranged a few
pleasure parties for the day and himself thoughtfully anticipated the different
tastes of his guests, he turned to Lady
Mainwaring.

"Don't forget that somebody ought to
go to the station to meet the Bradleys.
Frank writes from St. Moritz that they
are due here to-day."

Lady Mainwaring glanced quickly at
her husband, and said *sotto voce,* "Do you
think they'll care to come *now?* They
probably have heard all about it."

"Not how it affects me," returned Sir
Robert, in the same tone; "and as they
might think that because Frank was with
them on that California mountain we
would believe it had something to do with
Richardson involving the Bank in that
wretched company, we must really *insist*
upon their coming."

"Bradley!" echoed the Hon. Captain FitzHarry, overhearing the name during a late forage on the sideboard, "Bradley!— there was an awfully pretty American at Biarritz, travelling with a cousin, I think —a Miss Mason or Macy. Those sort of people, you know, who have a companion as pretty as themselves; bring you down with the other barrel if one misses—eh? Very clever, both of them, and hardly any accent."

"Mr. Bradley was a very dear friend of Frank's, and most kind to him," said Lady Mainwaring, gravely.

"Didn't know there *was* a Mr. Bradley, really. He didn't come to the fore, then," said the unabashed Captain. "Deuced hard to follow up those American husbands!"

"And their wives wouldn't thank you, if you did," said Lady Griselda Armiger, with a sweet smile.

"If it is the Mrs. Bradley I mean," said Lady Canterbridge from the lower end of the table, looking up from her letter, "who looks a little like Mrs. Summertree, and has a pretty cousin with her who has very good frocks, I'm afraid you won't be able to get her down here. She's booked with engagements for the next six weeks. She and her cousin made all the running at Grigsby Royal, and she has quite deposed that other American beauty in Northforeland's good graces. She regularly *affiché'd* him, and it is piteous to see him follow her about. No, my dear; I don't believe they'll come to any one of less rank than a Marquis. If they did, I'm sure Canterbridge would have had them at Buckenthorpe already."

"I wonder if there was ever anything in Frank's admiration of this Miss Macy?" said Lady Mainwaring a few moments later, lingering beside her husband in his study.

"I really don't know," said Sir Robert, abstractedly: "his letters were filled with her praises, and Richardson thought—"

"Pray don't mention that man's name again," said Lady Mainwaring, with the first indication of feeling she had shown. "I shouldn't trust him."

"But why do you ask?" returned her husband.

Lady Mainwaring was silent for a moment. "She is very rich, I believe," she said slowly. "At least, Frank writes that some neighbors of theirs whom he met in the Engadine told him they had sold the site of that absurd cottage where he was ill for some extravagant sum."

"My dear Geraldine," said the old man, affectionately, taking his wife's hand in his own, that now for the first time trembled, "if you have any hope based upon what you are thinking of now, let it be the last and least. You forget that Paget told us that with the best care he could scarcely ensure Frank's return to perfect health. Even if God in his mercy spared him long enough to take my place, what girl would be willing to tie herself to a man doomed to sickness and poverty? Hardly the one you speak of, my dear."

Lady Canterbridge proved a true prophet. Mrs. Bradley and Miss Macy did not come, regretfully alleging a previous engagement made on the continent with the Duke of Northforeland and the Marquis of Dungeness; but the unexpected and apocryphal husband *did* arrive. "I myself have not seen my wife and cousin since I returned from my visit to your son in Switzerland. I am glad they were able to

amuse themselves without waiting for me
at a London hotel, though I should have
preferred to have met them here." Sir
Robert and Lady Mainwaring were courte-
eous but slightly embarrassed. Lady
Canterbridge, who had come to the station
in bored curiosity, raised her clear blue
eyes to his. He did not look like a fool,
a complaisant or fashionably-cynical husband—this well-dressed, well-mannered,
but quietly and sympathetically observant
man. Did he really care for his selfish
wife? was it perfect trust or some absurd
Transatlantic custom? She did not understand him. It wearied her and she turned
her eyes indifferently away. Bradley, a
little irritated, he knew not why, at the
scrutiny of this tall, handsome, gentle-
manly-looking woman, who, however, in
spite of her broad shoulders and narrow
hips possessed a refined muliebrity superior to mere womanliness of outline,
turned slightly towards Sir Robert.
"Lady Canterbridge, Frank's cousin," explained Sir Robert, hesitatingly, as if
conscious of some vague awkwardness.
Bradley and Lady Canterbridge both
bowed,—possibly the latter's salutation

was the most masculine,—and Bradley, eventually forgetting her presence, plunged into an earnest, sympathetic, and intelligent account of the condition in which he found the invalid at St. Moritz. The old man at first listened with an almost perfunctory courtesy and a hesitating reserve; but as Bradley was lapsing into equal reserve and they drove up to the gates of the quadrangle, he unexpectedly warmed with a word or two of serious welcome. Looking up with a half-unconscious smile, Bradley met Lady Canterbridge's examining eyes.

The next morning, finding an opportunity to be alone with him, Bradley, with a tactful mingling of sympathy and directness, informed his host that he was cognizant of the disaster that had overtaken the Bank, and delicately begged him to accept any service he could render him. "Pardon me," he said, "if I speak as plainly to you as I would to your son: my friendship for him justifies an equal frankness to any one he loves; but I should not intrude upon your confidence if I did not believe that my knowledge and assistance might be of benefit to you. Although I did not sell my lands to Richardson or approve of his methods," he continued, "I fear it was some suggestion of mine that eventually induced him to form the larger and more disastrous scheme that ruined the Bank. So you see," he added lightly, "I claim a right to offer you my services." Touched by Bradley's sincerity and discreet intelligence, Sir Robert was equally frank. During the recital of his Californian investments—a chronicle of almost fatuous speculation and imbecile enterprise —Bradley was profoundly moved at the naive ignorance of business and hopeless ingenuousness of this old habitué of a cynical world and an intriguing and insincere society, to whom no scheme had been too wild for acceptance. As Bradley listened with a half-saddened smile to the grave visions of this aged enthusiast, he remembered the son's unsophisticated simplicity: what he had considered as the "boyishness" of immaturity was the taint of the utterly unpractical Mainwaring blood. It was upon this blood, and others like it, that Oldenhurst had for centuries waxed and fattened.

Bradley was true to his promise of assistance, and with the aid of two or three of his brother-millionaires, whose knowledge of the resources of the locality was no less powerful and convincing than the security of their actual wealth, managed to stay the immediate action of the catastrophe until the affairs of the Sierran Land and Timber Company could be examined and some plan of reconstruction arranged.

During this interval of five months, in which the credit of Sir Robert Mainwaring was preserved with the secret of his disaster, Bradley was a frequent and welcome visitor to Oldenhurst. Apart from his strange and chivalrous frendship for the Mainwarings—which was as incomprehensible to Sir Robert as Sir Robert's equally eccentric and Quixotic speculations had been to Bradley—he began to feel a singular and weird fascination for the place. A patient martyr in the vast London house he had taken for his wife and cousin's amusement, he loved to escape the loneliness of its autumn solitude or the occasional greater loneliness of his wife's social triumphs. The handsome, thoughtful man who sometimes appeared

at the foot of his wife's table or melted
away like a well-bred ghost in the hollow
emptiness of her brilliant receptions,
piqued the languid curiosity of a few.
A distinguished personage, known for his
tactful observance of *convenances* that
others forgot, had made a point of challenging this gentlemanly apparition, and
had followed it up with courteous civilities,
which led to exchange of much respect but
no increase of acquaintance. He had even
spent a week at Buckenthorpe, with Canterbridge in the coverts and Lady Canterbridge in the music-room and library. He
had returned more thoughtful, and for
some time after was more frequent in his
appearances at home, and more earnest in
his renewed efforts to induce his wife to
return to America with him.

"You'll never be happy anywhere but in
California, among those common people,"
she replied; "and while I was willing to
share your poverty *there,*" she added dryly,
"I prefer to share your wealth among civilized ladies and gentlemen. Besides," she
continued, "we must consider Louise. She
is as good as engaged to Lord Dunshunner,
and I do not intend that you shall make a

mess of her affairs here as you did in California."

It was the first time he had heard of
Lord Dunshunner's proposals; it was the
first allusion she had ever made to Louise
and Mainwaring.

Meantime, the autumn leaves had fallen
silently over the broad terraces of Oldenhurst with little changes to the fortunes of
the great house itself. The Christmas
house-party included Lady Canterbridge,
whose husband was still detained at Hom-
burg in company with Dunshunner; and
Bradley, whose wife and cousin lingered
on the continent. He was slightly embarrassed when Lady Canterbridge turned
to him one afternoon as they were returning from the lake and congratulated him
abruptly upon Louise's engagement.

"Perhaps you don't care to be congratulated," she said, as he did not immediately
respond, "and you had as little to do with
it as with that other? It is a woman's
function."

"What other?" echoed Bradley.

Lady Canterbridge slightly turned her
handsome head towards him as she walked
unbendingly at his side. "Tell me how

you manage to keep your absolute simplicity so fresh. Do you suppose it wasn't known at Oldenhurst that Frank had quite compromised himself with Miss Macy over there?"

"It certainly was not known 'over there,'" said Bradley, curtly.

"Don't be angry with me."

Such an appeal from the tall, indifferent woman at his side, so confidently superior to criticism, and uttered in a low tone, made him smile, albeit uneasily.

"I only meant to congratulate you," she continued carelessly. "Dunshunner is not a bad sort of fellow, and will come into a good property some day. And then, society is so made up of caprice, just now, that it is well for your wife's cousin to make the most of her opportunities while they last. She is very popular now; but next season—" Seeing that Bradley remained silent, she did not finish the sentence, but said with her usual abruptness, "Do you know a Miss Araminta Eulalie Sharpe?"

Bradley started. Could any one recognize honest Minty in the hopeless vulgarity which this fine lady had managed

to carelessly import into her name? His
eye kindled.

"She is an old friend of mine, Lady
Canterbridge."

"How fortunate! Then I can please you
by giving you good news of her. She is
the coming sensation. They say she is
very rich, but quite one of the people, you
know: in fact, she makes no scruples of
telling you her father was a blacksmith, I
think, and takes the dear old man with her
everywhere. FitzHarry raves about her,
and says her naïveté is something too delicious. She is regularly in with some of
the best people already. Lady Dungeness
has taken her up, and Northforeland is
only waiting for your cousin's engagement
to be able to go over decently. Shall I
ask her to Buckenthorpe?—come, now, as
an apology for my rudeness to your
cousin?" She was very womanly now in
spite of her high collar, her straight back,
and her tightly-fitting jacket, as she stood
there smiling. Suddenly, her smile faded;
she drew her breath in quickly.

She had caught a glimpse of his usually
thoughtful face and eyes, now illuminated
with some pleasant memory.

"Thank you," he said smilingly, yet with a certain hesitation, as he thought of The Lookout and Araminta Eulalie Sharpe, and tried to reconcile them with the lady before him. "I should like it very much."

"Then you have known Miss Sharpe a long time?" continued Lady Canterbridge as they walked on.

"While we were at The Lookout she was our nearest neighbor."

"And I suppose your wife will consider it quite proper for you to see her again at my house?" said Lady Canterbridge, with a return of conventional levity.

"Oh! quite," said Bradley.

They had reached the low Norman-arched side-entrance to the quadrangle. As Bradley swung open the bolt-studded oaken door to let her pass, she said carelessly,—

"Then you are not coming in now?"

"No; I shall walk a little longer."

"And I am quite forgiven?"

"I am thanking you very much," he said, smiling directly into her blue eyes. She lowered them, and vanished into the darkness of the passage.

The news of Minty's success was further

corroborated by Sir Robert, who later that evening called Bradley into the study. "Frank has been writing from Nice that he has renewed his acquaintance with some old Californian friends of yours—a Mr. and Miss Sharpe. Lady Canterbridge says that they are well known in London to some of our friends, but I would like to ask you something about them. Lady Mainwaring was on the point of inviting them here when I received a letter from Mr. Sharpe asking for a *business* interview. Pray who is this Sharpe?"

"You say he writes for a *business* interview?" asked Bradley.

"Yes."

Bradley hesitated for a moment and then said quietly, "Perhaps, then, I am justified in a breach of confidence to him, in order to answer your question. He is the man who has assumed all the liabilities of the Sierran Land and Timber Company to enable the Bank to resume payment. But he did it on the condition that you were never to know it. For the rest, he was a blacksmith who made a fortune, as Lady Canterbridge will tell you."

"How very odd—how kind, I mean. I

should like to have been civil to him on Frank's account alone."

"I should see him on business and be civil to him afterwards." Sir Robert received the American's levity with his usual seriousness.

"No, they must come here for Christmas. His daughter is— ?"

"Araminta Eulalie Sharpe," said Bradley, in defiant memory of Lady Canterbridge.

Sir Robert winced audibly. "I shall rely on you, my dear boy, to help me make it pleasant for them," he said.

Christmas came, but not Minty. It drew a large contingent from Oldenhurst to the quaint old church, who came to view the green-wreathed monuments, and walls spotted with crimson berries, as if with the blood of former Oldenhurst warriors, and to impress the wondering villagers with the ineffable goodness and bounty of the Creator towards the Lords of Oldenhurst and their friends. Sir Robert, a little gouty, kept the house, and Bradley, somewhat uneasy at the Sharpes' absence, but more distrait with other thoughts, wandered listlessly in the long library. At the

lower angle it was embayed into the octa-
gon space of a former tower, which was
furnished as a quaint recess for writing or
study, pierced through its enormous walls
with a lance-shaped window, hidden by
heavy curtains. He was gazing abstractedly at the melancholy eyes of Sir Percival, looking down from the dark panel
opposite, when he heard the crisp rustle of
a skirt. Lady Canterbridge, tightly and
stiffly buttoned in black from her long narrow boots to her slim, white-collared neck,
stood beside him with a prayer-book in her
ungloved hand. Bradley colored quickly;
the penetrating incense of the Christmas
boughs and branches that decked the walls
and ceilings, mingled with some indefinable intoxicating aura from the woman at
his side, confused his senses. He seemed
to be losing himself in some forgotten
past coeval with the long, quaintly-lighted
room, the rich hangings, and the painted
ancestor of this handsome woman. He
recovered himself with an effort, and
said,

"You are going to church?"

"I may meet them coming home; it's all
the same. You like *him?*" she said ab-

ruptly, pointing to the portrait. "I thought you did not care for that sort of man over there."

"A man like that must have felt the impotence of his sacrifice before he died, and that condoned everything," said Bradley, thoughtfully.

"Then you don't think him a fool? Bob says it was a fair bargain for a title and an office, and that by dying he escaped trial and the confiscation of what he had."

Bradley did not reply.

"I am disturbing your illusions again. Yet I rather like them. I think you are quite capable of a sacrifice—perhaps you know what it is already."

He felt that she was looking at him; he felt equally that he could not respond with a commonplace. He was silent.

"I have offended you again, Mr. Bradley," she said. "Please be Christian, and pardon me. You know this is a season of peace and goodwill." She raised her blue eyes at the same moment to the Christmas decorations on the ceiling. They were standing before the parted drapery of the lance window. Midway between the arched curtains hung a spray of mistletoe

—the conceit of a mischievous housemaid.
Their eyes met it simultaneously.

Bradley had Lady Canterbridge's slim,
white hand in his own. The next moment
voices were heard in the passage, and the
door nearly opposite to them opened deliberately. The idea of their apparent seclusion and half compromising attitude
flashed through the minds of both at the
same time. Lady Canterbridge stepped
quickly backward, drawing Bradley with
her, into the embrasure of the window;
the folds of the curtain swung together and
concealed them from view.

The door had been opened by the footman, ushering in a broad-shouldered man,
who was carrying a travelling-bag and an
umbrella in his hand. Dropping into an
arm-chair before the curtain, he waved
away the footman, who, even now, mechanically repeated a previously vain attempt to relieve the stranger of his luggage.

"You leave that 'ere grip sack where it
is, young man, and tell Sir Robert Mainwaring that Mr. Demander Sharpe, of
Californy, wishes to see him—on business
—on *business,* do ye' hear? You hang
onter that sentence—*on business!* it's about

ez much ez you kin carry, I reckon, and leave that grip sack alone."

From behind the curtain Bradley made a sudden movement to go forward; but Lady Canterbridge—now quite pale but collected—restrained him with a warning movement of her hand. Sir Robert's stick and halting step were next heard along the passage, and he entered the room. His simple and courteous greeting of the stranger was instantly followed by a renewed attack upon the "grip sack," and a renewed defence of it by the stranger.

"No, Sir Robert," said the voice argumentatively, "this yer's a *business* interview, and until it's over—if *you* please—we'll remain ez we air. I'm Demander Sharpe, of Californy, and I and my darter, Minty, oncet had the pleasure of knowing your boy over thar, and of meeting him agin the other day at Nice."

"I think," said Sir Robert's voice gently, "that these are not the only claims you have upon me. I have only a day or two ago heard from Mr. Bradley that I owe to your generous hands and your disinterested liberality the saving of my California fortune."

There was the momentary sound of a pushed-back chair, a stamping of feet, and then Mr. Sharpe's voice rose high with the blacksmith's old querulous aggrieved utterance:—

"So it's that finikin', conceited Bradley agin—that's giv' me away! Ef that man's all-fired belief in his being the Angel Gabriel and Dan'l Webster rolled inter one don't beat anythin'! I suppose that high-flyin' jay-bird kalkilated to put you and me and my gal and yer boy inter harness for his four hoss chariot and he sittin' kam on the box drivin' us! Why don't he tend to his own business, and look arter his own concerns—instead o' leaving Jinny Bradley and Loo Macy dependent on Kings and Queens and titled folks gen'rally, and he, Jim Bradley, philanderin' with another man's wife—while that thar man is hard at work tryin' to make a honest livin' fer his wife, buckin' agin faro an' the tiger gen'rally at Monaco! Eh? And that man a-inter-meddlin' with me! Ef," continued the voice, dropped to a tone of hopeless moral conviction, "ef there's a man I mor'aly despise—it's that finikin' Jim Bradley."

"You quite misunderstand me, my dear sir," said Sir Robert's hurried voice; "he told me you had pledged him to secrecy, and he only revealed it to explain why you wished to see me."

There was a grunt of half-placated wrath from Sharpe, and then the voice resumed, but more deliberately, "Well, to come back to business: you've got a boy, Francis, and I've got a darter, Araminty. They've sorter taken a shine to each other and they want to get married. Mind yer —wait a moment!—it wasn't allus so. No, sir; when my gal Araminty first seed your boy in Californy she was poor, and she didn't kalkilate to get inter anybody's family unbeknownst or on sufferance. Then she got rich and you got poor; and then—hold on a minit!—she allows, does my girl, that there ain't any nearer chance o' their making a match than they were afore, for she isn't goin' to hev it said that she married your son fur the chance of some day becomin' Lady Mainwaring."

"One moment, Mr. Sharpe," said the voice of the Baronet, gravely: "I am both flattered and pained by what I believe to be the kindly object of your visit. Indeed, I may say I have gathered a suspicion of what might be the sequel of this most unhappy acquaintance of my son and your daughter; but I cannot believe that he has kept you in ignorance of his unfortunate prospects and his still more unfortunate state of health."

"When I told ye to hold on a minit," continued the blacksmith's voice, with a touch of querulousness in its accent, "that was jist wot I was comin' to. I knowed part of it from my own pocket, she knowed the rest of it from his lip and the doctors she interviewed. And then she says to me —sez my girl Minty—'Pop,' she sez, 'he's got nothing to live for now but his title, and that he never may live to get, so that I think ye kin jist go, Pop, and fairly and squarely, as a honest man, ask his father to let me hev him.' Them's my darter's own words, Sir Robert, and when I tell yer that she's got a million o' dollars to back them, ye'll know she means business every time."

"Did Francis know that you were coming here?"

"Bless ye, no! He don't know that she

would have him. Ef it kem to that, he
ain't even asked her! She wouldn't let
him until she was sure of *you*."

"Then you mean to say there is no engagement?"

"In course not. I reckoned to do the
square thing first with ye."

The halting step of the Baronet crossing
the room was heard distinctly. He had
stopped beside Sharpe. "My dear Mr.
Sharpe," he said, in a troubled voice, "I
cannot permit this sacrifice. It is too—
too great!"

"Then," said Sharpe's voice querulously,
"I'm afraid we must do without your permission. I didn't reckon to find a sort o'
British Jim Bradley in you. If *you* can't
permit my darter to sacrifice herself by
marryin' your son, I can't permit her to
sacrifice her love and him by *not* marryin'
him. So I reckon this yer interview is
over."

"I am afraid we are both old fools, Mr.
Sharpe; but—we will talk this over with
Lady Mainwaring. Come—" There was
evidently a slight struggle near the chair
over some inanimate object. But the next
moment the Baronet's voice rose, persua-

sively, "Really, I must insist upon re-
lieving you of your bag and umbrella."

"Well, if you'll let me telegraph 'yes'
to Minty, I don't care if yer do."

When the room was quiet again, Lady
Canterbridge and James Bradley silently
slipped from the curtain, and, without a
word, separated at the door.

There was a merry Christmas at Oldenhurst and at Nice. But whether Minty's
loving sacrifice was accepted or not, or
whether she ever reigned as Lady Mainwaring, or lived an untitled widow, I cannot say. But as Oldenhurst still exists in
all its pride and power, it is presumed that
the peril that threatened its fortunes was
averted, and that if another heroine was
not found worthy of a frame in its picture-
gallery, at least it had been sustained as of
old by devotion and renunciation.

A DRIFT FROM REDWOOD CAMP.

THEY had all known him as a shiftless, worthless creature. From the time he first entered Redwood Camp, carrying his entire effects in a red handkerchief on the end of a long-handled shovel, until he lazily drifted out of it on a plank in the terrible inundation of '56, they never expected anything better of him. In a community of strong men with sullen virtues and charmingly fascinating vices, he was tolerated as possessing neither—not even rising by any dominant human weakness or ludicrous quality to the importance of a butt. In the *dramatis personæ* of Redwood Camp he was a simple "super"—who had only passive, speechless rôles in those fierce dramas that were sometimes unrolled beneath its green-curtained pines. Nameless and penniless, he was overlooked by the census and ignored by the tax collector, while in a

463

hotly-contested election for sheriff, when even the head-boards of the scant cemetery were consulted to fill the poll-lists, it was discovered that neither candidate had thought fit to avail himself of his actual vote. He was debarred the rude heraldry of a nickname of achievement, and in a camp made up of "Euchre Bills," "Poker Dicks," "Profane Pete," and "Snap-shot Harry," was known vaguely as "him," "Skeesicks," or "that coot." It was remembered long after, with a feeling of superstition, that he had never even met with the dignity of an accident, nor received the fleeting honor of a chance shot meant for somebody else in any of the liberal and broadly comprehensive encounters which distinguished the camp. And the inundation that finally carried him out of it was partly anticipated by his passive incompetency, for while the others escaped —or were drowned in escaping—he calmly floated off on his plank without an opposing effort.

For all that, Elijah Martin—which was his real name—was far from being unamiable or repellent. That he was cowardly, untruthful, selfish, and lazy, was undoubtedly the fact; perhaps it was his peculiar misfortune that, just then, courage, frankness, generosity, and activity were the dominant factors in the life of Redwood Camp. His submissive gentleness, his unquestioned modesty, his half refinement, and his amiable exterior consequently availed him nothing against the fact that he was missed during a raid of the Digger Indians, and lied to account for it; or that he lost his right to a gold discovery by failing to make it good against a bully, and selfishly kept this discovery from the knowledge of the camp. Yet this weakness awakened no animosity in his companions, and it is probable that the indifference of the camp to his fate in this final catastrophe came purely from a simple forgetfulness of one who at that supreme moment was weakly incapable.

Such was the reputation and such the antecedents of the man who, on the 15th of March, 1856, found himself adrift in a swollen tributary of the Minyo. A spring freshet of unusual volume had flooded the adjacent river until, bursting its bounds, it escaped through the narrow, wedge-shaped valley that held Redwood Camp. For a day and night the surcharged river poured half its waters through the straggling camp. At the end of that time every vestige of the little settlement was swept away; all that was left was scattered far and wide in the country, caught in the hanging branches of water-side willows and alders, embayed in sluggish pools, dragged over submerged meadows, and one fragment—bearing up Elijah Martin—pursuing the devious courses of an unknown tributary fifty miles away. Had he been a rash, impatient man, he would have been speedily drowned in some earlier desperate attempt to reach the shore; had he been an ordinary bold man, he would have succeeded in transferring himself to the branches of some obstructing tree; but he was neither, and he clung to his broken raft-like berth with an endurance that was half the paralysis of terror and half the patience of habitual misfortune. Eventually he was caught in a side current, swept to the bank, and cast ashore on an unexplored wilderness.

His first consciousness was one of hunger that usurped any sentiment of gratitude for his escape from drowning. As soon as his cramped limbs permitted, he crawled out of the bushes in search of food. He did not know where he was; there was no sign of habitation—or even occupation —anywhere. He had been too terrified to notice the direction in which he had drifted —even if he had possessed the ordinary knowledge of a backwoodsman, which he did not. He was helpless. In his bewildered state, seeing a squirrel cracking a nut on the branch of a hollow tree near him, he made a half-frenzied dart at the frightened animal, which ran away. But the same association of ideas in his torpid and confused brain impelled him to search for the squirrel's hoard in the hollow of the tree. He ate the few hazel-nuts he found there, ravenously. The purely animal instinct satisfied, he seemed to have borrowed from it a certain strength and intuition. He limped through the thicket not unlike some awkward, shy quadrumane, stopping here and there to peer out through the openings over the marshes that lay beyond. His sight, hearing, and even the sense of smell had become preternaturally acute. It was the latter which suddenly arrested his steps with the odor of dried fish. It had a significance beyond the mere instincts of hunger—it indicated the contiguity of some Indian encampment. And as such — it meant danger, torture, and death.

He stopped, trembled violently, and tried to collect his scattered senses. Redwood Camp had embroiled itself needlessly and brutally with the surrounding Indians, and only held its own against them by reckless courage and unerring marksmanship. The frequent use of a casual wandering Indian as a target for the practising rifles of its members had kept up an undying hatred in the heart of the aborigines and stimulated them to terrible and isolated reprisals. The scalped and skinned dead body of Jack Trainer, tied on his horse and held hideously upright by a cross of wood behind his saddle, had passed, one night, a slow and ghastly apparition, into camp; the corpse of Dick Ryner had been found anchored on the river-bed, disembowelled and filled with stone and gravel. The solitary and unprotected member of Redwood Camp who fell into the enemy's hands was doomed.

Elijah Martin remembered this, but his

fears gradually began to subside in a certain apathy of the imagination, which,
perhaps, dulled his apprehensions and allowed the instinct of hunger to become
again uppermost. He knew that the low
bark tents, or wigwams, of the Indians
were hung with strips of dried salmon,
and his whole being was new centered
upon an attempt to stealthily procure a
delicious morsel. As yet he had distinguished no other sign of life or habitation ;
a few moments later, however, and grown
bolder with an animal-like trustfulness in
his momentary security, he crept out of the
thicket and found himself near a long,
low mound or burrow-like structure of
mud and bark on the river-bank. A single
narrow opening, not unlike the entrance of
an Esquimau hut, gave upon the river.
Martin had no difficulty in recognizing the
character of the building. It was a "sweat-
house," an institution common to nearly
all the aboriginal tribes of California.
Half a religious temple, it was also half a
sanitary asylum, was used as a Russian
bath or superheated vault, from which the
braves, sweltering and stifling all night, by
smothered fires, at early dawn plunged,

perspiring, into the ice-cold river. The
heat and smoke were further utilized to
dry and cure the long strips of fish hanging from the roof, and it was through the
narrow aperture that served as a chimney
that the odor escaped which Martin had
detected. He knew that as the bathers
only occupied the house from midnight
to early morn, it was now probably empty.
He advanced confidently toward it.

He was a little surprised to find that the
small open space between it and the river
was occupied by a rude scaffolding, like
that on which certain tribes exposed their
dead, but in this instance it only contained
the feathered leggings, fringed blanket,
and eagle-plumed head-dress of some
brave. He did not, however, linger in this
plainly visible area, but quickly dropped
on all fours and crept into the interior of
the house. Here he completed his feast
with the fish, and warmed his chilled limbs
on the embers of the still smouldering
fires. It was while drying his tattered
clothes and shoeless feet that he thought
of the dead brave's useless leggings and
moccasins, and it occurred to him that he
would be less likely to attract the Indians'

attention from a distance and provoke a ready arrow, if he were disguised as one of them. Crawling out again, he quickly secured, not only the leggings, but the blanket and head-dress, and putting them on, cast his own clothes into the stream. A bolder, more energetic, or more provident man would have followed the act by quickly making his way back to the thicket to reconnoitre, taking with him a supply of fish for future needs. But Elijah Martin succumbed again to the recklessness of inertia; he yielded once more to the animal instinct of momentary security. He returned to the interior of the hut, curled himself again on the ashes, and weakly resolving to sleep until moonrise, and as weakly hesitating, ended by falling into uneasy but helpless stupor.

When he awoke, the rising sun, almost level with the low entrance to the sweat-house, was darting its direct rays into the interior, as if searching it with fiery spears. He had slept ten hours. He rose tremblingly to his knees. Everything was quiet without; he might yet escape. He crawled to the opening. The open space before it was empty, but the scaffolding

was gone. The clear, keen air revived
him. As he sprang out, erect, a shout that
nearly stunned him seemed to rise from
the earth on all sides. He glanced around
him in a helpless agony of fear. A dozen
concentric circles of squatting Indians,
whose heads were visible above the reeds,
encompassed the banks around the sunken
base of the sweat-house with successive
dusky rings. Every avenue of escape
seemed closed. Perhaps for that reason
the attitude of his surrounding captors
was passive rather than aggressive, and
the shrewd, half-Hebraic profiles nearest
him expressed only stoical waiting. There
was a strange similarity of expression in
his own immovable apathy of despair.
His only sense of averting his fate was a
confused idea of explaining his intrusion.
His desperate memory yielded a few common Indian words. He pointed auto-
matically to himself and the stream. His
white lips moved.

"I come—from—the river!"

A guttural cry, as if the whole assembly
were clearing their throats, went round the
different circles. The nearest rocked themselves to and fro and bent their feathered

heads toward him. A hollow-cheeked, decrepit old man arose and said, simply:—

"It is he! The great chief has come!"

. . . .

He was saved. More than that, he was re-created. For, by signs and intimations he was quickly made aware that since the death of their late chief, their medicine-men had prophesied that his perfect successor should appear miraculously before them, borne noiselessly on the river *from the sea,* in the plumes and insignia of his predecessor. This mere coincidence of appearance and costume might not have been convincing to the braves had not Elijah Martin's actual deficiencies contributed to their unquestioned faith in him. Not only his inert possession of the sweat-house and his apathetic attitude in their presence, but his utter and complete unlikeness to the white frontiersmen of their knowledge and tradition—creatures of fire and sword and malevolent activity—as well as his manifest dissimilarity to themselves, settled their conviction of his supernatural origin. His gentle, submissive voice, his yielding will, his lazy helplessness, the absence of strange weapons and fierce explosives in his possession, his unwonted sobriety—all proved him an exception to his apparent race that was in itself miraculous. For it must be confessed that, in spite of the cherished theories of most romances and all statesmen and commanders, that *fear* is the great civilizer of the savage barbarian, and that he is supposed to regard the prowess of the white man and his mysterious death-dealing weapons as evidence of his supernatural origin and superior creation, the facts have generally pointed to the reverse. Elijah Martin was not long in discovering that when the Minyo hunter, with his obsolete bow, dropped dead by a bullet from a viewless and apparently noiseless space, it was *not* considered the lightnings of an avenging Deity, but was traced directly to the ambushed rifle of Kansas Joe, swayed by a viciousness quite as human as their own; the spectacle of Blizzard Dick, verging on *delirium tremens,* and riding "amuck" into an Indian village with a revolver in each hand, did *not* impress them as a supernatural act, nor excite their respectful awe as much as the less harmful frenzy of one of their own medicine-men; they were

not influenced by implacable white gods,
who relaxed only to drive hard bargains
and exchange mildewed flour and shoddy
blankets for their fish and furs. I am
afraid they regarded these raids of Christian civilization as they looked upon grass-
hopper plagues, famines, inundations, and
epidemics; while an utterly impassive
God washed his hands of the means he had
employed, and even encouraged the faithful to resist and overcome his emissaries—
the white devils! Had Elijah Martin
been a student of theology, he would have
been struck with the singular resemblance
of these theories—although the application
thereof was reversed—to the Christian
faith. But Elijah Martin had neither the
imagination of a theologian nor the in-
sight of a politician. He only saw that
he, hitherto ignored and despised in a
community of half-barbaric men, now
translated to a community of men wholly
savage, was respected and worshipped!

It might have turned a stronger head
than Elijah's. He was at first frightened,
fearful lest his reception concealed some
hidden irony, or that, like the flower-
crowned victim of ancient sacrifice, he was

exalted and sustained to give importance
and majesty to some impending martyr-
dom. Then he began to dread that his
innocent deceit—if deceit it was—should
be discovered; at last, partly from meek-
ness and partly from the animal content-
ment of present security, he accepted the
situation. Fortunately for him it was
purely passive. The Great Chief of the
Minyo tribe was simply an expressionless
idol of flesh and blood. The previous in-
cumbent of that office had been an old
man, impotent and senseless of late years
through age and disease. The chieftains
and braves had consulted in council before
him, and perfunctorily submitted their de-
sions, like offerings, to his unresponsive
shrine. In the same way, all material
events—expeditions, trophies, industries—
were supposed to pass before the dull, impassive eyes of the great chief, for direct
acceptance. On the second day of Elijah's accession, two of the braves brought
a bleeding human scalp before him.
Elijah turned pale, trembled, and averted
his head, and then, remembering the danger of giving way to his weakness, grew
still more ghastly. The warriors watched

him with impassioned faces. A grunt—
but whether of astonishment, dissent, or
approval, he would not tell—went round
the circle. But the scalp was taken away
and never again appeared in his presence.

An incident still more alarming quickly
followed. Two captives, white men, se-
curely bound, were one day brought before
him on their way to the stake, followed by
a crowd of old and young squaws and children. The unhappy Elijah recognized in
the prisoners two packers from a distant
settlement who sometimes passed through
Redwood Camp. An agony of terror,
shame, and remorse shook the pseudo chief
to his crest of high feathers, and blanched
his face beneath its paint and yellow ochre.
To interfere to save them from the torture
they were evidently to receive at the hands
of those squaws and children, according to
custom, would be exposure and death to
him as well as themselves; while to assist
by his passive presence at the horrible
sacrifice of his countrymen was too much
for even his weak selfishness. Scarcely
knowing what he did as the lugubrious
procession passed before him, he hurriedly
hid his face in his blanket and turned his

back upon the scene. There was a dead silence. The warriors were evidently unprepared for this extraordinary conduct of their chief. What might have been their action it was impossible to conjecture, for at that moment a little squaw, perhaps impatient for the sport and partly emboldened by the fact that she had been selected, only a few days before, as the betrothed of the new chief, approached him slyly from the other side. The horrified eyes of Elijah, momentarily raised from his blanket, saw and recognized her. The feebleness of a weak nature, that dared not measure itself directly with the real cause, vented its rage on a secondary object. He darted a quick glance of indignation and hatred at the young girl. She ran back in startled terror to her companions, a hurried consultation followed, and in another moment the whole bevy of girls, old women, and children were on the wing, shrieking and crying, to their wigwams.

"You see," said one of the prisoners coolly to the other, in English, "I was right. They never intended to do anything to us. It was only a bluff. These Minyos are a different sort from the other tribes.

They never kill anybody if they can help it."

"You're wrong," said the other, excitedly. "It was that big chief there, with his head in a blanket, that sent those dogs to the right about. Hell! did you see them run at just a look from him? He's a high and mighty feller, you bet. Look at his dignity!"

"That's so—he ain't no slouch," said the other, gazing at Elijah's muffled head, critically. "D——d if he ain't a born king."

The sudden conflict and utter revulsion of emotion that those simple words caused in Elijah's breast was almost incredible. He had been at first astounded by the revelation of the peaceful reputation of the unknown tribe he had been called upon to govern; but even this comforting assurance was as nothing compared to the greater revelations implied in the speaker's praise of himself. He, Elijah Martin! the despised, the rejected, the worthless outcast of Redwood Camp, recognized as a "born king," a leader; his power felt by the very men who had scorned him! And he had done nothing—stop! had he actually done

16 Bret Harte

nothing? Was it not possible that he was *really* what they thought him? His brain reeled under the strong, unaccustomed wine of praise; acting upon his weak selfishness, it exalted him for a moment to their measure of his strength, even as their former belief in his inefficiency had kept him down. Courage is too often only the memory of past success. This was his first effort; he forgot he had not earned it, even as he now ignored the danger of earning it. The few words of unconscious praise had fallen like the blade of knighthood on his cowering shoulders; he had risen ennobled from the contact. Though his face was still muffled in his blanket, he stood erect and seemed to have gained in stature.

The braves had remained standing irresolute, and yet watchful, a few paces from their captives. Suddenly, Elijah, still keeping his back to the prisoners, turned upon the braves, with blazing eyes, violently throwing out his hands with the gesture of breaking bonds. Like all sudden demonstrations of undemonstrative men, it was extravagant, weird, and theatrical. But it was more potent than speech—

the speech that, even if effective, would still have betrayed him to his countrymen. The braves hurriedly cut the thongs of the prisoners; another impulsive gesture from Elijah, and they, too, fled. When he lifted his eyes cautiously from his blanket, captors and captives had dispersed in opposite directions, and he was alone—and triumphant!

From that moment Elijah Martin was another man. He went to bed that night in an intoxicating dream of power; he arose a man of will, of strength. He read it in the eyes of the braves, albeit at times averted in wonder. He understood, now, that although peace had been their habit and custom, they had nevertheless sought to test his theories of administration with the offering of the scalps and the captives, and in this detection of their common weakness he forgot his own. Most heroes require the contrast of the unheroic to set them off; and Elijah actually found himself devising means for strengthening the defensive and offensive character of the tribe, and was himself strengthened by it. Meanwhile the escaped packers did not fail to heighten the importance of their

adventure by elevating the character and
achievements of their deliverer; and it was
presently announced throughout the frontier settlements that the hitherto insignifi-
cant and peaceful tribe of Minyos, who in-
habited a large territory bordering on the
Pacific Ocean, had developed into a powerful nation, only kept from the war-path
by a more powerful but mysterious chief.
The Government sent an Indian agent to
treat with them, in its usual half-paternal,
half-aggressive, and wholly inconsistent
policy. Elijah, who still retained the imi-
tative sense and adaptability to surroundings which belong to most lazy, impressible
natures, and in striped yellow and ver-
milion features looked the chief he per-
sonated, met the agent with silent and
becoming gravity. The council was carried on by signs. Never before had an
Indian treaty been entered into with such
perfect knowledge of the intentions and de-
signs of the whites by the Indians, and such
profound ignorance of the qualities of the
Indians by the whites. It need scarcely be
said that the treaty was an unquestionable
Indian success. They did not give up their
arable lands; what they did sell to the

agent they refused to exchange for extrava-
gant-priced shoddy blankets, worthless
guns, damp powder, and mouldy meal.
They took pay in dollars, and were thus
enabled to open more profitable commerce
with the traders at the settlements for
better goods and better bargains; they
simply declined beads, whiskey, and Bibles
at any price. The result was that the
traders found it profitable to protect them
from their countrymen, and the chances of
wantonly shooting down a possible valuable
customer stopped the old indiscriminate
rifle-practice. The Indians were allowed
to cultivate their fields in peace. Elijah
purchased for them a few agricultural im-
plements. The catching, curing, and
smoking of salmon became an important
branch of trade. They waxed prosperous
and rich; they lost their nomadic habits—
a centralized settlement bearing the external signs of an Indian village took the
place of their old temporary encampments,
but the huts were internally an improvement on the old wigwams. The dried fish
were banished from the tent-poles to long
sheds especially constructed for that purpose. The sweat-house was no longer util-

ized for worldly purposes. The wise and mighty Elijah did not attempt to reform their religion, but to preserve it in its integrity.

That these improvements and changes were due to the influence of one man was undoubtedly true, but that he was necessarily a superior man did not follow. Elijah's success was due partly to the fact that he had been enabled to impress certain negative virtues, which were part of his own nature, upon a community equally constituted to receive them. Each was strengthened by the recognition in each other of the unexpected value of those qualities; each acquired a confidence begotten of their success. *"He-hides-his-face,"* as Elijah Martin was known to the tribe after the episode of the released captives, was really not so much of an autocrat as many constitutional rulers.

. . . .

Two years of tranquil prosperity passed. Elijah Martin, foundling, outcast, without civilized ties or relationship of any kind, forgotten by his countrymen, and lifted into alien power, wealth, security, and respect, became—homesick!

It was near the close of a summer afternoon. He was sitting at the door of his
lodge, which overlooked, on one side, the
far-shining levels of the Pacific and, on
the other, the slow descent to the cultivated
meadows and banks of the Minyo River,
that debouched through a waste of salt-
marsh, beach-grass, sand-dunes, and foamy
estuary into the ocean. The headland, or
promontory—the only eminence of the
Minyo territory—had been reserved by
him for his lodge, partly on account of its
isolation from the village at its base, and
partly for the view it commanded of his
territory. Yet his wearying and discontented eyes were more often found on the
ocean, as a possible highway of escape from
his irksome position, than on the plain and
the distant range of mountains, so closely
connected with the nearer past and his former detractors. In his vague longing he
had no desire to return to them, even in
triumph; in his present security there still
lingered a doubt of his ability to cope with
the old conditions. It was more like his
easy, indolent nature—which revived in his
prosperity—to trust to this least practical
and remote solution of his trouble. His

homesickness was as vague as his plan for escape from it; he did not know exactly what he regretted, but it was probably some life he had not enjoyed, some pleasure that had escaped his former incompetency and poverty.

He had sat thus a hundred times, as aimlessly blinking at the vast possibilities of the shining sea beyond, turning his back upon the nearer and more practicable mountains, lulled by the far-off beating of monotonous rollers, the lonely cry of the curlew and plover, the drowsy changes of alternate breaths of cool, fragrant reeds and warm, spicy sands that blew across his eyelids, and succumbed to sleep, as he had done a hundred times before. The narrow strips of colored cloth, insignia of his dignity, flapped lazily from his tent-poles, and at last seemed to slumber with him; the shadows of the leaf-tracery thrown by the bay-tree, on the ground at his feet, scarcely changed its pattern. Nothing moved but the round, restless, berry-like eyes of Wachita, his child-wife, the former heroine of the incident with the captive packers, who sat near her lord, armed with a willow wand, watchful of intruding wasps, sand-flies, and even the more ostentatious advances of a rotund and clerical-looking humble-bee, with his monotonous homily. Content, dumb, submissive, vacant, at such times, Wachita, debarred her husband's confidences through the native customs and his own indifferent taciturnity, satisfied herself by gazing at him with the wondering but ineffectual sympathy of a faithful dog. Unfortunately for Elijah her purely mechanical ministration could not prevent a more dangerous intrusion upon his security.

He awoke with a light start, and eyes that gradually fixed upon the woman a look of returning consciousness. Wachita pointed timidly to the village below.

"The Messenger of the Great White Father has come to-day, with his wagons and horses; he would see the chief of the Minyos, but I would not disturb my lord."

Elijah's brow contracted. Relieved of its characteristic metaphor, he knew that this meant that the new Indian agent had made his usual official visit, and had exhibited the usual anxiety to see the famous chieftain.

"Good!" he said. "White Rabbit [his lieutenant] will see the Messenger and exchange gifts. It is enough."

"The white messenger has brought his wangee [white] woman with him. They would look upon the face of him who hides it," continued Wachita, dubiously. "They would that Wachita should bring them nearer to where my lord is, that they might see him when he knew it not."

Elijah glanced moodily at his wife, with the half suspicion with which he still regarded her alien character. "Then let Wachita go back to the squaws and old women, and let her hide herself with them until the wangee strangers are gone," he said curtly. "I have spoken. Go!"

Accustomed to these abrupt dismissals, which did not necessarily indicate displeasure, Wachita disappeared without a word. Elijah, who had risen, remained for a few moments leaning against the tent-poles, gazing abstractedly toward the sea. The bees droned uninterruptedly in his ears, the far-off roll of the breakers came to him distinctly; but suddenly, with greater distinctness, came the murmur of a woman's voice.

"He don't look savage a bit! Why, he's real handsome."

"Hush! you—" said a second voice, in a frightened whisper.

"But if he *did* hear he couldn't understand," returned the first voice. A suppressed giggle followed.

Luckily, Elijah's natural and acquired habits of repression suited the emergency. He did not move, although he felt the quick blood fly to his face, and the voice of the first speaker had suffused him with a strange and delicious anticipation. He restrained himself, though the words she had naively dropped were filling him with new and tremulous suggestion. He was motionless, even while he felt that the vague longing and yearning which had possessed him hitherto was now mysteriously taking some unknown form and action.

The murmuring ceased. The humble-bees' drone again became ascendant—a sudden fear seized him. She was *going;* he should never see her! While he had stood there a dolt and sluggard, she had satisfied her curiosity and stolen away. With a sudden yielding to impulse, he darted quickly in the direction where he had heard her voice. The thicket moved, parted, crackled, and rustled, and then undulated thirty feet before him in a long wave, as if from the passage of some lithe, invisible figure. But at the same moment a little cry, half of alarm, half of laughter, broke from his very feet, and a bent manzanito-bush, relaxed by frightened fingers, flew back against his breast. Thursting it hurriedly aside, his stooping, eager face came almost in contact with the pink, flushed cheeks and tangled curls of a woman's head. He was so near, her moist and laughing eyes almost drowned his eager glance; her parted lips and white teeth were so close to his that her quick breath took away his own.

She had dropped on one knee, as her companion fled, expecting he would overlook her as he passed, but his direct onset had extracted the feminine outcry. Yet even then she did not seem greatly frightened.

"It's only a joke, sir," she said, coolly lifting herself to her feet by grasping his arm. "I'm Mrs. Dall, the Indian agent's wife. They said you wouldn't let anybody see you—and *I* determined I would.

That's all!" She stopped, threw back her tangled curls behind her ears, shook the briers and thorns from her skirt, and added: "Well, I reckon you aren't afraid of a woman, are you? So no harm's done. Good-by!"

She drew slightly back as if to retreat, but the elasticity of the manzanito against which she was leaning threw her forward once more. He again inhaled the perfume of her hair; he saw even the tiny freckles that darkened her upper lip and brought out the moist, red curve below. A sudden recollection of a playmate of his vagabond childhood flashed across his mind; a wild inspiration of lawlessness, begotten of his past experience, his solitude, his dictatorial power, and the beauty of the woman before him, mounted to his brain. He threw his arms passionately around her, pressed his lips to hers, and with a half-hysterical laugh drew back and disappeared in the thicket.

Mrs. Dall remained for an instant dazed and stupefied. Then she lifted her arm mechanically, and with her sleeve wiped her bruised mouth and the ochre-stain that his paint had left, like blood, upon her

cheek. Her laughing face had become instantly grave, but not from fear; her dark
eyes had clouded, but not entirely with
indignation. She suddenly brought down
her hand sharply against her side with a
gesture of discovery.

"That's no Injun!" she said, with
prompt decision. The next minute she
plunged back into the trail again, and the
dense foliage once more closed around her.
But as she did so the broad, vacant face
and the mutely wondering eyes of Wachita
rose, like a placid moon, between the
branches of a tree where they had been
hidden, and shone serenely and impassively
after her.

.   .   .   .

A month elapsed. But it was a month
filled with more experience to Elijah than
his past two years of exaltation. In the
first few days following his meeting with
Mrs. Dall, he was possessed by terror,
mingled with flashes of desperation, at the
remembrance of his rash imprudence. His
recollection of extravagant frontier chivalry to womankind, and the swift retribution of the insulted husband or guardian,
alternately filled him with abject fear or

extravagant recklessness. At times prepared for flight, even to the desperate
abandonment of himself in a canoe to the
waters of the Pacific: at times he was on
the point of inciting his braves to attack
the Indian agency and precipitate the war
that he felt would be inevitable. As the
days passed, and there seemed to be no
interruption to his friendly relations with
the agency, with that relief a new, subtle
joy crept into Elijah's heart. The image
of the agent's wife framed in the leafy
screen behind his lodge, the perfume of
her hair and breath mingled with the
spicing of the bay, the brief thrill and
tantalization of the stolen kiss still haunted
him. Through his long, shy abstention
from society, and his two years of solitary
exile, the fresh beauty of this young Western wife, in whom the frank artlessness of
girlhood still lingered, appeared to him
like a superior creation. He forgot his
vague longings in the inception of a more
tangible but equally unpractical passion.
He remembered her unconscious and spontaneous admiration of him; he dared to
connect it with her forgiving silence. If
she had withheld her confidences from her

husband, he could hope—he knew not exactly what!

One afternoon Wachita put into his hand a folded note. With an instinctive presentiment of its contents, Elijah turned red and embarrassed in receiving it from the woman who was recognized as his wife. But the impassive, submissive manner of this household drudge, instead of touching his conscience, seemed to him a vulgar and brutal acceptance of the situation that dulled whatever compunction he might have had. He opened the note and read hurriedly as follows:—

"You took a great freedom with me the other day, and I am justified in taking one with you now. I believe you understand English as well as I do. If you want to explain that and your conduct to me, I will be at the same place this afternoon. My friend will accompany me, but she need not hear what you have to say."

Elijah read the letter, which might have been written by an ordinary school-girl, as if it had conveyed the veiled rendezvous of a princess. The reserve, caution, and shyness which had been the safeguard of his weak nature were swamped in a flow of immature passion. He flew to the interview with the eagerness and inexperience of first love. He was completely at her mercy. So utterly was he subjugated by her presence that she did not even run the risk of his passion. Whatever sentiment might have mingled with her curiosity, she was never conscious of a necessity to guard herself against it. At this second meeting she was in full possession of his secret. He had told her everything; she had promised nothing in return—she had not even accepted anything. Even her actual after-relations to the dénouement of his passion are still shrouded in mystery.

Nevertheless, Elijah lived two weeks on the unsubstantial memory of this meeting. What might have followed could not be known, for at the end of that time an outrage—so atrocious that even the peaceful Minyos were thrilled with savage indignation—was committed on the outskirts of the village. An old chief, who had been specially selected to deal with the Indian agent, and who kept a small trading outpost, had been killed and his goods despoiled by a reckless Redwood packer. The murderer had coolly said that he was only "serving out" the tool of a fraudulent imposture on the Government, and that he dared the arch-impostor himself, the so-called Minyo chief, to help himself. A wave of ungovernable fury surged up to the very tent-poles of Elijah's lodge and demanded vengeance. Elijah trembled and hesitated. In the thraldom of his selfish passion for Mrs. Dall he dared not contemplate a collision with her countrymen. He would have again sought refuge in his passive, non-committal attitude, but he knew the impersonal character of Indian retribution and compensation—a sacrifice of equal value, without reference to the culpability of the victim—and he dreaded some spontaneous outbreak. To prevent the enforced expiation of the crime by some innocent brother packer, he was obliged to give orders for the pursuit and arrest of the criminal, secretly hoping for his escape or the interposition of some circumstance to avert his punishment. A day of sullen expectancy to the old men and squaws in camp, of gloomy anxiety to Elijah alone in his lodge, followed the departure of the braves on the war-path. It was midnight when they returned. Eli-

jah, who from his habitual reserve and the
accepted etiquette of his exalted station had
remained impassive in his tent, only knew
from the guttural rejoicings of the squaws
that the expedition had been successful and
the captive was in their hands. At any
other time he might have thought it an
evidence of some growing scepticism of his
infallibility of judgment and a diminution
of respect that they did not confront him
with their prisoner. But he was too glad
to escape from the danger of exposure and
possible arraignment of his past life by
the desperate captive, even though it might
not have been understood by the spectators.
He reflected that the omission might have
arisen from their recollection of his
previous aversion to a retaliation on other
prisoners. Enough that they would wait
his signal for the torture and execution at
sunrise the next day.

The night passed slowly. It is more
than probable that the selfish and ignoble
torments of the sleepless and vacillating
judge were greater than those of the prisoner who dozed at the stake between his
curses. Yet it was part of Elijah's fatal
weakness that his kinder and more human

instincts were dominated even at that moment by his lawless passion for the Indian
agent's wife, and his indecision as to the
fate of his captive was as much due to this
preoccupation as to a selfish consideration
of her relations to the result. He hated
the prisoner for his infelicitous and un-
timely crime, yet he could not make up his
mind to his death. He paced the ground
before his lodge in dishonorable incerti-
tude. The small eyes of the submissive
Wachita watched him with vague solicitude.

Toward morning he was struck by a
shameful inspiration. He would creep un-
perceived to the victim's side, unloose his
bonds, and bid him fly to the Indian
agency. There he was to inform Mrs.
Dall that her husband's safety depended
upon his absenting himself for a few days,
but that she was to remain and communicate with Elijah. She would understand
everything, perhaps; at least she would
know that the prisoner's release was to
please her, but even if she did not, no harm
would be done, a white man's life would
be saved, and his real motive would not be
suspected. He turned with feverish ea-

gerness to the lodge. Wachita had disappeared—probably to join the other women. It was well; she would not suspect him.

The tree to which the doomed man was bound was, by custom, selected nearest the chief's lodge, within its sacred enclosure, with no other protection than that offered by its reserved seclusion and the outer semicircle of warriors' tents before it. To escape, the captive would therefore have to pass beside the chief's lodge to the rear and descend the hill toward the shore. Elijah would show him the way, and make it appear as if he had escaped unaided. As he glided into the shadow of a group of pines, he could dimly discern the outline of the destined victim, secured against one of the larger trees in a sitting posture, with his head fallen forward on his breast as if in sleep. But at the same moment another figure glided out from the shadow and approached the fatal tree. It was Wachita!

He stopped in amazement. But in another instant a flash of intelligence made it clear. He remembered her vague uneasiness and solicitude at his agitation, her sudden disappearance; she had fathomed his perplexity, as she had once before. Of her own accord she was going to release the prisoner! The knife to cut his cords glittered in her hand. Brave and faithful animal!

He held his breath as he drew nearer. But, to his horror, the knife suddenly flashed in the air and darted down, again and again, upon the body of the helpless man. There was a convulsive struggle, but no outcry, and the next moment the body hung limp and inert in its cords. Elijah would himself have fallen, half-fainting, against a tree, but, by a revulsion of feeling, came the quick revelation that the desperate girl had rightly solved the problem! She had done what he ought to have done—and his loyalty and manhood were preserved. That conviction and the courage to act upon it—to have called the sleeping braves to witness his sacrifice —would have saved him, but it was ordered otherwise.

As the girl rapidly passed him he threw out his hand and seized her wrist. "Who did you do this for?" he demanded.

"For you," she said, stupidly.

"And why?"

"Because you no kill him—you love his squaw."

"*His* squaw!" He staggered back. A terrible suspicion flashed upon him. He dashed Wachita aside and ran to the tree. It was the body of the Indian agent! Aboriginal justice had been satisfied. The warriors had not caught the *murderer,* but, true to their idea of vicarious retribution, had determined upon the expiatory sacrifice of a life as valuable and innocent as the one they had lost.

.   .   .   .

"So the Gov'rment hev at last woke up and wiped out them cussed Digger Minyos," said Snap-shot Harry, as he laid down the newspaper, in the brand-new saloon of the brand-new town of Redwood. "I see they've stampeded both banks of the Minyo River, and sent off a lot to the reservation. I reckon the soldiers at Fort Cass got sick o' sentiment after those hounds killed the Injun agent, and are beginning to agree with us that the only 'good Injun' is a dead one."

"And it turns out that that wonderful chief, that them two packers used to rave about, woz about as big a devil ez any, and tried to run off with the agent's wife, only the warriors killed her. I'd like to know what become of him. Some says he was killed, others allow that he got away. I've heerd tell that he was originally some kind of Methodist preacher!—a kind o' saint that got a sort o' spiritooal holt on the old squaws and children."

"Why don't you ask old Skeesicks? I see he's back here ag'in—and grubbin' along at a dollar a day on tailin's. He's been somewhere up north, they say."

"What, Skeesicks? that shiftless, o'n'ry cuss! You bet he wusn't anywhere where there was danger of fighting. Why, you might as well hev suspected *him* of being the big chief himself! There he comes—ask him."

And the laughter was so general that Elijah Martin—alias Skeesicks—lounging shyly into the bar-room, joined in it weakly.

3771